THEY'RE HERE!

THEY'RE HERE!

Edited by
Hank Davis and
Sean CW Korsgaard

BAEN

THEY'RE HERE!

Copyright © 2023 by Hank Davis & Sean CW Korsgaard

A Baen Books Original

Baen Publishing Enterprises
P.O. Box 1403
Riverdale, NY 10471
www.baen.com

ISBN: 978-1-9821-9274-7

Cover art by Alan Pollack

First printing, August 2023

Distributed by Simon & Schuster
1230 Avenue of the Americas
New York, NY 10020

Library of Congress Cataloging-in-Publication Data: TK

Printed in the United States of America

10 9 8 7 6 5 4 3 2 1

ACKNOWLEDGMENTS

Our thanks to those authors who permitted the use of their stories, and to the estates and their representatives. Among the very helpful agents deserving thanks are Spectrum Literary Agency, Don Congdon Associates, The Lotts Agency, Writers House Literary Agency, Curtis Brown, Ltd, and the Virginia Kidd Literary Agency. And thanks for help and advice from others I'm unforgivably forgetting. Gratitude is also due to the Internet Speculative Fiction Database (ISFDB.org) for existing and being a handy source of raw data, and to the devoted volunteers who maintain that very useful site.

CONTENTS

INTRODUCTION
Will the Real E.T. Please Stand Up?
Hank Davis

The physicist Enrico Fermi (1901–1954) won a Nobel Prize, has a type of subatomic particle named after him (fermions), and has a lot to do with how the world after December 2, 1942, is very different from the way it was before that date, when Fermi's team at the University of Chicago activated the first atomic pile and created the first artificial self-sustaining nuclear reaction. Dr. Fermi was a heavy hitter, and had other honors named after him, and one of those concerns us here.

In 1950, when he was at Los Alamos, he and some other heavy hitters, including Edward Teller, broke for lunch. The table talk turned to recent reports of flying saucers, about which the diners were skeptical, but Fermi suddenly asked "Where are they?" (or, according to some accounts, "Where is everybody?"), which prompted a discussion which has been repeated with a different cast many times since then. It can be summed up, in my usual informal way, as there are billions of stars in our Milky Way galaxy (and there are billions more, we now know, than there were thought to be in 1950), and these stars have been around for billions of years, so why hasn't an extraterrestrial dropped by to say "Hey, monkey boys, what's new?" This absence of alien visitors has acquired several names, such as "The Great Silence," but most popularly, it has become known as "The Fermi Paradox."

There are many speculations why this is so, and this isn't the place to rehash them, particularly when the curious reader can consult the term "Fermi Paradox" on Wikipedia for a thorough treatment of possible reasons for the lack of alien visitors, but just suppose that there's no paradox at all and *They're Here!* (Hmmm, that might make a catchy book title...)

That's a fascinating topic for speculation, and speculation happens to be science fiction's stock in trade. No government grants are required, no one's tenure is hanging on the subject, and the reader can do a SETI investigation from the comfort of her or his armchair. Maybe nobody has found a single inscrutable black monolith on Earth or elsewhere (and, in view of the fourth volume in Clarke's series and the events therein, we should be grateful) and the *Chariots of the Gods* territory has a lack of hard evidence, but science fiction, unlike fantasy, begins with a possibility which is contrary to observed fact, including history in that category, but not contradicting the laws of nature as we know them, nor should the development of the implications of that possibility be contrary to logic. I'm not putting that forward as a definition of science fiction. When it comes to trying to define that slippery genre, there are nine and sixty ways of constructing tribal lays, and every one of them has a hole in it! (My apologies to Mr. Kipling.) I'm just trying to put down a ground rule for this discussion.

So, if the Fermi Paradox is not a paradox at all, but there are extraterrestrials among us, why haven't we noticed them?

The first possibility is obvious. They look human, or close enough to human, that the right clothing and maybe a little makeup, or even a bit of plastic surgery (for really dedicated aliens) allows them to walk among the monkey boys and girls unnoticed. (Hmmm...but would they fool a cat?) The idea that intelligent beings on other planets would look like us has a long lineage. Voltaire's *Micromégas*, for an early example, had Earth visited by two beings who were giants, since they came from larger worlds than Earth, but who had the standard human design: four limbs, erect bipeds, binocular vision, etc. (I don't recall if they wore powdered wigs.) Voltaire was writing satire, but he might have been serious about the human appearance, since the Bible says man was created in God's image, and He might not be interested in alternate blueprints. To paraphrase one of Voltaire's celebrated quips, if God did not exist, it would be necessary to invent Him...in man's image, probably.

The idea that aliens might look like us was taken seriously and not just in fiction until relatively recently. In the 1950s, scientist and science writer Willy Ley began an article on possible extraterrestrials by supposing a spaceship touched down and the crew began strolling down a road to the nearest town, and added that their appearance would probably not attract any undue attention from the natives because they would look much like humans. He went on to give reasons why he thought so.

Of course, there were at the same time counterarguments that such visitors wouldn't look like us. For example, that humans have four limbs because animals for millions of years previously had four limbs, and the quadrupedal design was due to early fish ancestors having had four fins, and once that design was in place, and it worked under evolutionary pressures, four limbs were the magic number. If those ancestral fish had instead possessed six fins, insects wouldn't be the only terrestrial animals with six legs. Seventy years after Ley wrote that article, the prevailing opinion is that extraterrestrials would look nothing like us, Star Trek universe, or no Star Trek universe. (Actually, the show has an explanation for the many humanoid species throughout the galaxy, but I'll leave researching that as an Exercise for the reader.)

Maybe so, but I'm suspicious of monolithic consensuses in general, and particularly in science, which is as prone to fads and group-think as other fields of thought. For two examples in astronomy/cosmology, take a look at books on the subject from the early twentieth century, when red giants were thought to be young stars that were still condensing and shrinking, and the collision hypothesis for the origin of the Solar System was considered all but proven. And good riddance to that last one, since it would imply that very few stars would have planets.

But even if aliens look nothing like us, so different that if they're very small, they might get sprayed with insecticide, or if they're as large or larger than, say a Great Dane, their appearance might cause the sort of fleeing panicked multitudes beloved by makers of horror movies with large enough budgets, a race that can cross interstellar space should have a few tricks up their technological sleeve in disguising themselves. For one such, check out Robert Silverberg's "The Reality Trip" in the pages which follow.

Then, there's the possibility that aliens might not be recognizable as aliens. I once wrote (modest cough) a story in which Antarctica turns out to be a very large alien which has been on the Earth for a very long time (the continent, that is; not including the icecap decorating it). Then there are problems in perception. A photographer once filmed buffalo herds up close by covering himself with a buffalo skin, complete with horns, and not panicking the herd. Maybe humans have limited enough perceptions that they can similarly be buffaloed, er, fooled. A more extreme case would be an ant crawling across the pages of a book. Not only is it incapable of reading the text, it has no *conception* of text, and might as well be walking across a leaf or rock. A page of *Alice's Adventures in Wonderland* might smell different to the ant from a page from *Ulysses*, but that would be the limit of its perceptions. And humans may have similar limits, of which we are unaware, and not notice a really strange alien. I'm reminded of Sir Arthur Eddington's quip that "The universe is not only stranger than we imagine. It is stranger than we *can* imagine."

If any of these fledgling speculations intrigue you, there are more polished thought experiments awaiting your attention in the pages which follow this introduction. So, I'll close with my usual regret that not all stories which I would like to have included were available, for one reason or another.

Among these were Kris Neville's "Bettyann," a story which hit me hard when I was still a rotten kid. Another was William Tenn's "Lisbon Cubed," with its sardonic ending typical of that gifted author. And while Donald Wollheim was better known as an editor and publisher for most of my lifetime, he also wrote many excellent short stories, and I regret the absence of his "Mimic," a story which has inspired two movie adaptations. Also missing is Avram Davidson's hilarious "Help! I am Doctor Morris Goldpepper" in which dentists save the world from undercover aliens with dental problems.

Particularly regrettable was the case of Ray Nelson's "Eight O'Clock in the Morning," which was freely adapted into the suspensefully paranoid movie, *They Live.* Mr. Nelson was agreeable to letting us reprint his story, but died before the contractual formalities could be completed. It, and the other four stories I've named, are well worth seeking out.

But I've kept you away from the real reasons for this book's existence long enough. The stories await your attention, each introduced by my coeditor, Sean CW Korsgaard, and I hope you'll enjoy the very good stories we were able to include. Have fun—but watch out for the body snatchers.

THE MEDDLER
Larry Niven

The story that in part inspired our cover, and even by the standards of a Larry Niven novelette, a uniquely original one. A neo noir mystery that might have been just as easily pulled from the pages of Black Mask *as the issue of* Fantasy & Science Fiction *that it did come from . . . if one could ignore the alien that has thrust himself right into the middle of it.*

As if one could. Private dick Bruce Cheseborough, Jr., is having a hard enough time of it with a mob boss gunning for his life when a shape-shifting, bulletproof alien claiming to have been sent to observe mankind decides to interfere. Throw in a few twists and turns, and you've got a hard-boiled detective thriller with enough of a science fiction flourish to satisfy devotees of either genre.

🐜 🐜 🐜

Someone was in my room.

It had to be one of Sinc's boys. He'd been stupid. I'd left the lights off. The yellow light now seeping under the door was all the warning I needed.

He hadn't used the door: the threads were still there. That left the fire escape outside the bedroom window. I pulled my gun, moved back a little in the corridor to get elbow room. Then—I'd practiced it often enough to drive the management crazy—I kicked the door open and was into the room in one smooth motion.

He should have been behind the door, or crouching behind a table, or hidden in the closet with his eye to the keyhole. Instead he was right out in the middle of the living room, facing the wrong way.

1

He'd barely started to turn when I pumped four GyroJet slugs into him. I saw the impacts twitching his shirt. One over the heart.

He was finished.

So I didn't slow down to watch him fall. I crossed the living room rug in a diving run and landed behind the couch. He couldn't be alone. There had to be others. If one had been behind the couch he might have gotten me, but there wasn't. I scanned the wall behind me, but there was nothing to hide under. So I froze, waiting, listening.

Where were they? The one I'd shot couldn't have come alone.

I was peeved at Sinc. As long as he'd sent goons to waylay me, he might have sent a few who knew what they were doing. The one I'd shot hadn't had time to know he was in a fight.

"Why did you do that?"

Impossibly, the voice came from the middle of the living room, where I'd left a falling corpse. I risked a quick look and brought my head down fast. The afterimage:

He hadn't moved. There was no blood on him. No gun visible, but I hadn't seen his right hand.

Bulletproof vest? Sinc's boys had no rep for that kind of thing, but that had to be it. I stood up suddenly and fired, aiming between the eyes.

The slug smashed his right eye, off by an inch, and I knew he'd shaken me. I dropped back and tried to cool off.

No noises. Still no sign that he wasn't alone.

"I said, 'Why did you do that?'"

Mild curiosity colored his high-pitched voice. He didn't move as I stood up, and there was no hole in either eye.

"Why did I do what?" I asked cleverly.

"Why did you make holes in me? My gratitude for the gift of metal, of course, but—" He stopped suddenly, like he'd said too much and knew it. But I had other worries.

"Anyone else here?"

"Only we two are present. I beg pardon for invasion of privacy, and will indemnify—" He stopped again, as suddenly, and started over. "Who were you expecting?"

"Sinc's boys. I guess they haven't caught on yet. Sinc's boys want to make holes in me."

"Why?"

Could he be that stupid? "To turn me off! To kill me!"

He looked surprised, then furious. He was so mad he gurgled. "I should have been informed! Someone has been unforgivably sloppy!"

"Yah. Me. I thought you must be with Sinc. I shouldn't have shot at you. Sorry."

"Nothing," he smiled, instantly calm again.

"But I ruined your suit..." I trailed off. Holes showed in his jacket and shirt, but no blood. "Just what are you?"

He stood about five feet four, a round little man in an old-fashioned brown one-button suit. There was not a hair on him, not even eyelashes. No warts, no wrinkles, no character lines. A nebbish, one of these guys whose edges are all round, like someone forgot to put in the fine details.

He spread smoothly manicured hands. "I am a man like yourself."

"Nuts."

"Well," he said angrily, "you would have thought so if the preliminary investigation team had done their work properly!"

"You're a—martian?"

"I am not a martian. I am—" He gurgled. "Also I am an anthropologist. Your word. I am here to study your species."

"You're from outer space?"

"Very. The direction and distance are secret, of course. My very existence should have been secret." He scowled deeply. Rubber face, I thought, not knowing the half of it yet.

"I won't talk," I reassured him. "But you came at a bad time. Any minute now, Sinc's going to figure out who it is that's on his tail. Then he'll be on mine, and this dump'll be ground zero. I hate to brush you. I've never met a... whatever."

"I too must terminate this interview, since you know me for what I am. But first, tell me of your quarrel. Why does Sinc want to make holes in you?"

"His name is Lester Dunhaven Sinclair the third. He runs every racket in this city. Look, we've got time for a drink—maybe. I've got scotch, bourbon—"

He shuddered. "No, I thank you."

"Just trying to set you at ease." I was a little miffed.

"Then perhaps I may adapt a more comfortable form, while you drink—whatever you choose. If you don't mind."

"Please yourself." I went to the rolling bar and poured bourbon and tap water, no ice. The apartment house was dead quiet. I wasn't surprised. I've lived here a couple of years now, and the other tenants have learned the routine. When guns go off, they hide under their beds and stay there.

"You won't be shocked?" My visitor seemed anxious. "If you are shocked, please say so at once."

And he melted. I stood there with the paper cup to my lip and watched him flow out of his one-button suit and take the compact shape of a half-deflated gray beach ball.

I downed the bourbon and poured more, no water. My hands stayed steady.

"I'm a private cop," I told the martian. He'd extruded a convoluted something I decided was an ear. "When Sinc showed up about three years ago and started taking over the rackets, I stayed out of his way. He was the law's business, I figured. Then he bought the law, and that was okay too. I'm no crusader."

"Crusader?" His voice had changed. Now it was deep, and it sounded like something bubbling up from a tar pit.

"Never mind. I tried to stay clear of Sinc, but it didn't work. Sinc had a client of mine killed. Morrison, his name was. I was following Morrison's wife, getting evidence for a divorce. She was shacking up with a guy named Adler. I had all the evidence I needed when Morrison disappeared.

"Then I found out Adler was Sinc's right hand."

"Right hand? Nothing was said of hive cultures."

"Huh?"

"One more thing the prelim team will have to answer for. Continue talking. You fascinate me."

"I kept working on it. What could I do? Morrison was my client, and he was dead. I collected plenty of evidence against Adler, and I turned it over to the cops. Morrison's body never turned up, but I had good corpus delicti evidence. Anyway, Sinc's bodies never do turn up. They just disappear.

"I turned what I had over to the cops. The case was squashed. Somehow the evidence got lost. One night I got beat up."

"Beat up?"

"Almost any kind of impact," I told him," can damage a human being."

"Really!" he gurgled. "All that water, I suppose."

"Maybe. In my line you have to heal fast. Well, that tore it. I started looking for evidence against Sinc himself. A week ago I sent Xeroxes off to the Feds. I let one of Sinc's boys find a couple of the copies. Bribery evidence, nothing exciting, but enough to hurt. I figured it wouldn't take Sinc long to figure out who made them. The Xerox machine I borrowed was in a building he owns."

"Fascinating. I think I will make holes in the Lady of Preliminary Investigation."

"Will that hurt?"

"She is not a—" Gurgle. "She is a—" Loud, shrill bird whistle.

"I get it. Anyway, you can see how busy I'm going to be. Much too busy to talk about, uh, anthropology. Any minute now I'll have Sinc's boys all over me, and the first one I kill I'll have the cops on me too. Maybe the cops'll come first. I dunno."

"May I watch? I promise not to get in your path."

"Why?"

He cocked his ear, if that was what it was. "An example. Your species has developed an extensive system of engineering using alternating current. We were surprised to find you transmitting electricity so far, and using it in so many ways. Some may even be worth imitating."

"That's nice. So?"

"Perhaps there are other things we can learn from you."

I shook my head. "Sorry, short stuff. This party's bound to get rough, and I don't want any bystanders getting hurt. What the hell am I talking about. Holes don't hurt you?"

"Very little hurts me. My ancestors once used genetic engineering to improve their design. My major weaknesses are susceptibility to certain organic poisons, and a voracious appetite."

"Okay, stay then. Maybe after it's all over you can tell me about Mars, or wherever you came from. I'd like that."

"Where I come from is classified. I can tell you about Mars."

"Sure, sure. How'd you like to raid the fridge while we wait? If you're so hungry all the time— Hold it."

Sliding footsteps.

They were out there. A handful of them, if they were trying to keep it a secret. And these had to be from Sinc, because all the neighbors were under their beds by now.

The martian heard it too. "What shall I do? I cannot reach human form fast enough."

I was already behind the easy chair. "Then try something else. Something easy."

A moment later I had two matching black leather footstools. They both matched the easy chair, but maybe nobody'd notice.

The door slammed wide open. I didn't pull the trigger, because nobody was there. Just the empty hallway.

The fire escape was outside my bedroom window, but that window was locked and bolted and rigged with alarms. They wouldn't get in that way. Unless—

I whispered, "Hey! How did you get in?"

"Under the door."

So that was all right. The window alarms were still working. "Did any of the tenants see you?"

"No."

"Good." I get enough complaints from the management without that.

More faint rustling from outside the door. Then a hand and gun appeared for an instant, fired at random, vanished. Another hole in my walls. He'd had time to see my head, to place me. I ran low for the couch. I was getting set again, both eyes on the door, when a voice behind me said, "Stand up slow."

You had to admire the guy. He'd got through the window alarms without a twitch, into the living room without a sound. He was tall, olive-skinned, with straight black hair and black eyes. His gun was centered on the bridge of my nose.

I dropped the GyroJet and stood up. Pushing it now would only get me killed.

He was very relaxed, very steady. "That's a GyroJet, isn't it? Why not use a regular heater?"

"I like this," I told him. Maybe he'd come too close, or take his eyes off me, or—anything. "It's light as a toy, with no recoil. The gun is just a launching chamber for the rocket slugs, and they pack the punch of a forty-five."

"But, man! The slugs cost a buck forty-five each!"

"I don't shoot that many people."

"At those prices, I believe it. Okay, turn around slow. Hands in the air." His eyes hadn't left me for a moment.

I turned my back. Next would be a sap—

Something metal brushed against my head, feather-light. I whirled, struck at his gun hand and his larynx. Pure habit. I'd moved the instant the touch told me he was in reach.

He was stumbling back with his hand to his throat. I put a fist in his belly and landed the other on his chin. He dropped, trying to curl up. And sure enough, he was holding a sap.

But why hadn't he hit me with it? From the feel of it, he'd laid it gently on top of my head, carefully, as if he thought the sap might shatter.

"All right, stand easy." The hand and gun came through the doorway, attached to six feet of clean living. I knew him as Handel. He looked like any blond brainless hero, but he wasn't brainless, and he was no hero.

He said, "You're going to hate yourself for doing that."

The footstool behind him began to change shape.

"Dammit," I said, "that's not fair."

Handel looked comically surprised, then smiled winningly. "Two to one?"

"I was talking to my footstool."

"Turn around. We've got orders to bring you to Sinc, if we can. You could still get out of this alive."

I turned around.

"I'd like to apologize."

"Save it for Sinc."

"No, honest. It wasn't my idea to have someone else mix in this. Especially—" Again I felt something brush against the side of my head. The martian must be doing something to stop the impact.

I could have taken Handel then. I didn't move. It didn't seem right that I could break Handel's neck when he couldn't touch me. Two to one I don't mind, especially when the other guy's the one. Sometimes I'll even let some civic-minded bystander help, if there's some chance he'll live through it. But this . . .

"What's not fair?" asked a high, complaining voice.

Handel screamed like a woman. I turned to see him charge into the door jamb, back up a careful two feet, try for the door again and make it.

Then I saw the footstool.

He was already changing, softening in outline, but I got an idea of the shape Handel had seen. No wonder it had softened his mind. I felt it softening my bones, melting the marrow, and I closed my eyes and whispered, "Dammit, you were supposed to watch."

"You told me the impact would damage you."

"That's not the point. Detectives are always getting hit on the head. We expect it."

"But how can I learn anything from watching you if your little war ends so soon?"

"Well, what do you learn if you keep jumping in?"

"You may open your eyes."

I did. The martian was back to his nebbish form. He had fished a pair of orange shorts out of his pile of clothes. "I do not understand your objection," he said. "This Sinc will kill you if he can. Do you want that?"

"No, but—"

"Do you believe that your side is in the right?"

"Yes, but—"

"Then why should you not accept my help?"

I wasn't sure myself. It felt wrong. It was like sneaking a suitcase bomb into Sinc's mansion and blowing it up.

I thought about it while I checked the hall. Nobody there. I closed the door and braced a chair under the knob. The dark one was still with us: he was trying to sit up.

"Look," I told the martian. "Maybe I can explain, maybe I can't. But if I don't get your word to stay out of this, I'll leave town. I swear it. I'll just drop the whole thing. Understand?"

"No."

"Will you promise?"

"Yes."

The Spanish type was rubbing his throat and staring at the martian. I didn't blame him. Fully dressed, the martian could have passed for a man, but not in a pair of orange undershorts. No hair or nipples marked his chest, no navel pitted his belly. The hood turned a flashing white smile on me and asked, "Who's he?"

"I'll ask the questions. Who're you?"

"Don Domingo." His accent was soft and Spanish. If he was worried, it didn't show. "Hey, how come you didn't fall down when I hit you?"

"I said I'll ask the—"

"Your face is turning pink. Are you embarrassed about something?"

"Dammit, Domingo, where's Sinc? Where were you supposed to take me?"

"The place."

"What place? The Bel Air place?"

"That's the one. You know, you have the hardest head—"

"Never mind that!"

"Okay okay. What will you do now?"

I couldn't call the law in. "Tie you up, I guess. After this is over, I'll turn you in for assault."

"After this is over, you won't be doing much, I think. You will live as long as they shoot at your head, but when—"

"Now drop that!"

The martian came out of the kitchen. His hand was flowing around a tin of corned beef, engulfing it tin and all. Domingo's eyes went wide and round.

Then the bedroom exploded.

It was a fire bomb. Half the living room was in flames in an instant. I scooped up the GyroJet, stuck it in my pocket.

The second bomb exploded in the hall. A blast of flame blew the door inward, picked up the chair I'd used to brace the door and flung it across the room.

"No!" Domingo yelled. "Handel was supposed to wait! Now what?"

Now we roast, I thought, stumbling back with my arm raised against the flames. A calm tenor voice asked, "Are you suffering from excessive heat?"

"Yes! Dammit, yes!"

A huge rubber ball slammed into my back, hurling me at the wall. I braced my arms to take up some of the impact. It was still going to knock me silly. Just before I reached it, the wall disappeared. It was the outside wall. Completely off balance, I dashed through an eight-foot hole and out into the empty night, six floors above concrete.

I clenched my teeth on the scream. The ground came up—the ground came up—where the hell was the ground? I opened my eyes. Everything was happening in slow motion. A second stretched to eternity. I had time to see strollers turning to crane upward, and to spot Handel near a corner of the building, holding a handkerchief to his bleeding nose. Time to look over my shoulder as Domingo stood against a flaming background, poised in slow motion in an eight-foot circle cut through the wall of my apartment. Flame licked him. He jumped. Slow motion?

He went past me like a falling safe. I saw him hit; I heard him hit. It's not a good sound. Living on Wall Street during November '80, I heard it night after night during the weeks following the election. I never got used to it.

Despite everything my belly and groin were telling me, I was not falling. I was sinking, like through water. By now half a dozen people were watching me settle. They all had their mouths open. Something poked me in the side, and I slapped at it and found myself clutching a .45 slug. I plucked another off my cheek. Handel was shooting at me.

I fired back, not aiming too well. If the martian hadn't been "helping" me I'd have blown his head off without a thought. As it was—anyway, Handel turned and ran.

I touched ground and walked away. A dozen hot, curious eyes bored into my back, but nobody tried to stop me.

There was no sign of the martian. Nothing else followed me either. I spent half an hour going through the usual contortions to shake a tail, but that was just habit. I wound up in a small, anonymous bar.

My eyebrows were gone, giving me a surprised look. I found myself studying my reflection in the bar mirror, looking for other signs that I'd been in a fight.

My face, never particularly handsome, has been dignified by scar tissue over the years, and my light brown hair never wants to stay in place. I had to move the part a year back to match a bullet crease in my scalp. The scars were all there, but I couldn't find any new cuts or bruises. My clothes weren't mussed. I didn't hurt anywhere. It was all unreal and vaguely dissatisfying.

But my next brush with Sinc would be for real.

I had my GyroJet and a sparse handful of rocket slugs in one pocket. Sinc's mansion was guarded like Fort Knox. And Sinc would be expecting me; he knew I wouldn't run.

We knew a lot about each other, considering we'd never met.

Sinc was a teetotaler. Not a fanatic; there was liquor on the premises of his mansion/fort. But it had to be kept out of Sinc's sight.

A woman usually shared his rooms. Sinc's taste was excellent. He changed his women frequently. They never left angry, and that's unusual. They never left poor, either.

I'd dated a couple of Sinc's exes, letting them talk about Sinc if they cared to. The consensus:

Sinc was an all-right guy, a spender, inventive and enthusiastic where it counted.

And neither particularly wanted to go back.

Sinc paid well and in full. He'd bail a man out of jail if the occasion arose. He never crossed anyone. Stranger yet, nobody ever crossed him. I'd had real trouble learning anything about Sinc. Nobody had wanted to talk.

But he'd crossed Domingo. That had caught us both by surprise.

Put it different. Someone had crossed Domingo. Domingo had been waiting for rescue, not bombs. So had I. It was Sinc's policy to pull his boys out if they got burned.

Either Domingo had been crossed against Sinc's orders, or Sinc was serious about wanting me dead.

I meet all kinds of people. I like it that way. By now I knew enough about Sinc to want to know more, much more. I wanted to meet him. And I was damn glad I'd shaken the martian, because...

Just what was it that bugged me about the martian?

It wasn't the strangeness. I meet all kinds. The way he shifted shape could throw a guy, but I don't bug easy.

Manners? He was almost too polite. And helpful.

Much too helpful.

That was part of it. The lines of battle had been drawn...and then something had stepped in from outer space. He was deus ex machina, the angel who descends on a string to set everything right, and incidentally to ruin the story. Me tackling Sinc with the martian's help was like a cop planting evidence. It was wrong. But more than that, it seemed to rob the thing of all its point, so that nothing mattered.

I shrugged angrily and had another drink. The bartender was trying to close. I drank up fast and walked out in a clump of tired drunks.

My car had tools I could use, but by now there'd be a bomb under the hood. I caught a cab and gave him an address on Bellagio, a couple of blocks from Sinc's place, if you can number anything in that area in "blocks." It's all hills, and the streets can drive you nuts. Sinc's home ground was a lumpy triangle with twisted sides, and big. It must have cost the Moon to landscape. One afternoon I'd walked past it, casing it. I couldn't see anything except through the gate. The fence was covered by thick climbing ivy. There were alarms in the ivy.

I waited till the taxi was gone, then loaded the GyroJet and started walking. That left one rocket slug still in my pocket.

In that neighborhood there was something to duck behind every time a car came by. Trees, hedges, gates with massive stone pillars. When I saw headlights I ducked, in case Sinc's boys were patrolling. A little walking took me to within sight of the ivy fence. Any closer and I'd be spotted.

So I ducked onto the property of one of Sinc's neighbors.

The place was an oddity: a rectangular pool with a dinky poolhouse at one end, a main house that was all right angles, and, between the two, a winding brook with a small bridge across it and trees hanging over the water. The brook must have been there before the house, and some of the trees too. It was a bit of primal wilderness that jarred strangely with all the right angles around it. I stuck with the brook, naturally.

This was the easy part. A burglary rap was the worst that could happen to me.

I found a fence. Beyond was asphalt, streetlamps, and then the ivy barrier to Sinc's domain.

Wire cutters? In the car. I'd be a sitting duck if I tried to go over. It could have been sticky, but I moved along the fence, found a rusty gate, and persuaded the padlock to open for me. Seconds later I was across the street and huddled against the ivy, just where I'd taken the trouble to hunt out a few of the alarms.

Ten minutes later I went over. Sitting duck? Yes. I had a clear view of the house, huge and mostly dark. In the moment before I dropped, someone would have had a clear view of me too, framed by lamplight at the top of the fence.

I dropped between the inner and outer fences and took a moment to think. I hadn't expected an inner fence. It was four feet of solid brick topped by six feet of wiring; and the wiring had a look of high voltage. Now what?

Maybe I could find something to short out the fence. But that would alert the house just as I was going over. Still, it might be the best chance.

Or I could go back over the ivy and try the gate defenses. Maybe I could even bluff my way through. Sinc must be as curious about me by now as I was about him. Everything I knew about Sinc was in the present tense. Of his past I knew only that there were no records of his past. But if Sinc had heard about my floating lightly down from a sixth-floor window, not unlike Mary Poppins . . . it might be worth a try. At least I'd live long enough to see what Sinc looked like.

Or—

"Hello. How does your war proceed?"

I sighed. He drifted down beside me, still man-shaped, dressed in a dark suit. I saw my mistake when he got closer. He'd altered his skin color to make a suit, shirt, and tie. At a distance it would pass. Even close up, he had nothing that needed hiding.

"I thought I'd got rid of you," I complained. "Are you bigger?" At a guess, his size had nearly doubled.

"Yes. I became hungry."

"You weren't kidding about your appetite."

"The war," he reminded me. "Are you planning to invade?"

"I was. I didn't know about this fence."

"Shall I—?"

"No! No, you shall not whatever you were thinking about. Just watch!"

"What am I to watch? You have done nothing for several minutes."

"I'll think of something."

"Of course."

"But whatever I do, I won't use your help, now or ever. If you want to watch, fine, be my guest. But don't help."

"I do not understand why not."

"It's like bugging a guy's telephone. Sinc has certain rights, even if he is a crook. He's immune from cruel and unusual punishment. The FBI can't bug his phone. You can't kill him unless you try him first, unless he's breaking a law at the time. And he shouldn't have to worry about armed attack by martians!"

"Surely if Sinc himself breaks the rules—"

"There are rules for dealing with lawbreakers!" I snapped.

The martian didn't answer. He stood beside me, seven feet tall and pudgy, a dark, manlike shape in the dim light from the house.

"Hey. How do you do all those things you do? Just a talent?"

"No. I carry implements." Something poked itself out of his baby-smooth chest, something hard that gleamed like metal. "This, for instance, damps momentum. Other portable artifacts lessen the pull of gravity, or reprocess the air in my lung."

"You keep them all inside you?"

"Why not? I can make fingers of all sizes inside me."

"Oh."

"You have said that there are rules for dealing with rule breakers. Surely you have already broken those rules. You have trespassed on private property. You have departed the scene of an accident, Don Domingo's death. You have—"

"All right."

"Then—"

"All right, I'll try again." I was wasting too much time. Getting over the fence was important. But so, somehow, was this. Because in a sense the martian was right. This had nothing to do with rules ...

"It has nothing to do with rules," I told him. "At least, not exactly. What counts is power. Sinc has taken over this city, and he'll want others too, later. He's got too much power. That's why someone has to stop him.

"And you give me too much power. A—a man who has too much power loses his head. I don't trust myself with you on my side. I'm a detective. If I break a law I expect to be jailed for it unless I can explain why. It makes me careful. If I tackle a crook who can whip me, I get bruised. If I shoot someone who doesn't deserve it, I go to prison. It all tends to make me careful. But with you around—"

"You lose your caution," said the dark bulk beside me. He spoke almost musingly, with more of human expression than I'd heard before. "You may be tempted to take more power than is good for you. I had not expected your species to be so wise."

"You thought we were stupid?"

"Perhaps. I had expected you to be grateful and eager for any help I might give. Now I begin to understand your attitude. We, too, try to balance out the amount of power given to individuals. What is that noise?"

It was a rustling, a scampering, barely audible but not at all furtive.

"I don't know."

"Have you decided upon your next move?"

"Yes. I—damn! Those are dogs!"

"What are dogs?"

Suddenly they were there. In the dark I couldn't tell what breed, but they were big, and they didn't bark. In a rustling of claws scrabbling on cement, they rounded the curve of the brick wall, coming from both sides, terribly fast. I hefted the GyroJet and knew there were twice as many dogs as I had shots.

Lights came on, bright and sudden, all over the grounds. I fired, and a finger of flame reached out and touched one of the dogs. He fell, tumbling, lost in the pack.

All the lights went deep red, blood red. The dogs stopped. The noise stopped. One dog, the nearest, was completely off the ground, hovering in mid-leap, his lips skinned back from sharp ruby teeth.

"It seems I have cost you time," the martian murmured. "May I return it?"

"What did you do?"

"I have used the damper of inertia in a projected field. The effect is as if time has stopped for all but us. In view of the length of time I have kept you talking, it is the least I can do."

Dogs to the left and dogs to the right, and lights all the hell over the place. I found men with rifles placed like statues about the wide lawn.

"I don't know if you're right or wrong," I said. "I'll be dead if you turn off that time stopper. But this is the last time. Okay?"

"Okay. We will use only the inertia damper."

"I'll move around to the other side of the house. Then you turn off the gadget. It'll give me some time to find a tree."

We went. I stepped carefully among the statues of dogs. The martian floated behind like a gigantic, pudgy ghost.

The channel between inner and outer fence went all the way around to the gate at the front of the house. Near the gate the inner fence pinched against the outer, and ended. But before we reached that point I found a tree. It was big and it was old, and one thick branch stretched above the fence to hover over our heads.

"Okay, turn off the gadget." The deep red lights glared a sudden white. I went up the ivy. Long arms and oversized hands are a big help to my famous monkey act. No point now in worrying about alarms. I had to balance standing on the outer fence to reach the branch with my fingers. When I put my weight on it, it dipped three feet and started to creak. I moved along hand over hand, and swung up into the leaves before my feet could brush the inner fence. At a comfortable crouch I settled myself to take stock.

There were at least three riflemen on the front lawn. They were moving in a search pattern, but they didn't expect to find anything. All the action was supposed to be in back.

The martian floated into the air and moved across the fence.

He nicked the top going over. A blue spark snapped, and he dropped like a sack of wheat. He landed against the fence, grounded now, and electricity leaped and sizzled. Ozone and burnt meat mixed in the cold night air. I dropped out of the tree and ran to him. I didn't touch him. The current would have killed me.

It had certainly killed him.

And that was something I'd never thought of. Bullets didn't faze him. He could produce miracles on demand. How could he be killed by a simple electric fence? If he'd only mentioned that! But he'd been surprised even to find that we had electricity.

I'd let a bystander be killed. The one thing I'd sworn I would never do again . . .

Now he was nothing like human. Metal things poked gleaming from the dead mass that had been an anthropologist from the stars.

The rustle of current had stopped seconds ago. I pulled one of the metal gadgets out of the mass, slid it in a pocket, and ran.

They spotted me right away. I took a zigzag course around a fenced tennis court, running for the front door. There were man-length windows on either side of the door. I ran up the steps, brought the GyroJet down in a hurried slashing blow that broke most of the panes in one window, and dove off the steps into a line of bushes.

When things happen that fast, your mind has to fill the gaps between what you saw and what you didn't. All three gunmen chased me frantically up the steps and through the front door, shouting at the tops of their lungs.

I moved along the side of the house, looking for a window.

Somebody must have decided I couldn't go through all that jagged glass. He must have outshouted the others, too, because I heard the hunt start again. I climbed a piece of wall, found a little ledge outside a darkened second-floor window. I got the window up without too much noise.

For the first time on this crazy night, I was beginning to think I knew what I was doing. That seemed odd, because I didn't know much about the layout of the house, and I hadn't the faintest idea where I was. But at least I knew the rules of the game. The variable, the martian, the deus ex machina, was out of the picture.

The rules were: whoever saw me would kill me if he could. No bystanders, no good guys would be here tonight. There would be no complex moral choices. I would not be offered supernatural help, in return for my soul or otherwise. All I had to do was try to stay alive.

(But a bystander had died.)

The bedroom was empty. Two doors led to a closet and a bathroom. Yellow light seeped under a third door. No choice here. I pulled the GyroJet and eased the third door open.

A face jerked up over the edge of a reading chair. I showed it the gun, kept it aimed as I walked around in front of the chair. Nobody else was in the room.

The face could have used a shave. It was beefy, middle-aged, but symmetrical enough except for an oversized nose. "I know you," it said, calmly enough considering the circumstances.

"I know you too." It was Adler, the one who'd gotten me into this mess, first by cohabiting with Morrison's wife and then by killing Morrison.

"You're the guy Morrison hired," said Adler. "The tough private eye. Bruce Cheseborough. Why couldn't you let well enough alone?"

"I couldn't afford to."

"You couldn't afford not to. Have some coffee."

"Thanks. You know what'll happen if you yell or anything?"

"Sure." He picked up a water glass, dumped the water in the wastebasket. He picked up a silver thermos and poured coffee into his own coffee cup and into the water glass, moving slowly and evenly. He didn't want to make me nervous.

He himself was no more than mildly worried. That was reassuring, in a way, because he probably wouldn't do anything stupid. But . . . I'd seen this same calm in Don Domingo, and I knew the cause. Adler and Domingo and everyone else who worked for Sinc, they all had perfect faith in him. Whatever trouble they were in, Sinc would get them out.

I watched Adler take a healthy gulp of coffee before I touched the glass. The coffee was black and strong, heavily laced with good brandy. My first gulp tasted so good I damn near smiled at Adler.

Adler smiled back. His eyes were wide and fixed, as if he were afraid to look away from me. As if he expected me to explode. I tried to think of a way he could have dropped something in the coffee without drinking it himself. There wasn't any.

"You made a mistake," I told him, and gulped more coffee. "If my name had been Rip Hammer or Mike Hero, I might have dropped the whole thing when I found out you were with Sinc's boys. But when your name is Bruce Cheseborough, Junior, you can't afford to back out of a fight."

"You should have. You might have lived." He said it without concentrating on it. A puzzled frown tugged at the corners of his eyes and mouth. He was still waiting for something to happen.

"Tell you what. You write me out a confession, and I can leave here without killing anyone. Won't that be nice?"

"Sure. What should I confess to?"

"Killing Morrison."

"You don't expect me to do that."

"Not really."

"I'm going to surprise you." Adler got up, still slow, and went behind the desk. He kept his hands high until I was around behind him. "I'll write your damn confession. You know why? Because you'll never use it. Sinc'll see to that."

"If anyone comes through that door—"

"I know, I know." He started writing. While he was at it, I examined the tool I'd taken from the martian's corpse. It was white shiny metal, with a complex shape that was like nothing I'd ever seen. Like the plastic guts in a toy gun, half melted and then cooled, so that all the parts were merged and rounded. I had no idea what it did. Anyway, it was no good to me. I could see slots where buttons or triggers were buried, but they were too small for fingers. Tweezers might have reached them, or a hatpin.

Adler handed me the paper he'd been writing on. He'd made it short and pointed: motive, means, details of time. Most of it I already knew.

"You don't say what happened to the body."

"Same thing that happened to Domingo."

"Domingo?"

"Domingo, sure. When the cops came to pick him up in back of your place, he was gone. Even the bloodstains were gone. A miracle, right?" Adler smiled nastily. When I didn't react he looked puzzled.

"How?" I asked him.

Adler shrugged uncomfortably. "You already know, don't you? I won't write it down. It would bring Sinc in. You'll have to settle for what you've got."

"Okay. Now I tie you up and wend my way homeward."

Adler was startled. He couldn't have faked it. "Now?"

"Sure. You killed my client, not Sinc."

He grinned, not believing me. And he still thought something was about to happen.

I used the bathrobe sash for his arms and a handkerchief for a gag. There were other bathrobes in the closet to finish the job. He still didn't believe I was going to leave, and he was still waiting for something to happen. I left him on the bed, in the dark.

Now what?

I turned off the lights in the sitting room and went to the window.

The lawn was alive with men and dogs and far too much light. That was the direct way out.

I had Adler's hide in my pocket. Adler, who had killed my client. Was I still chasing Sinc? Or should I try to get clear with that piece of paper?

Get clear, of course.

I stood by the window, picking out shadows. There was a lot of light, but the shadows of bushes and trees were jet black. I found a line of hedge, lighted on this side; but I could try the other. Or move along that side of the tennis court, then hop across to that odd-looking statue—

The door opened suddenly, and I whirled.

A man in dark slacks and a smoking jacket stood facing my gun. Unhurriedly, he stepped through the door and closed it behind him.

It was Sinc. Lester Dunhaven Sinclair III was a man in perfect condition, not a pound overweight or underweight, with gymnasium muscles. I guessed his age at thirty-four or so. Once before I'd seen him, in public, but never close enough to see what I saw now: that his thick blond hair was a wig.

He smiled at me. "Cheseborough, isn't it?"

"Yah."

"What did you do with my . . . lieutenant?" He looked me up and down. "I gather he's still with us."

"In the bedroom. Tied up." I moved around to lock the door to the hall.

I understood now why Sinc's men had made him into something like a feudal overlord. He measured up. He inspired confidence. His confidence in himself was total. Looking at him, I could almost believe that nothing could stand against him.

"I gather you were too intelligent to try the coffee. A pity," said Sinc. He seemed to be examining my gun, but with no trace of fear. I tried to think it was a bluff, but I couldn't. No man could put across such a bluff. His twitching muscles would give him away. I began to be afraid of Sinc.

"A pity," he repeated. "Every night for the past year Adler has gone to bed with a pot of coffee spiked with brandy. Handel too."

What was he talking about? The coffee hadn't affected me at all. "You've lost me," I said.

"Have I?" Smiling as if he'd won a victory, Sinc began to gurgle. It was eerily familiar, that gurgle. I felt the rules changing again, too fast to follow. Smiling, gurgling rhythmically, Sinc put a hand in his pants pocket and pulled out an automatic. He took his time about it.

It was not a big gun, but it was a gun; and the moment I knew that, I fired.

A GyroJet rocket-slug burns its solid fuel in the first twenty-five feet, and moves from there on momentum. Sinc was twenty-five feet away. Flame reached out to tap him on the shoulder joint, and Sinc smiled indulgently. His gun was steady on the bridge of my nose.

I fired at his heart. No effect. The third shot perforated the space between his eyes. I saw the hole close, and I knew. Sinc was cheating too.

He fired.

I blinked. Cold fluid trickled down from my forehead, stung my eyes, dribbled across my lips. I tasted rubbing alcohol.

"You're a martian too," I said.

"No need for insult," Sinc said mildly. He fired again. The gun was a squirtgun, a plastic kid's toy shaped like an automatic. I wiped the alcohol out of my eyes and looked at him.

"Well," said Sinc. "Well." He reached up, peeled his hair off, and dropped it. He did the same with his eyebrows and eyelashes. "Well, where is he?"

"He told me he was an . . . anthropologist. Was he lying?"

"Sure, Cheseborough. He was the Man. The Law. He's tracked me over distances you couldn't even write down." Sinc backed up against a wall. "You wouldn't even understand what my people called my crime. And you've no reason to protect him. He used you. Every time he stopped a bullet for you, it was to make me think you were him. That's why he helped you on a floating act. That's why he's disposed of Domingo's body. You were his stalking-horse. I'm supposed to kill you while he's sneaking up on me. He'll sacrifice you without a qualm. Now *where is he*?"

"Dead. He didn't know about electric fences." A voice from the hall, Handel's voice, bellowed, "Mr. Sinclair! Are you all right in there?"

"I have a guest," Sinc called out. "He has a gun."

"What do we do?"

"Don't do anything," Sinc called to him. And then he started to laugh. He was losing his human contours, "relaxing" because I already knew what he was.

"I wouldn't have believed it," he chuckled. "He tracked me all that way to die on an electric fence!" His chuckles cut off like a broken tape, making me wonder how real they were, how real his laughter could be with his no doubt weird breathing system. "The current couldn't kill him, of course. It must have shorted his airmaker and blown the battery."

"The spiked coffee was for him," I guessed. "He said he could be killed by organic poisons. He meant alcohol."

"Obviously. And all I did was give you a free drink," he chuckled.

"I've been pretty gullible. I believed what your women told me."

"*They* didn't know." He did a pretty accurate double take. "You thought . . . Cheseborough, have I made rude comments about your sex life?"

"No. Why?"

"Then you can leave mine alone."

He had to be kidding. No he didn't; he could take any shape he liked. Wow, I thought. Sinc's really gone native. Maybe he *was* laughing, or thought he was.

Sinc moved slowly toward me. I backed away, holding the useless gun.

"You realize what happens now?"

I took a guess. "Same thing that happened to Domingo's body. All your embarrassing bodies."

"Exactly. Our species is known for its enormous appetite." He moved toward me, the squirt gun forgotten in his right hand. His muscles had sagged and smoothed. Now he was like the first step in making a clay model of a man. But his mouth was growing larger, and his teeth were two sharp-edged horseshoes.

I fired once more.

Something smashed heavily against the door. Sinc didn't hear it. Sinc was melting, losing all form as he tried to wrap himself around his agony. From the fragments of his shattered plastic squirt gun, rubbing alcohol poured over what had been his hand and dripped to the floor.

The door boomed again. Something splintered.

Sinc's hand was bubbling, boiling. Sinc, screaming, was flowing out of his slacks and smoking jacket. And I...I snapped out of whatever force was holding me rooted, and I picked up the silver thermos and poured hot spiked coffee over whatever it was that writhed on the floor.

Sinc bubbled all over. White metal machinery extruded itself from the mass and lay on the rug.

The door crackled and gave. By then I was against the wall, ready to shoot anything that looked my way. Handel burst into the room and stopped dead.

He stood there in the doorway, while the stars grew old and went out. Nothing, I felt, could have torn his eyes from that twitching, bubbling mass. Gradually the mass stopped moving...and Handel gulped, got his throat working, shrieked, and ran from the room.

I heard the meaty thud as he collided with a guard, and I heard him babbling, "Don't go in there! Don't...oh, don't..." and then a sob, and the sound of uneven running feet.

I went into the bedroom and out the window. The grounds still blazed with light, but I saw no motion. Anyway, there was nothing out there but dogs and men.

CITIZEN JELL
Michael Shaara

Michael Shaara is best remembered today for his sports and historical fiction, most famously for The Killer Angels, *a terrific novel about the Battle of Gettysburg which won the 1975 Pulitzer Prize for Fiction, and was both adapted into the movie* Gettysburg *and inspired the TV series* Firefly. *While perhaps overshadowed, it shouldn't be overlooked that Shaara cut his teeth as an author writing short fiction for science fiction magazines in the 1950s and was one of the early names in military science fiction, with a knack for world-weary characters facing hard choices.*

Here we have one such story, originally published in the August 1959 issue of Galaxy Magazine. *It follows an alien who has retired to Florida, as one does, where he spends his days fishing and entertaining the local children, desperately seeking to avoid the notice of his people and live out his days in paradise. So naturally, he now faces a choice where he must sacrifice one to save the other* ...

🦅 🦅 🦅

None of his neighbors knew Mr. Jell's great problem. None of his neighbors, in truth, knew Mr. Jell at all. He was only an odd old man who lived alone in a little house on the riverbank. He had the usual little mail box, marked "E. Jell," set on a post in front of his house, but he never got any mail, and it was not long before people began wondering where he got the money he lived on.

Not that he lived well, certainly; all he ever seemed to do was just fish, or just sit on the riverbank watching the sky, telling tall stories to small children. And none of that took any money to do.

But still, he was a little odd; people sensed that. The stories he told all his young friends, for instance—wild, weird tales about spacemen and other planets—people hardly expected tales like that from such an old man. Tales about cowboys and Indians they might have understood, but spaceships?

So he was definitely an odd old man, but just how odd, of course, no one ever really knew. The stories he told the children, stories about space travel, about weird creatures far off in the Galaxy—those stories were all true.

Mr. Jell was, in fact, a retired spaceman.

Now that was part of Mr. Jell's problem, but it was not all of it. He had very good reasons for not telling anybody the truth about himself—no one except the children—and he had even more excellent reasons for not letting his own people know where he was.

The race from which Mr. Jell had sprung did not allow this sort of thing—retirement to Earth. They were a fine, tolerant, extremely advanced people, and they had learned long ago to leave undeveloped races, like the one on Earth, alone. Bitter experience had taught them that more harm than good came out of giving scientific advances to backward races, and often just the knowledge of their existence caused trouble among primitive peoples.

No, Mr. Jell's race had for a long while quietly avoided contact with planets like Earth, and if they had known Mr. Jell had violated the law, they would have come swiftly and taken him away—a thing Mr. Jell would have died rather than let happen.

Mr. Jell was unhuman, yes, but other than that he was a very gentle, usual old man. He had been born and raised on a planet so overpopulated that it was one vast city from pole to pole. It was the kind of place where a man could walk under the open sky only on rooftops, where vacant lots were a mark of incredible wealth. Mr. Jell had passed most of his long life under unbelievably cramped and crowded conditions—either in small spaceships or in the tiny rooms of unending apartment buildings.

When Mr. Jell had happened across Earth on a long voyage some years ago, he had recognized it instantly as the place of his dreams. He had had to plan very carefully, but when the time came for his retirement, he was able to slip away. The language of Earth was already on record; he had no trouble learning it, no trouble buying a small cottage on the river in a lovely warm place called Florida. He settled down quietly, a retired old man of one hundred and eighty-five, looking forward to the best days of his life.

And Earth turned out to be more wonderful than his dreams. He discovered almost immediately that he had a great natural aptitude for fishing, and though the hunting instinct had been nearly bred out of him and he could no longer summon up the will to kill, still he could walk in the open woods and marvel at the room, the incredible open, wide, and unoccupied room, live animals in a real forest, and the sky above, clouds seen through the trees—real trees, which Mr. Jell had seldom seen before. And, for a long while, Mr. Jell was certainly the happiest man on Earth.

He would arise, very early, to watch the sun rise. After that, he might fish, depending on the weather, or sit home just listening to the lovely rain on the roof, watching the mighty clouds, the lightning. Later in the afternoon, he might go for a walk along the riverbank, waiting for school to be out so he could pass some time with the children.

Whatever else he did, he would certainly go looking for the children.

A lifetime of too much company had pushed the need for companionship pretty well out of him, but then he had always loved children, and they made his life on the river complete. They believed him; he could tell them his memories in safety, and there was something very special in that, to have secrets with friends. One or two of them, the most trustworthy, he even allowed to see the Box.

Now the Box was something extraordinary, even to so advanced a man as Mr. Jell. It was a device which analyzed matter, made a record of it, and then duplicated it. The Box could duplicate anything.

What Mr. Jell would do, for example, would be to put a loaf of bread into the Box, and press a button, and presto, there would be two loaves of bread, each perfectly alike, atom for atom. It would be absolutely impossible for anyone to tell them apart. This was the way Mr. Jell made most of his food, and all of his money. Once he had gotten one original dollar bill, the Box went on duplicating it—and bread, meat, potatoes, anything else Mr. Jell desired was instantly available at the touch of a button.

Once the Box duplicated a thing, anything, it was no longer necessary to have the original. The Box filed a record in its electronic memory, describing, say, bread, and Mr. Jell had only to dial a number any time he wanted bread. And the Box needed no fuel except dirt, leaves, old pieces of wood, just anything made out of atoms—most of which it would arrange into bread or meat or whatever Mr. Jell wanted, and the rest of which it would use as a source of power.

So the Box made Mr. Jell entirely independent, but it did even more than that; it had one other remarkable feature. It could be used also as a transmitter and receiver. Of matter. It was, in effect, the Sears Roebuck catalogue of Mr. Jell's people, with its own built-in delivery service.

If there was an item Mr. Jell needed, any item at all, and that item was available on any of the planets ruled by Mr. Jell's people, Mr. Jell could dial for it, and it would appear in the Box in a matter of seconds.

The makers of the Box prided themselves on the speed of their delivery, the ease with which they could transmit matter instantaneously across light-years of space. Mr. Jell admired this property, too, but he could make no use of it. For once he had dialed, he would also be billed. And of course his Box would be traced to Earth. That Mr. Jell could not allow.

No, he would make do with whatever was available on Earth. He had to get along without the catalogue.

And he really never needed the catalogue, not at least for the first year, which was perhaps the finest year of his life. He lived in perfect freedom, ever-continuing joy, on the riverbank, and made some special friends: one Charlie, aged five, one Linda, aged four, one Sam, aged six. He spent a great deal of his time with these friends, and their parents approved of him happily as a free baby-sitter, and he was well into his second year on Earth when the first temptation arose.

Bugs.

Try as he might, Mr. Jell could not learn to get along with bugs.

His air-conditioned, antiseptic, neat and odorless existence back home had been an irritation, yes, but he had never in his life learned to live with bugs of any kind, and he was too old to start now. But he had picked an unfortunate spot. The state of Florida was a heaven for Mr. Jell, but it was also a heaven for bugs.

There is probably nowhere on Earth with a greater variety of insects, large and small, winged and stinging, than Florida, and the natural portion of all kinds found their ways into Mr. Jell's peaceful existence. He was unable even to clear out his own house—never mind the endless swarms of mosquitoes that haunted the riverbank—and the bugs gave him some very nasty moments. And the temptation was that he alone, of all people on Earth, could have exterminated the bugs at will.

One of the best-selling export gadgets on Mr. Jell's home world was a small, flying, burrowing, electronic device which had been built specifically to destroy bugs on planets they traded with. Mr. Jell was something of a technician, and he might not even have had to order a Destroyer through the catalogue, but there were other problems.

Mr. Jell's people had not been merely capricious when they formed their policy of non-intervention. Mr. Jell's bug-destroyer would kill all the bugs, but it would undoubtedly ruin the biological balance upon which the country's animal life rested. The birds which fed on the bugs would die, and the animals which fed on the birds, and so on, down a course which could only be disastrous. And even one of the little Destroyers would put an extraordinary dent in the bug population of the area; once sent out into the woods, it could not be recalled or turned off, and it would run for years.

No, Mr. Jell made the valiant decision to endure little itchy bumps on his arms for the rest of his days.

Yet that was only the first temptation. Soon there were others, much bigger and more serious. Mr. Jell had never considered this problem at all, but he began to realize at last that his people had been more right than he knew. He was in the uncomfortable position of a man who can do almost anything, and does not dare do it. A miracle man who must hide his miracles.

The second temptation was rain. In the middle of Mr. Jell's second year, a drought began, a drought which covered all of Florida. He sat by helplessly, day after day, while the water level fell in his own beloved river, and fish died gasping breaths, trapped in little pockets upstream. Several months of that produced Mr. Jell's second great temptation. Lakes and wells were dry all over the country, farms and orange groves were dry, there were great fires in the woods, birds and animals died by the thousands.

All that while, of course, Mr. Jell could easily have made it rain. Another simple matter, although this time he would have had to send away for the materials, through the Box. But he couldn't do that. If he did, they would come for him, and he consoled himself by arguing that he had no right to make it rain. That was not strictly controllable, either. It might rain and rain for several days, once started, filling up the lakes, yes, and robbing water from somewhere else, and then what would happen when the normal rainy season came?

Mr. Jell shuddered to think that he might be the cause, for all his good intentions, of vast floods, and he resisted the second temptation. But that was relatively easy. The third temptation turned out to be infinitely harder.

Little Charlie, aged five, owned a dog, a grave, sober, studious dog named Oscar. On a morning near the end of Mr. Jell's second year, Oscar was run over by a truck. And Charlie gathered the dog up, all crumpled and bleeding and already dead, and carried him tearfully but faithfully off to Mr. Jell, who could fix anything.

And Mr. Jell could certainly have fixed Oscar. Hoping to guard against just such an accident, he had already made a "recording" of Oscar several months before. The Box had scanned Oscar and discovered exactly how he was made—for the Box, as has been said, could duplicate anything—and Mr. Jell had only to dial the Oscar number to produce a new Oscar. A live Oscar, grave and sober, atom for atom identical with the Oscar that was dead.

But young Charlie's parents, who had been unable to comfort the boy, came to Mr. Jell's house with him. And Mr. Jell had to stand there, red-faced and very sad, and deny to Charlie that there was anything he could do, and watch the look in Charlie's eyes turn into black betrayal. And when the boy ran off crying, Mr. Jell had the worst temptation of all.

He thought so at the time, but he could not know that the dog had not been the worst. The worst was yet to come.

He resisted a great many temptations after that, but now for the first time doubt had begun to seep in to his otherwise magnificent existence. He swore to himself that he could never give this life up. Here on the riverbank, dry and buggy as it well was, was still the most wonderful life he had ever known, infinitely preferable to the drab crowds he would face at home. He was an old man, grimly aware of the passage of time. He would consider himself the luckiest of men to be allowed to die and be buried here.

But the temptations went on.

First there was the Red Tide, a fish-killing disease which often sweeps Florida's coast, murdering fish by the hundreds of millions. He could have cured that, but he would have had to send off for the chemicals.

Next there was an infestation of the Mediterranean fruit fly, a bug which threatened most of Florida's citrus crop and very nearly ruined little Linda's father, a farmer. There was a Destroyer available which could be set to kill just one type of bug, Mr. Jell knew, but he would have had to order it, again, from the catalogue. So he had to let Linda's father lose most of his life's savings.

Shortly after that, he found himself tempted by a young, gloomy couple, a Mr. and Mrs. Ridge, whom he visited one day looking for their young son, and found himself in the midst of a morbid quarrel. Mr. Ridge's incredible point of view was that this was too terrible a world to bring children into. Mr. Jell found himself on the verge of saying that he himself had personally visited forty-seven other worlds, and not one could hold a candle to this one.

He resisted that, at last, but it was surprising how close he had come to talking, even over such a relatively small thing as that, and he had concluded that he was beginning to wear under the strain, when there came the day of the last temptation.

Linda, the four-year-old, came down with a sickness. Mr. Jell learned with a shock that everyone on Earth believed her incurable.

He had no choice then. He knew that from the moment he heard of the illness, and he wondered why he had never until that moment anticipated this. There was, of course, nothing else he could do, much as he loved this Earth, and much as he knew little Linda would certainly have died in the natural order of things. All of that made no difference; it had finally come home to him that if a man is able to help his neighbors and does not, then he ends up something less than a man.

He went out on the riverbank and thought about it all that afternoon, but he was only delaying the decision. He knew he could not go on living here or anywhere with the knowledge of the one small grave for which he would be forever responsible. He knew Linda would not begrudge him those few moments, that one afternoon more. He waited, watching the sun go down, and then he went back into the house and looked through the catalogue. He found the number of the serum and dialed for it.

The serum appeared within less than a minute. He took it out of the Box and stared at it, the thought of the life it would bring to Linda driving all despair out of his mind. It was a universal serum; it would protect her from all disease for the rest of her life. They would be coming for him soon, but he knew it would take them a while to get here, perhaps even a full day. He did not bother to run. He was much to old to run and hide.

He sat for a while thinking of how to get the serum to her, but that was no problem. Her parents would give her anything she asked now, and he made up some candy, injecting the serum microscopically into the chunks of chocolate, and then suddenly had a wondrous idea. He put the chunks into the Box and went on duplicating candy until he had several boxes.

When he was finished with that, he went visiting all the houses of all the good people he knew, leaving candy for them and their children. He knew he should not do that, but, he thought, it couldn't really do much harm, could it? Just those few lives altered, out of an entire world?

But the idea had started wheels turning in his mind, and toward the end of that night, he began to chuckle with delight. Might as well be flashed for a rogg as a zilb.

He ordered out one special little bug Destroyer, from the Box, set to kill just one bug, the medfly, and sent it happily down the road toward Linda's farm. After that, he duplicated Oscar and sent the dog yelping homeward with a note on his collar. When he was done with that, he ordered a batch of chemicals, several tons of it, and ordered a conveyor to carry it down and dump it into the river, where it would be washed out to sea and so end the Red Tide.

By the time that was over, he was very tired; he had been up the whole night. He did not know what to do about young Mr. Ridge, the one who did not want children. He decided that if the man was that foolish, nothing could help him. But there was one other thing he could do. Praying silently that once he started this thing, it would not get out of hand, he made it rain.

In this way, he deprived himself of the last sunrise. There was nothing but gray sky, misty, blowing, when he went out onto the riverbank that morning. But he did not really mind. The fresh air and the rain on his face were all the good-bye he could have asked for. He was sitting on wet grass wondering the last thought—why in God's name don't more people here realize what a beautiful world this is?—when he heard a voice behind him.

The voice was deep and very firm.

"Citizen Jell," it said.

The old man sighed.

"Coming," he said, "coming."

DESIGNATED DESTROYER
Steve Diamond

As someone who often enjoys his science fiction and fantasy tinged with just the right amount of horror, it has been a joy to see Steve Diamond joining the Baen roster with Servants of War, *cowritten by Larry Correia. High fantasy World War I with mech suits of dead golems, lobotomized shock troopers, trench lines with poison gas and raining blood, and malevolent gods manipulating the war for their own ends . . . it's grimdark fantasy at its best, and if the words "Do you believe in fate, Illarion?" don't turn your guts to ice by the end, you don't have a pulse.*

Here in our first original story of the anthology, Steve has set aside the blood magic and mech suits for a claustrophobic tale of post-apocalyptic science fiction. A survivor stumbles out of cryogenic freezing to a future where mankind lingers by a thread—and whatever drove us to the brink might still be too close for comfort.

🕷 🕷 🕷

Bright, pulsing red lights were the first thing my mind registered.

I tried blinking away the haze of sleep, but couldn't focus. All I saw was red light through a fog. When I reached up to rub my eyes, my hands hit something solid directly in front of me. Glass? Where was I?

Keeping my hands close to my body, I got them to my face and attempted to rub away the sleep and confusion. My eyes cleared somewhat, and I found myself in a tube filled with thick fog. I wiped against the inside of the glass, clearing away the moisture buildup so

I could look outside. Again I tried to blinked away the exhaustion with no success.

I looked around my pod unable to remember how I got here. The answer was there, just out of reach. If I could clear my head I'd know the answer. Pressing my hands against the inside of the glass, I pushed. Nothing happened. My arms felt oddly weak.

My vision darkened, then returned. Outside the pod, I could see a dark room, roughly circular. Evenly spaced along the walls were other tall, cylindrical tubes. Other people, then? Like me?

A dark shadow moved around the room.

I pushed back into my pod, for all the good it would do. My heart pounded, and for the first time since waking up, I felt the grip of fear tightening around my chest. Between the red light, fog inside the tube, and my confused brain, I couldn't make out the shape moving from pod to pod. It moved to the left out of my line of sight, then suddenly popped up in front of me on the other side of the glass.

My mouth opened to scream, but nothing came out. I blinked a few times, and the figure resolved. A woman.

She looked frantic, eyes looking all around the outside of my tube for . . . for what? For something, I was sure. Something important. Fear gave way to exhaustion. I was so tired, and all I wanted was to close my eyes again . . .

Thumping against the glass pulled me from the edges of sleep. The woman pounded on the outside of the glass with her fists and waved to get my attention. She pointed down near my waist, insistently. The inside of the pod lacked room to move around, but I shifted to the side and looked down by my right side. I could barely see with the swirling fog inside the tube, so I felt around. My fingers brushed a handle. The woman pressed her face against the glass, black hair matting between her skin and the clear barrier. She nodded and lifted a hand pantomiming a pulling motion.

Pull? Pull what? I looked down again, confused. What had I just been doing? The interior fog cleared momentarily, and I saw my hand gripped a lever. The woman made the pulling motion again.

I pulled up on the handle, and with a hiss of air escaping the tube, the glass pushed outward, then lifted up and away.

The fog cleared, and I took a deep breath. When I pushed away from the pod, my knees buckled, sending me crashing to the floor.

"James? James are you all right?"

The voice came from so far away. Was it even real? Maybe it was just the memory of a voice I once knew.

"James?"

Louder this time. Closer. I felt a cold hand on my shoulder and jerked away from it, falling the rest of the way to the floor. I rolled to my back and held my hands up to ward off... to ward off... something. Someone?

A woman knelt by my side, hands up and palms out.

"It's okay, James. It's me, Sara. Take a few deep breaths."

I did as she instructed, and felt a wave of nausea roll through me. I rolled to my side and vomited, heaving until nothing more came out. I laid there for a few minutes. Maybe hours. Nothing was clear.

"Better?"

I nodded. I did feel a little better. "Where?" I barely got the word out. My throat was raw and bone dry.

"We're in Prometheus Bunker. North America."

Bunker? Prometheus? Something about those words sparked a memory. I remembered being escorted underground, one soldier with a hand on my arm, pulling me along. I remembered looking back, seeing more soldiers firing their guns through the opening of a huge, closing hangar door.

"Who?" I rasped.

"I'm Sara. Sara Addison. You know me."

I shook my head and tapped on my chest.

"Oh," she said, then nodded in understanding. "You're James Conroy. I'm sorry, I should have realized pulling you out of cryo out of sequence would have some side effects. Are you having trouble focusing?"

I nodded. James Conroy. My name was James Conroy. It felt right. Snippets of memories flooded me, random faces all calling me James. With the name came other memories of me working on elaborate computer systems, and machinery. I remembered working on these pods. Cryo pods. But... but I couldn't remember *why*.

"Look, James, I know you have a lot of questions, and your mind is muddled and fuzzy. That will all go away in time. You weren't scheduled to be woken up for another fifty years, when we were about to launch. But we have a problem, and we need you now."

Launch? Fifty years? What was she talking about? I pretended I understood and nodded my agreement.

"James, I'm going to take you to the medbay. You can rest for a little bit while your body reacclimatizes. You have cryo-stasis sickness. Do you remember what that means?"

I nodded automatically. I did know. A light reaction to cryo sleep was normal. Nausea, disorientation, and lethargy. Everyone experienced it to a small degree. No calibration of equipment could be completely perfect, and everyone's physiology differed. But the person-by-person setup was as accurate as possible. Age, gender, weight, height. All of it taken into account. To be removed from cryo too late or too early resulted in extreme versions of the usual side effects, plus more. In extreme circumstances, memory loss, physical weakness, hallucinations, and even death.

Sara walked me to the medbay, which thankfully was just down the hallway. I had a vague recollection of medical being situated near all the cryo pod rooms . . . but I just didn't know. I had to pause numerous times to dry heave, but with each one I felt a little better. Granted, every minute improvement felt like a massive one in this state.

The red emergency lighting pulsed, the only light in these halls directed us toward medical, and runners in the center of the ceiling pointed to the facility's exits. Though somewhere in my mind, I knew using the exits would be bad.

Sara pulled me into the medbay and sat me on a low bed. At each corner of the bed stood a small, freestanding light. She flicked them all on, illuminating the room in bright, white fluorescent light.

"Can't keep them on too long," she said. "Taxes the generators. Anything coming back?"

"Yes." My throat still felt like it had been scrubbed with a wire brush. "Water?"

She blinked at me in confusion, said, "Oh. Right. I'll get you some." She went to the back corner of the room and returned with a small ration bag. "Here. This should help."

The top of the bag ripped free easily, and I downed the water greedily. It wasn't cold, but it still soothed the rawness I felt. As I drank, she wrapped a blanket around my shoulders. "Thank you. I'm sorry, I don't remember you. I remember a..." I thought hard, conjuring up the image of a beautiful blond doctor. What was her name? Easton? No, Eaton. "I think her name was Eaton. Can't remember her first name."

Sara shrugged. "She's still in cryo, I think. I'm an assistant medical physician, so I'm still a little lost. She isn't scheduled to wake up for thirty years."

"Then why are you awake?"

"I don't know. My pod just opened, and I woke up on the ground. I'm not sure how. My whole pod group . . . it's all gone. All flatlined."

A bad way to go. You go into cryo expecting it to feel like a quick dream. But to never wake? Some people called the pods coffins.

Memories and facts floated into my consciousness. Hundreds of people in cryo. Schedules of sleep and wakefulness. My time to wake was . . . was . . . seventy years from entry? But why? Why the schedule? Why the Prometheus Bunker? We'd gone down because . . . because . . .

I pressed my palms to my eyes. I could barely see straight. Every few seconds my vision doubled. Nausea still took hold of me in waves. My head began aching, a stabbing pain in the front of my head behind my left eye.

"Why am I awake?"

Sara sat down next to me. She seemed smaller, more worn. "I didn't know what else to do. Cryo systems are failing. The facility's backups won't hold much longer. If we don't do something, the AI will—"

"Begin prioritizing power allocation." The words came automatically. "And if we are already on emergency power, then life support can't handle waking up a lot of people. How many people are awake?"

"Just the two of us, I think. But I haven't explored that much. Lots of places in the bunker are locked down, and I don't have access."

"Okay. And you're sure we are still in the bunker?" Why did that question matter? Something she'd said earlier. A . . . launch? Yes. The bunker was the first stage. At a designated time, it was supposed to launch a surface bombardment. But I couldn't remember why. "We haven't . . . launched?"

"No. And I can't get to the control center to see why? I don't have clearance."

That didn't seem right. "Something must be wrong. Everyone should have emergency access. Your biometrics should be keyed in everywhere."

"I know, but it doesn't work. I keep getting errors."

I closed my eyes. If I had five minutes, I could be blissfully asleep. But no. I didn't have time for that, regardless of my exhaustion or the side effects. With cryo pods failing, our facility's viability was in jeopardy. Even with my struggles to remember where I was—*who* I was—the need to protect the other people in stasis was ingrained in me.

A shiver passed through me. For the first time since falling out of the pod, my mind registered my appearance. I wore only a pair of fitted shorts, little more than underwear. The chill of cryo felt bone-deep, and the blanket couldn't drive it away. I remembered . . . lockers.

"Where are the clothing and equipment lockers? I need to get dressed."

"Oh!" Sara's face reddened in embarrassment. "Of course. I'll walk you over there. But let's take it slow. You'll be under the effects of cryo sickness for a while, I'm afraid."

She powered down the fluorescent lights and handed me a flashlight. I didn't turn it on. Instead I pulled the blanket closer around me. My body began shivering, lightly at first, then heavy until I had to clench my jaw to keep my teeth from chattering. I followed her from the medbay and down another identical hallway and into another. Evenly bolted along the walls of the hall, signs pointed directions to other areas of the facility. Medbay was back the way we came. At a junction, the sign directed us to Operations to the right, or Locker Rooms to the left.

Operations. That would be the control center Sara mentioned. We'd need to go there to check the system status throughout the bunker. But for now, clothes.

The hall split into a wall with two doors, each with handprint scanners outside the door. The left showed MEN, and the right WOMEN. I pressed my palm against the pad next to the men's door and it lit up blue, then flashed green. My name scrolled across the top of it, and the door's magnetic lock clicked. Sara pulled the door open, then followed me inside.

The emergency lighting shone dimmer in the room, and the rows of lockers cast heavy shadows. Again that feeling of fear spiked inside me as I looked into the dark rows. A long, narrow bench split the space between the banks of lockers.

"Do you remember which locker is yours?"

I shook my head and forced myself to walk into the closest row. When I looked down the long row, the darkness between stretched, going back away from me for an eternity. And there, in the very back of it, the blackness swirled, threatening to suck me in. I shut my eyes and leaned against the cold metal of the lockers.

"James, are you all right?"

I opened my eyes again and that swirling darkness had been replaced by a normal, shadowed row of lockers in which red lights pulsed. I pressed my forehead against the nearest locker door. Despite my shivering, the cool metal felt good against my skin. I looked up and saw a nameplate that read D SANTOS. The next one in line showed P RYDER. Alphabetical.

"I think my locker is deeper in. You go right. I'll go left." I didn't wait for her to acknowledge me. I needed a moment alone, and this would have to do.

I kept a hand up, constantly brushing against the lockers. I stopped frequently, leaning against the metal to catch my breath and to ward off the dizziness plaguing me. But I never sat down, knowing I'd struggle to get back up.

My locker was in the back, left side of the room. A brief memory of opening it flashed in my mind. Nothing important, nothing major. But the confirmation lifted a burden from my shoulders I hadn't realized I'd been carrying. I pressed my thumb onto the scanner, and the door popped open.

Inside, I found a few sets of clothes on hangers, a jacket, shoes at the bottom, and a badge on a lanyard on a small shelf. The badge showed my picture—and I instantly recognized myself—with my name and title. The title read: Chief System Architect.

Aside from the clothes and badge, I didn't find anything else inside. No pictures. No personal effects. No guidebook for being woken up early from cryo with a spotty memory and seeing things that weren't there.

I slipped into the clothes then pulled on the jacket. They didn't drive away the cold, but they helped a little. I pulled the blanket around me, knowing I looked silly. But who would judge me? Sara, the assistant physician?

Thinking of the woman, I noticed how quiet the locker room had become.

I didn't shut my locker. Some part of me didn't want to make a noise, no matter how insignificant or small. I walked back deeper into the shadows, heart pounding. Even my breathing sounded too loud in my own ears. Keeping close to the lockers, I peeked out behind their back edge. Nothing but shadows in the red light greeted me. As quietly as I could manage, I circled around, heading toward the opposite side of the room. On my way, I noticed an open locker.

The nameplate on it said K HICKS. Inside hung empty hangers. No badge like in my locker, but when I stepped in closer, glass crunched under my shoes. I bent down and picked up a picture frame, the glass in pieces under my feet. The picture was of a black man with a beautiful blond woman, both all smiles in front of a worn-down building with a sign proclaiming GUN RANGE. I didn't recognize the man, but the girl looked familiar. This was the doctor I'd barely remembered earlier, Eaton. Her first name still eluded me. Which meant the black guy was Hicks.

I gently set the picture on the locker's shelf. When I withdrew my hand, I noticed a slick substance on my fingers where they'd touched the broken frame. I rubbed it between my fingers. It felt like grease, or oil, but I couldn't see any color on it. I brought my hand to my face and sniffed. It smelled rotten. I took a step back from the locker and quietly half-shut the door. The same substance covered the outside of the door and the thumbpad.

What was going on?

"What are you looking at?"

I nearly jumped out of my skin at Sara's loud voice, just behind me. I spun around and found her staring at me, confusion obvious in her expression. When had she come up behind me?

"Sorry... I... I found my locker. I ended up over here and found an open locker."

Sara stepped by me and opened the locker all the way, then pulled out the picture. "Do you know them?"

"Just the . . . wait . . . you don't recognize Dr. Eaton? She's your boss, right?"

She frowned and held the picture up into the red lights, squinting at it before setting it back in the locker. "Sorry, I have trouble with the red light. I can hardly see. It's been days in the emergency lights, and I swear they are burning my retinas. You're right. It is her. I don't recognize the other person, though. Do you?"

I rubbed my eyes. She was right, the red light made my eyes hurt, and my head throb worse. "No. I just saw the locker open, and the clothes gone. And there's some weird residue on the picture and on the door."

"Residue?" She rubbed her fingers together and looked at the door. "I don't see anything."

"It's right here . . ." I pointed at the thumb scanner and blinked. Nothing was there. I pushed Sara aside and grabbed the picture. Nothing. The oily substance was gone. I looked down at my own hands in disbelief. Nothing. "I . . . it . . ."

"James, it's all right. It's just the symptoms. There's nothing here."

"How . . . where's this guy, then?"

"I don't know, James. You're the only other person I've seen since waking up, and that's because I woke you up. Maybe he's in one of the other locations I can't get to? If there is someone else, we should find them. They might be in as bad of shape as you are."

I nodded, pushing down the feeling of losing my grip on sanity. Sara waved me to follow her, and we left the men's locker room.

We walked directly to Operations, following the signs through the passageways. Other hallways led to separate cryo pod groups. Little by little, the layout of the place became familiar again. I remembered four different cryo hubs, each with their own medical bay and locker rooms. A sign pointed to Cryo Hub Four, and I began walking that way.

"James, where are you going? We need to get to Operations."

I stopped, not even realizing I'd turned away from our destination. "I . . . I don't know. I think I just wanted to check on the pods here. There's . . . there's something important in Hub Four."

"Some*thing* or some*one*?"

"I'm not sure. Maybe both."

"Well, they can wait. It won't do any good to check on them if we just let them die because their pods fail. Come on, we need to get to the control center."

She resumed walking to Operations, not waiting for me to agree, and I followed after.

A wave of nausea hit me, sending me to the ground. I kept myself from retching, but just barely. I began to push back to my feet, when Sara offered her hand to me. As I reached out to take it, the veins under her skin wiggled and moved like worms. I squeezed my eyes shut hard and took a few breaths. Sara's hand was fine when I opened my eyes again. Veins fine. I took her hand and let her help me up.

"Are you all right?"

No, I really wasn't. But what could I say? I was obviously sick, weak, and hallucinating. There weren't too many other side effects I could experience besides death. "I'm good. Let's just get to Operations."

The handprint scanner outside the control center wasn't the garden variety access point like the one outside the lockers. The latter only read a handprint, while the former did subtle DNA checks. Sara pressed her hand against the screen, which flashed red, denying her access. She turned back to me and pointed at the scanner.

"You see? I've tried a dozen times. Different times of day, my hand hot or cold, sweaty or dry. It doesn't matter. Something is wrong with it."

I waved her aside and pressed my hand on the pad. It pulsed blue, then lit up green. The door's magnetic locks disengaged.

"Of course it works for you," she said. She shook her head in disgust and pulled the door open.

"I'll check it out inside. Maybe some permissions got crossed."

"Don't bother. I'd rather you fix the cryo pods. The inconvenience of not being able to get into a few areas isn't the end of the world. I'll just follow you around, or have you remotely open them. Let's get inside."

Operations had the feeling of a mausoleum. The dead-quiet state of the room felt unnatural. Even if I had been woken up off schedule, someone should have been in here. Pieces of the plan resolved as I looked around the room. A skeleton crew should always be around, waking from cryo in shifts to manage the bunker's systems.

Instead, it looked like no one had been here for a long time.

I ran a finger over the top of a bank of screens, and it came away thick with dust. When was the last time someone had been in here?

The control center was shaped like a giant octagon. Banks of equipment and consoles sat dark at every side of the room, with a similarly shaped table in the center. The table typically displayed holographic images of the facility, or the world outside.

The first order of business was starting up the systems.

My body moved on autopilot as I went from control to control, cycling the power on the various systems. They blinked on slowly, like they hadn't been used in years. Sara stood by the door, wearing her discomfort openly. She had the look of a girl alone at her first dance, not sure what to do. I couldn't blame her. An assistant physician wouldn't know much of what to do here with the systems off.

The main control bank blossomed to life on the screen in front of me, the glare harsh in the dim, red light. I scrolled through the options quicky until I found life support. Hub One—the one I'd woken up in—was in bad shape. Hub Two was on the verge of being shut down to prioritize support to the other Hubs. Number Three showed all green and active. Four was the worst of all the groups of pods.

"Which Hub were you in, Sara?"

"Two."

"I thought you said it was a complete loss?"

"It was. The displays on every pod were black."

"Looks like they aren't dead yet. I'll need you to go there and verify as I make adjustments here. Can you do that?"

"We can still save them?" For the first time, I heard hope in her voice.

I bent down and opened a panel under the console and pulled out two radios. They, too, were covered in dust, but when I switched them on, they crackled to life. I tossed one to her.

"Take this to Hub Two. I'll need you to check the pods as I go through some systems."

"All right." She ran out of the control room, and a few minutes later the radio squawked.

"I'm here. Let me know when you do something."

"Okay, hold tight," I said.

Error messages cascaded across the screen. Nearly everything was down. But as I looked through the system malfunctions, I realized they were all simple fixes. Regular review and maintenance would have found and eliminated all these. One by one I corrected them, and Hub Two's status went green. Hub One lit up green. Four, though, stayed down.

Sara's voice came through the radio again. "Have you done anything? All the pods show as down."

"They should all be fine now, even if the individual screens don't show it. We'll likely have to do a reboot on just the screens later. The master display here shows them all good."

"I'm going to stay here and see if they come on, or see if I can get anything working on my end."

"That's fine. I've got a lot to do here. There are system errors all over the place."

"You can fix them all? Make this place work again?"

"I think so. And then I'll wake a few of the other people and get things back on schedule."

"Sounds good."

I double-checked Hub Two's status. Still green. I wasn't sure what she thought she'd be able to do there, but I didn't need her around at the moment. Plus I needed to look up some information. I couldn't very well tell Sara that I couldn't even remember the reason we were here. Why were we supposed to launch a bombardment on the planet? What were we hiding from?

I found the information easily enough.

It was odd to read it without remembering it. In the year 2050 a meteor hit earth, and the world's leaders had declared a national emergency. Except the meteor had actually been an alien ship. Within months entire countries had gone dark. They turned our own weapons and systems against us. So we took our best minds and put them in stasis as a preventative measure. Prometheus Bunker. Home of two thousand individuals. Some of America's best and brightest. Within the facility we constructed isolated systems to keep the individuals inside safe, and silos to launch missiles in their defense. Either the aliens would leave our world or die off, or we'd bombard the planet and wait out the fallout.

The odd thing was that no one had a firm grasp of what the aliens looked like. None of the documents about the invaders had any real details.

But as I read over the reports, all the feelings came back. The paranoia and hysteria. The frantic project to build the bunkers. I remembered getting pulled into this facility, soldiers shooting out the open door. I was the last one in before locking it all down. They rushed me to cryo and put me immediately under.

And here I was, twenty years later.

Except... this all felt off. This looked more like an old, decommissioned facility from a hundred years earlier.

I pulled up the error logs again and looked at the time stamps. The year jumped out at me.

2272.

I shut my eyes, assuming this was another hallucination. But the number was still there when I opened them again. This couldn't be right. Every check I ran pulled the same result. I hadn't woken up fifty years early, I was over one hundred and fifty years *late*.

Even if Sara hadn't been able to get into the control center, any number of access points would have told her the year. So why had she lied?

Another check told me the bombardment had never been launched. Our entire plan had failed.

After all this time, somehow the cryo systems were still active, if barely. I'd managed to fix them for the time being. But to truly save the people in the pods, I'd have to bring them all out, let them recover, then put them back under. But I didn't know the situation topside. For all I knew, the place was a barren wasteland, or some alien utopia.

Hub Four. My earlier intuition told me important people were there. I pulled up a personnel list for each Hub, seeing if any of the names stood out. Few did, but in Hub Four their titles did. Generals, physicists, mathematicians. They even had some professional soldiers. The other Hubs contained assistants to most of those people. That I hadn't been included in Hub Four seemed strange. But I had been the last person brought in from the outside. Maybe I'd just filled a spot.

If I could wake up some of those VIPs in Hub Four, maybe we

could figure out this situation together. But I couldn't do it from here. With the status of that Hub in jeopardy, and with it not being resolved through my fixes here, I knew I'd have to go physically evaluate the issue.

I picked up the radio to tell Sara where I was heading, but stopped before keying it live. Through the fog and exhaustion, my mind screamed at me to stop.

On a whim I pulled up the personnel list for Hub Two again and looked for Sara Addison.

Nothing.

I searched her name, finding a Sara Addison from Hub Four. Not a medical doctor, but a politician. When I pulled up her image, it was a completely different woman. Red hair instead of dark. The woman's skin in the picture was pale and covered in freckles. This wasn't the person who'd pulled me from cryo.

So who *was* this person acting as Sara?

I kept the radio with me as I left the control center and headed to Hub Four—every mystery led to that section of the facility. I kept an eye behind me, not wanting Sara—or whoever she was—to sneak up on me like she had in the lockers. As the head cryo engineer, my access should get me into the Hub without any issue. It wasn't locked behind biometrics like the control center . . .

The biometrics. Was that why Sara couldn't get into Operations? Her handprint somehow got her in, but her DNA was being rejected.

She obviously wasn't Sara. Who was she?

A random, more chilling question slid behind the previous one. *What* as she?

Questions about Sara died off instantly when I reached the door to the Hub. On the dim red, the seal around the door dripped a clear liquid, and the hand scanner on the side gleamed wet with the same substance. Just like the locker. Pain still stabbed in my head, and the sight of the dripping fluid made double over and throw up. As I heaved, my radio hissed, and Sara's voice came on.

"How are things going in the control center, James?"

I took a few deep breaths to force the nausea down.

"James? Are you there?"

"Uh, yeah." I couldn't let her know where I was, or what I'd figured out. "Sorry, I was on the other side of the room from the radio."

"I still haven't noticed anything come back online here. I thought you were fixing it? I need these pods."

"Yeah . . . no . . . there are a ton of errors here. It's like the systems haven't been used in a hundred years. It's going to take me a while to get through them. Just keep working on them on your end."

Silence. I stared down at the radio for a few minutes, not sure what to expect from her. Then finally, "Are the information libraries working?"

"No," I lied. "There's some data corruption. I'm not sure when I'll get to them. Getting the pods working is more important."

"Do you want me to come help?"

"No," I replied quickly. Probably too quickly. "There really isn't much you can help with here. I'd . . . I'd rather you, uh, get things squared away in medical back there. With pods stabilizing, we'll have to bring a few more people out to help fix other things. I don't know what kind of state they'll be in, so I'll be relying on you." I hoped the lie sounded convincing.

"I guess that makes sense," Sara said. "I'll get that all put together."

"Great. I'll call you if I need you back here."

I turned my attention back to the Hub door. The clear fluid was still there. I rubbed my eyes. Still there. I walked up to the hand pad and pressed my hand against it. The oily, clear substance clung to my hand. It made me want to take a shower. The pad went green, and the door clicked open.

When I opened the door, a blast of humid, hot air hit me. It reeked of decay. Air this warm shouldn't have been possible in the controlled systems of the bunker. I clicked on the flashlight and stabbed the beam into the darkness.

The walls inside dripped with moisture and more of the clear oil. The first door on my right led down a short hallway to a closed door with the sign that said 4-1. The handprint scanner still functioned, but the door didn't pop open as far as it should have when the locks disengaged. I grabbed at its edge and pulled. My weakened muscles strained, and I braced a foot against the outside of the doorframe to give me more leverage.

With a sucking squelch, I pulled the door open. The full force of the rotting smell enveloped me, making me gag. I pointed my flashlight inside and felt my eyes go wide.

The inside of the room was shaped the same as the one I'd woken up inside. Roughly circular, with standing cryo pods evenly spaced along the walls. But the similarities ended there. If I hadn't know what the room was supposed to be, I'd never have recognized it.

A sickly yellow slime covered nearly every surface and dripped from the ceiling. The cryo pods were completely covered in it, but the glass doors had been ripped away and discarded around the room. The pods no longer looked mechanical, but rather biological, like they'd grown muscle and skin . . . and that skin had been ripped open. They reminded me of a person who had been gutted, intestines spilling to the floor . . . and now rotted with the passage of time.

I pointed the flashlight across the room into the open cavity of the pod. Inside was the ripped open cadaver of a human, barely recognizable. The light from my flashlight illuminated mounds of flesh on the floor, revealing pieces of humans.

I pushed back away from the door and tripped, falling to the floor. I covered my eyes with one hand, gasping for breath and silently pleading for this all to be a hallucination. But when I pulled my hand away, the mess was still there.

Going door to door in Hub Four, I found every room in the charnel house to be the same. Nearly five hundred people gone. The biological material covered every surface, and as I got to the back of the Hub, it spilled out from the individual cryo rooms into the halls. Veins of the matter dripped yellow and clear fluid to the floors, and embedded inside it all were body parts. Red emergency lights cast the scene as a hellscape I'd never be able to forget.

Nothing came out when I tried to throw up. I dry heaved. I was too horrified to even weep for the people my cryo systems were supposed to protect.

"James?"

I nearly dropped the radio as Sara's voice erupted from it.

"Yeah?"

"Are you still working on the pods?"

"Yes. It's . . ." I looked around at all the death around me. "It's a mess."

"And you're still in the control center?"

"Yeah."

"Strange. Because I don't see you here."

The silence following her statement hung heavy in the dying air. If she was there, she'd be able to see the last things I'd pulled up. She'd been so insistent on fixing Hub Two. And Hub Three showed all green. Did that mean...

I ran from Hub Four and turned the corner leading to Three.

"James? Where are you?"

Responding to her seemed like the last thing I should do. My weak legs gave out, and I crashed to the floor. The door to Hub Three stood just ahead. Even from here I could see the clear sheen covering it and the access pad.

Bracing against the wall, I stumbled to the door and opened it. Just like in Hub Four, a blast of hot air hit me, but the smell of rotting flesh was substantially less.

The door to the first cryo room hung partially open. I pulled it the rest of the way. Inside, the flesh covering the surfaces looked almost healthy. The fluid dripping off it more clear than yellow. Where it enveloped the pods, it seemed to breathe, pushing out, then settling back.

"You aren't supposed to be here. She said she'd take care of you."

A man stepped out from the back shadows between two pods. Though *it* was a man only in the loosest terms. The left half of his body was a black man I barely recognized as Hicks from the photo in the locker room. The right ride was somewhere in transition between Hicks and... something else. As the thing walked toward me, the right side of the face stretched, hair falling from it, and skin going translucent. The creature—the alien, I knew—paused and reached out an arm to touch the nearest pod. The appendage flowed out, fluidlike, and spread out over the surface of the skin covering the pod.

"What... what are you..."

"It's feeding time." The alien cocked its head to the side in an almost doglike motion. "This one is almost ready to hatch." Then it sniffed the air. "I can tell you've seen our failures. No matter. I can also smell the other eggs have been saved. The air here carries the scent of their renewed health. You have my thanks. It seems she was right about you."

"Eggs?" What else could I say? I knew the answer already, but my mind bent like a toothpick on the verge of shattering.

"Yes. We nearly lost them. We just need a few more of your human years, and we can finally abandon this disposable world." Loathing filled the alien's words. "We can finally go home. You've saved us all, human. We can learn from your actions and save the others around the world you thought to hide in your . . . what is the human word you use . . . bunkers? Yes. You thought to hide from us, but we were already among you in your hidden projects."

It was all for nothing. All our work. All our secrecy.

"We will do you a great honor, human. For saving us. We will use your body—your genetic matter—to create a new queen for our species. You will live on in all of us. Forever. Come. Embrace your . . . reward."

I screamed and threw the flashlight at the alien. It cracked against the thing's head, but the alien barely reacted.

"You shouldn't resist." The alien's voice was so calm, ambivalent to the harm I'd tried to cause. "Even if you flee, we'll just wake up others like we did before you. Another will give us what we want. We'll convert you into us . . . just like we are doing inside this egg."

I ran as fast as I could, leaving the alien behind. When I looked back over my shoulder, it was exiting the room, walking slowly after me.

I needed a plan. I need to escape and stop them. Had they infiltrated every bunker around the world? Surely there were a few left. But this one . . . this one was compromised beyond hope. I wished someone would have launched the bombardment right away.

As I rounded the corner in the hall leading to Operations, an idea managed to take root in my confused mind.

I switched my direction and ran to Hub Two. The alien masquerading as Sara had abandoned it when she'd gone looking for me in the control center. I needed to lure her—it—away from the controls.

Hub Two's door was already open when I arrived, and I ran to the back of the Hub, as far from the entrance as I could. Alien flesh spilled out from the rooms into the hall. I stepped around it and into the cryo pod room. At the far back, a cabinet hung on the wall between pods, partially covered in the skin. I ripped the alien matter away, throwing it to the side. Some clung to me, and it felt like it was biting into my skin, trying to get inside.

In the cabinet was the small emergency pack I'd hoped to find. Flares.

I removed one of the flares, ignited it, and stuck it into one of the breathing eggs. The clear fluid caught fire in a whoosh and spread up and out around the room. The cooking flesh reminded me of burning pork from a long-forgotten barbeque I could barely remember.

After leaving the burning room, I tossed the flare into the cryo room across from it, then keyed my radio.

"Sara, you may want to check on Hub Two. I don't think the eggs there are going to make it."

"James? Where are you?"

"Did you know that clear fluid dripping from all your alien skin is flammable? Hub Two isn't going to make it."

"What have you done? We need those pods!"

"Better come and save them, then."

I walked the long way around the facility back to Operations. Running wasn't possible anymore. My legs shook, and my breath came out ragged. A sharp pain stabbed at my hand where the alien skin still clung. Dark, writhing lines—my veins—spread up my forearm away from my hand. Not a hallucination this time. Maybe not on Sara either. I didn't know anymore, but the pain brought with it a small measure of clarity, driving away some of the fog and confusion that had clouded my mind since waking up.

When I reached Operations, I closed the doors behind me and sealed them. I didn't know if Sara's inability to get inside had been an act, but if they were indeed changing our DNA into theirs, then the biometrics might not be able to read it.

The bunker systems were isolated from all other systems except the one connecting them all. I scrolled through status reports of all the bunkers around the country and world. The vast majority— Prometheus Bunker included—had their main doors open.

My gamble rested on the ones with closed door still being secure. I remotely activated the pods in those specific bunkers, then sent a message to each one.

"This is James Conroy, though I barely remember being that man. The year is 2272. When you wake up and hear this message, you'll be as confused as I am. But you need to check your bunker. Nearly every facility around the world is compromised. Look for stuff that looks like this." I held up my hand to the video recorder to show the alien skin clinging to me. "Burn it. Burn it all. Don't go outside yet. The aliens got to us and prevented the bombardment. I'm activating it now. Good luck."

As I sent the message, I heard a pounding on the control center door. My radio went live again.

"You've killed them all, James. Why would you do that?"

I flipped on security feeds and skipped through them until I found the one showing Sara outside the door. The other alien wearing Hicks's body was there too, pressing his hand against the access pad, which denied him access. I set the radio down, not bothering to answer.

"You were offered the highest reward from us. To be reborn as a queen for our species. Now you will be punished. Open the door."

I found the bombardment sequence, and started it. I hoped it still worked. A countdown flashed to life.

Three minutes.

When I looked back at the security feed, Sara had morphed into a blond beauty. Dr. Eaton.

"James, please, let me in. It's me, Dr. Eaton. Don't you remember me?"

The alien next to her now looked completely like Hicks again. They pounded on the door, and stared up into the camera. They looked panicked, tears running down their cheeks.

Two minutes.

"Please, James, let us in? What is going on? Why did you lock us out? We woke you up, and you just ran from us. What are you doing?"

I pressed my hand to the side of my head, trying to push away the stabbing pain in my skull. Her words shouldn't have worked. I knew exactly what she was. What they both were. But could I have been wrong? Hallucinating them, too?

One minute.

The pain in my hand brought me back to reality. The black veins crept up my bicep. What would happen when they reached my heart or brain?

The countdown on the bombardment hit zero.

The bunker shook as missiles launched from the attached silos. I tracked their progress all across the world as they began landing and detonating.

"We are lost," the alien version of Hicks said.

A missile hit near the entrance to Prometheus Bunker. The payload of the missile brought its destruction through the facility's open door, annihilating everything inside.

As the world went white, burning me away, I hoped my decision to kill the world would ultimately save it.

FIRST ANNIVERSARY
Richard Matheson

The transition for newlyweds out of the honeymoon period can be an awkward one for any married couple. Sometimes the bonds grow stronger, and those early years form a foundation for a partnership that will last a lifetime. For others, the cracks begin to form, the passions begin to fade, lies reveal themselves, and the beginning of the end has begun.

You'd be hard-pressed to find a first anniversary more consequential—or more tragic—than the one presented here. Originally printed in Playboy in 1960 and appearing in print for the first time in nearly two decades, we have one of the stranger selections from Richard Matheson's bibliography. This is the tale of Norman and Adeline, and their marriage at that moment that newlywed glow has just begun to fade...

Just before he left the house on Thursday morning, Adeline asked him, "Do I still taste sour to you?"

Norman looked at her reproachfully.

"Well, do I?"

He slipped his arms around her waist and nibbled at her throat. "Tell me now," said Adeline.

Norman looked submissive.

"Aren't you going to let me live it down?" he asked.

"Well, you said it, darling. And on our first anniversary too!"

He pressed his cheek to hers. "So I said it," he murmured. "Can't I be allowed a faux pas now and then?"

"You haven't answered me."

"Do you taste sour? Of course you don't." He held her close and breathed the fragrance of her hair. "Forgiven?"

She kissed the tip of his nose and smiled and, once more, he could only marvel at the fortune which had bestowed on him such a magnificent wife. Starting their second year of marriage, they were still like honeymooners.

Norman raised her face and kissed her.

"Be damned," he said.

"What's wrong? Am I sour again?"

"No." He looked confused. "Now I can't taste you at all."

"Now you can't taste her at all," said Dr. Phillips.

Norman smiled. "I know it sounds ridiculous," he said.

"Well, it's unique, I'll give it that," said Phillips.

"More than you think," added Norman, his smile grown a trifle labored.

"How so?"

"I have no trouble tasting anything else."

Dr. Phillips peered at him awhile before he spoke. "Can you smell her?" he asked then.

"Yes."

"You're sure."

"*Yes*. What's that got to do with—" Norman stopped. "You mean that the senses of taste and smell go together," he said.

Phillips nodded. "If you can smell her, you should be able to taste her."

"I suppose," said Norman, "but I can't."

Dr. Phillips grunted wryly. "Quite a poser."

"No ideas?" asked Norman.

"Not offhand," said Phillips, "though I suspect it's an allergy of some kind."

Norman looked disturbed.

"I hope I find out soon," he said.

Adeline looked up from her stirring as he came into the kitchen. "What did Dr. Phillips say?"

"That I'm allergic to you."

"He didn't say that," she scolded.

"Sure he did."

"Be serious now."

"He said I have to take some allergy tests."

"He doesn't think it's anything to worry about, does he?" asked Adeline.

"No."

"Oh, good." She looked relieved.

"Good, nothing," he grumbled. "The taste of you is one of the few pleasures I have in life."

"You stop that." She removed his hands and went on stirring. Norman slid his arm around her and rubbed his nose on the back of her neck. "Wish I could taste you," he said. "I like your flavor."

She reached up and caressed his cheek. "I love you," she said.

Norman twitched and made a startled noise.

"What's wrong?" she asked.

He sniffed. "What's that?" He looked around the kitchen. "Is the garbage out?" he asked.

She answered quietly. "Yes, Norman."

"Well, something sure as hell smells awful in here. Maybe—" He broke off, seeing the expression on her face. She pressed her lips together and, suddenly, it dawned on him. "Honey, you don't think I'm saying—"

"Well, aren't you ?" Her voice was faint and trembling.

"Adeline, come on."

"First, I taste sour. Now—"

He stopped her with a lingering kiss.

"I love you," he said, "understand? I love you. Do you think I'd try to hurt you?"

She shivered in his arms. "You *do* hurt me," she whispered.

He held her close and stroked her hair. He kissed her gently on the lips, the cheeks, the eyes. He told her again and again how much he loved her.

He tried to ignore the smell.

Instantly, his eyes were open and he was listening. He stared up sightlessly into the darkness. Why had he woken up? He turned his head and reached across the mattress. As he touched her, Adeline stirred a little in her sleep.

Norman twisted over on his side and wriggled close to her. He pressed against the yielding warmth of her body, his hand slipping languidly across her hip. He lay his cheek against her back and started drifting downward into sleep again.

Suddenly, his eyes flared open. Aghast, he put his nostrils to her skin and sniffed. An icy barb of dread hooked at his brain; my God, what's wrong? He sniffed again, harder. He lay against her, motionless, trying not to panic.

If his senses of taste and smell were atrophying, he could understand, accept. They weren't, though. Even as he lay there, he could taste the acrid flavor of the coffee that he'd drunk that night. He could smell the faint odor of mashed-out cigarettes in the ashtray on his bedside table. With the least effort, he could smell the wool of the blanket over them.

Then why? She was the most important thing in his life. It was torture to him that, in bits and pieces, she was fading from his senses.

It had been a favorite restaurant since their days of courtship. They liked the food, the tranquil atmosphere, the small ensemble which played for dining and for dancing. Searching in his mind, Norman had chosen it as the place where they could best discuss this problem. Already, he was sorry that he had. There was no atmosphere that could relieve the tension he was feeling and expressing.

"What else can it be?" he asked, unhappily. "It's nothing physical." He pushed aside his untouched supper. "It's got to be my mind."

"But why, Norman?"

"*If I only knew,*" he answered.

She put her hand on his. "Please don't worry," she said.

"How can I help it?" he asked. "It's a nightmare. I've lost part of you, Adeline."

"Darling, don't," she begged. "I can't bear to see you unhappy."

"I am unhappy," he said. He rubbed a finger on the tablecloth. "And I've just about made up my mind to see an analyst." He looked up. "It's got to be my mind," he repeated. "And—damnit!—I resent it. I want to root it out."

He forced a smile, seeing the fear in her eyes.

"Oh, the hell with it," he said. "I'll go to an analyst; he'll fix me up. Come on, let's dance."

She managed to return his smile.

"Lady, you're just plain gorgeous," he told her as they came together on the dance floor.

"*Oh, I love you so,*" she whispered.

It was in the middle of their dance that the feel of her began to change.

Norman held her tightly, his cheek forced close to hers so that she wouldn't see the sickened expression on his face.

"And now it's gone?" finished Dr. Bernstrom.

Norman expelled a burst of smoke and jabbed out his cigarette in the ashtray. "Correct," he said, angrily.

"When?"

"This morning," answered Norman. The skin grew taut across his cheeks. "No taste. No smell." He shuddered fitfully. "And now no sense of touch."

His voice broke. "What's wrong?" he pleaded. "What kind of breakdown is this?"

"Not an incomprehensible one," said Bernstrom.

Norman looked at him anxiously. "What then?" he asked. "Remember what I said: it has to do only with my wife. Outside of her—"

"I understand," said Bernstrom.

"Then what is it?"

"You've heard of hysterical blindness."

"Yes."

"Hysterical deafness."

"Yes, but—"

"Is there any reason, then, there couldn't be an hysterical restraint of the other senses as well?"

"All right, but why?"

Dr. Bernstrom smiled. "That, I presume," he said, "is why you came to see me."

Sooner or later, the notion had to come. No amount of love could stay it. It came now as he sat alone in the living room, staring at the blur of letters on a newspaper page.

Look at the facts. Last Wednesday night, he'd kissed her and, frowning, said, "You taste sour, honey." She'd tightened, drawn away. At the time, he'd taken her reaction at its obvious value: she felt insulted. Now, he tried to summon up a detailed memory of her behavior afterward.

Because, on Thursday morning, he'd been unable to taste her at all.

Norman glanced guiltily toward the kitchen where Adeline was cleaning up. Except for the sound of her occasional footsteps, the house was silent.

Look at the facts, his mind persisted. He leaned back in the chair and started to review them.

Next, on Saturday, had come that dankly fetid stench. Granted, she should feel resentment if he'd accused her of being its source. But he hadn't; he was sure of it. He looked around the kitchen, asked her if she'd put the garbage out. Yet, instantly, she'd assumed that he was talking about her.

And, that night, when he'd woken up, he couldn't smell her.

Norman closed his eyes. His mind must really be in trouble if he could justify such thoughts. He loved Adeline; needed her.

How could he allow himself to believe that she was, in any way, responsible for what had happened?

Then, in the restaurant, his mind went on, unbidden, while they were dancing, she'd, suddenly, felt cold to him. She'd suddenly felt— he could not evade the word—*pulpy*.

And, then, this morning—

Norman flung aside the paper. *Stop it!* Trembling, he stared across the room with angry, frightened eyes. It's me, he told himself, *me!* He wasn't going to let his mind destroy the most beautiful thing in his life. He wasn't going to let—

It was as if he'd turned to stone, lips parted, eyes widened, blank. Then, slowly—so slowly that he heard the delicate crackling of bones in his neck—he turned to look toward the kitchen. Adeline was moving around.

Only it wasn't footsteps he heard.

He was barely conscious of his body as he stood. Compelled, he drifted from the living room and across the dining alcove, slippers noiseless on the carpeting. He stopped outside the kitchen door, his face a mask of something like revulsion as he listened to the sounds she made in moving.

Silence then. Bracing himself, he pushed open the door. Adeline was standing at the opened refrigerator. She turned and smiled.

"I was just about to bring you—" She stopped and looked at him uncertainly. "Norman?" she said.

He couldn't speak. He stood frozen in the doorway, staring at her.

"Norman, what is it?" she asked.

He shivered violently.

Adeline put down the dish of chocolate pudding and hurried toward him. He couldn't help himself; he shrank back with a tremulous cry, his face twisted, stricken.

"Norman, what's the matter?"

"I don't know," he whimpered.

Again, she started for him, halting at his cry of terror. Suddenly, her face grew hard as if with angry understanding.

"What is it now?" she asked. "I want to know."

He could only shake his head.

"I want to know, Norman!"

"No." Faintly, frightenedly.

She pressed trembling lips together. "I can't take much more of this," she said. "I mean it, Norman."

He jerked aside as she passed him. Twisting around, he watched her going up the stairs, his expression one of horror as he listened to the noises that she made. Jamming palsied hands across his ears, he stood shivering uncontrollably. *It's me!* he told himself again, again; until the words began to lose their meaning—*me, it's me, it's me, it's me!*

Upstairs, the bedroom door slammed shut. Norman lowered his hands and moved unevenly to the stairs. She had to know that he loved her, that he wanted to believe it was his mind. She had to understand.

Opening the bedroom door, he felt his way through the darkness and sat on the bed. He heard her turn and knew that she was looking at him.

"I'm sorry," he said, "I'm . . . sick."

"No," she said. Her voice was lifeless.

Norman stared at her. "What?"

"There's no problem with other people, our friends, tradesmen . . ." she said. "They don't see me enough. With you, it's different. We're together too often. The strain of hiding it from you hour after hour, day after day, for a whole year, is too much for me. I've lost the power to control your mind. All I can do is—blank away your senses one by one."

"You're not—"

"—telling you those things are real? I am. They're real. The taste, the smell, the—and what you heard tonight."

He sat immobile, staring at the dark form of her.

"I should have taken all your senses when it started," she said. "It would have been easy then. Now it's too late."

"What are you talking about?" He could barely speak.

"It isn't fair!" cried her voice. "I've been a good wife to you! Why should I have to go back? I won't go back! I'll find somebody else. I won't make the same mistake next time!"

Norman jerked away from her and stood on wavering legs, his fingers clutching for the lamp.

"Don't touch it!" ordered the voice. The light flared blindingly into his eyes. He heard a thrashing on the bed and whirled. He couldn't even scream. Sound coagulated in his throat as he watched the shapeless mass rear upward, dripping decay.

"All right!" The words exploded in his brain with the illusion of sound. "All right, then *know* me!"

All his senses flooded back at once. The air was clotted with the smell of her. Norman recoiled, lost balance, fell. He saw the moldering bulk rise from the bed and start for him. Then his mind was swallowed in consuming blackness and it seemed as if he fled along a night-swept hall pursued by a suppliant voice which kept repeating endlessly, "Please! I don't want to go back! *None of us want to go back!* Love me, let me stay with you! Love me, love me, love me . . ."

INTERLOPER
Poul Anderson

It's actually something of a thrill to be able to share a Poul Anderson short story that hasn't been in print in just over forty years, not since a collection of Anderson's fantasy stories assembled by Jim Baen himself. And like a bottle of finely aged scotch, this one is distinctive, unique, and well worth the wait.

"Interloper" is a perfect marriage of Anderson's love for classical myth that made Three Hearts and Three Lions *and* The Broken Sword *dear favorites to so many readers and gripping golden age science fiction. A tale of aliens who have come to Earth, only to find several other alien races already living here, preying on mankind from the shadows, and inspiring some of our darkest myths.*

☙ ☙ ☙

The spaceboat slipped down, slowly and stealthily on its gravitic beams, toward the sea which rolled restlessly under the moon. For a moment the broken moonlight seemed to spread outward in little ripples of cold fire, then the boat had gone beneath the water's surface.

It struck bottom not far down, for the beach was only half a mile distant, and lay there wrapped in darkness. Briefly, there was no movement or sound. Then the outer airlock valve opened and Beoric swam to the surface.

The night was vast and dark around him. He saw with complete clarity, in the thin fickle moonlight, but he could not make out any living thing. Sea and sky and the shadowy shoreline—momentarily, the thought of what must be waiting for him was utterly daunting, his heart felt cold in his breast, in all the centuries of his life he had never been so alone. He felt something of the ultimate loneliness of death.

A thought slipped into his mind, cool and unhuman as the sea depths from which it rose: *The creature is waiting. He has been waiting for an hour or more, in the shadows under the trees.*

Beoric's answering thought was a reaction of near panic: *Don't! They may be able to detect us, after all—*

In all the thousands of years, they have given no sign of being responsive to our special wave band. It is, of course, best not to take chances, not to communicate directly with you oftener than necessary. But we will be listening to your thoughts all the time.

You are not alone. The new thought came from the shore, somewhere behind the line of trees under which the alien waited. *We are with you, Beoric.*

It heartened him immensely. Whatever came, whatever happened—he was not altogether alone. Though all the powers of the universe be ranged against him, he had a few on his side. But—so few!

He struck out for the shore, swimming with long easy strokes that seemed to ride the waves. The moon-whitened beach came nearer, until he was wading through the shallows and up onto dry ground.

The creature who had been waiting stirred in the shadows. Beoric's nightseeing eyes swept over the gross black bulk of him, and for another moment fear was cold along his own spine. But—it was too late now. Even had he wanted to back out after the long centuries of which this night might be the culmination, it was too late.

He ran across the beach and ducked behind a tree, as if he hoped the creature had not seen him. And he sent his thoughts probing forth at the mind of the other, as if he were trying to detect whether the thing were intelligent or not. If it should be a member of the dominant race here, the next logical step would be to seize control of its brain and—

The defensive reaction was so swift and savagely strong that Beoric's own mind reeled. For an instant his head swam, he seemed to be sinking into an illimitable darkness—almost the thing had control of him! Then his nervous energy urged back, he threw a hard shield about his brain and sent a thought stabbing along the universally detectable wave band:

"Apparently your race has mastered the secrets of telepathy. If you are that far advanced, you will probably be able to guess my origin."

"Not guess—know!" The answering thought shivered violently in his brain. There must be an incredible force housed in that great scaly body. Beoric caught overtones of a dark amusement: "I thought at first you must be one of the natives—your appearance is almost identical—but obviously you are not."

"Then—you don't belong here—either?"

"Of course not. Wherever you are from, it must be from quite a distance or we would have encountered your people before. But your initial reaction to my presence suggests that you are used to the concept and techniques of visiting someone else's planet."

"I am." In the closed circle of his private thoughts, Beoric felt a sudden harsh laughter of his own. Indeed he was! "But I had not expected to find other—guests—on this world."

He stepped out into the open. The moonlight gleamed coldly on his wet, waterproof tunic and kilts. His strange slant eyes, all cloudy blue without pupil or white, roved into the darkness where the monster still crouched. "Come out," he invited. "Come out and bid me welcome."

"Of course." The squat, enormously thick creature waddled out and stood under the moon. His blank reptilian eyes glittered as they swept over Beoric. Instinctively, the newcomer cocked his long pointed ears toward the monster, though the words that rolled and boomed in his skull had no sonic origin. "Yes—yes, you look very like a native. Except for those eyes and ears—but dark glasses and a hat will cover it very well. That highcheeked cast of face, and very white skin, would also be considered unusual, but not so much so as to arouse great comment."

"Let me get my facts straight," thought Beoric. "Just what planet is this? I mean, what is it called?"

"The natives call it Earth, of course. Don't all land dwelling races call their world Earth? The pronunciation in the local language—they still speak many separate tongues—is—" The monster thought the sound. "The sun is called Sol by them, and we use that term since it is easy to pronounce and all our names differ. This is Sol III, as you probably know."

"I knew it was the third planet, yes. But who are 'we'? Is there more than one race of—visitors?"

"Indeed. Indeed." With sudden suspicion: "But I am answering all the questions. Who are you? Where are you from? Where are your companions? What is your purpose? Why is there no iron in your spaceship? What sort of civilization has your race evolved?"

"One thing at a time." Beoric's answer was taut and wary. "I will not give information away, but I will trade it for what you know. You cannot expect me, on finding a whole new interstellar civilization, to reveal all the secrets of my own until I am convinced of your good intentions."

"Fair enough. But who are you, then?"

"My name, in the spoken language of my race, is Beoric, though that hardly matters. My home star lies clear across the Galaxy, near the periphery; I will not at present be more specific than that. My race, the Alfar, evolved a faster-than-light drive quite a long time ago, several centuries past in fact, and visited the nearer stars. Finally the expedition to which I belong was sent out on a survey which was to swing clear around the Galaxy, investigating stars picked at random so as to get a rough idea of overall conditions. But since we necessarily had to select only a small fraction of suns for study, it is not surprising that we passed right through your civilization without realizing it."

"Where is your ship? That little boat in which you landed could only hold one or two."

"You cannot expect me to reveal the ship's orbit. I came down alone in the boat. The presence of cities here indicated intelligent life with some degree of technology, so I landed—secretly, of course—to investigate more thoroughly. Apparently you detected us some distance out."

"We spotted your boat, yes, by its gravitic vibrations. But not your ship. What sort of screen do you have for star drive vibrations? We've never been able to conceal them that well. And why is your boat chemically powered?"

"The vibration screen must remain my secret. As for the oil-burning spaceboat—well, we have evolved an unusual oil technology on Alfar. With the extreme efficiency of the gravity beam, we just don't need atomic energy for such a small craft."

"I see. But I could detect no iron or silver in your boat—"

"Both metals are hard to obtain on Alfar. We manage quite well with alloys and with copper." Beoric leaned forward, as if suddenly realizing he was giving away too much. "But it is your turn now. Who are you? Why are you here? Why this inquisition, rather than a free welcome?"

"It is a long story," thought the monster. "Nor have you been a model of openness. However—welcome to Earth. Perhaps you would like to come to our headquarters—?"

"Well—it would certainly be the most convenient starting point— I warn you, if I do not return to my ship within three rotations of this planet, they will be coming down after me—with weapons."

"You need have no fear. We are not greedy. Earth has plenty for all."

Beoric stood watching the bony, snouted face of the monster. It seemed to him that he could almost follow the being's private thoughts:

Wherever this creature is from, whether or not he is telling the truth, he must be alone on this planet. We would have detected any other space vessel landing anywhere. Also, he is cut off from his companions. The inverse square law makes it impossible to send a thought more than a few hundred miles at most, and his ship must be further out or we would detect it. He is alone, unarmed, and incommunicado. In three days we can decide what to do—

"My vocal name is Hraagung. Come, we have a car waiting."

"A car—?"

"Yes, of course." Hraagung chuckled, with a certain horrible sardonicism. "I was chosen to meet you, since my own senses could follow the metal of your boat without elaborate instruments. But for obvious reasons, I cannot move about openly on this planet."

"I have to get inside before dawn," thought Beoric. "Alfar's sun is dim and red, nearly extinct. For that reason, I can see very easily in this moon light, but cannot endure the glare and the ultraviolet light of a G-type star."

"So?" Hraagung paused, and Beoric could almost see him turning this revelation over in his cold brain. It was an admission of weakness, to be sure, but it had to be made. And, to a highly advanced civilization with its screens and protective suits, the handicap was not serious. "What would you have done if you hadn't met us?"

"Hidden away by day and slept, of course. The fact that the cities were lighted showed that the natives would be diurnal, which would make my work of spying all the easier."

"Yes—to be sure. Well, we haven't far to go. This way." The monster lumbered in advance. Beoric wrung the water from his shoulder-length silvery-blond hair and followed.

They came through the line of trees on to a paved highway. A native automobile was parked there—four-wheeled, enclosed, obviously chemical powered. As he neared it, Beoric felt the sudden nerve-chill that meant *iron*.

He had expected it, but that made it none the easier. Every ingrained instinct screamed at him to come no closer. Iron, iron, iron—touch it and see your hand go up in smoke! Iron, cold iron, crouched there under the moon!

And he must enter that metal box, and not for an instant must he show the fear that ripped along his shrinking nerves and dinned in his brain. If they knew, if they found the fatal weakness of the Alfar, he was done. A thousand years of slow work and scheming and waiting were done—Earth was done. And it all depended on him.

For a moment he couldn't do it. In spite of his resolve, in spite of his many rehearsals, in spite of the bleak fact that he *must* go through with it—he couldn't. He couldn't deny the reflexes that knotted his muscles and locked his will and brought sweat cold and bitter out on his body.

Courage. The thought quivered deep in his brain. It came from the sea, from the fields beyond the road, from the trees that stood whispering in the night wind. *Courage, Beoric. You are not alone.*

They were sending him more than unspoken word. There was an actual flow of nervous energy into his body, an almost physical force suddenly entering him, bracing him, stilling the thunder of his heart and the panic-storm in brain. Calmness came, and he walked boldly forward.

A man stood beside the car. No—not a man, not an Earthling, though he looked like one and wore the conventional shirt, trousers, coat, and whatnot else of the planet. He was tall, as tall as Beoric, and the Alf could feel the strength that was in him, coiled in his lean body and his long skull like a great cold snake. The sheer aura of that tremendous intellect and neural force could not be hidden, it forced itself out into the telepathic bands and shouted arrogantly along the nerves of Beoric and Hraagung.

The stranger had been listening to the conversation on the beach. His thought came slow and—deep—"Welcome, Beoric of Alfar. I trust your stay will be pleasant and mutually profitable. I am—my race has abandoned vocal language altogether. But on this planet I use the spoken name of Adam Kane." He caught a question in Beoric's thoughts, the Alf had detected overtones. "Yes, my race is so nearly like the Earthling—outwardly!—that only a little surgery enabled us to pass unquestioned. Someone must act as intermediary between aliens and natives, and so the choice falls on us. Which is very useful—in fact, it is necessary to the enterprises we maintain here."

Hraagung crawled into the rear of the car and crouched low so he could not be seen from the outside. His immense body filled the back seat, and the rank reptile smell of him filled the whole vehicle. Kane slid behind the wheel. "Come along," he thought impatiently.

Fear was cold in Beoric as he touched the righ-hand door handle. It was chrome-plated, safe enough for him, but the near presence of iron shuddered in his nerves. With a convulsive movement, he opened the door and slipped in beside Kane. The car purred into motion.

"Where are you from?" thought Beoric. "You still haven't told me."

"From various stars hereabouts," answered Kane. "I come from the most distant." Beoric recognized Deneb in this thought. "But"—arrogantly—"we Vaettir arrived here first. Somewhat later, other races mastered the secret of faster-than-light travel and came to Sol in the course of their explorations. Hraagung is from—" Beoric translated the thought-image, in his own private mind, as Sirius. "And so forth. Today a number of planets have vested interests in Earth. Under the leadership of the Vaettir, they have set up a system such that their various enterprises do not conflict."

He looked at Beoric. The eyes fairly blazed in his lean face, an intolerable glare which the Alf fought to meet, and his hard thought vibrated like vicious lightning in the other's brain: "We are not hostile to newcomers who will respect the system. If they wish to open some project here or on some other of our subject planets which does not clash with established interests, they are free to do so under the rules and direction of the Vaettir. But if they violate the code, they will be destroyed."

Beoric sat quiescent, trying to think how he should react. After a while, he thought slowly: "That seems fair enough. As a matter of fact, a similar system is not unknown in my civilization. It is possible that our two cultures could have mutually profitable intercourse."

"Perhaps!" The answering vibrations lashed back, hard and suspicious.

"Precisely what forms of exploitation are carried on here?" asked the Alf.

"Various ones, depending on the race," said Hraagung. "The Procyonites find Earthlings an excellent source of blood. The Altairians simply want to observe historical processes, as part of their project of mass-action study. The Arcturian economy depends on controlling the productive facilities of a great number of subject planets, skimming the cream off their industry and agriculture. We of Sirius find Earth a convenient military outpost and refueling station—also—" The thought was like a tiger licking its lips—"the natives serve other purposes."

Beoric flashed a question at Kane: "What of your race, the—Denebian Vaettir?"

The answer was steel-hard, with a bleak amusement shimmering over the surface: "We have many interests in this part of the Galaxy."

The Alf leaned back and tried to relax. The almost empty land was beginning to show houses here and there, and the horizon ahead was lit with a dull glow. The car sped smoothly, swiftly over the highway, at a pace that an Earthling could hardly have controlled. It was dark inside the body, a thickness of shadows rank with the Sirian reptile stink. The reflected headlights threw a dim luminance on the harsh bony features of Adam Kane, limning them against the darkness in a nightmare tracing of cheekbones and jaw and cruel jutting nose. The nervous force of the Denebian could not be hidden, it swirled and eddied in the car like an atmosphere. Beoric had to fight its overwhelming power.

"Our headquarters are in the city ahead—New York, it's called," thought Hraagung. "We are on Long Island now."

"Your spaceships don't land there, though?" asked Beoric. He did not try to cover his interest, it would only be natural in a traveler from a distant star—nor could he hope to hide any emotional overtones of his thoughts from the blazing intellect of the Denebian.

"Not in the city, no, though we do have one there for emergency use—in fact, our building is little more than a disguised ship. The actual bases and landing fields are elsewhere—"

No matter how he fought to suppress his emotions Beoric could not keep a shout out of his thoughts. Ye gods—the building was a ship—the building was a ship! Why—that meant—

He grew aware of the cold Sirian eyes focusing on him. The Denebian driver's gaze did not turn from the unwinding road, but Beoric felt his senses—and the gods knew how many uncanny perceptions he had—licking at the Alf's hard-held mental bloc, tongues of fire that—

He laughed, a little shakily, and explained: "I was startled. I had never heard of putting up such a construction without the natives knowing about it. How did you manage it?"

The Denebian's slow deep thought rolled through his brain: "It was simple. We put up the apartment building as a shell. It was only necessary to control the minds of a few city inspectors, since casual observers would not realize the difference. Then, one stormy night, we brought the ship down into the shell. Our laborers completed the disguise with a roof, interior walls and floors."

"You used native labor?"

"Of course. Even at the time, none of them realized the fact that they were not putting up an ordinary structure."

"I see." Beoric saw indeed, and in spite of knowing most of it beforehand he was utterly shaken. What sort of brains did the Vaettir have, that they could casually supply hundreds of men with false memories, prevent them even during their work from taking conscious notice of incongruities—? What was the extent of their power?

Tonight, he thought grimly, *I'll find out!*

Tonight—indeed! The answering thought, on the Alf band, came from behind the racing car. They must be following, in their own vehicles, and—

"You must realize," thought Kane, almost conversationally, "that the exploitation of Earth is quite old. In fact, the first Vaettir arrived here—" he thought of a length of time which Beoric rendered as about four thousand years ago. "We began to colonize extensively about seven centuries back, at which time the native civilization was less complex and it was very easy to pass oneself off as whatever one desired. Thus our organization is firmly established. Through the corporations we control on Earth, the governments which we influence—or run outright whenever it is necessary, through the old and highly reputable family connections of some of the Vaettir, through a number of other means which you can easily imagine, we can do exactly as we please, under the very noses of the natives." For a moment his iron features split in a grin. "The only ones who suspect that Earthlings are not their own property are labelled cranks—and generally the label is quite correct."

Beoric thought of the ruthlessness he had read in Hraagung's mind and asked, "Why do you take so much trouble? Why not annex Earth outright?"

"That would not suit the purposes of the Vaettir." The cold answer was like a suddenly drawn sword. "It is part of our plan that the directed evolution of Earthly civilization be thought a native project—for some time to come."

Beoric nodded. He slumped back in his seat, watching the blurred buildings reel crazily past. It was plain enough who really ran this corner of the Galaxy. The Sirians, for one, would probably like nothing better than to come as conquerors, treating Earthlings frankly as cattle. But if Deneb said "no," then "no" it was.

And—we are pitting ourselves against—that! We, who could not prevail against—

"You cannot hope to conceal your presence entirely?" he thought.

"We don't try," shrugged Hraagung. "In earlier times, we went about almost openly, and were often seen by natives, thereby giving rise to much legendry—"

Yes, thought Beoric, within the locked chambers of his own skull. *Yes, I know the myths. Frightened glimpses of unhuman beings stalking over the world, of a science from beyond the stars, became trolls, goblins, ifrits, dragons, all the horrors of the old stories were grounded in more horrible fact. What brought on the wave of medieval devil-worship if not the growing influx from outer space? Who was the Satan they worshipped at the Black Mass if not a Denebian or a Sirian or some other monster who found a cult of fanatics useful—and who must often have laughed as he conferred with his brethren highly placed in church and state?*

They are most of Earth's mythology. But planets have at least a few myths of their own—

"Later," went on the Sirian, "when too obvious evidence of our presence might have led some sophisticated minds to suspect the truth, we resorted to a measure of—precaution. Who knows what goes on in some lonely part of a great cattle ranch—or in his neighbor's house in a great city? To whom does it occur that the silent partners controlling key industries may not be on Earth at all—?

"There are glimpses. Why bother to conceal them? A man who spied me on a dark night would hardly put his own reputation in jeopardy telling of it—or, if he did, it would be the ravings of delirium, not so? On occasions where someone knows too much, his memories are removable. Almost daily, sign of us is seen—objects in the sky, poltergeist phenomena, vanishings and appearances, all the rest. But who will be able to make anything of such scattered and fragmentary evidence?" Hraagung's deep vocal chuckle vibrated in the body of the car. "Those few who have collected any sort of coherent proof and tried to deduce the truth, are laughed at as paranoiacs."

Kane's wolf-grin flashed out. "The beauty of it is," thought the Denebian, "that almost all such people really are paranoid. It is an obvious sign of instability to attribute the world's trouble to outside persecutors—even if such an attribution should happen to be correct!"

The hurtling car was moving more slowly now as it entered frequented streets. Buildings loomed on either side, blotting out the stars, and there was iron, iron everywhere, the city was a cage of steel. For an instant of blind horror, Beoric fought not to scream. Then slowly, shakily, his resolution returned. After all, the metal wouldn't harm him unless he touched it. And too many centuries depended on him now. And it was too late to back out.

That's right, Beoric. The strong reassuring thoughts beat in the back of his head. *We're after you. We're entering the city too—*

For a moment, he savored the realization. He was, at least, a part of his people, they were with him.

It came to him, not for the first time, that if the Alfar brain structure permitted them to telepath on a wave band undetectable to any other race, then doubtless the Sirians and the others—above all, the Vaettir—could also think on levels unreadable to him. And— what thoughts were flashing back and forth in the night around him?

If—oh, gods, if the incredible Vaettir really could listen in on his thoughts, if that was the secret of their power, if Kane was simply leading the Alfar into a trap—But the chance had to be taken. Earth itself was a trap.

He sat in silence. The car wound smoothly through darkened streets where only the duil yellow lamps and an occasional furtive movement in the shadows and alleys had life. It was near the ebb time of the great city's life; it slept like a sated beast under the sinking moon.

The fields and woods, hills and waters and sky, never slept. There was always life, a rustle of wings, a pattering of feet, a gleam of eyes out of the night, there was always the flowing tide of nervous energy, wakeful, alert. Life lay like a sea beyond the city, and Beoric had never been really alone.

Until now. But the city slept, and there was nothing wild to run in the fields and leap in the moonlit waters. Beoric's straining mind sensed a few rodents scuttering in the ground, a slinking cat or two, the threadlike nervous impulses of insects fluttering around the one-eyed street lamps. Now and again there would be a human thought, someone wakeful—and the thought seemed to echo in the vast hollow silence of the city, it was alone, alone.

The city slept. Beoric could sense the life force of the sleeping humans, nervous, jagged-feeling, even now. It was like an overwhelming lethargy, a million and a million and a million sleeping bodies with all their pain and sorrow and longing turned loose to wander in their minds. The Alf locked his brain to the sticky tide, but it rolled around him, it lay like a sweat-dampened cloak over his nervous system.

They are too many. The sheer magnitude of life force of—how many millions? Ten?—is more than we can endure. And yet we dare challenge the rulers of this world.

They were in the outer edges of the decadent zone surrounding the main business district. It was the logical location for the headquarters—not so evilly situated as to be suspect to police, but in a relatively idle area which would be empty of traffic at night. And now—yes, the quiver of life force up ahead, impulses of a wave-form not quite Earthly, it came from *that* building.

Beoric looked at the darkened bulk before which the automobile came to a halt. It was a ten-story apartment building, as drab and dingy as any of its neighbors. A dim light glowed in the door, picking out a sign: NO VACANCY. *Of course not!* thought Beoric, and suppressed an impulse to hysterical laughter.

"No one watching," flashed Kane's thought. "We can go right in."

Hraagung's unwieldy bulk crossed the sidewalk with surprising speed. The three entered into a hall like that of any other building of this type. Beoric's sensitive nostrils wrinkled at the odors of stale cookery, but he had to admit the disguise was complete.

Even to an elderly human who sat half dozing at the desk. Beoric dipped into his mind for an instant and withdrew with a shudder from the—hollowness.

But the haughty Vaettir would not trouble to pose as menials. They would need a few authentic natives, to act as janitors and whatever other fronts were necessary. Natives who could pass for normal individuals, but whom their vampire masters had sucked dry of all personality. Flesh and blood robots—

Kane led the way into an elevator. "This runs directly into the spaceship," he explained. "You will find more suitable accommodations there."

Such as a coffin, maybe? Or more probably a dissecting table. They'll want to know what I really am.

They emerged into a short corridor lit by coldly gleaming fluorotubes. Kane gestured at a door, which opened to reveal a small, richly furnished room.

"This is one of the guest quarters we keep for transient visitors to Earth," thought the Denebian. "I hope you will find it suitable. The furniture adjusts itself to the shape of the user's body, and you can set temperature, humidity, air pressure, and the rest to whatever is most comfortable for you."

The thought of being set in an airtight chamber was not at all to Beoric's liking. "I am not tired, now, thanks," he vibrated. "I would be more interested in seeing the other colonists."

"This is only headquarters, as I told you," answered Kane. "But most members of the grand control council for Sol are already here, and I have summoned the rest mentally. They should arrive soon."

"All the councilors? That is an honor."

Kane skinned his teeth in a humorless smile. "Not too much of an honor for a visitor from so far away," his thought almost purred. And then, a naked rapier flash: "After all, we have to decide what to do about you!"

Beoric knew, suddenly and bleakly, that he was not intended to leave the ship still in possession of his own personality. It should not take more than two or three of the Vaettir brains to smash through his mental defenses and get complete control of him. And when they knew all he knew about the Alfar, he would go as their depersonalized agent to his ship.

The Alf's fingers touched the sheathed knife strapped under his tunic. He should be able to hold off such an assault long enough to whip out the weapon, and its iron blade would burn through his heart. The Vaettir no doubt had techniques for reviving the dead, but they wouldn't work on him—in minutes his brain and its knowledge would be crumbled, in hours his rapidly proteolyzed flesh would be dust, even his bones would not last many years. The metabolism which was at once their strength and weakness had at least been the cloak of the Alfar.

He was no longer afraid of death. He more than half expected it. But he could not control the inward shudder that racked him at the thought that the Vaettir might somehow be able to upset the plan. There was so little that the Alfar knew about them—so horribly little.

Kane started down the hall. Beoric followed, uneasily aware of Hraagung coming ponderously after. He was between the two monsters, no chance of escape. It lay with the others now, and he didn't dare call on them.

They entered a cubicle which shot into sudden motion. Beoric judged that it was carrying them toward the center of the ship. He flashed out an impulse on the Alf band, to guide the others, but there was no answer.

The ship was silent. He could hear nothing but the purr of the moving cube, the breathing of Hraagung crouched hard and cold beside him. He could feel the surge of inhuman nerve flows, swirling through his own telepathic receptive center like a dark tide, and he could feel the iron frame of the ship, its faint residual magnetism seemed to chill his nerves. Thank all the gods, the metal floor and wall and ceilings were nonferrous. But he was in a cage of iron, a spiderweb, and the breath choked in his throat.

The cube stopped, its door opening on a little antechamber. As the three passengers stepped out, another creature flashed into sight on a metal plate and stalked toward the room beyond.

Beoric started. "What the devil—!" Then, catching himself with the native quick-mindedness of his race: "I take it you've somehow managed to apply the interstellar drive principle to short distances. But how? Our civilization was never able to use it for other than hops of a light-year or more."

"The true minimum distance is about a hundred miles," answered Kane. "Thus we can summon the whole Solar control council in almost no time. Even the officers from the other planets should be present tonight."

"The planets! But—but gods, that's millions of miles off! How can your thought reach—"

Kane's intolerably brilliant eyes rested speculatively on the Alf. "The Vaettir have mastered certain principles of telepathy unattainable by lesser races," he thought haughtily.

And—how much else have they mastered? It's no wonder they rule their civilization.

They entered the council chamber. It was long and high, and the icy white light shimmering on the metal walls made them seem peculiarly unreal, as if the room were of infinite extent. There was a table near the center, around which, on adjustable couches, sat and lay and squatted the rulers of Earth.

Beoric's eyes swept over them, and the shrinking, ingrained fear of all his people's fugitive generations screamed along his nerves and shouted in his brain. He stood still, fighting for calm, and met their gaze with his own blind blue stare. He knew their races already, though he let Hraagung point out which each of them belonged to.

There were two each from Sirius, Procyon, Arcturus, and Altair, and five Denebians. Here, if nowhere else, the utter dominance of the Vaettir was open and arrogant. They sat at the head of the table, wrapped in their own pride, and Beoric could not meet the flame of their eyes.

He looked over the others. Besides the Denebians, only the Sirians seemed really formidable. The Procyonites were wizened little insectile horrors that sucked blood from Earthlings asleep and fed on radiated nervous energy of the wakeful, a completely parasitic species which, though it lowered the energy and intelligence of its victims, did less harm than the vampire legends tracing to its activities suggested. The Arcturians were cunning, ruthless—their muzzled faces even looked vulpine—and highly intelligent, but physically comparatively small and weak. The placid Altairians, coiled in their tentacles and watching the scene with calm cool eyes, were here only as scientific observers. They had no sympathy for the natives, and cooperated willingly enough in the control of Earth, but they did no direct harm.

He had to reckon with all of them, thought Beoric tautly. But it was the raw imperialism of Sirius and the absolute mastery of Deneb which were the real shadows over Earth.

Over—the Galaxy? Who knew? Just how far did the shadow empire reach?

He grew aware that Kane and Hraagung had taken their places. The council table was full now. And there was no place for him, he had to stand in front of them. They were hardly bothering not to slap him in the face with the knowledge that he was a prisoner.

"By now all of you know the stranger's story," flashed Kane's thought. "The question before us is what action to take."

The slow, almost drowsy, and keenly penetrating thought of an Altairian came: "I would suggest that first we settle whether or not the story is true."

"Of course," answered Kane. Sardonically: "But it would be most discourteous to our guest not to accept it for the time being, at least."

"To be sure." The Altairian's gray gaze swung to Beoric. "Suppose we simply trade a few questions and answers, to clear up mutual ignorance."

"Gladly," bowed the Alf. Suddenly, he felt almost at home. This was like the court intrigue of the old days, the swift fencing with words, the subtle mockery—if he couldn't at least hold his own, he didn't deserve to.

"I can understand a certain natural suspicion on your part," he began. "But it does seem a little extreme for a great civilization to be so concerned about one ship."

"A ship from a culture of we know not what strength, a ship with at least one magnificent weapon, the vibration screen, of which we know nothing," flashed Hraagung bluntly. "What word will you carry back to your home sun?"

"Friendly word, I assure you. What use would it be to conquer on the other side of the Galaxy? What use would Earth be to us, who need armor to venture out on its daylight?"

"There are plenty of nocturnal races who never see their own sun if they can avoid it," grunted Hraagung. "You would find Earth's night perfectly comfortable. However, I assume that you would be after higher stakes than one insignificant planet."

"The trouble with you Sirians," thought an Arcturian sarcastically, "is that you cannot imagine any mentality different from your own. You, who simply conquer planets to loot them, still cannot comprehend the attitude of, say, my race, which deliberately builds up Earth in order to gain thereby. You—why, you are on Earth, you have a military base here, simply because you fear that otherwise we'll put one up to use against Sirius."

"Oh, I suppose they like an occasional snack, too," jeered a Procyonite. "They like to arrange a disappearance of a native—into their own bellies. They're good butchers—but they never heard of a milking."

The Sirians stirred dangerously, and Beoric felt the tide of anger that rose in the room. They hated each other, these rival races. If it weren't for the steel grip of the Vaettir, they'd be at each other's throats in a minute.

A Denebian thought cut through the emotional fog. "That will do." It was a chill peremptory command, and Beoric could feel the sudden throttling of rage within the others. "We have more important business than simply squabbling. This arrival constitutes a major crisis."

"I tell you," thought Beoric, "we are only peaceful explorers. If you wish to be isolated, the Alfar will be glad to give your territory a wide berth."

"That is not the point," vibrated Kane. "The very existence of another, comparable civilization is a danger to our plans. To be perfectly frank, the Vaettir intend to expand their activities. Even if the Alfar remained neutral, their suns would constitute foci of resistance for such races as already have the vibratory engine but have not yet had contact with other equal cultures. The history of the Galaxy has been planned carefully in advance, with many developments set to take place of themselves without the supervision of the comparatively small number of Vaettir. We thought we knew all races which had interstellar spaceships. Now the Alfar appear, a totally unforeseen factor. Even with the friendliest intentions, you will upset our calculations.

"Thus—" The terrible eyes blazed at the Alf, "you see why this emergency council is necessary. So great, indeed, is the emergency that all the Vaettir in the Solar System are here tonight to settle your case."

All of them! For a moment, utter exultation flamed in Beoric. *All of them? Every last damned one! That was as much as we dared hope for.*

And then, in a sudden sickening backwash of dismay: *But—if they really only need five to run the Solar System—how colossal are not their powers? What may these five not be able to do tonight?*

He grew aware of the eyes on him, of the thoughts and senses probing at him, studying and analyzing and drawing unguessable conclusions. He laughed, shakily, and thought: "This is quite a surprise. And, naturally, somewhat alarming to me."

"You need not fear conquest," thought Kane almost contemptuously. "The Vaettir permit only certain planets to be taken over outright. The rest, according to our plans, are controlled in more subtle ways. Such as Earth, for instance."

Beoric licked his lips. They seemed suddenly dry. "How—many—stars—to date?"

There was a moment of hesitation, then: "No reason why you should not know," answered an Altairian. "The civilization—which is to say, the Denebian dominance—covers about five hundred stars so far, and is becoming increasingly influential on a thousand or more other systems. Eventually, of course—" He shrugged, a sinuous movement of boneless arms.

"You can't—expect me—to like the idea."

"Not at first," The Arcturian's thought was ingratiating. "But actually such civilization can be very beneficial to the subjects."

"How—"

"Why, take our own activities here on Earth, for instance. The meager natural resources of the Arcturian System have long been almost exhausted, yet our race lives well by building up industry on backward planets like Earth and taking a certain part of the produce. About two hundred years ago we started an industrial revolution here and made its progress as rapid as the Denebians permitted. *We* controlled the booming industry, through the various fronts of the organization, and as much of what was produced as we needed went to Arcturus. We led native researchers to take the lines leading to success—and they thought they were responsible for it. Workers in, say, aircraft factories still don't know that a number of the parts they make go into Arcturian aircars and ships; all who are in a position to know are misled by carefully arranged records, or simply come under sufficient mental control to be incapable of noticing the discrepancies. Oil, iron, alloys, grain, machine parts—some of it all goes to Arcturus. Not much from any one planet—but there are many planets."

"But—governments—"

"Governments!" The foxy face grinned. "*We* are the governments, or as much of them as necessary. Why, a number of backward nations have been forcibly industrialized by revolutionary governments which we arranged in the first place. If you knew how many dictators and commissioners and industrialists and whatnot else are depersonalized natives with a direct mental link to some extra-terrestrial, you would appreciate how completely Earth is in thrall. And—when we are done with them, when some new development is commanded—they go. They are defeated in war, or die, or—fade out of the picture one way or another.

"And yet—" The thought was swift, persuasive—"yet think how Earth has benefited from it. The population has been approximately doubling every century. The standard of living has gone steadily up. The latent resources of the planet are being put to work. Earthlings are pawns, yes—but very well treated pawns."

I wonder. What about the endless, senseless wars that rack them, what about the pollution of the fair green fields with smoke and waste, what about poverty and misery and the loss of all control over their own destiny? What about the time when the purposes of the Vaettir call for the lash? Call for the—discarding—of the human race? But I'm not supposed to know that.

"There is no need to employ euphemisms," came the icy thought of Kane. "Earthlings receive whatever sort of treatment the particular situation calls for. If an individual native comes to prominence and carries out policies contrary to our desires, he dies. There were presidents of this country, for instance, who would have changed the planned course of events. They died—the bullet of a controlled assassin, the hemorrhage of a focused supersonic beam, whatever means was most convenient. The Vaettir will not tolerate interference with their purposes."

"Yes—and what are those aims?" Beoric swung to the five grim-faced monsters at the head of the table. His thoughts were tinged with a fear that was not all feigned. "I take it that as the oldest and most powerful mentally of the local races you have established control over them, so that even your supposed equals jump to your bidding. But—why? What do you want? Where is this great plan of yours leading?"

"That is not for you or anyone else to question," came the bleak reply. "You would not understand the truth anyway. If you said that the Vaettir aimed to rule the attainable universe, it would be an imputation of your own childish motivations to us, for that aim is only a means to an end. If you said that the Vaettir intelligence can draw on the directed minds of whole planets, increasing its own potential correspondingly, and that for this reason it is necessary to direct the history of those planets toward the most useful, easily regimented type of thinking, you would be closer to the truth. Perhaps—" for a bare instant, the lightning-like thought sagged under a burden of vast and intolerable weariness, the despair of the ultimately evolved being who has nothing left to achieve—"perhaps, if you said that there is really nothing else to do, except die, you would almost realize the truth. Almost."

Where are they? Where are the others? Gods, why don't they come?

Beoric thought slowly and bitterly: "So that is why there must be war and misery and evolution of slave states. That is why men—why natives of all the planets you rule must be fettered by old mistakes which even they can see are wrong. You say there are still separate nations on this world. But a race capable of understanding the technology I have glimpsed must surely be intelligent enough to realize that only a unified planetary government can end the horrors of their destinies. Yet—they don't have it. Because it wouldn't suit the purposes of the Vaettir."

"They will have it, eventually," answered Kane. "But it will be the sort of state *we* want. And stop wasting sympathy on the natives. Do you feel sorry for your own domestic animals?"

Suddenly his thought rang out, chill and deadly, overwhelming in its sheer volume of savage energy: "This farce has gone far enough. I think you have trapped yourself sufficiently, and we can begin finding out who you really are."

"Eh—*huh?*" The surprise flashed around the council table. Only the five great Vaettir were in possession of themselves—*they* had known what was coming.

"Of course." Kane's thought roared and boomed in their skulls. The Alf sagged under that rush of devastating cold fury. "Surely you were not taken in by his story—Yes, you were. And it was not without a certain ingenuity.

"But how could an obviously inferior race find a way of screening off stardrive vibrations when the Vaettir had vainly sought such a means for millennia? Why was the stranger, who claimed to come from a civilization not unused to this sort of arrangement, so interested in the details of how Earth is run—and so shocked by them? Yes—shocked in the wrong way, at the wrong times. From the moment I met him, I was studying his emotional reactions. They fitted no reasonable pattern if his story were true. He was too interested in some details, too indifferent to others. Only a Denebian might have noticed the anomalies, for he covered up very well, but they were there.

"There is only one answer." The terrible vibrations filled the room in a sudden soundless thunder. *"There is no interstellar spaceship. There is no planet Alfar. He came from within the Solar System!"*

For an instant there was a silence in which Beoric's sudden horror spurted numbingly along his spine. Lost, lost, the Vaettir had known after all—

No. They still don't know. The thought was like a strong arm suddenly laid about his sagging body. *But we expected that they might deduce this much. And we're just outside the building now.*

For an instant Beoric saw through the eyes of the communicating Alf. A dozen automobiles were parking all around the block. That they were constructed entirely of nonferrous alloys was not evident to the vision, and the beings who tumbled out of them wore conventional native clothes, could pass for human in the vague light. But—they had weapons.

Hold them off, Beoric. Hold their attention for the few minutes it will take us to get to the council chamber and cut off their escape—or their access to their defense. Keep them from noticing our radiations as we approach.

The hurried message ended. And now the minds of the council were crashing against Beoric's brain, drowning his own thoughts in a roar of invading energy. His consciousness reeled toward an abysmal darkness—no, he had to keep them occupied, had to.

"Wait!" he gasped vocally. "Wait—I'll tell you—"

Kane's mind was like a steel band around his. "Start telling, then. But you won't save your miserable personality if you let slip even one falsehood."

"We—we're from—Earth itself—" *Gods, am I telling? There's no need for it—But if even one councilor manages to get word of this to Deneb—*

"You aren't Earthlings!"

"No, we—yes, we are. But not—human Earthlings."

"How could you evolve on a planet to which you are so ill adapted?"

"We aren't. We are extremely well adapted to Earth's night. We haven't yet deduced just how our type of life got started. Obviously it has a common origin with the ordinary sort, but it must lie far back, perhaps in the Archeozoic. Somehow forms of life evolved which could not stand actinic light but which could thrive in darkness, seeing by infrared waves—In spite of their great differences, which are metabolic rather than chemical, the two types of flesh are mutually digestible, so the nocturnal sort did not lack for food—There was quite a variety of such life forms once, and eventually they even evolved a manlike species—us!"

"Nonsense!" Beoric gasped with the pain of the Vaettir assault on his brain. "There are no such geological or paleontological indications that such forms ever existed."

"Of course not." The Alf's thoughts flowed frantically. Would they never come? Where were they? What was keeping them? "I said that the nocturnal life's metabolism is peculiar. The natural balance, involving high rates of both anabolism and catabolism, makes very long life spans possible. I am five hundred years old, and still young. But it means that the body decays very quickly on death. Even the bones are soon oxidized, being organic. No fossil traces would remain at all. Perhaps a few have been preserved by freak accidents, though I doubt it, but they would be very few and human paleontologists simply haven't chanced to find them. And, of course, there was never any possibility of interbreeding with the dominant forms."

"Dominant? But why should the nocturnals have become—"

"Extinct? Yes, they nearly are. They couldn't really compete with the other type, which could endure both day and night, and which reproduced much faster. The Alfar have few children in their long lives. Our numbers have been on the wane for centuries, and almost all other animals of our sort are extinct."

"That still doesn't account—"

"We have other weaknesses, too." *There's no harm in telling now. If the others don't come soon, it's all over anyhow.* "Certain metals, silver and iron, are fatal to us. They catalyze rapid proteolysis and oxidation of our tissues." Beoric saw Kane's eyes widen the tiniest fraction, and knew what icy calculations must be going on in that long skull. He went on, drearily: "Even in neolithic times, humans had the edge on us, and once they had learned metallurgy our doom was sealed. They drove us out of all lands they inhabited and, for religious and superstitious reasons, destroyed most of our cities and other works. The invention of firearms, which we could not duplicate, was simply the last blow. We gave up the fight and retreated into wastelands and into the night, living in hidden dwellings and having little contact with humans. Once in a while, there might be a brief encounter, but the last of these was three hundred years ago, and since then we have lived so remotely that men no longer believe we ever existed."

"And yet—" Kane paused. "It is not illogical. If a human, say, were to be told that there are several nonhuman races sharing the planet with him, he would hardly balk at one more. Even if such an extra race were—native!" For a moment he sat quiescent, then: "What is that?"

His thought lashed like a fist at Beoric, and the other Vaettir hurled their rage with him. The Alf fell to the floor, screaming with the pain of it.

"Strangers—I feel their vibrations—*Strangers in the ship!*" Kane made one tigerish bound toward the door, toward escape—or the atomic guns of the vessel.

An arrow whined, and through blurring eyes Beoric saw the Denebian pitch forward with the feathered shaft through his breast. He saw his fellows, the warriors of the Alfar, coming through the door, and they had cast off their human coats and hats, they wore the golden-shining beryllium-copper helmets and byrnies of the old days, and they carried the old weapons. Longbow, spear, sword, ax, and a shrieking fury that clamored between the metal walls, the blood-howl for vengeance.

The air was thick with the sighing arrows. All were aimed at the Denebians, who fell before their terrible mental force, that might yet have annihilated the invaders, could utter more than a snarl. And now the warriors were on the councilors, ax and sword rising and falling and rising bloodily again.

"Save one!" cried the king. "Save an Altairian!"

Beoric sat dizzily up. Strength was flowing back into him, strength and a gasping incredulous realization that he was still alive. That—they had won. The Vaettir were dead.

"How are you, Beoric?" The anxious voice was close to his ear.

"I'm all right." The Alf climbed unsteadily to his feet. "How—is it?"

"All well. I can't detect anybody else on the ship. It's ours," said the king.

He turned to the surviving Altairian, who lay coiled in his tentacles under the spears of the warriors and watched them with calm eyes. "Your people were always the most decent," thought the king, "and I think you will be the most cooperative. We want you to show us how to run this ship. If you do we'll release you on some planet from which you can find your way home."

"Agreed," answered the octopoid. "Would you mind explaining exactly who you are and what is your purpose and how you accomplished all this?"

"We are the nocturnal equivalent of Earth humankind," answered Beoric. "We were almost powerless, but being telepathic we did know of the interstellar exploitation which was going on. It menaced us just as much as it did our old human enemies—but it also offered us an opportunity.

"In time, we learned how to make nonferrous alloys which would substitute for iron and steel. And by telepathic 'spying' on the invaders, over a period of centuries, we picked up enough hints to be able to generate gravity beams and eventually, to build a small spaceboat.

"We knew we could never enter the Denebian stronghold if they realized our true nature. The remnants of our race would simply be hunted down. But if we could send an agent—myself—to pose as a visitor from some great formidable civilization beyond their own, they would treat him with respect—for a while, anyway. He could get into one of their ships. And his fellows, whom the aliens would not expect to be on Earth with him, could use the diversion he created to come in after him and take possession of the ship."

"And so you have it," murmured the Altairian's thought. "And you have wiped out all the Vaettir in the Solar System, completely disorganizing their rule here till they can send someone else. Well done! But—what now?"

"First," said the king, "the whole race of the Alfar is leaving the Solar System. This ship should be big enough to carry them all. There are so few of us left—But when we find a planet which suits us, an uninhabited world we can hold without fear, hidden from the Vaettir by the vastness of the Galaxy, we can begin to make our comeback. After that—a warned, roused union of free stars, equipped with ships such as this, can do something about the Vaettir." His thought was grim. "And I know what that something will be."

"It's strange," mused Beoric. "The aliens knew that they had caused most of the demon-myths of Earth. It did not occur to them that the myths of Faerie might also have an origin in reality. That I might be—an elf! That peris and nixies and kobolds and brownies and fairies and the Sea People and all the rest might, in a way, really exist . . . And so man's old enemy, the shifty unreliable folk of the night, becomes in the end his savior. And Alfheim changes from myth to a real planet."

"Aye. And—well done, Beoric," said King Oberon.

DEAD RINGER
Lester del Rey

As someone who worked as a reporter, and served in the Army before that, I shouldn't be surprised that this short story from Lester del Rey spoke to me as it did. It's not just that "Dead Ringer" manages to include zombies, aliens, and conspiracy all in under 4K words, but how the story is cleverly told from the POV of a potentially unreliable narrator.

Is Dane Phillips a crusading reporter who has uncovered a horrifying truth he has to share at any cost? A victim of trauma from an abusive father and combat in World War II, whose grasp on reality has finally slipped? An unlucky fool who has stumbled into an alien bid for dominance . . . or a pawn in that game?

Dane Phillips slouched in the window seat, watching the morning crowds on their way to work and carefully avoiding any attempt to read Jordan's old face as the editor skimmed through the notes. He had learned to make his tall, bony body seem all loose-jointed relaxation, no matter what he felt. But the oversized hands in his pockets were clenched so tightly that the nails were cutting into his palms.

Every tick of the old-fashioned clock sent a throb racing through his brain. Every rustle of the pages seemed to release a fresh shot of adrenalin into his blood stream. *This time*, his mind was pleading. *It has to be right this time. . . .*

Jordan finished his reading and shoved the folder back. He

reached for his pipe, sighed, and then nodded slowly. "A nice job of researching, Phillips. And it might make a good feature for the Sunday section, at that."

It took a second to realize that the words meant acceptance, for Phillips had prepared himself too thoroughly against another failure. Now he felt the tautened muscles release, so quickly that he would have fallen if he hadn't been braced against the seat. He groped in his mind, hunting for words, and finding none. There was only the hot, sudden flame of unbelieving hope. And then an almost blinding exultation.

Jordan didn't seem to notice his silence. The editor made a neat pile of the notes, nodding again. "Sure. I like it. We've been short of shock stuff lately and the readers go for it when we can get a fresh angle. But naturally you'd have to leave out all that nonsense on Blanding. Hell, the man's just buried, and his relatives and friends—"

"But that's the proof!" Phillips stared at the editor, trying to penetrate through the haze of hope that had somehow grown chilled and unreal. His thoughts were abruptly disorganized and out of his control. Only the urgency remained. "It's the key evidence. And we've got to move fast! I don't know how long it takes, but even one more day may be too late!"

Jordan nearly dropped the pipe from his lips as he jerked upright to peer sharply at the younger man. "Are you crazy? Do you seriously expect me to get an order to exhume him now? What would it get us, other than lawsuits? Even if we could get the order without cause—which we can't!"

Then the pipe did fall as he gaped open-mouthed. "My God, you believe all that stuff. You expected us to publish it *straight*!"

"No," Dane said thickly. The hope was gone now, as if it had never existed, leaving a numb emptiness where nothing mattered. "No, I guess I didn't really expect anything. But I believe the facts. Why shouldn't I?"

He reached for the papers with hands he could hardly control and began stuffing them back into the folder. All the careful documentation, the fingerprints—smudged, perhaps, in some cases, but still evidence enough for anyone but a fool—

"Phillips?" Jordan said questioningly to himself, and then his voice was taking on a new edge. "Phillips! Wait a minute, I've got it now! *Dane* Phillips, not *Arthur*! Two years on the *Trib*. Then you turned up on the *Register* in Seattle? Phillip Dean, or some such name there."

"Yeah," Dane agreed. There was no use in denying anything now. "Yeah, Dane Arthur Phillips. So I suppose I'm through here?"

Jordan nodded again and there was a faint look of fear in his expression. "You can pick up your pay on the way out. And make it quick, before I change my mind and call the boys in white!"

It could have been worse. It had been worse before. And there was enough in the pay envelope to buy what he needed—a flash camera, a little folding shovel from one of the surplus houses, and a bottle of good scotch. It would be dark enough for him to taxi out to Oakhaven Cemetery, where Blanding had been buried.

It wouldn't change the minds of the fools, of course. Even if he could drag back what he might find, without the change being completed, they wouldn't accept the evidence. He'd been crazy to think anything could change their minds. And they called *him* a fanatic! If the facts he'd dug up in ten years of hunting wouldn't convince them, nothing would. And yet he had to see for himself, before it was too late!

He picked a cheap hotel at random and checked in under an assumed name. He couldn't go back to his room while there was a chance that Jordan still might try to turn him in. There wouldn't be time for Sylvia's detectives to bother him, probably, but there was the ever-present danger that one of the aliens might intercept the message.

He shivered. He'd been risking that for ten years, yet the likelihood was still a horror to him. The uncertainty made it harder to take than any human-devised torture could be. There was no way of guessing what an alien might do to anyone who discovered that all men were not human—that some were...zombies.

There was the classic syllogism: *All men are mortal; I am a man; therefore, I am mortal.* But not Blanding—or Corporal Harding.

It was Harding's "death" that had started it all during the fighting on Guadalcanal. A grenade had come flying into the foxhole where Dane and Harding had felt reasonably safe. The concussion had

knocked Dane out, possibly saving his life when the enemy thought
he was dead. He'd come to in the daylight to see Harding lying there,
mangled and twisted, with his throat torn. There was blood on
Dane's uniform, obviously spattered from the dead man. It hadn't
been a mistake or delusion; Harding had been dead.

It had taken Dane two days of crawling and hiding to get back to
his group, too exhausted to report Harding's death. He'd slept for
twenty hours. And when he awoke, Harding had been standing
beside him, with a whole throat and a fresh uniform, grinning and
kidding him for running off and leaving a stunned friend behind.

It was no ringer, but Harding himself, complete to the smallest
personal memories and personality traits.

The pressures of war probably saved Dane's sanity while he
learned to face the facts. All men are mortal; Harding is not mortal;
therefore, Harding is not a man! Nor was Harding alone—Dane
found enough evidence to know there were others.

The *Tribune* morgue yielded even more data. A man had faced
seven firing squads and walked away. Another survived over a dozen
attacks by professional killers. Fingerprints turned up mysteriously
"copied" from those of men long dead. Some of the aliens seemed to
heal almost instantly; others took days. Some operated completely
alone; some seemed to have joined with others. But they were legion.

Lack of a clearer pattern of attack made him consider the
possibility of human mutation, but such tissue was too wildly
different, and the invasion had begun long before atomics or X-rays.
He gave up trying to understand their alien motivations. It was
enough that they existed in secret, slowly growing in numbers while
mankind was unaware of them.

When his proof was complete and irrefutable, he took it to his
editor—to be fired, politely but coldly. Other editors were less polite.
But he went on doggedly trying and failing. What else could he do?
Somehow, he had to find the few people who could recognize facts
and warn them. The aliens would get him, of course, when the story
broke, but a warned humanity could cope with them. *Ye shall know
the truth, and the truth shall make you free.*

Then he met Sylvia by accident after losing his fifth job—a girl
who had inherited a fortune big enough to spread his message in

paid ads across the country. They were married before he found she was hard-headed about her money. She demanded a full explanation for every cent beyond his allowance. In the end, she got the explanation. And while he was trying to cash the check she gave him, she visited Dr. Buehl, to come back with a squad of quiet, refined strong-arm boys who made sure Dane reached Buehl's "rest home" safely.

Hydrotherapy . . . Buehl as the kindly firm father image . . . analysis . . . hypnosis that stripped every secret from him, including his worst childhood nightmare.

His father had committed a violent, bloody suicide after one of the many quarrels with Dane's mother. Dane had found the body.

Two nights after the funeral, he had dreamed of his father's face, horror-filled, at the window. He knew now that it was a normal nightmare, caused by being forced to look at the face in the coffin, but the shock had lasted for years. It had bothered him again, after his discovery of the aliens, until a thorough check had proved without doubt that his father had been fully human, with a human, if tempestuous, childhood behind him.

Dr. Buehl was delighted. "You see, Dane? You *know* it was a nightmare, but you don't really believe it even now. Your father was an alien monster to you—no adult is quite human to a child. And that literal-minded self, your subconscious, saw him after he died. So there are alien monsters who return from death. Then you come to from a concussion. Harding is sprawled out unconscious, covered with blood—probably your blood, since you say he wasn't wounded, later.

"But after seeing your father, you can't associate blood with yourself—you see it as a horrible wound on Harding. When he turns out to be alive, you're still in partial shock, with your subconscious dominant. And that has the answer already. There are monsters who come back from the dead! An exaggerated reaction, but nothing really abnormal. We'll have you out of here in no time."

No non-directive psychiatry for Buehl. The man beamed paternally, chuckling as he added what he must have considered the clincher.

"Anyhow, even zombies can't stand fire, Dane, so you can stop worrying about Harding. I checked up on him. He was burned to a crisp in a hotel fire two months ago."

It was logical enough to shake Dane's faith, until he came across Milo Blanding's picture in a magazine article on society in St. Louis. According to the item, Milo was a cousin of *the* Blandings, whose father had vanished in Chile as a young man, and who had just rejoined the family. The picture was of Harding!

An alien could have gotten away by simply committing suicide and being carried from the rest home, but Dane had to do it the hard way, watching his chance and using commando tactics on a guard who had come to accept him as a harmless nut.

In St. Louis, he'd used the "Purloined Letter" technique to hide— going back to newspaper work and using almost his real name. It had seemed to work, too. But he'd been less lucky about Harding- Blanding. The man had been in Europe on some kind of a tour until his return only this last week.

Dane had seen him just once then—but long enough to be sure it was Harding—before he died again.

This time, it was in a drunken auto accident that seemed to be none of his fault, but left his body a mangled wreck.

It was almost dark when Dane dismissed the taxi at the false address, a mile from the entrance to the cemetery. He watched it turn back down the road, then picked up the valise with his camera and folding shovel. He shivered as he moved reluctantly ahead. War had proved that he would never be a brave man and the old fears of darkness and graveyards were still strong in him. But he had to know what the coffin contained now, if it wasn't already too late.

It represented the missing link in his picture of the aliens. What happened to them during the period of regrowth? Did they revert to their natural form? Were they at all conscious while the body reshaped itself into wholeness? Dane had puzzled over it night after night, with no answer.

Nor could he figure how they could escape from the grave. Perhaps a man could force his way out of some of the coffins he had inspected. The soil would still be soft and loose in the grave and a lot of the coffins and the boxes around them were strong in appearance only. A determined creature that could exist without much air for long enough might make it. But there were other caskets that couldn't be cracked, at least without the aid of outside help.

What happened when a creature that could survive even the poison of embalming fluids and the draining of all the blood woke up in such a coffin? Dane's mind skittered from it, as always, and then came back to it reluctantly.

There were still accounts of corpses turned up with the nails and hair grown long in the grave. Could normal tissues stand the current tricks of the morticians to have life enough for such growth? The possibility was absurd. Those cases had to be aliens—ones who hadn't escaped. Even they must die eventually in such a case—after weeks and months! It took time for hair to grow.

And there were stories of corpses that had apparently fought and twisted in their coffins still. What was it like for an alien then, going slowly mad while it waited for true death? How long did madness take?

He shivered again, but went steadily on while the cemetery fence appeared in the distance. He'd seen Blanding's coffin—and the big, solid metal casket around it that couldn't be cracked by any amount of effort and strength. He was sure the creature was still there, unless it had a confederate. But that wouldn't matter. An empty coffin would also be proof.

Dane avoided the main gate, unsure about whether there would be a watchman or not. A hundred feet away, there was a tree near the ornamental spikes of the iron fence. He threw his bag over and began shinnying up. It was difficult, but he made it finally, dropping onto the soft grass beyond. There was the trace of the Moon at times through the clouds, but it hadn't betrayed him, and there had been no alarm wire along the top of the fence.

He moved from shadow to shadow, his hair prickling along the base of his neck. Locating the right grave in the darkness was harder than he had expected, even with an occasional brief use of the small flashlight. But at last he found the marker that was serving until the regular monument could arrive.

His hands were sweating so much that it was hard to use the small shovel, but the digging of foxholes had given him experience and the ground was still soft from the gravediggers' work. He stopped once, as the Moon came out briefly. Again, a sound in the darkness above left him hovering and sick in the hole. But it must have been only some animal.

He uncovered the top of the casket with hands already blistering.

Then he cursed as he realized the catches were near the bottom, making his work even harder.

He reached them at last, fumbling them open. The metal top of the casket seemed to be a dome of solid lead, and he had no room to maneuver, but it began swinging up reluctantly, until he could feel the polished wood of the coffin.

Dane reached for the lid with hands he could barely control. Fear was thick in his throat now. What could an alien do to a man who discovered it? Would it be Harding there—or some monstrous thing still changing? How long did it take a revived monster to go mad when it found no way to escape?

He gripped the shovel in one hand, working at the lid with the other. Now, abruptly, his nerves steadied, as they had done whenever he was in real battle. He swung the lid up and began groping for the camera.

His hand went into the silk-lined interior and found nothing! He was too late. Either Harding had gotten out somehow before the final ceremony or a confederate had already been here. The coffin was empty.

There were no warning sounds this time—only hands that slipped under his arms and across his mouth, lifting him easily from the grave. A match flared briefly and he was looking into the face of Buehl's chief strong-arm man.

"Hello, Mr. Phillips. Promise to be quiet and we'll release you. Okay?" At Dane's sickened nod, he gestured to the others. "Let him go. And, Tom, better get that filled in. We don't want any trouble from this."

Surprise came from the grave a moment later. "Hey, Burke, there's no corpse here!"

Burke's words killed any hopes Dane had at once. "So what? Ever hear of cremation? Lots of people use a regular coffin for the ashes."

"He wasn't cremated," Dane told him. "You can check up on that." But he knew it was useless.

"Sure, Mr. Phillips. We'll do that." The tone was one reserved for humoring madmen. Burke turned, gesturing. "Better come along, Mr. Phillips. Your wife and Dr. Buehl are waiting at the hotel."

The gate was open now, but there was no sign of a watchman; if one worked here, Sylvia's money would have taken care of that, of course. Dane went along quietly, sitting in the rubble of his hopes while the big car purred through the morning and on down Lindell Boulevard toward the hotel. Once he shivered, and Burke dug out hot brandied coffee. They had thought of everything, including a coat to cover his dirt-soiled clothes as they took him up the elevator to where Buehl and Sylvia were waiting for him.

She had been crying, obviously, but there were no tears or recriminations when she came over to kiss him. Funny, she must still love him—as he'd learned to his surprise he loved her. Under different circumstances . . .

"So you found me?" he asked needlessly of Buehl. He was operating on purely automatic habits now, the reaction from the night and his failure numbing him emotionally. "Jordan got in touch with you?"

Buehl smiled back at him. "We knew where you were all along, Dane. But as long as you acted normal, we hoped it might be better than the home. Too bad we couldn't stop you before you got all mixed up in this."

"So I suppose I'm committed to your booby-hatch again?"

Buehl nodded, refusing to resent the term. "I'm afraid so, Dane— for a while, anyhow. You'll find your clothes in that room. Why don't you clean up a little? Take a hot bath, maybe. You'll feel better."

Dane went in, surprised when no guards followed him. But they had thought of everything. What looked like a screen on the window had been recently installed and it was strong enough to prevent his escape.

Blessed are the poor, for they shall be poorly guarded!

He was turning on the shower when he heard the sound of voices coming through the door. He left the water running and came back to listen.

Sylvia was speaking.

"—seems so logical, so completely rational."

"It makes him a dangerous person," Buehl answered, and there was no false warmth in his voice now. "Sylvia, you've got to admit it to yourself. All the reason and analysis in the world won't convince him he's wrong. This time we'll have to use shock treatment. Burn over those memories, fade them out. It's the only possible course."

There was a pause and then a sigh. "I suppose you're right."

Dane didn't wait to hear more. He drew back, while his mind fought to accept the hideous reality. Shock treatment! The works, if what he knew of psychiatry was correct. Enough of it to erase his memories—a part of himself. It wasn't therapy Buehl was considering; it couldn't be.

It was the answer of an alien that had a human in its hands—one who knew too much!

He might have guessed. What better place for an alien than in the guise of a psychiatrist? Where else was there the chance for all the refined, modern torture needed to burn out a man's mind? Dane had spent ten years in fear of being discovered by them—and now Buehl had him.

Sylvia? He couldn't be sure. Probably she was human. It wouldn't make any difference. There was nothing he could do through her. Either she was part of the game or she really thought him mad.

Dane tried the window again, but it was hopeless. There would be no escape this time. Buehl couldn't risk it. The shock treatment—or whatever Buehl would use under the name of shock treatment—would begin at once. It would be easy to slip, to use an overdose of something, to make sure Dane was killed. Or there were ways of making sure it didn't matter. They could leave him alive, but take his mind away.

In alien hands, human psychiatry could do worse than all the medieval torture chambers!

The sickness grew in his stomach as he considered the worst that could happen. Death he could accept, if he had to. He could even face the chance of torture by itself, as he had accepted the danger while trying to have his facts published. But to have his mind taken from him, a step at a time—to watch his personality, his ego, rotted away under him—and to know that he would wind up as a drooling idiot . . .

He made his decision, almost as quickly as he had come to realize what Buehl must be.

There was a razor in the medicine chest. It was a safety razor, of course, but the blade was sharp and it would be big enough. There was no time for careful planning. One of the guards might come in at any moment if they thought he was taking too long.

Some fear came back as he leaned over the wash basin, staring at his throat, fingering the suddenly murderous blade. But the pain wouldn't last long—a lot less than there would be under shock treatment, and less pain. He'd read enough to feel sure of that.

Twice he braced himself and failed at the last second. His mind flashed out in wild schemes, fighting against what it knew had to be done.

The world still had to be warned! If he could escape, somehow... if he could still find a way... He couldn't quit, no matter how impossible things looked.

But he knew better. There was nothing one man could do against the aliens in this world they had taken over. He'd never had a chance. Man had been chained already by carefully developed ridicule against superstition, by carefully indoctrinated gobbledegook about insanity, persecution complexes, and all the rest.

For a second, Dane even considered the possibility that he was insane. But he knew it was only a blind effort to cling to life. There had been no insanity in him when he'd groped for evidence in the coffin and found it empty!

He leaned over the wash basin, his eyes focused on his throat, and his hand came down and around, carrying the razor blade through a lethal semicircle.

Dane Phillips watched fear give place to sickness on his face as the pain lanced through him and the blood spurted.

He watched horror creep up to replace the sickness while the bleeding stopped and the gash began closing.

By the time he recognized his expression as the same one he'd seen on his father's face at the window so long ago, the wound was completely healed.

KNOTWORK
Nina Kiriki Hoffman

Few authors have the knack for making their readers—or especially in the context of this story, their characters—see the world from a different perspective quite like Nina Kiriki Hoffman.

One of the newer stories reprinted for the anthology, "Knotwork" may well also be among its more unusual. Hell hath no fury like a woman scorned—especially when the spouse you've been cheating on is an alien whose needlecraft can alter human will and personality. In addition to mulling over potential justice, we get a contemplation on how relationships change over time, the nature of free will, and how much give-and-take there is in all the ties that bind us together.

When we married, my husband and I tied knots in ourselves and in each other.

I am not from around here, and to me all knots mean special things. Where I come from, one moves through a lacework of knots; one learns to tie one's own knots; one learns how knots limit one. I came here to get away from knotwork, and yet, four years after I arrived, I consciously brought my skills into play, and crafted a tangle to bind two people together, as local custom seemed to dictate.

I thought the knots meant the same things to my husband that they meant to me. We had been seven years married, and somewhere along the way our wild mutual madness faded into something I found comfortable in its complex sameness. To me, the knots remained, even though the passion had died. To my husband...

103

"So, Nuala, what's this we hear about your husband?" Marie asked me when I joined my three best friends for our weekly Tuesday lunch at Le Chèvre et Les Trois Framboises. This week Marie's hair was purple and shellacked into a fountain of lazy curls. She was a live mannequin in the window of the largest department store in town, and this week the clothing she advertised was severe in pink and black. Everyone in the restaurant stared at her, which gave the others of us a measure of anonymity.

I put my beaded purse on the table beside my place setting. "So what is it you hear?"

Anika, who worked in the same corporate office as my husband—in fact, she was the person who had introduced me to my husband—said, "We hear he takes Jacy Hines, one of the associates, everywhere with him."

"He took her shopping in my store," Marie said. "I saw them come in together from my window, and later I asked the clerks where they went. To fishing equipment. When's the last time a man asked a woman to look at fishing equipment?"

"Perhaps she knows something about it." I had met Jacy at one of the firm's office parties. She was a small pigeon woman, comforting and round, with short brown hair and bright brown eyes, ruddy of complexion and neat of hand, and I had liked her. She hadn't borne any of the marks of threat one learns to look for when one leases her husband to a job for the bulk of the day. Jacy and I had discussed knotwork and the mysteries of coffee. If she had had the energy of a spouse-taker, wouldn't I have felt it? I had given up several of my special senses when I bound myself, but not that one.

"He took her out to buy you a birthday present last week," Anika said. "Last year he sent his secretary. This year he took Jacy, and they shopped together."

My birthday celebration would happen on Saturday. It was something Hugh and I always did alone together. I hadn't realized that selecting my gift was a task he delegated; the gifts I had received from him had been sensitive and thoughtful, and I had been touched.

I had not smelled them closely enough. The stink of someone else must have been on them. I used my eyes too much these days; I had lost some of the vital information streams I used to fish.

"He took her to coffee yesterday in my restaurant," said Polly, who owned a diner two blocks from Le Chèvre. We never met at Polly's for lunch; she liked to get away and eat somebody else's food once in a while. "They sat on the same side of the booth instead of across from each other."

Hugh had taken Jacy to Polly's restaurant? Then he intended me to know; he knew about my friendship with Polly, certainly knew she would tell me what she had seen. Perhaps the other things could be explained somehow; Jacy had special knowledge of fishing; Jacy had a woman's feel for a gift. But to have coffee with her in Polly's place. Why?

I had signed up for three new classes through community education this term, but I always signed up for classes. Hugh hadn't wanted me to work when we married, and I was satisfied not to. Instead I taught myself the intricacies of housekeeping and mankeeping and cooking, which were not overnight things to learn, but now I had them mastered and had time for other things. I took classes: two of them this term were night classes, which meant I left him to sketchy dinners and his own company twice a week. Was that enough reason for him to slip my knots?

I waited for him to come home that evening, even though I should have packed my portfolio for life drawing class and left before he pressed the garage door opener.

Hugh came into the kitchen from the garage. I studied his dark suit, his strong, square hand around the handle of his briefcase, his dark hair disarrayed because he pulled it when stuck in traffic, the shadows under his blue-gray eyes: my first thought was fondness.

"Oh! Nu! Still here?" he said.

He must have seen my car in the garage. "Why pretend surprise?" I asked, more direct than usual. I did not want to take the time for our usual dance.

"I know you have class tonight. I thought maybe one of your friends picked you up."

"This is only the second week. I have no friends in class yet. I understand you've been more friendly than you should be, though."

A flush of red touched his cheeks and was gone. "We said long ago that we would keep our old friends."

"And make new ones? The rule was we could keep our old friends, but the new ones we would make together or not at all."

"That was the rule," he said. "You break it every time you take one of these classes."

"Those aren't real friends. Those are driving-together-and-discussing-class-material friends. Any of them I want to keep, I introduce to you. And you always say no. And I always listen." On occasion, I had listened with regret. I liked a boy from madrigals class. Hugh nixed him, and I unknotted him; not the easiest unlove I had ever done, either, since the origin of his attraction was natural rather than induced.

"I've known Jacy longer than I've known you." Hugh set his briefcase on the kitchen table and ran his hand through his hair.

"Have you?"

"We went to grade school together."

I twisted my hands in my lap. He had never told me. We told each other things of this sort; it was part of our pact.

Our pact. Established in passion, a heat I thought would never die. Where had it run to? It had drained from us both as surely as snowmelt leaves mountains in summer.

Eventually, I said, "If you have something to say to me, I wish you would just say it, rather than sending my friends as your messengers."

"I have nothing to say to you except what's for supper?"

A chill lodged in my heart. I opened the freezer compartment of the fridge. "You decide." I grabbed my portfolio and left.

That night at life drawing class we had a male model, a man who drove city busses during the day. He was an older man, in his fifties at a guess, with a black beard streaked with white, his hair thinning on top. He had folds of fat at his waist and kind eyes, and I liked drawing him much more than I had liked drawing the model last week, a Greek god who could not hold a pose more than a minute without wavering, and when I complained, he moved even more to spite me.

I laid down line with my darkest, fastest pencil, trying to be pleased with the exercise, the model, everyone else in class looking at skewed views of this same pose, our instructor walking around to stand behind us for a while, then leaning forward to discuss technique with us when she sensed an opening.

I laid down line. I could not stop thinking about the early days with my husband, how we had pledged our lives to each other, so deeply had we felt our love, how we had bound ourselves tight, thinking that what we wanted at the time was what we would want always.

Now a small brown woman whom my husband had known before he had met me inched between us, though truth to tell there was a big enough gap between us that anyone could have fit into it.

"Ouch," said the model, dropping out of pose and clapping a hand to his buttocks.

I looked at my picture, realized I had laid down the line of his buttocks with too much heat in my hand. Smoke rose from the page. My face burned. I touched the paper with my ice hand.

This should not have happened. I had locked all these touch powers away when I had woven the vows that bound me to Hugh. Something had broken, and now my vows were coming unthreaded.

I had done nothing. Hugh. It was Hugh.

"Cramp?" the teacher asked the model.

The model nodded. What else could he say? Or maybe he *had* experienced it as a cramp. He wouldn't have a mental opening to experience a line of fire along his buttocks; what couldn't happen couldn't be called by its true name, a human law that allowed me to operate within this realm without too much risk of discovery.

I set down my pencil and clasped one hand in the other, letting my hands speak to each other until both were in the middle of their range.

I came here to find friends I could not discover where I lived before, and I had made these friends: Marie, Anika, Polly at college, young, naked, trusting as unfledged birds who opened their mouths for whatever a parent would put inside. I had shaped myself by learning what had shaped them, and how they operated in their worlds. Anything they did that produced a reaction I liked, I learned to do. They fed me a human character. I learned from the other people we spent time with, as well. The dorm, the cafeteria, classes, fraternity parties, football games, bars, the student union, road trips over the breaks. It was my perfect nursery.

I watched my three friends fall in and out of love, and practiced a little myself. I met boys and enjoyed them, but none touched my heart.

It was four years later, after we had left college for the world, that

Anika introduced me to Hugh. When I first saw him, I felt a flare of heat that surprised me, and I judged I had waited long enough to try the rest of the accoutrements of love. I dropped some of my walls and let love consume me.

It seemed to me that Hugh too lost himself in love. We were both mad in the best ways.

"Nuala? Something the matter?" asked my art teacher.

"My hands hurt."

She rubbed my shoulder. "Maybe you were holding the pencil too tight."

I smiled at her and picked up my pencil, then flipped to a fresh page. The model had dropped into a new pose, and I hadn't drawn a line of it. These were five-minute poses, and I had no idea how much longer I had with this pose, so I scrawled lines quickly, flowed in the outline of where the model was. Pencilwork was one form of knotwork, though I had not let myself play with that before. I tried to keep these parts separate: knotwork from what everyone else did here. One of my vows to myself when I bound myself to Hugh had been that I would remain undiscovered.

"Wow," said the teacher. "I've never seen you work so fast and well."

I glanced over my shoulder at her, then looked at my drawing. I had let some of the other world out of my fingers, the merest caress of that which speaks touch-power. I set down my pencil again.

"Don't stop," said the teacher. "I didn't mean to interrupt your process."

"I'm sorry," I said. "I'm having trouble concentrating."

The madness had seeped out of our marriage so slowly I hadn't noticed it leaving. One day I woke up after Hugh left for work, and I knew I didn't care if I saw Hugh again that day. I couldn't remember the last time joy leapt into my heart at the sight of him. I still had my vows and agreements, though, which I must honor, or I feared I would dissolve. So I looked around for other things here that could excite me. Classes woke up a sleeping part of me for moments at a time. Friends helped too. I settled into an existence that was gray with small spikes of color here and there. It was enough.

So I thought. Eventually, Hugh would die; my vows would end, and I could choose where to go next, whether back to my home where I could live as myself, to a new world, or somewhere else in this world, perhaps to find someone else, perhaps to try a different kind of sharing, a shorter one, or a more intricate one, or a more unbalanced one. The possibility of finding joy again existed. I had found it once.

Waiting has always been one of my skills.

I was not willing to wait while my husband betrayed me in public. Perhaps I could have let it go if he had been discreet. If he had been discreet, and our vows dissolved because of his actions, I could have moved on. But to do it so all my friends knew. This seemed a deliberate act.

If he had nothing to say about it, I wondered if perhaps Jacy would tell me something.

"Maybe you should always draw when you're having trouble concentrating," the art teacher told me. "This is wonderful."

"It's a mistake." I ripped the page off my easel and tore it to bits, severing the lines and their touch-power. Who knew what they had already carried to the model? At least he didn't seem to be suffering.

Or did he? He had held the pose surprisingly well for a long time while I thought things over. When I ripped up the page, he collapsed and breathed hard for a moment. He shook his head like a bull shaking off a bee, then slapped his face.

"You okay?" the teacher asked.

"I think I'm coming down with something," the model answered. "Hot flashes, then this weird paralysis. Maybe I better take a break."

The teacher checked the clock. Half an hour earlier than the model's scheduled break. "All right," she said. "Everybody take ten minutes and then come back. Nuala?"

I closed my pad. "I better go home," I said. "I'm not feeling well either."

Hugh would not be expecting me home for forty-five minutes or an hour. I couldn't decide if I would rather surprise him or wait. In the end, I stopped for coffee at the 24-hour coffee shop and sat in a booth, thinking about what to do.

I went to a phone booth and checked the listings, found Jacy Hines. I called her number and she answered.

"This is Nuala. May I come and see you?"

She hesitated. I waited.

"Let me meet you somewhere," she said at last. I wondered if Hugh were there with her now.

I told her where I was, and she came fifteen minutes later. She wore a brown jacket over a dark orange dress, and black tights and shoes. She looked small and comforting, like someone I should like for a friend.

We both got coffee and sat across from each other in the booth. I waited.

She had drunk half of her coffee when she finally spoke. "What do you want?"

"What are you doing with my husband?"

She stared into her cup. "He said you wouldn't mind."

"You have been misinformed."

She glanced up then, and I drew that look on the tabletop with my darkest pencil, letting touch-power enter her outline.

"You see," I whispered when I knew I had her attention, that her gaze would not waver, "I made promises when I married him, and he gave me promises in return. Are his promises mist? Does that make mine water, to melt and flow instead of staying hard as ice?"

"He said you were no longer sexual with each other." Her whisper was strained.

"I don't remember by whose desire." I rubbed my fingertips over my forehead.

"Do you want him still? I didn't know."

"I am bound to him by vows I hold sacred."

For a moment she said nothing. "I'm sorry."

"He has drawn you in. Does that mean I pull you farther into our vows, or that I let go of our vows?" I got a different pencil out of my box and drew carefully on the portrait of Jacy, added lines of warmth where I had learned they would most affect a human. She twitched and shuddered as I worked, and red flowed across her face.

"What are you doing?" she asked in an agonized whisper.

Another touch there. Three tweaks. I slid my eyes sideways, watched her shudder again.

"Whatever I like." I watched her for a while, left her suspended almost all the way to where she would find release, not quite there, just the itchy anxious side short of it. Then I touched my drawing, and she shook and shuddered, her breath panting in and out of her. Finally she melted back against her bench.

I traced the lines of my picture with summon power until the picture released the tabletop. It eased into my hand. Jacy's shoulders shifted. "What are you doing?" she whispered again. A tear leaked from one of her eyes.

"Knotwork." I tied the lines of her drawing in several complicated knots and slipped it into my pocket. This was so easy for me that I knew my vows had indeed melted. Since I had not stepped outside them, I knew Hugh had destroyed them.

Did I want to reinstate them? Or should I leave him now? I ran my fingers over the small knot of lines in the bottom of my pocket. Jacy jumped and twitched.

"Please," she said. "Please don't do that."

I rubbed the warm places in my knots with the ball of my thumb. She leaned back, eyes closed, mouth open. Low gasps rang from her. I rubbed slower, then faster, until she melted down under the table. People at nearby tables watched her when her gasps grew loud enough. "Stop," she moaned. I gave her lines one last rub, and she cried out, loud enough for everyone in the restaurant to hear.

I took my hand out of my pocket. I finished my coffee. I glanced at the waitress, who came over to me after a couple minutes.

"Is your friend all right?" she asked as she refilled my cup.

"She's fine." I pointed to Jacy's cup and the waitress refilled that too, and went away. I poured two creams into Jacy's coffee, as I had seen her do when she first sat down. I sipped my coffee. Then I leaned down and spoke under the table. "You can come out now."

She had curled into a ball. "I'm never coming out." Tears streaked her face.

"You can come out, or I can make you come out."

She rubbed her eyes. A little later she crept out from under the table and settled herself in her seat. People stared. She looked toward the wall, her cheeks flushed.

"Drink your coffee."

She drank. "What do you want?" she asked.

"I don't know yet."

"I'm sorry. I'm so sorry. He said—"

I nodded. I dropped money on the table to cover our coffees and a tip. "Let's go."

She collected her purse and her jacket from the bench and tried to stand. Staggered.

I slipped my hand into my pocket and stroked strength into her lines. She straightened, took a deep breath, and followed me out of the restaurant.

"Are you a witch?" she asked in the parking lot.

"Not exactly."

"But you can make me feel things." She blushed again.

"Did you like it?"

She stared at the ground. She shook her head. She smiled a tiny smile, the smile one smiles for oneself. "I can never go into that restaurant again."

"Let's go back right now."

She touched my arm. "Please. Don't."

I stared at her hand until she dropped it. "Please," she whispered.

I cupped her knotwork in my hand. She tensed.

"Let's go to your apartment."

She relaxed.

I let her drive us in her car.

My husband's scent was in her living room.

It was a small and comforting place. I sat on her brown velvet couch, and she dropped into a red armchair across a walnut coffee table from me. Bookshelves lined one wall, most of the books hardcovers and well worn. A plant stand held a number of leggy, healthy plants. A red and blue Persian carpet the size of a bathroom stall in a hotel covered a patch of floor between furniture.

Brown velvet smelled of my husband, his satisfied scent.

"I bound myself to him, and he to me," I told Jacy.

"I'm sorry. I didn't realize. He acted as if there were nothing between you anymore."

"When I met you, you didn't smell like a threat."

She shook her head. "I never thought of it. I was surprised when he came into my office and asked me to help him evaluate a portfolio. He's my senior. I thought perhaps he was grooming me for a higher-level position. I thought it was because of my merits. Then he kept asking my help. Things that seemed natural at first, and then things that seemed outside our jobs. Step by step he walked me away from what I thought was right, and I did not notice. Until one night we were up here together. I thought we were talking about work. And then it was different somehow. He sat close to me. I've been alone a long time. People don't see me that way, and I— I'm so sorry, Mrs. Breton."

"I don't know if that's my name anymore."

She covered her face with her hands. "I never meant—I don't know how it happened. I should have listened to Barry. He told me to stay away from Hugh. But it seemed like nothing at first, so innocent. I am such a fool. I am deeply sorry."

"Was he here tonight?"

She lowered her head. Her lips tightened.

"Why did he make your relationship public?" I wondered. "If he doesn't mind my taking classes—if he knows it means he can see you—why let me find out about it?"

"I don't think that's right," she said in a low voice. "I think he minds."

I slipped my hand into my pocket, cradled her lines inside it. "Does he speak to you of me?"

Her gaze fixed on my hand in my pocket. She was frightened. "Sometimes," she whispered.

"What does he tell you?"

"He says you don't care about him anymore. That you're gone a lot. That he's a passionate man and you no longer want him."

I tried to view this as Hugh did. Had he told Jacy his own truth? I was not gone a lot. Perhps twice a week seemed like a lot. Perhaps he resented the time I spent with my friends while he was at the office. Did I signal Hugh that I no longer wanted him? We climbed into bed and went to sleep. We never turned to each other anymore.

All the knotwork I had made with Hugh was what we had woven together; in my vows I had decided that I would not hold him in my hand the way I held Jacy now. That was part of the risk and wonder of our marriage for me. Where I came from, one wove knots on knots. That was what one knew: the skill of the knotmaker determined who ruled the connection between any two people. I had come here to find something new.

No knots but first knots. Shelve that skill and try something new. So I had new skills, but it was time, past time, to reclaim the old ones.

I took Jacy's knotwork out of my pocket and sat with it in my hand. She shivered and leaned forward to look. "Is that me?" she asked.

"It is not you, but what I use on you. We spoke of this when we first met."

"We did?" She reached out a hand, touched the edge of her knot, jerked the hand back, her eyes widening. "I felt that."

I smiled at her and drew a finger along an edge, watched as she straightened. This was a stroke up her side. She stared at me. I stroked down her other side. She glanced at her side, then at me.

"It's not fair," she said. "How can you do that to me?"

"Fair has nothing to do with it." I had woven myself tight in a lace of rules, played at being one of them. All of that was gone.

I set Jacy's knotwork on the table between us and leaned back against her couch. Again I smelled my husband's satisfaction.

All his actions told me that he wanted everything to change. Did he want to go back to what we were? Did he want to move on, join with Jacy and abandon me? He was no longer the person I married; and nor was I the person who had married him any longer.

What did I want?

I thought of my friends, the knots we had tied in our lives where they intersected, our weekly lunches, our telephone conversations, our movie dates, the occasional friend emergency where we met one or two or three or four together, to comfort someone in trouble. I thought of my studies, the greatest of which was my study of how to mimic a human, all the rest subsidiary. I thought of the pleasures Hugh and I had shared, how they had swallowed every other consideration until I had thought nothing else mattered.

I took a pencil out of my purse, pulled out my grocery list, flipped to a blank page, and drew Hugh.

I had never knotted him in this way before. I had knotted spirit in him, but never body. I had abdicated that power after our marriage.

This time I drew on all my memories of our days and nights, on how I had touched him everywhere, and how he had touched me. I drew his spark points and his dull points, the parts of himself he groomed and those small spaces that escaped him.

I left these lines blank, open to whichever power I would choose to pour into them when I was ready. I took out the other two pencils and laid lines on top, the warmth lines, the pain lines. I turned my husband from equal to object.

I dropped the pad on the table beside Jacy's knotwork.

"What is it a picture of?" she asked.

I startled. I had forgotten she was there.

I turned the pad so she could see it better and looked at her, my eyebrows up. How well did she know Hugh?

Her eyes shifted as she studied the knotwork. Slowly a frown pulled the edges of her mouth down. "Is it—" She sat back suddenly, eyes wide, cheeks pale. "This is Hugh?"

I smiled.

"What are you going to do?" she whispered.

"I don't know yet." I leaned forward and picked up her lines. She hunched her shoulders, then relaxed them, but bit her lower lip. I set her knotwork on top of the picture of Hugh's, wondering what would happen. Hugh's work was not active yet; I had not powered it; but Jacy knew what it was.

Her lines curled away from the image of Hugh's. No attempt to tangle.

Jacy and I stared at one another.

"You renounce him?" I asked.

"I never meant . . . I can't stay with someone who betrays someone else that way. I trusted what he told me, that you wouldn't mind. He lied to me. I don't want a person who does that."

I lifted her knotwork, held it between my hands and talked the knots into dissolving, let the power loose. Some of it came back to me, and some went into the air.

I rubbed my hands against each other, then took a napkin from my purse and wiped off the stain.

"What?" Jacy said. She patted her chest, her face. "What?"

I showed her my empty hands.

She heaved a big sigh and smiled at me. "Thank you." Then she frowned. "What do you want me to do?"

"I have let go of wanting to dictate your actions."

"But with Hugh—"

I picked up my pad and looked at my knotwork. "I don't know what I want." I lifted a finger of my fire hand and held it just above the knotwork, ready to charge the picture with power. "What would you do if you were me?"

She shook her head.

"What is the human response?" I asked.

She swallowed. "There is no one answer. Some wives look the other way and nurse their pain. Some talk it over with the husbands and decide that they can work it out. Some leave. Some kill their husbands." She covered her mouth with her hand. "Forget I said that!"

"Among my people, killing another is a sign of lack of imagination. So many other things are more satisfying, and hurt more."

She dropped her hand from her mouth, clasped her other hand in it. "Where do you come from?"

"Somewhere else."

She frowned, then crossed her arms, hiding her hands in her armpits. "Why did you come here?" she whispered.

"To learn."

She stared down at her feet for a moment, then gazed at me again. "Does Hugh know what you are?"

"No." I had let him bind me, but had not told him what powers I gave him, what powers I gave up. I knew, and that was enough.

"He's an idiot," Jacy said.

I cocked my head and stared at her.

"Did you try to keep what you were a secret from him?"

"I became something else in the framework of our marriage. I gave up my powers. How could he know what I was when I wasn't myself?"

"You said we talked about the pictures—the strings?—when we first met?"

"Knotwork," I said.

"Knotwork. Like macrame?"

"I don't know that word."

"What do you remember about that conversation?"

I thought back to the party. So many drunk people. I don't like talking to drunken people. They don't make sense, and they don't remember what they said later. It's as though the conversation never took place. So why have it take place?

Only if I want information, and by that time I was not looking for information about my husband's daytime environment. I was content to own the sphere of home.

At the party, Jacy had held a glass, and only took little sips. So I talked to her. She spoke to me about coffee grinders in supermarkets, which ones had the best blends and which blends were not good; and we spoke of knotwork. "You told me who everyone in the room was, and how they were knotted to each other."

"Oh." She frowned. "I didn't call it that, though, did I?"

"I don't remember. That's how it made sense to me, so that's how I remember it."

"Knots are—" she began.

The phone rang. It sat beside the couch. I looked at it, then at Jacy. She licked her lip and picked up the phone. "Hello?"

She listened a moment, then said, "I don't think—"

She put her hand over the mouthpiece and whispered, "Hugh."

"What does he want?" I whispered back.

"To come over."

Strange feelings eeled through me. I picked up my drawing of my husband and nodded to Jacy.

"I don't think that's a good idea," she said into the mouthpiece, "but if you really want to—"

She listened a little longer. "All right." She hung up the phone and looked at me. "He said you should be home by now. He said you should have a little of your own medicine. If you're going to make him wait, he will make you wait."

"He'll make me wait while he's with you."

She nodded. "I don't think he would have heard me even if I said no. I've never heard him talk like this before. If I had—"

I waited.

She twisted one hand in the other, shook her head. "I would suspect that there was something else going on, something I wouldn't like. Obviously there's still an emotional charge. He still cares, or he wouldn't want you home on time."

"I heard you went shopping for my birthday present together," I said.

Her face went crimson. "He told me you liked silver," she whispered, "and that if I picked it, it would be better. Something delicate, Celtic knots, he thought, but he said he didn't know what looked good."

"Did you find me something good?"

She ducked her head, twisted her hands. After a moment, she nodded.

"Thank you."

A knock on Jacy's door, then the sound of a key in the lock. I lifted my knotwork from the table and touched both ice and fire to it.

"Jacy?" Hugh said. All he saw was her. He came across the room, stooped beside her armchair, and kissed her. Her hands clenched on the arms of the chair. "Honey?"

She lifted one hand and pushed his face away until he could not help but see me. He straightened. "Nuala."

"Hugh." I stroked summon power into my drawing until it pulled free of the page, and then I knotted it. The knot for power over another's body. The knot for power over another's speech. I hesitated a moment, thinking of other knots: power over another's heart, power over another's mind, power over another's spirit. Without the knots, I could still stroke the pain and pleasure lines, manipulate the knotwork and cause strong but temporary effects, as I had with Jacy. With the knots, my power would be absolute, unless the person I knotted had his own knot power. I did not think Hugh had such power.

I looked at my husband. Great sadness struck me. I still loved him. Just the sight of him made me soft and fond, even here in the apartment where he had taken another woman in the way he had promised he would only take me.

I did not put the other three knots into my work. There was always time for that if I needed it.

"Nuala, what are you doing?" Hugh asked, an uneasy edge to his voice. He gripped Jacy's shoulder.

"I am choosing a future for us, my love."

"What do you mean?"

I looked at the knotwork I held, the complex and the simple parts, a diagram of my husband, by necessity flat where he had depths, no true image of all there was about him, but true enough that I could capture him in it.

"By betraying me, you have set me free. I don't know what I want from this freedom. I will discover it."

"Honey—"

"Don't call me by the same name you use for her."

He glanced down, saw that he had his hand on Jacy's shoulder, that she glared up at him. He sucked air in and released her.

Jacy rose and came to sit beside me on the couch. "You told me she didn't care anymore, Hugh," she said. "You lied."

"Do you care?" Hugh sat in the chair Jacy had left.

I said, "I do. I would never have left you as long as you lived."

"But we had nothing left."

"We had everything. Some parts of it were asleep. Why didn't you tell me you wanted to wake them?"

"Didn't I? All those nights I reached for you, and you turned your back."

Had he reached for me? I remembered his touch on my shoulder, on my back. I had cherished that touch, but hadn't thought it meant anything more. Had it been a request? We were speaking different languages with our bodies, after those years when we had known without words what would please the other and ourselves. When had we lost our language?

"I thought you just wanted to touch my back. I didn't know it was a request for something else. Why didn't you say something?"

"I thought you were telling me it was over."

"That's so strange," Jacy said. "You don't talk with words?"

"Everything with him is a dance," I said. "He approaches what he wants, but he never says it out loud. This is not my first or second or even third language. Sometimes I know what he wants, and sometimes I get tired of trying to figure it out and give up."

"I can't talk about these things," Hugh said.

I looked at the knotwork in my hands. There was the knot I had put on his speech. If I twisted it one way, words would spill out of him. If I kinked it with skill, they would be words I was interested in hearing.

"Do you know what she's holding?" Jacy asked Hugh.

"Knitting?" Hugh guessed.

Jacy reached into my hand and stroked the knotwork. Hugh jerked, clapped a hand to his side. Jacy pressed a different place, and

Hugh clapped his knees together. "What are you doing?" he asked in a choked voice.

"You don't know what you're touching," I told Jacy.

"Yes, but this is fun." She touched the knot for speech.

"I am so confused and scared," Hugh said. "I wanted something to happen, but I didn't know how to direct it, so I flailed around and tried things, and this is what happened, but what is it? I don't understand it, and I'm terrified."

Jacy lifted her finger and looked at me, then frowned at Hugh. "What do you feel for Nuala?" she asked, and touched the speech knot again.

"She frightens me and I love her. I know she has a secret life she will never share, and I'm jealous. I think she's leaving me. I think she's found someone else. I think she no longer likes me. I want to hurt her. I want to wake her up and make her remember what she's losing. I want her to come back. I want her to notice that I've left. I don't know what's going on in her head."

"Why don't you ask her?"

"I can't ask questions like that. I'll get smacked."

"Smacked by who?"

"My mother will hit me if I ask for anything. She always says no questions, no wishes. Every answer is a smack." Hugh writhed in the chair, covered his mouth with his hands. Sweat beaded on his forehead.

Jacy jerked her finger off the knot.

Hugh collapsed, breathing hard. "What are you doing to me?"

I closed my hand around my knotwork, then opened my hand again and stroked lines. Hugh settled back. His breathing eased.

"Whatever I want," I whispered.

After a moment he opened his eyes. A tear ran across his cheek. "Nuala, what is this?"

"Ah, husband, this is my secret side, the side I gave up to be with you, but since you left me, I reclaimed it."

"I haven't left you."

"You broke our vows. You left me."

"I wanted to stir things up. I wanted things to change between us."

"You got your wish." I glanced at Jacy, who had been used like an instrument. My husband had made her an object and a weapon, just as I had made him. Once you make a person an object, everything changes between you. The climb back up to person is much harder than the first climb.

Jacy had made that climb.

I studied the knotwork. I could use it to bend Hugh any way I liked.

If I bent Hugh, would I want to go home with him? If all that he was was what I chose—I could choose good things. I could tie knots to make him trustworthy and loyal. But I would always know that I chose it, and in time I would not be able to tell what was left of who he had really been.

"Nuala," he said.

"Hugh. Now that you've changed everything, what do you want?"

He groaned. "I want to go back to when things were good between us."

I glanced at Jacy. She frowned.

"What do you want?" I asked.

She slumped back against the couch and sighed. "It doesn't matter," she said.

Cupping Hugh's knotwork in my left hand, I sketched another Jacy with my right. She straightened as she watched. Her tongue darted out to lick her upper lip.

I charged the work with both hands to encompass her complexity.

"What do you want?" I asked her again.

"Not to be lonely," she whispered, and then, "I want to learn what you know."

Happiness heated my chest. I began to see work I could do, a direction I could go; stay here, keep Hugh, learn new things. The old vows were gone. I was through playing fair.

I set aside the knotwork of Jacy. "Watch carefully," I told her. She bent her head over my hands as I manipulated Hugh's knotwork. "This is the knot for power over another's heart. This is how you stroke it when you want him to be true." We both studied what I had done, then looked across the table at Hugh.

Heat had kindled in his eyes. He leaned forward, his gaze fixed on my face, and I felt my own heat rise within. He wanted me, and that excited me.

We couldn't go back, but we could go forward into a second love. I could add Jacy into the mix, and make Hugh like it.

I would bend him in increments. I might lose who he had been, it was true; but who he had been had chosen to betray me.

I could always bend him back.

DIAMONDS IN THE ROUGH
Alex Shvartsman

At the time of publication, with Russia in the news for the sort of aggressive belligerence all too familiar to those who lived through the Cold War, it's sometimes hard to remember there was a time when many thought—and some hoped—that the Russian bear was dead and buried for good. Those were the '90s, the heady days when the collapse of the USSR and the lingering spirit of glasnost *meant anyone with a big enough bank account and small enough moral compass could have a turn picking the Soviet's bones clean—and plenty of Russians desperately doing anything to survive.*

From Alex Shvartsman, and originally published in Galaxy's Edge *magazine, we have the tale of one such young Russian dealing with surviving the collapse of the Iron Curtain, that involves gunrunning, blood diamonds, and a group of aliens looking to profit off both, before the deal goes south for all parties involved.*

🐝 🐝 🐝

"I'm going out, Mom," Igor called out from his room. He grabbed a leather jacket, then retrieved the shoebox he kept atop the wardrobe where his younger siblings couldn't reach.

"Dinner is almost ready, Igor," his mother shouted back from the kitchen over the sound of the radio. "Can you wait?"

"Can't, Mom. It's work." Cheap posters of Hollywood action stars stared at him from where they were affixed to the fading wallpaper. Igor opened the box and took out an old police-issue Makarov pistol.

His boss, whose last name was also Makarov, had laughed when he'd given it to him. "This is the official handgun for anyone in my crew. No Nagants or Tokarevs, not for my men." This Makarov had no connection to his namesake gun designer from the '40s, but he acted as though the ongoing popularity of this model fifty years later was somehow his personal accomplishment.

Igor checked the pistol and put it into the inner pocket of his jacket. Although he never fired it outside of the shooting range, it made him feel like the badass heroes from the foreign films, the ones who could walk away from explosions and mayhem behind them without flinching or looking back.

"Keep out of trouble." His mother's cracking voice betrayed her apprehension.

Neither of them liked the idea of him working for Makarov, but he had little choice. Ever since Gorbachev let loose with this Perestroika business, the country was coming apart at the seams. With no government funds coming in, the newly privatized factories had cut their staff. Igor's father was laid off and couldn't find steady work. Hyperinflation wiped out whatever meager savings his family had. The money seventeen-year-old Igor was able to bring in was indispensable to their family's survival.

A brand-new 1990 Mercedes-Benz 600 was parked halfway on the sidewalk in front of the building. It was painted a garish shade of dark purple, clearly an aftermarket job.

Makarov was one of the New Russians, a small group of opportunists who'd found a way to grow rich by appropriating the crumbling bits of the Soviet empire. Among the New Russians it was not merely acceptable but expected to flaunt their wealth, and Makarov was no exception. In the city where unemployment soared toward fifty percent, his fleet of purple foreign cars paraded his opulence.

Igor climbed in the back.

"You're late," said Sharik without turning.

The driver was a grim older man. No one knew his real name save for, perhaps, Makarov himself. To everyone else he was just Sharik, and he didn't seem to mind being called by a common dog's name. He wore a sleeveless shirt displaying heavily tattooed forearms which told the story of years spent within the Russian penal system.

"I'm right on time. You're early," Igor snapped back, then turned to the man in the front passenger seat. "Hello, Leonid Nikolayevich."

"Hello, Igor," said the geologist.

They rode in silence for a time. Leonid looked more fidgety than usual, chewing his lower lip. "This is a bad idea," he told Sharik. "I don't think Mak should be double-crossing those Chechens. They're bandits, not businessmen. They don't play nice."

"Shut up, four-eyes," said Sharik. "You're not paid to think. Besides, this is not something you should be yapping about in front of the kid."

Igor frowned. He knew what Makarov was up to. He was young, not stupid. Sharik didn't trust him, but then Sharik didn't trust anyone except for the boss, as best as he could tell.

They rode the rest of the way in silence and arrived at a warehouse on the outskirts of the city, where several armed guards were posted at the entrance. Sharik dropped him and the geologist off, waved to the guards, and left on another errand.

The large industrial building was mostly empty, with only a handful of wooden crates stacked by one of the walls. A few stools were placed near the crates. Makarov and a group of his men sat there. Another stool housed several glasses and a half-empty bottle of vodka.

Makarov was telling some kind of a raunchy joke. He raised his glass in greeting, the clear liquid sloshing inside. His hand was steady and he didn't slur his words, which meant he had kept his drinking to a minimum.

"Good evening, Mak." Igor knew his employer preferred to be called by his nickname.

Makarov wore a bright-red jacket over a yellow T-shirt and black jeans. A thick gold chain hung around his neck and a large Rolex gleamed on his arm. On his face was a self-satisfied smirk of a man who was denied nothing, and he carried himself with the swagger of a 1920s gangster from an American movie. Igor thought that Makarov couldn't act or look any more a stereotype of a New Russian if he tried.

"My customers will be here soon. For now, relax, have a drink or two. Just not so many that it will affect your skills, eh, Leonid?" Makarov chuckled and filled their glasses.

After imbibing some liquid courage, Leonid spoke up. "This isn't right, boss. We have a good thing going with the Chechens. Why rock the boat?"

Makarov looked his underling up and down. "This is business," he said. "The Chechens aren't our friends, they aren't our family. They're just customers, and they were outbid."

"But when you made the deal with the Chechens you said you wanted to sell them the guns because they'd take them far away from here." The geologist gesticulated as he talked. "Who knows what these new people might do?"

Igor agreed with Leonid's sentiment, but he was smart enough to keep his mouth shut.

Selling weapons was a recent thing, but not entirely unexpected. Makarov earned enormous profits by selling off whatever he could get his hands on to anyone who would pay: heavy machinery from the now-shuttered factories, reams of copper wiring meant for maintaining the city infrastructure, even Soviet-era statues of Lenin that foreign collectors wanted for some reason. All of these things belonged to the Russian people, but in the post-Soviet chaos there was no strong government, no police force with authority and will to stop the profiteers. As things deteriorated, it became possible for Makarov to pilfer even military supplies, and he jumped at the opportunity.

Igor figured Makarov would blow up at Leonid for his questions, but the boss was in a good mood.

"The Chechens are crazy and they're still in our backyard, not so far away," said Makarov. "But these new people, they'll export the guns to Africa or South America, to some nasty little war in a place you can't even find on the map. And they'll pay extra for the privilege. Blood diamonds they can't easily move in Europe, so we get them at a discount rate. Once you examine them, of course." He saluted Leonid with his glass. "It's a win-win. You see that now?"

Leonid nodded reluctantly. "Yes, Mak."

"Good." Makarov grinned. "Stick with me, boys, and I'll keep you in vodka. I've got plans for us, big plans." He drained the rest of his glass.

Makarov's business associates showed up fifteen minutes later. There were two of them, a man and a woman, dressed in nearly identical black business suits. The man carried a shoulder bag.

Something was strange about the pair, though Igor couldn't quite put his finger on it. They walked and carried themselves in a slightly odd way. Their facial features were exotic: round eyes that were just a little too large, ruddy complexions, weak chins, and short earlobes. Igor wondered where they were from, wondered if Makarov knew, or cared.

Makarov and the foreigners greeted each other. They spoke Russian fluently and with only the vaguest hint of an accent, as though they were used to Slavic pronunciations. Could they be from Poland? Czechoslovakia?

The man handed over a bag. Makarov opened it, peered inside, and passed it to Leonid. "Do your thing."

The geologist propped the bag on one of the stools, revealing the rough diamonds inside. They looked like chunks of glass. Still embedded in rock and dirt, they glinted in the pale light that emanated from the incandescent bulbs suspended along the ceiling.

Igor craned his neck and peered over Leonid's shoulder. "Whoa, those are some big rocks."

"They aren't cut. Cutting them will make them lose over half of their total volume," said Leonid. He retrieved tools from his own bag: a jeweler's loupe, a microscope, and a few other items Igor didn't recognize.

Makarov relied on Leonid to authenticate precious stones and metals, which were the standard currency among the wealthy and the connected because the value of the ruble was in constant freefall.

Igor always thought his boss an eccentric for hiring a geologist. Any jeweler could have handled the task. Igor went to the library once, and read about identifying diamonds. He thought that even he could probably do a reasonable job of it, given a magnifying glass and a lighter. But, as was the case with his cars and his women, Makarov was accustomed to buying the best of everything, and that included hiring experts.

Leonid was taking his time, running all sorts of tests on the stones, and even studying some of the dirt they came with. Makarov opened one of the crates and was showing off a Kalashnikov to the two foreigners.

Igor studied the stones from a distance. In their rough form, they looked nothing like the gems he'd seen in the windows of expensive jewelry shops. It took a trained eye to recognize their true value, and a trained hand to cut the stone properly and bring all that potential to fruition. He couldn't help thinking how modern Russia was so much like a rough diamond: all that potential locked inside. But would it ever truly blossom into a gem if men like Makarov did the cutting?

Leonid carefully returned the stones to the bag, got up and waved Makarov over. While the foreigners were busy examining the merchandise, Makarov joined him. The two of them walked away and engaged in an animated discussion that lasted for nearly two minutes.

Makarov's men knew their boss; the expression on his face made them focus, primed them to expect trouble.

He confronted the foreigners. "What are you trying to pull?"

"Is there a problem?" asked the woman. She was holding a Kalashnikov, but Igor knew it wasn't loaded.

"You tell me." Makarov crossed his arms. "My expert tells me something is wrong about these stones."

"The precious stones were selected to your specifications," said the man.

Neither of the foreigners seemed nervous to Igor, but then, he supposed, arms merchants were accustomed to dangerous dealings.

"My geologist isn't happy," said Makarov. "And when he isn't happy, I get upset. Me being upset isn't good for business."

"Where are they from?" Leonid interjected himself into the conversation before Makarov could lose his cool and go too far with the threats. "There's no question these are authentic diamonds, but the impurities are highly unusual, and the lamproite matrix material is like nothing I've ever seen."

The two foreigners exchanged glances.

"You've already confirmed their authenticity," said the woman. "This should suffice. We prefer not to reveal the location of our mines."

"Not good enough," said Makarov. "If Leonid is suspicious, anyone I try to sell the diamonds to will be dubious as well."

"Meteoroid!" said Leonid. "They must've found extraterrestrial material with diamonds in it."

Everyone looked at the geologist.

"What, like from space?" asked Makarov.

"Earth has been bombarded by matter from space over the course of millions of years," said Leonid. "Some of it contains diamonds thought to be formed from the shock of collision between asteroids. All the ones I've heard of have been tiny, not like these." He puffed up, clearly proud of his deduction. "Most people wouldn't figure this out, but I was educated in Leningrad."

Makarov began to say something but was interrupted by the sound of gunfire outside.

Makarov's men reached for their weapons. It was what they were there for: extra muscle for a deal that presented an alluring target for anyone brazen enough to take advantage. No one outside of this warehouse was supposed to know when and where the exchange was going down. Igor didn't even know where he'd end up when Sharik picked him up earlier that evening. *Sharik!* He wasn't in the building. Could he have double-crossed them?

Makarov made eye contact with Igor and pointed at the foreigners. "Watch these two!" He turned to the others. "That crate over there. The guns in it are loaded."

Igor ushered his charges toward the far corner of the warehouse. He didn't think they were behind the attack. They'd arrived unarmed and had brought the gemstones. There was little for them to gain from the violence. Makarov must've made the same calculation, or his orders would have been different.

The deafening sound of an explosion nearly stunned Igor. It took him a few seconds to recover, and when he did he saw at least a dozen men with automatic rifles pouring in through the jagged hole blasted in the wall, advancing through the debris and the smoke.

The Chechens! Igor recognized a few of them from Makarov's past dealings. It couldn't have been Sharik, then. He hated the Chechens; if the dog was ever to betray his master, it wouldn't be to *them*.

The attackers advanced into the warehouse. Then they saw Makarov's men, armed with AK-47s. The two sides opened fire.

It was a bloodbath. Men on both sides died in a hail of bullets.

It must have been the adrenaline, but everything seemed to move very slowly to Igor. He thought the Chechens must have expected token resistance, must not have realized how many men Makarov would have or how well they would be armed, else they wouldn't walk into the enemy line of fire like this.

He held his pistol in both hands, reluctant to fire, reluctant to draw attention to himself and his unarmed wards. It worked for a short while. Then one of the Chechens turned his attention to him and the foreigners.

Igor and the attacker stared right at each other. Somehow, Igor was focusing on the wrong details: the bead of sweat on the man's forehead, the charcoal stain on his tan shirt. Igor couldn't bring himself to fire at a live target. The man turned his rifle toward him and squeezed the trigger.

A curtain of light, far brighter than the dim glow produced by the light bulbs, materialized between him and the attackers. Bullets bounced against the rectangular barrier as though it was a concrete wall. The impossible shield was pellucid and yet bright. Now everyone in the room was facing them.

Igor turned around to find one of the strangers focusing intently on a small sphere in his palm. The woman held a similar gadget, and cast wary glances at both groups of armed men.

It didn't take long for the Chechens to realize their bullets couldn't penetrate the barrier, and they went back to firing at Makarov and his men. The battle resumed, with Igor and the two foreigners stuck as spectators behind the light shield.

The entire skirmish couldn't have taken more than a minute, but it felt far longer to Igor. Powerless to act, but also thankful for the protection—however strange and incomprehensible the source of it was to him—he watched men die.

He saw Leonid fall backward, his body riddled with bullets. The light went out from the geologist's eyes.

This was what the guns Makarov was selling were meant to do, be it in Grozny, Chechnya or in some remote part of the world where they had palm trees. And now this violence was happening in front of him. Was happening to him.

He was too young to have personally experienced the horrors of the Soviet regime that he'd read about in the papers, but whatever atrocities the communists were guilty of, at least criminals hadn't battled it out openly in their time. He felt like he was seeing the end of civilization, the preview of things to come.

And who were these arms dealers exactly? Wizards? Time travelers? Aliens? He thought back to the extraterrestrial diamonds.

Aliens fit the bill. He'd read Efremov, and Lem, and Bulychev. Aliens weren't supposed to be like this. Sinister or benevolent, what could they possibly want with a bunch of old AK-47 rifles? Although his mind was working in overdrive, it refused to process the surprise of the discovery, refused to cope with it. For now, whoever the foreigners were, they were keeping him safe and that was enough.

The fight ended with most of the Chechens dead or dying on the ground, and only a handful of the defenders, including Makarov himself, left standing. The last couple of intruders fled through the opening their explosive had created in the wall, Makarov's men firing at their backs.

The foreigner made the light shield disappear. Then they heard more shots from the outside, and more screams.

"Follow me," shouted Makarov as he raced toward Igor and the foreigners.

Whatever was coming next, he wanted the protection of the light shield, too. He and his men positioned themselves around the foreigners when yet another group entered the warehouse.

This time it was Sharik. He and his men advanced more carefully than the Chechens, entering the warehouse simultaneously through the front door and the blast hole in the wall.

Makarov held off ordering his men to fire, perhaps holding out hope that Sharik was still his loyal dog, that he had brought reinforcements to fight the Chechens. Igor thought his boss was a fool; Sharik was clearly making a power play and Makarov let his men come in and disperse along the walls. The foreigners were not so trusting. Both of them activated their light shields this time.

Sharik took a step forward and addressed Makarov's men.

"I'm in charge now." He pointed at Makarov. "There's room in my organization for whoever kills that pompous windbag."

A few of Makarov's men glanced at their boss, trying to figure out which way the wind was blowing.

"Are you kidding?" shouted Makarov. "You sicced the Chechens on us, tried to have us all killed. You think my men will trust you after that?"

"That wasn't personal," said Sharik. There was no remorse in his voice. "I let the two problems take care of each other; all my men have to do now is mop up. That's the kind of leadership those who join me can expect. You see, I take initiative." As he said that, he raised his pistol and shot at Makarov. The bullet made a whining sound as it ricocheted off the light barrier.

Sharik whistled. "I'll be damned." He cocked his head and stared at the foreigners with newfound interest. "You two, turn off your fancy American light-fence and I'll allow you to walk out of here."

The foreigners made no move to lower their shields.

"You have not proven yourself to be trustworthy," said the woman.

Sharik chuckled. "Suit yourselves." He waved to his men. "Take them."

Sharik's men had already dispersed throughout the warehouse. The defenders positioned themselves near the edges of the two light shields. The two groups sniped at one another, bullets whizzing across the warehouse.

Igor clutched his handgun in sweaty palms. A Hollywood action star would have taken charge, would have eliminated a half dozen opponents by himself. Igor thought he understood this sort of violence having seen it on badly dubbed videotapes, but real life was different. In real life he couldn't bring himself to engage. He huddled next to the foreigners and watched the events unfold around him.

Sharik ran along the far wall of the warehouse while his men laid cover fire. He got to the point where he had a clear shot, crouched and aimed.

The male arms dealer gasped and fell backward, a wet spot blossoming on his chest. The sphere rolled out of his hand and one of the light barriers flickered and went out. The woman screamed and dropped to her knees next to him, her barrier winking out of existence as well.

With their protection suddenly gone, the corner of the warehouse became a killing field. Sharik's men mowed down the defenders in a matter of seconds.

Igor crouched low, expecting a bullet to find him. He heard about people's lives flashing before their eyes in the final moments, but for him there was only terror and images of his family; how would they react when he didn't come home tonight? He imagined his parents arguing. Mom would want to file a missing persons report while Dad would say he was probably fine and they should wait until morning...

Makarov dove for the gadget dropped by the fallen foreigner. He grabbed hold of it but couldn't bring the defensive shield back to life. In his hands it was only a dead chunk of metal.

The woman cradled her partner's lifeless body and her wail turned into a scream of rage. She let go of his corpse, got up, grasped her own sphere with both hands and concentrated on it.

An intense wall of light formed several meters out, encircling the foreigners, Igor, Makarov and Tolya, one of his men. It blocked the bullets but left the rest of Makarov's people exposed to enemy fire.

The woman ignored the cacophony of gunfire and the screams of the wounded as she went on staring at the sphere. Suddenly the light burst outward like a sun going nova and bathed the entire warehouse. Then, less than a second later, it disappeared.

The warehouse was completely silent. Once Igor's eyes recovered from the flash of light, he could see that everyone on the outside of the barrier, Sharik's people and Makarov's alike, were dead. Their bodies were crumpled on the floor with no outward signs of any damage.

Makarov stared at the scene of the carnage for several long seconds, then turned to the woman who still held the sphere in both hands. Her wide eyes seemed unfocused, large tears pooling in their corners.

Makarov placed the sphere he'd been holding on the ground, took a step toward her and punched her in the face.

The woman crumpled onto the concrete. The sphere fell from her hands and Makarov kicked it out of reach. She clutched at her nose and blood poured through her fingers.

Igor noticed that the blood was orange. The same color as the bloodstain that covered the chest of her partner.

"What the devil are you?" asked Makarov.

The woman moaned softly, but made no response.

Makarov grabbed her by the shoulders and lifted her up. Then he forced her hands away from her face and studied her up close.

"You're some kind of a space alien, aren't you?" He shook her. "Answer me, or I'll put a bullet through your head."

"Yes," she whispered, her voice barely loud enough for Igor to hear. "We're from another world."

"Why are you here? What do you want with us?" Makarov asked.

"We told the truth. We want to trade for your weapons."

Makarov chuckled bitterly. "What do you want with guns, when you have . . . this." He nodded toward one of the spheres on the ground.

"We can't trade high technology on interdicted planets," she said. "Only mechanical weapons." She wiped the blood from her face with the sleeve of her jacket. "Our business model is like yours—outside the framework of our laws."

Makarov nodded, then called over his shoulder. "Guard her, Tolya. Igor, go find some rope and tie her up."

His remaining underling stepped up and trained his gun on the woman.

"We can still complete our transaction," she said. "You have the diamonds, and I can get you more."

"After all this, I'll need the guns and the diamonds," said Makarov. "Recruit new men, arm them. Besides, I have a feeling the CIA or some big corporation will pay me whatever I ask for you and your—what did you call it?—high technology. Enough to build an empire so strong no one will dare challenge me." He grinned savagely at Tolya. "Told you, stick with me and you'll make it big-time."

Igor thought it wasn't fair. The woman had saved their lives. He thought of the guns in the streets of his hometown, of the sort of violence a man like Makarov might unleash given the opportunity.

Makarov and Tolya were focused on the woman. They didn't see Igor raise his pistol. Even though his hands shook, it was impossible to miss at point-blank range. He put a bullet in the back of Makarov's head. Tolya began to turn, but he never had a chance: another pull of the trigger, and Igor and the woman remained the only ones alive in the building.

She trembled, no doubt expecting that the third bullet would be meant for her.

Igor stared at the carnage. "Tell me the truth, is it better . . . out there?" he asked, pointing upward with his gun.

She thought it over.

"No," she said, her voice small and resigned. "It is the same, everywhere."

Igor lowered his gun slowly.

"The weapons are yours," he said. "Get them out of here."

He understood that these guns would be used to kill, somewhere. He couldn't fix the whole universe. The only thing he could do, the only thing within his power, was to protect his tiny corner of it. Perhaps the heroes from Hollywood films would have found a better way, but Igor was no hero, and this wasn't a movie.

"Don't leave any behind, all right?"

Some of the tension slowly drained from the woman's face and she nodded.

Igor picked up the bag of diamonds, hefted it over his shoulder, and walked away without looking back.

THE REALITY TRIP
Robert Silverberg

As a relative greenhorn as an author, editor and anthologist, I find introducing Robert Silverberg feels like being a rookie ballplayer trying to introduce Michael Jordan. His body of work on all fronts is so large, the awards and praise heaped upon them so many, that they speak for themselves more than I ever could. It should come as no surprise that his contribution to our anthology of stories of aliens on Earth stands among its most unique.

An alien observer in a biomechanical carapace is on a mission to observe and report on Earth, now nearly a dozen years into his mission. He laments Earth's oppressive gravity, has come to savor the air pollution that reminds him of his homeworld, and recently has to deal with fending off a nosy and flirtatious neighbor and his own depression and isolation with the assignment. Through that isolation, at last, our alien may yet discover just what it means to be human.

I am at a reclamation project for her. She lives on my floor of the hotel, a dozen rooms down the hall: a lady poet, private income. No, that makes her sound too old, a middle-aged eccentric. Actually she is no more than thirty. Taller than I am, with long kinky brown hair and a sharp, bony nose that has a bump on the bridge. Eyes are very glossy. A studied raggedness about her dress; carefully chosen shabby clothes. I am in no position really to judge the sexual attractiveness of Earthfolk but I gather from remarks made by men living here that she is not considered good-looking. I pass her often on my way to my room. She smiles fiercely at me. Saying to herself, no doubt, You poor lonely man. Let me help you bear the burden of your unhappy life. Let me show you the meaning of love, for I too know what it is like to be alone.

Or words to that effect. She's never actually said any such thing. But her intentions are transparent. When she sees me, a kind of hunger comes into her eyes, part maternal, part (I guess) sexual, and her face takes on a wild crazy intensity. Burning with emotion. Her name is Elizabeth Cooke. "Are you fond of poetry, Mr. Knecht?" she asked me this morning, as we creaked upward together in the ancient elevator. And an hour later she knocked at my door. "Something for you to read," she said. "I wrote them." A sheaf of large yellow sheets, stapled at the top; poems printed in smeary blue mimeography. The Reality Trip, the collection was headed. Limited Edition: 125 Copies. "You can keep it if you like," she explained. "I've got lots more." She was wearing bright corduroy slacks and a flimsy pink shawl through which her breasts plainly showed. Small tapering breasts, not very functional-looking. When she saw me studying them her nostrils flared momentarily and she blinked her eyes three times swiftly. Tokens of lust?

I read the poems. Is it fair for me to offer judgment on them? Even though I've lived on this planet eleven of its years, even though my command of colloquial English is quite good, do I really comprehend the inner life of poetry? I thought they were all quite bad. Earnest, plodding poems, capturing what they call slices of life. The world around her, the cruel, brutal, unloving city. Lamenting the failure of people to open to one another. The title poem began this way:

He was on the reality trip. Big black man,
bloodshot eyes, bad teeth. Eisenhower jacket,
frayed. Smell of cheap wine. I guess a knife
in his pocket. Looked at me mean. Criminal
record. Rape, child-beating, possession of drugs.
In his head saying, slavemistress bitch, and me in
my head saying, black brother, let's freak in
together, let's trip on love—

And so forth. Warm, direct emotion; but is the urge to love all wounded things a sufficient center for poetry? I don't know. I did put her poems through the scanner and transmit them to Homeworld, although I doubt they'll learn much from them about Earth. It would flatter Elizabeth to know that while she has few readers here, she has acquired some ninety light-years away. But of course I can't tell her that.

She came back a short while ago. "Did you like them?" she asked.

"Very much. You have such sympathy for those who suffer."

I think she expected me to invite her in. I was careful not to look at her breasts this time.

The hotel is on West Twenty-third Street. It must be over a hundred years old; the facade is practically baroque and the interior shows a kind of genteel decay. The place has a bohemian tradition. Most of its guests are permanent residents and many of them are artists, novelists, playwrights, and such. I have lived here nine years. I know a number of the residents by name, and they me, but I have discouraged any real intimacy, naturally, and everyone has respected that choice. I do not invite others into my room. Sometimes I let myself be invited to visit theirs, since one of my responsibilities on this world is to get to know something of the way Earthfolk live and think. Elizabeth is the first to attempt to cross the invisible barrier of privacy I surround myself with. I'm not sure how I'll handle that. She moved in about three years ago; her attentions became noticeable perhaps ten months back, and for the last five or six weeks she's been a great nuisance. Some kind of confrontation is inevitable: either I must tell her to leave me alone, or I will find myself drawn into a situation impossible to tolerate. Perhaps she'll find someone else to feel even sorrier for, before it comes to that.

My daily routine rarely varies. I rise at seven. First Feeding. Then I clean my skin (my outer one, the Earthskin, I mean) and dress. From eight to ten I transmit data to Homeworld. Then I go out for the morning field trip: talking to people, buying newspapers, often some library research. At one I return to my room. Second Feeding. I transmit data from two to five. Out again, perhaps to the theater, to a motion picture, to a political meeting. I must soak up the flavor of this planet. Often to saloons; I am equipped for ingesting alcohol, though of course I must get rid of it before it has been in my body very long, and I drink and listen and sometimes argue. At midnight back to my room. Third Feeding. Transmit data from one to four in the morning. Then three hours of sleep, and at seven the cycle begins anew. It is a comforting schedule. I don't know how many agents Homeworld has on Earth, but I like to think that I'm one of the most diligent and useful. I miss very little. I've done good service, and, as they say here, hard work is its own reward. I won't deny that I hate the physical discomfort of it and frequently give way to real despair over my isolation from my own kind. Sometimes I even think of asking for a transfer to Homeworld. But what would become of me there? What services could I perform? I have shaped my life to one end: that of dwelling among the Earthfolk and reporting on their ways. If I give that up, I am nothing.

Of course there is the physical pain. Which is considerable.

The gravitational pull of Earth is almost twice that of Homeworld. It makes for a leaden life for me. My inner organs always sagging against the lower rim of my carapace. My muscles cracking with strain. Every movement a willed effort. My heart in constant protest. In my eleven years I have as one might expect adapted somewhat to the conditions; I have toughened, I have thickened. I suspect that if I were transported instantly to Homeworld now I would be quite giddy, baffled by the lightness of everything. I would leap and soar and stumble, and might even miss this crushing pull of Earth. Yet I doubt that. I suffer here; at all times the weight oppresses me. Not to sound too self-pitying about it. I knew the conditions in advance. I was placed in simulated Earth gravity when I volunteered, and was given a chance to withdraw, and I decided to go anyway. Not realizing that a week under double gravity is not the same thing as a lifetime. I could always have stepped out of the simulation chamber. Not here. The eternal drag on every molecule of me. The pressure. My flesh is always in mourning.

And the outer body I must wear. This cunning disguise. Forever to be swaddled in thick masses of synthetic flesh, smothering me, engulfing me. The soft slippery slap of it against the self within. The elaborate framework that holds it erect, by which I make it move: a forest of struts and braces and servoactuators and cables, in the midst of which I must unendingly huddle, atop my little platform in the gut. Adopting one or another of various uncomfortable positions, constantly shifting and squirming, now jabbing myself on some awkwardly placed projection, now trying to make my inflexible body flexibly to bend. Seeing the world by periscope through mechanical eyes. Enwombed in this mountain of meat. It is a clever thing; it must look convincingly human, since no one has ever doubted me, and it ages ever so slightly from year to year, graying a bit at the temples, thickening a bit at the paunch. It walks. It talks. It takes in food and drink, when it has to. (And deposits them in a removable pouch near my leftmost arm.) And I within it. The hidden chess player; the invisible rider. If I dared, I would periodically strip myself of this cloak of flesh and crawl around my room in my own guise. But it is forbidden. Eleven years now and I have not been outside my protoplasmic housing. I feel sometimes that it has come to adhere to me, that it is no longer merely around me but by now a part of me.

In order to eat I must unseal it at the middle, a process that takes many minutes. Three times a day I unbutton myself so that I can stuff the food concentrates into my true gullet. Faulty design, I call that. They could just as easily have arranged it so I could pop the food into my Earth-mouth and have it land in my own digestive tract. I suppose the newer models have that. Excretion is just as troublesome for me; I unseal, reach in, remove the cubes of waste, seal my skin again. Down the toilet with them. A nuisance.

And the loneliness! To look at the stars and know Homeworld is out there somewhere! To think of all the others, mating, chanting, dividing, abstracting, while I live out my days in this crumbling hotel on an alien planet, tugged down by gravity and locked within a cramped counterfeit body—always alone, always pretending that I am not what I am and that I am what I am not, spying, questioning, recording, reporting, coping with the misery of solitude, hunting for the comforts of philosophy—

In all of this there is only one real consolation, aside, that is, from the pleasure of knowing that I am of service to Homeworld. The atmosphere of New York City grows grimier every year. The streets are full of crude vehicles belching undigested hydrocarbons. To the Earthfolk, this stuff is pollution, and they mutter worriedly about it. To me it is joy. It is the only touch of Homeworld here: that sweet soup of organic compounds adrift in the air. It intoxicates me. I walk down the street breathing deeply, sucking the good molecules through my false nostrils to my authentic lungs. The natives must think I'm insane. Tripping on auto exhaust! Can I get arrested for overenthusiastic public breathing? Will they pull me in for a mental checkup?

Elizabeth Cooke continues to waft wistful attentions at me. Smiles in the hallway. Hopeful gleam of the eyes. "Perhaps we can have dinner together some night soon, Mr. Knecht. I know we'd have so much to talk about. And maybe you'd like to see the new poems I've been doing." She is trembling. Eyelids flickering tensely; head held rigid on long neck. I know she sometimes has men in her room, so it can't be out of loneliness or frustration that she's cultivating me. And I doubt that she's sexually attracted to my outer self. I believe I'm being accurate when I say that women don't consider me sexually magnetic. No, she loves me because she pities me. The sad shy bachelor at the end of the hall, dear unhappy Mr. Knecht; can I bring some brightness into his dreary life? And so forth. I think that's how it is. Will I be able to go on avoiding her? Perhaps I should move to another part of the city. But I've lived here so long; I've grown accustomed to this hotel. Its easy ways do much to compensate for the hardships of my post. And my familiar room. The huge many-paned window; the cracked green floor tiles in the bathroom; the lumpy patterns of replastering on the wall above my bed. The high ceiling; the funny chandelier. Things that I love. But of course I can't let her try to start an affair with me. We are supposed to observe Earthfolk, not to get involved with them. Our disguise is not that difficult to penetrate at close range. I must keep her away somehow. Or flee.

Incredible! There is another of us in this very hotel!

As I learned through accident. At one this afternoon, returning from my morning travels: Elizabeth in the lobby, as though lying in wait for me, chatting with the manager. Rides up with me in the elevator. Her eyes looking into mine. "Sometimes I think you're afraid of me," she begins. "You mustn't be. That's the great tragedy of human life, that people shut themselves up behind walls of fear and never let anyone through, anyone who might care about them and be warm to them. You've got no reason to be afraid of me." I do, but how to explain that to her? To sidestep prolonged conversation and possible entanglement I get off the elevator one floor below the right one. Let her think I'm visiting a friend. Or a mistress. I walk slowly down the hall to the stairs, using up time, waiting so she will be in her room before I go up. A maid bustles by me. She thrusts her key into a door on the left: a rare faux pas for the usually competent help here, she forgets to knock before going in to make up the room. The door opens and the occupant, inside, stands revealed. A stocky, muscular man, naked to the waist. "Oh, excuse me," the maid gasps, and backs out, shutting the door. But I have seen. My eyes are quick. The hairy chest is split, a dark gash three inches wide and some eleven inches long, beginning between the nipples and going past the navel. Visible within is the black shiny surface of a Homeworld carapace. My countryman, opening up for Second Feeding. Dazed, numbed, I stagger to the stairs and pull myself step by leaden step to my floor. No sign of Elizabeth. I stumble into my room and throw the bolt. Another of us here? Well, why not? I'm not the only one. There may be hundreds in New York alone. But in the same hotel? I remember, now, I've seen him occasionally: a silent, dour man, tense, hunted-looking, unsociable. No doubt I appear the same way to others. Keep the world at a distance. I don't know his name or what he is supposed to do for a living.

We are forbidden to make contact with fellow Homeworlders except in case of extreme emergency. Isolation is a necessary condition of our employment. I may not introduce myself to him; I may not seek his friendship. It is worse now for me, knowing that he is here, than when I was entirely alone. The things we could reminisce about! The friends we might have in common! We could reinforce one another's endurance of the gravity, the discomfort of our disguises, the vile climate. But no. I must pretend I know nothing. The rules. The harsh, unbending rules. I to go about my business, he his; if we meet, no hint of my knowledge must pass.

So be it. I will honor my vows. But it may be difficult.

He goes by the name of Swanson. Been living in the hotel eighteen months; a musician of some sort, according to the manager. "A very peculiar man. Keeps to himself; no small talk, never smiles. Defends his privacy. The other day a maid barged into his room without knocking and I thought he'd sue. Well, we get all sorts here." The manager thinks he may actually be a member of one of the old European royal families, living in exile, or something romantic. The manager would be surprised.

I defend my privacy too. From Elizabeth, another assault on it.

In the hall outside my room. "My new poems," she said. "In case you're interested." And then: "Can I come in? I'd read them to you. I love reading out loud." And: "Please don't always seem so terribly afraid of me. I don't bite, David. Really I don't. I'm quite gentle."

"I'm sorry."

"So am I." Anger, now, lurking in her shiny eyes, her thin taut lips. "If you want me to leave you alone, say so, I will. But I want you to know how cruel you're being. I don't demand anything from you. I'm just offering some friendship. And you're refusing. Do I have a bad smell? Am I so ugly? Is it my poems you hate and you're afraid to tell me?"

"Elizabeth—"

"We're only on this world such a short time. Why can't we be kinder to each other while we are? To love, to share, to open up. The reality trip. Communication, soul to soul." Her tone changed. An artful shading. "For all I know, women turn you off. I wouldn't put anybody down for that. We've all got our ways. But it doesn't have to be a sexual thing, you and me. Just talk. Like, opening the channels. Please? Say no and I'll never bother you again, but don't say no, please. That's like shutting a door on life, David. And when you do that, you start to die a little."

Persistent. I should tell her to go to hell. But there is the loneliness. There is her obvious sincerity. Her warmth, her eagerness to pull me from my lunar isolation. Can there be harm in it? Knowing that Swanson is nearby, so close yet sealed from me by iron commandments, has intensified my sense of being alone. I can risk letting Elizabeth get closer to me. It will make her happy; it may make me happy; it could even yield information valuable to Homeworld. Of course I must still maintain certain barriers.

"I don't mean to be unfriendly. I think you've misunderstood,

Elizabeth. I haven't really been rejecting you. Come in. Do come in."
Stunned, she enters my room. The first guest ever. My few books; my
modest furnishings; the ultrawave transmitter, impenetrably
disguised as a piece of sculpture. She sits. Skirt far above the knees.
Good legs, if I understand the criteria of quality correctly. I am
determined to allow no sexual overtures. If she tries anything, I'll
resort to—I don't know—hysteria. "Read me your new poems," I say.
She opens her portfolio. Reads.

In the midst of the hipster night of doubt and
Emptiness, when the bad-trip god came to me with
Cold hands, I looked up and shouted yes at the
Stars. And yes and yes again. I groove on yes;
The devil grooves on no. And I waited for you to
Say yes, and at last you did. And the world said
The stars said the trees said the grass said the
Sky said the streets said yes and yes and yes—

She is ecstatic. Her face is flushed; her eyes are joyous. She has
broken through to me. After two hours, when it becomes obvious
that I am not going to ask her to go to bed with me, she leaves. Not
to wear out her welcome. "I'm so glad I was wrong about you, David,"
she whispers. "I couldn't believe you were really a life-denier. And
you're not." Ecstatic.

I am getting into very deep water.
We spend an hour or two together every night. Sometimes in my
room, sometimes in hers. Usually she comes to me, but now and
then, to be polite, I seek her out after Third Feeding. By now I've read
all her poetry; we talk instead of the arts in general, politics, racial
problems. She has a lively, well-stocked, disorderly mind. Though
she probes constantly for information about me, she realizes how
sensitive I am, and quickly withdraws when I parry her. Asking about
my work; I reply vaguely that I'm doing research for a book, and
when I don't amplify she drops it, though she tries again, gently, a
few nights later. She drinks a lot of wine, and offers it to me. I nurse
one glass through a whole visit. Often she suggests we go out together
for dinner; I explain that I have digestive problems and prefer to eat

alone, and she takes this in good grace but immediately resolves to help me overcome those problems, for soon she is asking me to eat with her again. There is an excellent Spanish restaurant right in the hotel, she says. She drops troublesome questions. Where was I born? Did I go to college? Do I have family somewhere? Have I ever been married? Have I published any of my writings? I improvise evasions. Nothing difficult about that, except that never before have I allowed anyone on Earth such sustained contact with me, so prolonged an opportunity to find inconsistencies in my pretended identity. What if she sees through?

And sex. Her invitations grow less subtle. She seems to think that we ought to be having a sexual relationship, simply because we've become such good friends. Not a matter of passion so much as one of communication: we talk, sometimes we take walks together, we should do that together too. But of course it's impossible. I have the external organs but not the capacity to use them. Wouldn't want her touching my false skin in any case. How to deflect her? If I declare myself impotent she'll demand a chance to try to cure me. If I pretend homosexuality she'll start some kind of straightening therapy. If I simply say she doesn't turn me on physically she'll be hurt. The sexual thing is a challenge to her, the way merely getting me to talk with her once was. She often wears the transparent pink shawl that reveals her breasts. Her skirts are hip high. She does herself with aphrodisiac perfumes. She grazes my body with hers whenever opportunity arises. The tension mounts; she is determined to have me.

I have said nothing about her in my reports to Homeworld. Though I do transmit some of the psychological data I have gathered by observing her.

"Could you ever admit you were in love with me?" she asked tonight.

And she asked, "Doesn't it hurt you to repress your feelings all the time? To sit there locked up inside yourself like a prisoner?"

And, "There's a physical side of life too, David. I don't mind so much the damage you're doing to me by ignoring it. But I worry about the damage you're doing to you."

Crossing her legs. Hiking her skirt even higher.

We are heading toward a crisis. I should never have let this

begin. A torrid summer has descended on the city, and in hot
weather my nervous system is always at the edge of eruption. She
may push me too far. I might ruin everything. I should apply for
transfer to Homeworld before I cause trouble. Maybe I should
confer with Swanson. I think what is happening now qualifies as
an emergency.

Elizabeth stayed past midnight tonight. I had to ask her finally to
leave: work to do. An hour later she pushed an envelope under my
door. Newest poems. Love poems. In a shaky hand: "David you
mean so much to me. You mean the stars and nebulas. Can't you let
me show my love? Can't you accept happiness? Think about it. I
adore you."

What have I started?

103°F. today. The fourth successive day of intolerable heat. Met
Swanson in the elevator at lunch time; nearly blurted the truth about
myself to him. I must be more careful. But my control is slipping.
Last night, in the worst of the heat, I was tempted to strip off my
disguise. I could no longer stand being locked in here, pivoting and
ducking to avoid all the machinery festooned about me. Resisted the
temptation; just barely. Somehow I am more sensitive to the gravity
too. I have the illusion that my carapace is developing cracks. Almost
collapsed in the street this afternoon. All I need: heat exhaustion,
whisked off to the hospital, routine fluoroscope exam. "You have a
very odd skeletal structure, Mr. Knecht." Indeed. Dissecting me, next,
with three thousand medical students looking on. And then the
United Nations called in. Menace from outer space. Yes. I must be
more careful. I must be more careful. I must be more—

Now I've done it. Eleven years of faithful service destroyed in a
single wild moment. Violation of the Fundamental Rule. I hardly
believe it. How was it possible that I—that I—with my respect for
my responsibilities—that I could have—even considered, let alone
actually done—

But the weather was terribly hot. The third week of the heat wave.
I was stifling inside my false body. And the gravity: was New York
having a gravity wave too? That terrible pull, worse than ever.
Bending my internal organs out of shape. Elizabeth a tremendous

annoyance: passionate, emotional, teary, poetic, giving me no rest, pleading for me to burn with a brighter flame. Declaring her love in sonnets, in rambling hip epics, in haiku. Spending two hours in my room, crouched at my feet, murmuring about the hidden beauty of my soul. "Open yourself and let love come in," she whispered. "It's like giving yourself to God. Making a commitment; breaking down all walls. Why not? For love's sake, David, why not?" I couldn't tell her why not, and she went away, but about midnight she was back knocking at my door. I let her in. She wore an ankle-length silk housecoat, gleaming, threadbare. "I'm stoned," she said hoarsely, voice an octave too deep. "I had to bust three joints to get up the nerve. But here I am. David, I'm sick of making the turnoff trip. We've been so wonderfully close, and then you won't go the last stretch of the way." A cascade of giggles. "Tonight you will. Don't fail me. Darling." Drops the housecoat. Naked underneath it: narrow waist, bony hips, long legs, thin thighs, blue veins crossing her breasts. Her hair wild and kinky. A sorceress. A seeress. Berserk. Approaching me, eyes slit-wide, mouth open, tongue flickering snakily. How fleshless she is! Beads of sweat glistening on her flat chest. Seizes my wrists; tugs me roughly toward the bed. We tussle a little. Within my false body I throw switches, nudge levers. I am stronger than she is. I pull free, breaking her hold with an effort. She stands flat-footed in front of me, glaring, eyes fiery.

So vulnerable, so sad in her nudity. And yet so fierce. "David! David! David!" Sobbing. Breathless. Pleading with her eyes and the tips of her breasts. Gathering her strength; now she makes the next lunge, but I see it coming and let her topple past me. She lands on the bed, burying her face in the pillow, clawing at the sheet. "Why? Why why why WHY?" she screams.

In a minute we will have the manager in here. With the police.

"Am I so hideous? I love you, David, do you know what that word means? Love. Love." Sits up. Turns to me. Imploring. "Don't reject me," she whispers. "I couldn't take that. You know, I just wanted to make you happy, I figured I could be the one, only I didn't realize how unhappy you'd make me. And you just stand there. And you don't say anything. What are you, some kind of machine?"

"I'll tell you what I am," I said.

That was when I went sliding into the abyss. All control lost; all prudence gone. My mind so slathered with raw emotion that survival itself means nothing. I must make things clear to her, is all. I must show her. At whatever expense. I strip off my shirt. She glows, no doubt thinking I will let myself be seduced. My hands slide up and down my bare chest, seeking the catches and snaps. I go through the intricate, cumbersome process of opening my body. Deep within myself something is shouting NO NO NO NO NO, but I pay no attention. The heart has its reasons.

Hoarsely: "Look, Elizabeth. Look at me. This is what I am. Look at me and freak out. The reality trip."

My chest opens wide.

I push myself forward, stepping between the levers and struts, emerging halfway from the human shell I wear. I have not been this far out of it since the day they sealed me in, on Homeworld. I let her see my gleaming carapace. I wave my eyestalks around. I allow some of my claws to show. "See? See? Big black crab from outer space. That's what you love, Elizabeth. That's what I am. David Knecht's just a costume, and this is what's inside it." I have gone insane. "You want reality? Here's reality, Elizabeth. What good is the Knecht body to you? It's a fraud. It's a machine. Come on, come closer. Do you want to kiss me? Should I get on you and make love?"

During this episode her face has displayed an amazing range of reactions. Open-mouthed disbelief at first, of course. And frozen horror: gagging sounds in throat, jaws agape, eyes wide and rigid. Hands fanned across breasts. Sudden modesty in front of the alien monster? But then, as the familiar Knecht-voice, now bitter and impassioned, continues to flow from the black thing within the sundered chest, a softening of her response. Curiosity. The poetic sensibility taking over. Nothing human is alien to me: Terence, quoted by Cicero. Nothing alien is alien to me. Eh? She will accept the evidence of her eyes. "What are you? Where did you come from?" And I say, "I've violated the Fundamental Rule. I deserve to be plucked and thinned. We're not supposed to reveal ourselves. If we get into some kind of accident that might lead to exposure, we're supposed to blow ourselves up. The switch is right here." She comes close and peers around me, into the cavern of David Knecht's chest. "From some other planet? Living here in disguise?" She understands the picture. Her shock is fading. She even laughs. "I've seen worse than you on acid," she says. "You don't frighten me now, David. David? Shall I go on calling you David?"

This is unreal and dreamlike to me. I have revealed myself, thinking to drive her away in terror; she is no longer aghast, and smiles at my strangeness. She kneels to get a better look. I move back a short way. Eyestalks fluttering: I am uneasy, I have somehow lost the upper hand in this encounter.

She says, "I knew you were unusual, but not like this. But it's all right. I can cope. I mean, the essential personality, that's what I fell in love with. Who cares that you're a crab-man from the Green Galaxy? Who cares that we can't be real lovers? I can make that sacrifice. It's your soul I dig, David. Go on. Close yourself up again. You don't look comfortable this way." The triumph of love. She will not abandon me, even now. Disaster. I crawl back into Knecht and lift his arms to his chest to seal it. Shock is glazing my consciousness: the enormity, the audacity. What have I done? Elizabeth watches, awed, even delighted. At last I am together again. She nods. "Listen," she tells me, "you can trust me. I mean, if you're some kind of spy, checking out the Earth, I don't care. I don't care. I won't tell anybody. Pour it all out, David. Tell me about yourself. Don't you see, this is the biggest thing that ever happened to me. A chance to show that love isn't just physical, isn't just chemistry, that it's a soul trip, that it crosses not just racial lines but the lines of the whole damned species, the planet itself—"

It took several hours to get rid of her. A soaring, intense conversation, Elizabeth doing most of the talking. She putting forth theories of why I had come to Earth, me nodding, denying, amplifying, mostly lost in horror at my own perfidy and barely listening to her monologue. And the humidity turning me into rotting rags. Finally: "I'm down from the pot, David. And all wound up. I'm going out for a walk. Then back to my room to write for a while. To put this night into a poem before I lose the power of it. But I'll come to you again by dawn, all right? That's maybe five hours from now. You'll be here? You won't do anything foolish? Oh, I love you so much, David! Do you believe me? Do you?"

When she was gone I stood a long while by the window, trying to reassemble myself. Shattered. Drained. Remembering her kisses, her lips running along the ridge marking the place where my chest opens. The fascination of the abomination. She will love me even if I am crustaceous beneath.

I have to have help.

I went to Swanson's room. He was slow to respond to my knock; busy transmitting, no doubt. I could hear him within, but he didn't answer. "Swanson?" I called. "Swanson?" Then I added the distress signal in the Homeworld tongue. He rushed to the door. Blinking, suspicious. "It's all right," I said. "Look, let me in. I'm in big trouble." Speaking English, but I gave him the distress signal again.

"How did you know about me?" he asked.

"The day the maid blundered into your room while you were eating, I was going by. I saw."

"But you aren't supposed to—"

"Except in emergencies. This is an emergency." He shut off his ultrawave and listened intently to my story. Scowling. He didn't approve. But he wouldn't spurn me. I had been criminally foolish, but I was of his kind, prey to the same pains, the same loneliness, and he would help me.

"What do you plan to do now?" he asked. "You can't harm her. It isn't allowed."

"I don't want to harm her. Just to get free of her. To make her fall out of love with me."

"How? If showing yourself to her didn't—"

"Infidelity," I said. "Making her see that I love someone else. No room in my life for her. That'll drive her away. Afterwards it won't matter that she knows: who'd believe her story? The FBI would laugh and tell her to lay off the LSD. But if I don't break her attachment to me I'm finished."

"Love someone else? Who?"

"When she comes back to my room at dawn," I said, "she'll find the two of us together, dividing and abstracting. I think that'll do it, don't you?"

So I deceived Elizabeth with Swanson.

The fact that we both wore male human identities was irrelevant, of course. We went to the room and stepped out of our disguises—a bold, dizzying sensation!—and suddenly we were just two Homeworlders again, receptive to one another's needs. I left the door unlocked. Swanson and I crawled up on my bed and began the chanting. How strange it was, after these years of solitude, to feel those vibrations again! And how beautiful. Swanson's vibrissae touching mine. The interplay of harmonies. An underlying sternness to his technique—he was contemptuous of me for my idiocy, and rightly so—but once we passed from the chanting to the dividing all was forgiven, and as we moved into the abstracting it was truly sublime. We climbed through an infinity of climactic emptyings. Dawn crept upon us and found us unwilling to halt even for rest.

A knock at the door. Elizabeth.

"Come in," I said.

A dreamy, ecstatic look on her face. Fading instantly when she saw the two of us entangled on the bed. A questioning frown. "We've been mating," I explained. "Did you think I was a complete hermit?" She looked from Swanson to me, from me to Swanson. Hand over her mouth. Eyes anguished. I turned the screw a little tighter. "I couldn't stop you from falling in love with me, Elizabeth. But I really do prefer my own kind. As should have been obvious."

"To have her here now, though—when you knew I was coming back—"

"Not her, exactly. Not him exactly either, though."

"—so cruel, David! To ruin such a beautiful experience." Holding forth sheets of paper with shaking hands. "A whole sonnet cycle," she said. "About tonight. How beautiful it was, and all. And now—and now—" Crumpling the pages. Hurling them across the room. Turning. Running out, sobbing furiously. Hell hath no fury like. "David!" A smothered cry. And slamming the door.

She was back in ten minutes. Swanson and I hadn't quite finished donning our bodies yet; we were both still unsealed. As we worked, we discussed further steps to take: he felt honor demanded that I request a transfer back to Homeworld, having terminated my usefulness here through tonight's indiscreet revelation. I agreed with him to some degree but was reluctant to leave. Despite the bodily torment of life on Earth I had come to feel I belonged here. Then Elizabeth entered, radiant.

"I mustn't be so possessive," she announced. "So bourgeois. So conventional. I'm willing to share my love." Embracing Swanson. Embracing me. "A ménage à trois," she said. "I won't mind that you two are having a physical relationship. As long as you don't shut me out of your lives completely. I mean, David, we could never have been physical anyway, right, but we can have the other aspects of love, and we'll open ourselves to your friend also. Yes? Yes? Yes?"

Swanson and I both put in applications for transfer, he to Africa, me to Homeworld. It would be some time before we received a reply. Until then we were at her mercy. He was blazingly angry with me for involving him in this, but what choice had I had? Nor could either of us avoid Elizabeth. We were at her mercy. She bathed both of us in shimmering waves of tender emotion; wherever we turned, there she was, incandescent with love. Lighting up the darkness of our lives. You poor lonely creatures. Do you suffer much in our gravity? What about the heat? And the winters. Is there a custom of marriage on your planet? Do you have poetry?

A happy threesome. We went to the theater together. To concerts. Even to parties in Greenwich Village. "My friends," Elizabeth said, leaving no doubt in anyone's mind that she was living with both of us. Faintly scandalous doings; she loved to seem daring. Swanson was sullenly obliging, putting up with her antics but privately haranguing me for subjecting him to all this. Elizabeth got out another mimeographed booklet of poems, dedicated to both of us. Triple Tripping, she called it. Flagrantly erotic. I quoted a few of the poems in one of my reports to Homeworld, then lost heart and hid the booklet in the closet. "Have you heard about your transfer yet?" I asked Swanson at least twice a week. He hadn't. Neither had I.

Autumn came. Elizabeth, burning her candle at both ends, looked gaunt and feverish. "I have never known such happiness," she announced frequently, one hand clasping Swanson, the other me. "I never think about the strangeness of you anymore. I think of you only as people. Sweet, wonderful, lonely people. Here in the darkness of this horrid city." And she once said, "What if everybody here is like you, and I'm the only one who's really human? But that's silly. You must be the only ones of your kind here. The advance scouts.

Will your planet invade ours? I do hope so! Set everything to rights. The reign of love and reason at last!"

"How long will this go on?" Swanson muttered.

At the end of October his transfer came through. He left without saying good-bye to either of us and without leaving a forwarding address. Nairobi? Addis Ababa? Kinshasa?

I had grown accustomed to having him around to share the burden of Elizabeth. Now the full brunt of her affection fell on me. My work was suffering; I had no time to file my reports properly. And I lived in fear of her gossiping. What was she telling her Village friends? ("You know David? He's not really a man, you know. Actually inside him there's a kind of crab-thing from another solar system. But what does that matter? Love's a universal phenomenon. The truly loving person doesn't draw limits around the planet.") I longed for my release. To go home; to accept my punishment; to shed my false skin. To empty my mind of Elizabeth.

My reply came through the ultrawave on November 13. Application denied. I was to remain on Earth and continue my work as before. Transfers to Homeworld were granted only for reasons of health.

I debated sending a full account of my treason to Homeworld and thus bringing about my certain recall. But I hesitated, overwhelmed with despair. Dark brooding seized me. "Why so sad?" Elizabeth asked. What could I say? That my attempt at escaping from her had failed? "I love you," she said. "I've never felt so real before." Nuzzling against my cheek. Fingers knotted in my hair. A seductive whisper. "David, open yourself up again. Your chest, I mean. I want to see the inner you. To make sure I'm not frightened of it. Please? You've only let me see you once." And then, when I had: "May I kiss you, David?" I was appalled.

But I let her. She was unafraid. Transfigured by happiness. She is a cosmic nuisance, but I fear I'm getting to like her.

Can I leave her? I wish Swanson had not vanished. I need advice.

Either I break with Elizabeth or I break with Homeworld. This is absurd. I find new chasms of despondency every day. I am unable to do my work. I have requested a transfer once again, without giving details. The first snow of the winter today.

Application denied.

"When I found you with Swanson," she said, "it was a terrible shock. An even bigger blow than when you first came out of your chest. I mean it was startling to find out you weren't human, but it didn't hit me in any emotional way, it didn't threaten me. But then, to come back a few hours later and find you with one of your own kind, to know that you wanted to shut me out, that I had no place in your life—Only we worked it out, didn't we?" Kissing me. Tears of joy in her eyes. How did this happen? Where did it all begin? Existence was once so simple. I have tried to trace the chain of events that brought me from there to here, and I cannot. I was outside of my false body for eight hours today. The longest spell so far. Elizabeth is talking of going to the islands with me for the winter. A secluded cottage that her friends will make available. Of course, I must not leave my post without permission. And it takes months simply to get a reply.

Let me admit the truth: I love her.

January 1. The new year begins. I have sent my resignation to Homeworld and have destroyed my ultrawave equipment. The links are broken. Tomorrow, when the city offices are open, Elizabeth and I will go to get the marriage license.

THE CLINIC
Theodore Sturgeon

Nemo is a long-term patient at a psychiatric hospital with a perplexing condition. He seems to be suffering from an extreme case of amnesia, possessing absolutely no memory of his life before his arrival, be it his own identity or even how to feed and clothe himself, and can only speak in a broken form of English. He also has a mind that processes the world around him very differently, letting him learn rapidly and view those around him with unusual insight. His caretakers aren't quite sure if he's a fugitive faking the condition, a medical marvel, or something not of this Earth entirely.

This 1953 short story from Theodore Sturgeon is remarkable for a few reasons, not the least of which is Sturgeon's deft hand with the often abstract and surrealist prose, but also for the skillful and compassionate execution of making a disabled person the point-of-view character.

The policemen and the doctors men and most of the people outside, they all helped me, they were very nice but nobody helped me as many-much as Elena.

De la Torre liked me very nice I think, but number one because what I am is his work. The Sergeant liked me very nice too but inside I think he say not real, not real. He say in all his years he know two for-real amnesiacs but only in police book. Unless me. Some day, he say, some day he find out I not-real amnesiac trying to fool him. De la Torre say I real. Classic case, he say. He say plenty men forget talk forget name forget way to do life-work but *por Dios* not forget buttons forget eating forget every damn thing like me. The Sergeant say yes Doc you would rather find a medical monstrosity than turn up a faker. De la Torre say yes you would rather find out he is a fugitive than a phenomenon, well this just shows you what expert opinion is worth when you get two experts together. He say, one of us has to be wrong.

Is half right. Is both wrong.

If I am a fugitive I must be very intelligent. If I am an amnesiac I could be even intelligenter as a fugitive. Anyway I be intelligent better than any man in the world, as how could conversation as articulo-fluent like this after only six days five hours fifty-three minutes?

Is both wrong. I be Nemo.

But now comes Elena again, de la Torre is look happy-face, the Sergeant is look watch-face, Elena smile so warm, and we go.

"How are you tonight, Nemo?"

"I am very intelligent."

She laughs. "You can say that again," and then she puts hand on my mouth and more laughs. "No, don't say it again. Another figure of speech... Remember any yet?"

"What state what school what name, all that? No."

"All right." Now de la Torre, he ask me like that and when I no him, he try and try ask some other how. The Sergeant, he ask me like that and when I no him, he try and try ask me the same asking, again again. Elena ask and when I no her, she talk something else. Now she say, "What would you like to do tonight?"

I say," Go with you whatever."

She say, "Well we'll start with a short beer," so we do.

The short beer is in a room with long twisty blue lights and red lights and a noise-machine looks like two sunsets with bubbles and sounds unhappy out loud. The short beer is wet, high as a hand, color like Elena's eyes, shampoo on top, little bubbles inside. Elena drink then I drink all. Little bubbles make big bubble inside me, big bubble come right back up so roaring that all people look to see, so it is bigger as the noise-machine. I look at people and Elena laugh again. She say, "I guess I shouldn't laugh. Most people don't do that in public, Nemo."

"Was largely recalcitrant bubble and decontrolled," I say. "So what do—keep for intestinals?"

She laugh again and say, "Well, no. Just try to keep it quiet." And now come a man from high long table where so many stand, he has hair on face, low lip flaccid, teeth brown black and gold, he smell as waste-food, first taste of mouth-thermometer, and skin moisture after drying in heavy weavings. He say, "You sound like a pig, Mac, where you think you are, home?"

I look at Elena and I look at he, I say, "Good evening." That what de la Torre say in first speak to peoples after begin night. Elena quick touch arm of mine, say, "Don't pay any attention to him, Nemo." Man bend over, put hand forward and touches it to ear of me with velocity, to make a large percussive effect. Same time bald man run around end of long high table exhibiting wooden device, speaking the prognosis: "Don't start nothing in my place, Purky, or I'll feed you this bung-starter."

I rub at ear and look at man who smells. He say, "Yeah, but you hear this little pig here? Where he think he's at?"

The man with bung-starter device say, "Tell you where you'll be at, you don't behave yourself, you'll be out on the pavement with a knot on your head," and he walk at Purky until Purky move and walk again until Purky is back to old place. I rub on ear and look at Elena and Elena has lip-paint of much bigger red now. No it is not bigger red, it is face skin of more white. Elena say, "Are you all right, Nemo? Did he hurt you?"

I say, "He is destroyed no part. He is create algesia of the middle ear. This is usual?"

"The dirty rat. No, Nemo, it isn't usual. I'm sorry, I'm so sorry. I shouldn't've brought you in here.... Some day someone'll do the world a favor and knock his block off."

"I have behavior?"

She say, "You what? Oh—did you act right." She gives me diagnostic regard from sides of eyes. "I guess so, Nemo. But...you can't let people push you around like that. Come on, let's get out of here."

"But then this is no more short beer, yes?"

"You like it? You want another?"

I touch my larynx. "It localizes a euphoria."

"Does it now. Well, whatever that means, I guess you can have another." She high display two fingers and big bald man gives dispensing of short beer more. I take all and large bubble forms and with concentration I exude it through nostrils quietly and gain Elena's approval and laughter. I say my thanks about the kindlies, about de la Torre and the Sergeant but it is Elena who helps with the large manymuchness.

"Forget it," she say.

"Is figure of speech? Is command?"

She say low-intensity to shampoo on short beer, "I don't know, Nemo. No, I guess I wouldn't want you to forget me." She look up at me and I know she will say again, "You'll never forget your promise, Nemo?" and she say it. And I say, "I not go away before I say, Elena, 'I going away.'"

She say, "What's the matter, Nemo? What is it?"

I say, "You think I go away, so I think about I go away too. I like you think about I here. And that not all of it."

"I'm sorry. It's just that I—well, it's important to me, that's all. I couldn't bear it if you just disappeared some day.... What else, Nemo?"

I say, "Two more short beer."

We drink the new short beer with no talk and with thinks. Then she say she go powder she nose. She nose have powder but she also have behavior so I no say why. When she go in door-place at back angle, I stand and walk.

I walk to high long table where stand the smelly man Purky, I push on him, he turn around.

He say, "Well look what crawled up! What you want, piggy?"

I say, "Where you block?"

He say, "Where's *what*?" He speak down to me from very tall, but he speak more noise than optimum.

I say, "You block. Block. You know, knock off block. Where you block? I knock off."

Big man who bring short beer, he roar. Purky, he roar. Mens jump back, looking, looking. Purky lift high big bottle, approach it at me swiftly. I move very close swiftlier, impact the neck of Purky by shoulder, squeeze flesh of Purky in and down behind pelvis, sink right thumb in left abdomen of Purky—one-two-three and go away again. Purky still swing down bottle but I not there for desired encounter now. Bottle go down to floor, Purky go down to floor, I walk back to chair, Purky lie twitching, men look at he, men look at me, Purky say "Uh-uh-uh." I sit down.

Elena come out of door running, say "What happened? Nemo..." and she look at Purky and all men looking.

I say, "Sorry. Sorry."

"Did you do that, Nemo?"

I make the head-nod, yes.

"Well what are you sorry about?" she say, all pretty with surprise and fierce.

I say, "I think you happy if I knock block off, but not know block. Where is block? I knock off now."

"No you don't!" she say. "You come right along out of here! Nemo, you're dynamite!"

I puzzle. "Is good?"

"Just now, is good."

We go out and big man call, "Hey, how about one on the house, Bomber?"

I puzzle again. EIena say, "He means he wants to give you a drink."

"Short beer?"

Big man put out short beer, I drink all. Purky sit up on floor. I feel big bubble come; I make it roar. I look at Purky. Purky not talk. Elena pull me, we go.

We walk by lakeshore long time. People foot-slide slowly to pulse from mens with air-vibrators, air-column wood, air-column metal, vibrating strings single and sets. "Dancing," Elena say and I say, "Nice. Is goodly nice." We have a happy, watching. Pulse fast, pulse slow, mens cry with pulse and vibrations, womens, two at once, cry together. "Singing," Elena say, and the lights move on the dancing, red and yellow-red and big and little blue; clouds shift and change, pulse shift and change, stars come, stars go and the wind, warm. Elena say, "Nemo, honey, do you know what love is?"

I say no.

She look the lake, she look the lights, she wave the arm of her to show all, with the wind and stars; she make her voice like whisper and like singing too and she say, "It's something like this, Nemo. I hope you find out some day."

I say yes, and I have sleepy too. So she take me back to the hospital.

It is the day and de la Torre is tired with me. He fall into chair, wipe the face of he with a small white weaving.

He say, "*Por Dios*, Nemo, I don't figure you at all. Can I be frank with you?"

I say, "Yes," but I know all he be is de la Torre.

He say, "I don't think you're trying. But you must be trying; you couldn't get along so fast without trying. You don't seem to be interested; I have to tell you some things fifty times before you finally get them. Yet you ask questions as if you *were* interested. What are you? What do you want?"

I lift up the shoulders once, quickly, just like de la Torre when he not know.

He say, "You grasp all the complicated things at sight, and ignore the simple ones. You use terms out of *Materia Medica* and use them right, and all the time you refuse to talk anything but a highly individualized pidgin-English. Do you know what I'm talking about?"

I say, "Yes."

He say, "*Do* you? Tell me: what is *Materia Medica*? What is 'Individualized'? What is 'Pidgin-English'?"

I do the shoulders thing.

"So don't tell me you know what I'm talking about."

I turn the head little, raise the one finger like he do sometime, I say, "I do. I do."

"Tell me then. Tell it in your own words. Tell me why you won't learn to talk the way I do."

"No use," I say. Then I say, "No use for me." Then I say, "Not interest me." And still he sit and puzzle at me.

So I try. I say, "De la Torre, I see peoples dancing in the night."

"When? With Elena?"

"Elena, yes. And I see mens make pulse and cries for dancing."

"An orchestra?" I puzzle. He say, "Men with instruments, making noises together?" I make a yes. He say, "Music. That's called music."

I say, "What this?" and I move the arms.

He say, "Violin?"

I say, "Yes. Make one noise, a new noise, a new noise—one and one and one. Now," I say, "what this?" and I move again.

"Banjo," he say. "Guitar, maybe."

"Make many noise, in set. Make a new set. And a new set. Yes?"

"Yes," he say. "It's played in chords, mostly. What are you getting at?"

I bump on side of head. "You have think word and word and word and you make set. I have think set and set and set."

"You mean I think like a violin, one note at a time, and you think like a guitar, a lot of related notes at a time?" He quiet, he puzzle. "Why do you want to think like that?"

"Is my thinks."

"You mean, that's the way you think? Well, for Pete's sake, Nemo, you'll make it a lot easier to convey your thinks—uh—thoughts if you'll learn to come out with them like other people."

I make the no with the head. "No use for me."

"Look," he say. He blow hard through he nostrils, bang-bang on table, eyes close. He say, "You've got to understand this. I'll give you an example. You know how an automobile engine works?"

I say no.

He grab white card and mark-stick and start to mark, start to conversation swift, say all fast about they call this a four-cycle engine because it acts in four different phases, the piston goes down, this valve opens, that valve closes, the piston goes up, this makes a fire . . . and a lot, all so swift. "This the intake cycle," and many words. "This is the crankshaft, spark plug, fuel line, compression stroke . . ." Much and much.

And stops, whump. Points mark-stick. "Now, you and your thinking in concepts. That's how it works, basically. Don't tell me you got any of that, with any real understanding."

"Don't tell?"

"No, no," he say. He tired, he smile. He say, "Name the four cycles of this engine."

I say, "Suck. Squeeze. Pop. Phooey."

He drop he mark-stick. A long quiet. He say, "I can't teach you anything."

I say, "I not intelligent?"

He say, "*I* not intelligent."

Is many peoples in eat-place but I by my own with my plate and my thinks, I am alone. Is big roughness impacting on arm, big noise say, "What's your *name?*"

I bend to look up and there is the Sergeant. I say, "Nemo." He sit down. He look. He make me have think: he like me, he not believe me. He not believe anybody. He say: "Nemo, Nemo. That's not your name."

I do the thing with the shoulders.

He say, "You weren't surprised when I jolted you then. Don't you ever get surprised? Don't you ever get sore?"

I say, "Surprise, no. Sore?"

He say, "Sore, mad, angry."

I have a think. I say, "No."

He say, "Ought to be something that'll shake you up. Hm . . . They pamper you too much around here, you walking around like Little Eva or Billy Budd or somebody. Sweetness and light. Dr. de la Torre says you're real bright."

"De la Torre real bright."

"Maybe. Maybe." He eyes have like coldness, like so cold nothing move. He say, "That Elena. How you like Elena, Nemo?"

I say, "I like." And I say, "High music, big color-gentle."

He say, "Thought so." He poke sharp into my chest. "Now I'm gonna tell you the truth about your Elena. She's crazy as a coot. She went bad young. She was a mainliner, understand me? She was an addict. She did a lot of things to get money for the stuff. She had to do more'n most of 'em, with a face like that, and it didn't get any prettier. De la Torre pulled her through a cure. He's a good man. Three different times he cured her.

"So one time she falls off again and what do you know, she picks up with a looney just like you. A guy they called George. I figured from the start he was a faker. Showed up wandering, just like you. And she goes for him. She goes for him bigger'n she ever went for anything else, even hash. And he went over the hill one fine day and was never seen again.

"So she's off the stuff, sure. And you know what? The only thing she has any use for is amnesiacs. Yeah, I mean it. You're the sixth in a row. They come in, she sticks with 'em until they get cured or fade. Between times she just waits for the next one.

"And that's your Elena. De la Torre strings along with her because she does 'em good. So that's your light o' love, Nemo boy. A real twitch. If it isn't dope it's dopes. You get cured up, she'll want no part of you. Wise up, fella."

He look at me. He has a quiet time. He say, "God awmighty, you don't give a damn for her after all . . . or maybe you just don't know how to get mad . . . or you didn't understand a word of what I said."

I say, "Every people hurt Elena. Some day Elena be happy, always. Sergeant hurt every people. Sergeant not be happy. Never."

He look at me. Something move in the cold, like lobster on ice; too cold to move much. I say, "Poor Sergeant."

He jump up, he make a noise, not word, he raise a big hand. I look up at him, I say, "Poor Sergeant." He go away. He bump de la Torre who is quiet behind us.

De la Torre say, "I heard that speech of yours, you skunk. I'd clobber you myself if I didn't think Nemo'd done it better already. You'd better keep your big flat feet the hell out of this hospital."

Sergeant run away. De la Torre stand a time, go away. I eat.

It is night by the lake, the moon is burst and leaking yellow to me over the black alive water and Elena by me. I say, "I go soonly."

She breathe, I hear.

I say, "Tree finish, tree die. Sickness finish, sickness gone. House finish, workmens leave. Is right."

"Don't go. Don't go yet, Nemo."

"Seed sprout, child grow, bird fly. Something finish, something change. I finish."

She say, "Not so soon."

"Bury plant? Tie boy to cradle? Nail wings to nest?"

She say, "All right." We sit.

I say, "I promised."

She say, "You kept your promise, Nemo. Thank you." She cry. I watch leaking moon float free, lost light flattening and flattening at the black lake. Light tried, light tried, water would not mix.

Elena say, "What world do you live in, Nemo?"

I say, "My world."

She say, "Yes . . . yes, that's the right answer. You live in your world, I live in my world, a hundred people, a hundred worlds.

Nobody lives with me, nobody. Nemo, you can travel from one world to another."

I do the head, yes.

"But just one at a time. I'm talking crazy, but you don't mind. I had a world I don't remember, soft and safe, and then a world that hurt me because I was too stupid to duck when I saw hurt coming. And a world that was better than real where I couldn't stay, but I had to go there . . . and I couldn't stay . . . and I had to go . . . and then I had a world where I thought, just for a little while—such a little while—I thought it was a world for me and . . ."

I say, "—and George."

She say, "*You can read my mind!*"

"No!" I say, big; loud. Hurt. I say, "Truly no, not do that, I can't do that."

She touch on my face, say, "It doesn't matter. But George, then, about George . . . I was going to be lost again, and this time forever, and I saw George and spoke right up like a—a—" She shake. "You wouldn't know what I was like. And instead, George was gentle and sweet and he made me feel as if I was . . . well and whole. In all my life nobody ever treated me gently, Nemo, except Dr. de la Torre, and he did it because I was sick. George treated me as if I was healthy and fine, and he . . . admired me for it. Me. And he came to love me like those lights, those lights I showed you, all the colors, slipping among the dancers under the sky. He came to love me so much he wanted to stay with me for ever and ever, and then he went away sometime between a morning and a snowstorm."

The moon is gone up, finished and full, the light, left on the water frightened and yearning to it, thinning, breaking and fusing, pointing at the moon, the moon not caring, it finished now.

She say, "I was dead for a long time."

She passes through a think and lets her face be dead until she say, "Dr. de la Torre was so kind, he used to tell me I was a special princess, and I could go anywhere. I went in all the places in the hospital, and I found out a thing I had not known; that I had these hands, these legs, eyes, this body, voice, brains. It isn't much and nobody wants it . . . now . . . but I had it all. And some of those people in there, without all of it, they were happier than I was, brave and good. There's a place with people who have their voices taken out of their throats, Nemo, you know that? And they learn to speak there. You know how they do it? I tell some people this, they laugh, but you won't laugh. You won't laugh, Nemo?"

I am not laugh.

She say, "You know that noise you made when you drank the beer so fast? That's what they do. On purpose. They do it and they practice and practice and work hard, work together. And bit by bit they make a voice that sounds like a voice. It's rough and it's all on one note, but it's a real voice. They talk together and laugh, and have a debating society...

"There's a place in there where a man goes in without legs, and comes out dancing, yes twirling and swirling a girl around, her ballgown a butterfly and he smiling and swift and sure. There's a place for the deaf people, and they must make voices out of nothing too, and ears. They do it, Nemo! And together they understand each other. Outside, people don't understand the deaf. People don't mean to be unkind, but they are. But the deaf understand the deaf, and they understand the hearing as well, better than the hearing understand themselves.

"So one day I met a soldier there, with the deaf. He was very sad at first. Many of the people there are born deaf, but he had a world of hearing behind him. And there was a girl there and they fell in love. Everyone was happy, and one day he went away.

"She cried, she cried so, and when she stopped, it was even worse.

"And Dr. de la Torre went and found the soldier, and very gently and carefully he dug out why he had run away. It was because he was handicapped. It was because he had lost a precious thing. And he wouldn't marry the girl, though he loved her, because she was as she had been born and he felt she was perfect. She was perfect and he was damaged. She was perfect and he was unfit. And that is why he ran away.

"Dr. de la Torre brought him back and they were married right there in the hospital with such fine banquet and dance; and they got jobs there and went to school and now they are helping the others, together...

"So then I went into another world, and this is my world; and if I should *know* that it is not a real world I would die.

"My world is here, and somewhere else there are people like us but different. One of the ways they are different is that they need not speak; not words anyway. And something happens to them sometimes, just as it does to us: through sickness, through accident, they lose forever their way of communicating, like our total deaf. But they can learn to speak, just as you and I can learn Braille, or make a voice without a larynx, and then at least they may talk among themselves. And if you are to learn Braille, you should go among the blind. If you are to learn lip-reading you do it best among the deaf. If you have something better than speech and lose it, you must go among a speaking people.

"And that is what I believe, because I must or die. I think George was such a one, who came here to learn to speak so he could rejoin others who also had to learn. And I think that anyone who has no memory of this Earth or anything on it, and who must be taught to speak, might be another. They pretend to be amnesiacs so that they will be taught *all* of a language. I think that when they have learned, they understand themselves and those like them, and also the normal ones of their sort, better than anyone, just as the deaf can understand the hearing ones better.

"I think George was such a one, and that he left me because he thought of himself as crippled and of me as whole. He left me for love. He was humble with it.

"This is what I believe and I can't . . ."

She whisper.

". . . I can't believe it . . . very much . . . longer . . ."

She listen to grief altogether until it tired, and when she can listen to me I say, "You want me to be George, and stay."

She sit close, she put she wet face on my face and say, "Nemo, Nemo, I wish you could, I do *so* wish you could. But you can't be my George, because I love him, don't you see? You can be my de la Torre, though, who went out and found a man and explained why and brought him back. All he has to know is that when love is too humble it can kill the lovers . . . Just tell him that, Nemo. When you . . . when you go back."

She look past me at the moon, cold now, and down and out to the water and sky, and she here altogether out of memory and hope-thinks. She say with strong daytime voice, "I talk crazy sometimes, thanks, Nemo, you didn't laugh. Let's have a beer some time."

🧑 🧑 🧑

I wish almost the Sergeant knows where I keep anger. It would please him I have so much. Here in the bare rocks, here in the night, I twist on anger, curl and bite me like eel on spear.

It is night and with anger, I alone in cold hills, town and hospital a far fog of light behind. I stand to watch it the ship and around it, those silents who watch me, eight of them, nine, all silent.

This is my anger: that they are silent. They share all thinks in one thinking instant, each with one other, each with all others. All I do now is talk. But the silents, there stand by ship, share and share all thinks, none talks. They wait, I come. They have pity.

They have manymuch pity, so I angry.

Then I see my angry is envy, and envy never teach to dance a one-legged man. Envy never teach the lip-reading.

I see that and laugh at me, laugh but it sting my eyes.

"*Hello!*"

One comes to me, not silent, but have conversation! Surprise. I say, "Good evening."

He shake hand of me, say, "We thought you were not going to come." His speak slow, very strong, steadily.

I say, "I ready. I surprise you have talk."

He say, "Oh, I spent some time here. I studied very carefully. I have come back to live here."

I say, "You conversation goodly. I have learn talk idea, good enough. You have word and word and word, like Earth peoples. Good. Why you come returning?"

He look my face, very near, say, "I did not like it at home. When you go back there, everyone will be kind. But they will have their own lives to live, and there is not much they can share with you any more. You will be blind among the seeing, deaf among those who hear. But they will be kind, oh yes: very kind."

Then he look back at the silents, who stand watching. He say, "But here, I speak among the speaking, and it is a better sharing than even a home planet gone all silent." He point at watchers. He laugh. He say, "We speak together in a way they have never learned to speak, like two Earth mutes gesticulating together in a crowd. It is as if we were the telepaths and not they—see them stare and wonder!"

I laugh too. "Not need to telepath here!"

He say, "Yes, on Earth we can be blind with the blind, and we will never miss our vision. While I was here I was happy to share myself by speaking. When I went home I could share only with other . . . damaged . . . people. I had to go home to find out that I did not feel damaged when I was here, so I came back."

I look to ship, to wondering silents. I say, "What name you have here?"

He say, "They called me George."

I think, I have message for you: Elena dying for you. I say, "Elena waiting for you."

He make large shout and hug on me and run. I cry, "Wait! Wait!" He wait, but not wanting. I say, "I learn talk like you, word and word, and one day find Elena for me too."

He hit on me gladly, say, "All right. I'll help you."

We go down hill togetherly, most muchly homelike. Behind, ship wait, ship wait, silents watch and wonder. Then ship load up with all pity I need no more, scream away up to stars.

I have a happy now that I get sick lose telepathy come here learn talk find home, *por Dios*.

HOW TO TALK TO GIRLS AT PARTIES

Neil Gaiman

Of all the things I might miss about my youth, those awkward fumbling attempts at courting the opposite sex as a fresh-faced teenager will never be one of them. The title of a popular book at the time comes to mind, Men Are from Mars, Women Are from Venus, *because with all the wild changes in hormones, body and brain development, and social anxieties, and so uncomfortable in your own body, those other teens and romance might as well be on another planet.*

I don't know if the girls in this story are from Venus, but two teen boys in 1970s South London are in for an out-of-this-world experience with the opposite sex they won't soon forget. Toss in Neil Gaiman's signature knack for the surreal, the unsettling, and fantastic, with a little punk-rock flair thrown in, and neither will you.

🧑 🧑 🧑

"Come on," said Vic. "It'll be great."

"No, it won't," I said, although I'd lost this fight hours ago, and I knew it.

"It'll be brilliant," said Vic, for the hundredth time. "Girls! Girls! Girls!" He grinned with white teeth.

We both attended an all-boys' school in south London. While it would be a lie to say that we had no experience with girls—Vic seemed to have had many girlfriends, while I had kissed three of my sister's friends—it would, I think, be perfectly true to say that we both chiefly spoke to, interacted with, and only truly understood, other boys. Well, I did, anyway. It's hard to speak for someone else, and I've not seen Vic for thirty years. I'm not sure that I would know what to say to him now if I did.

We were walking the backstreets that used to twine in a grimy maze behind East Croydon station—a friend had told Vic about a party, and Vic was determined to go whether I liked it or not, and I didn't. But my parents were away that week at a conference, and I was Vic's guest at his house, so I was trailing along beside him.

"It'll be the same as it always is," I said. "After an hour you'll be off somewhere snogging the prettiest girl at the party, and I'll be in the kitchen listening to somebody's mum going on about politics or poetry or something."

"You just have to talk to them," he said. "I think it's probably that road at the end here." He gestured cheerfully, swinging the bag with the bottle in it.

"Don't you know?"

"Alison gave me directions and I wrote them on a bit of paper, but I left it on the hall table. S'okay. I can find it."

"How?" Hope welled slowly up inside me.

"We walk down the road," he said, as if speaking to an idiot child. "And we look for the party. Easy."

I looked, but saw no party: just narrow houses with rusting cars or bikes in their concreted front gardens; and the dusty glass fronts of newsagents, which smelled of alien spices and sold everything from birthday cards and secondhand comics to the kind of magazines that were so pornographic that they were sold already sealed in plastic bags. I had been there when Vic had slipped one of those magazines beneath his sweater, but the owner caught him on the pavement outside and made him give it back.

We reached the end of the road and turned into a narrow street of terraced houses. Everything looked very still and empty in the Summer's evening. "It's all right for you," I said. "They fancy you. You don't actually have to talk to them." It was true: one urchin grin from Vic and he could have his pick of the room.

"Nah. S'not like that. You've just got to talk."

The times I had kissed my sister's friends I had not spoken to them. They had been around while my sister was off doing something elsewhere, and they had drifted into my orbit, and so I had kissed them. I do not remember any talking. I did not know what to say to girls, and I told him so.

"They're just girls," said Vic. "They don't come from another planet."

As we followed the curve of the road around, my hopes that the party would prove unfindable began to fade: a low pulsing noise, music muffled by walls and doors, could be heard from a house up ahead. It was eight in the evening, not that early if you aren't yet sixteen, and we weren't. Not quite.

I had parents who liked to know where I was, but I don't think Vic's parents cared that much. He was the youngest of five boys. That in itself seemed magical to me: I merely had two sisters, both younger than I was, and I felt both unique and lonely. I had wanted a brother as far back as I could remember. When I turned thirteen, I stopped wishing on falling stars or first stars, but back when I did, a brother was what I had wished for.

We went up the garden path, crazy paving leading us past a hedge and a solitary rosebush to a pebble-dashed facade. We rang the doorbell, and the door was opened by a girl. I could not have told you how old she was, which was one of the things about girls I had begun to hate: when you start out as kids you're just boys and girls, going through time at the same speed, and you're all five, or seven, or eleven, together. And then one day there's a lurch and the girls just sort of sprint off into the future ahead of you, and they know all about everything, and they have periods and breasts and makeup and God-only-knew-what-else—for I certainly didn't. The diagrams in biology textbooks were no substitute for being, in a very real sense, young adults. And the girls of our age were.

Vic and I weren't young adults, and I was beginning to suspect that even when I started needing to shave every day, instead of once every couple of weeks, I would still be way behind.

The girl said, "Hello?"

Vic said, "We're friends of Alison's." We had met Alison, all freckles and orange hair and a wicked smile, in Hamburg, on a German exchange. The exchange organizers had sent some girls with us, from a local girls' school, to balance the sexes. The girls, our age, more or less, were raucous and funny, and had more or less adult boyfriends with cars and jobs and motorbikes and—in the case of one girl with crooked teeth and a raccoon coat, who spoke to me about it sadly at the end of a party in Hamburg, in, of course, the kitchen—a wife and kids.

"She isn't here," said the girl at the door. "No Alison."

"Not to worry," said Vic, with an easy grin. "I'm Vic. This is Enn." A beat, and then the girl smiled back at him. Vic had a bottle of white wine in a plastic bag, removed from his parents' kitchen cabinet. "Where should I put this, then?"

She stood out of the way, letting us enter. "There's a kitchen in the back," she said. "Put it on the table there, with the other bottles." She had golden, wavy hair, and she was very beautiful. The hall was dim in the twilight, but I could see that she was beautiful.

"What's your name, then?" said Vic.

She told him it was Stella, and he grinned his crooked white grin and told her that that had to be the prettiest name he had ever heard. Smooth bastard. And what was worse was that he said it like he meant it.

Vic headed back to drop off the wine in the kitchen, and I looked into the front room, where the music was coming from. There were people dancing in there. Stella walked in, and she started to dance, swaying to the music all alone, and I watched her.

This was during the early days of punk. On our own record players we would play the Adverts and the Jam, the Stranglers and the Clash and the Sex Pistols. At other people's parties you'd hear ELO or 10cc or even Roxy Music. Maybe some Bowie, if you were lucky. During the German exchange, the only LP that we had all been able to agree on was Neil Young's *Harvest*, and his song "Heart of Gold" had threaded through the trip like a refrain: *I crossed the ocean for a heart of gold. . . .*

The music playing in that front room wasn't anything I recognized.

It sounded a bit like a German electronic pop group called Kraftwerk, and a bit like an LP I'd been given for my last birthday, of strange sounds made by the BBC Radiophonic Workshop. The music had a beat, though, and the half-dozen girls in that room were moving gently to it, although I only looked at Stella. She shone.

Vic pushed past me, into the room. He was holding a can of lager.

"There's booze back in the kitchen," he told me. He wandered over to Stella and he began to talk to her. I couldn't hear what they were saying over the music, but I knew that there was no room for me in that conversation.

I didn't like beer, not back then. I went off to see if there was something I wanted to drink. On the kitchen table stood a large bottle of Coca-Cola, and I poured myself a plastic tumblerful, and I didn't dare say anything to the pair of girls who were talking in the underlit kitchen. They were animated and utterly lovely. Each of them had very black skin and glossy hair and movie star clothes, and their accents were foreign, and each of them was out of my league.

I wandered, Coke in hand.

The house was deeper than it looked, larger and more complex than the two-up two-down model I had imagined. The rooms were underlit—I doubt there was a bulb of more than 40 watts in the building—and each room I went into was inhabited: in my memory, inhabited only by girls. I did not go upstairs.

A girl was the only occupant of the conservatory. Her hair was so fair it was white, and long, and straight, and she sat at the glass-topped table, her hands clasped together, staring at the garden outside, and the gathering dusk. She seemed wistful.

"Do you mind if I sit here?" I asked, gesturing with my cup. She shook her head, and then followed it up with a shrug, to indicate that it was all the same to her. I sat down.

Vic walked past the conservatory door. He was talking to Stella, but he looked in at me, sitting at the table, wrapped in shyness and awkwardness, and he opened and closed his hand in a parody of a speaking mouth. Talk. Right.

"Are you from around here?" I asked the girl.

She shook her head. She wore a low-cut silvery top, and I tried not to stare at the swell of her breasts.

I said, "What's your name? I'm Enn."

"Wain's Wain," she said, or something that sounded like it. "I'm a second."

"That's uh. That's a different name."

She fixed me with huge, liquid eyes. "It indicates that my progenitor was also Wain, and that I am obliged to report back to her. I may not breed."

"Ah. Well. Bit early for that anyway, isn't it?"

She unclasped her hands, raised them above the table, spread her fingers. "You see?" The little finger on her left hand was crooked, and it bifurcated at the top, splitting into two smaller fingertips. A minor deformity. "When I was finished a decision was needed. Would I be retained, or eliminated? I was fortunate that the decision was with me. Now, I travel, while my more perfect sisters remain at home in stasis. They were firsts. I am a second.

"Soon I must return to Wain, and tell her all I have seen. All my impressions of this place of yours."

"I don't actually live in Croydon," I said. "I don't come from here." I wondered if she was American. I had no idea what she was talking about.

"As you say," she agreed, "neither of us comes from here." She folded her six-fingered left hand beneath her right, as if tucking it out of sight. "I had expected it to be bigger, and cleaner, and more colorful. But still, it is a jewel."

She yawned, covered her mouth with her right hand, only for a moment, before it was back on the table again. "I grow weary of the journeying, and I wish sometimes that it would end. On a street in Rio at Carnival, I saw them on a bridge, golden and tall and insect-eyed and winged, and elated I almost ran to greet them, before I saw that they were only people in costumes. I said to Hola Colt, 'Why do they try so hard to look like us?' and Hola Colt replied, 'Because they hate themselves, all shades of pink and brown, and so small.' It is what I experience, even me, and I am not grown. It is like a world of children, or of elves." Then she smiled, and said, "It was a good thing they could not any of them see Hola Colt."

"Um," I said, "do you want to dance?"

She shook her head immediately. "It is not permitted," she said. "I can do nothing that might cause damage to property. I am Wain's."

"Would you like something to drink, then?"

"Water," she said.

I went back to the kitchen and poured myself another Coke, and filled a cup with water from the tap. From the kitchen back to the hall, and from there into the conservatory, but now it was quite empty.

I wondered if the girl had gone to the toilet, and if she might change her mind about dancing later. I walked back to the front room and stared in. The place was filling up. There were more girls dancing, and several lads I didn't know, who looked a few years older than me and Vic. The lads and the girls all kept their distance, but Vic was holding Stella's hand as they danced, and when the song ended he put an arm around her, casually, almost proprietorially, to make sure that nobody else cut in.

I wondered if the girl I had been talking to in the conservatory was now upstairs, as she did not appear to be on the ground floor.

I walked into the living room, which was across the hall from the room where the people were dancing, and I sat down on the sofa. There was a girl sitting there already. She had dark hair, cut short and spiky, and a nervous manner.

Talk, I thought. "Um, this mug of water's going spare," I told her, "if you want it?"

She nodded, and reached out her hand and took the mug, extremely carefully, as if she were unused to taking things, as if she could trust neither her vision nor her hands.

"I love being a tourist," she said, and smiled hesitantly. She had a gap between her two front teeth, and she sipped the tap water as if she were an adult sipping a fine wine. "The last tour, we went to sun, and we swam in sunfire pools with the whales. We heard their histories and we shivered in the chill of the outer places, then we swam deepward where the heat churned and comforted us.

"I wanted to go back. This time, I wanted it. There was so much I had not seen. Instead we came to world. Do you like it?"

"Like what?"

She gestured vaguely to the room—the sofa, the armchairs, the curtains, the unused gas fire.

"It's all right, I suppose."

"I told them I did not wish to visit world," she said. "My parent-teacher was unimpressed. 'You will have much to learn,' it told me. I said, 'I could learn more in sun, again. Or in the deeps. Jessa spun webs between galaxies. I want to do that.'

"But there was no reasoning with it, and I came to world. Parent-teacher engulfed me, and I was here, embodied in a decaying lump of meat hanging on a frame of calcium. As I incarnated I felt things deep inside me, fluttering and pumping and squishing. It was my first experience with pushing air through the mouth, vibrating the vocal cords on the way, and I used it to tell parent-teacher that I wished that I would die, which it acknowledged was the inevitable exit strategy from world."

There were black worry beads wrapped around her wrist, and she fiddled with them as she spoke. "But knowledge is there, in the meat," she said, "and I am resolved to learn from it."

We were sitting close at the center of the sofa now. I decided I should put an arm around her, but casually. I would extend my arm along the back of the sofa and eventually sort of creep it down, almost imperceptibly, until it was touching her. She said, "The thing with the liquid in the eyes, when the world blurs. Nobody told me, and I still do not understand. I have touched the folds of the Whisper and pulsed and flown with the tachyon swans, and I still do not understand."

She wasn't the prettiest girl there, but she seemed nice enough, and she was a girl, anyway. I let my arm slide down a little, tentatively, so that it made contact with her back, and she did not tell me to take it away.

Vic called to me then, from the doorway. He was standing with his arm around Stella, protectively, waving at me. I tried to let him know, by shaking my head, that I was onto something, but he called my name and, reluctantly, I got up from the sofa and walked over to the door. "What?"

"Er. Look. The party," said Vic, apologetically. "It's not the one I thought it was. I've been talking to Stella and I figured it out. Well, she sort of explained it to me. We're at a different party."

"Christ. Are we in trouble? Do we have to go?"

Stella shook her head. He leaned down and kissed her, gently, on the lips. "You're just happy to have me here, aren't you, darlin'?"

"You know I am," she told him.

He looked from her back to me, and he smiled his white smile: roguish, lovable, a little bit Artful Dodger, a little bit wide-boy Prince Charming. "Don't worry. They're all tourists here anyway. It's a foreign exchange thing, innit? Like when we all went to Germany."

"It is?"

"Enn. You got to talk to them. And that means you got to listen to them, too. You understand?"

"I did. I already talked to a couple of them."

"You getting anywhere?"

"I was till you called me over."

"Sorry about that. Look, I just wanted to fill you in. Right?"

And he patted my arm and he walked away with Stella. Then, together, the two of them went up the stairs.

Understand me, all the girls at that party, in the twilight, were lovely; they all had perfect faces but, more important than that, they had whatever strangeness of proportion, of oddness or humanity it is that makes a beauty something more than a shop window dummy.

Stella was the most lovely of any of them, but she, of course, was Vic's, and they were going upstairs together, and that was just how things would always be.

There were several people now sitting on the sofa, talking to the gap-toothed girl. Someone told a joke, and they all laughed. I would have had to push my way in there to sit next to her again, and it didn't look like she was expecting me back, or cared that I had gone, so I wandered out into the hall. I glanced in at the dancers, and found myself wondering where the music was coming from. I couldn't see a record player or speakers.

From the hall I walked back to the kitchen.

Kitchens are good at parties. You never need an excuse to be there, and, on the good side, at this party I couldn't see any signs of someone's mum. I inspected the various bottles and cans on the kitchen table, then I poured a half an inch of Pernod into the bottom of my plastic cup, which I filled to the top with Coke. I dropped in a couple of ice cubes and took a sip, relishing the sweet-shop tang of the drink.

"What's that you're drinking?" A girl's voice.

"It's Pernod," I told her. "It tastes like aniseed balls, only it's alcoholic." I didn't say that I only tried it because I'd heard someone in the crowd ask for a Pernod on a live Velvet Underground LP.

"Can I have one?" I poured another Pernod, topped it off with Coke, passed it to her. Her hair was a coppery auburn, and it tumbled around her head in ringlets. It's not a hair style you see much now, but you saw it a lot back then.

"What's your name?" I asked.

"Triolet," she said.

"Pretty name," I told her, although I wasn't sure that it was. She was pretty, though.

"It's a verse form," she said, proudly. "Like me."

"You're a poem?"

She smiled, and looked down and away, perhaps bashfully. Her profile was almost flat—a perfect Grecian nose that came down from her forehead in a straight line. We did Antigone in the school theater the previous year. I was the messenger who brings Creon the news of Antigone's death. We wore half-masks that made us look like that. I thought of that play, looking at her face, in the kitchen, and I thought of Barry Smith's drawings of women in the Conan comics: five years later I would have thought of the Pre-Raphaelites, of Jane Morris and Lizzie Siddall. But I was only fifteen then.

"You're a poem?" I repeated.

She chewed her lower lip. "If you want. I am a poem, or I am a pattern, or a race of people whose world was swallowed by the sea."

"Isn't it hard to be three things at the same time?"

"What's your name?"

"Enn."

"So you are Enn," she said. "And you are a male. And you are a biped. Is it hard to be three things at the same time?"

"But they aren't different things. I mean, they aren't contradictory." It was a word I had read many times but never said aloud before that night, and I put the stresses in the wrong places. Contradictory.

She wore a thin dress made of a white, silky fabric. Her eyes were a pale green, a color that would now make me think of tinted contact lenses; but this was thirty years ago; things were different then. I remember wondering about Vic and Stella, upstairs. By now, I was sure that they were in one of the bedrooms, and I envied Vic so much it almost hurt.

Still, I was talking to this girl, even if we were talking nonsense, even if her name wasn't really Triolet (my generation had not been given hippie names: all the Rainbows and the Sunshines and the Moons, they were only six, seven, eight years old back then). She said, "We knew that it would soon be over, and so we put it all into a poem, to tell the universe who we were, and why we were here, and what we said and did and thought and dreamed and yearned for. We wrapped our dreams in words and patterned the words so that they would live forever, unforgettable. Then we sent the poem as a pattern of flux, to wait in the heart of a star, beaming out its message in pulses and bursts and fuzzes across the electromagnetic spectrum, until the time when, on worlds a thousand sun systems distant, the pattern would be decoded and read, and it would become a poem once again."

"And then what happened?"

She looked at me with her green eyes, and it was as if she stared out at me from her own Antigone half-mask; but as if her pale green eyes were just a different, deeper, part of the mask. "You cannot hear a poem without it changing you," she told me. "They heard it, and it colonized them. It inherited them and it inhabited them, its rhythms becoming part of the way that they thought; its images permanently transmuting their metaphors; its verses, its outlook, its aspirations becoming their lives. Within a generation their children would be born already knowing the poem, and, sooner rather than later, as these things go, there were no more children born. There was no need for them, not any longer. There was only a poem, which took flesh and walked and spread itself across the vastness of the known."

I edged closer to her, so I could feel my leg pressing against hers.

She seemed to welcome it: she put her hand on my arm, affectionately, and I felt a smile spreading across my face.

"There are places that we are welcomed," said Triolet, "and places where we are regarded as a noxious weed, or as a disease, something immediately to be quarantined and eliminated. But where does contagion end and art begin?"

"I don't know," I said, still smiling. I could hear the unfamiliar music as it pulsed and scattered and boomed in the front room.

She leaned into me then and—I suppose it was a kiss. . . . I suppose. She pressed her lips to my lips, anyway, and then, satisfied, she pulled back, as if she had now marked me as her own.

"Would you like to hear it?" she asked, and I nodded, unsure what she was offering me, but certain that I needed anything she was willing to give me.

She began to whisper something in my ear. It's the strangest thing about poetry—you can tell it's poetry, even if you don't speak the language. You can hear Homer's Greek without understanding a word, and you still know it's poetry. I've heard Polish poetry, and Inuit poetry, and I knew what it was without knowing. Her whisper was like that. I didn't know the language, but her words washed through me, perfect, and in my mind's eye I saw towers of glass and diamond; and people with eyes of the palest green; and, unstoppable, beneath every syllable, I could feel the relentless advance of the ocean.

Perhaps I kissed her properly. I don't remember. I know I wanted to.

And then Vic was shaking me violently. "Come on!" he was shouting. "Quickly. Come on!"

In my head I began to come back from a thousand miles away.

"Idiot. Come on. Just get a move on," he said, and he swore at me. There was fury in his voice.

For the first time that evening I recognized one of the songs being played in the front room. A sad saxophone wail followed by a cascade of liquid chords, a man's voice singing cut-up lyrics about the sons of the silent age. I wanted to stay and hear the song.

She said, "I am not finished. There is yet more of me."

"Sorry, love," said Vic, but he wasn't smiling any longer. "There'll be another time," and he grabbed me by the elbow and he twisted and pulled, forcing me from the room. I did not resist. I knew from experience that Vic could beat the stuffing out me if he got it into his head to do so. He wouldn't do it unless he was upset or angry, but he was angry now.

Out into the front hall. As Vic pulled open the door, I looked back one last time, over my shoulder, hoping to see Triolet in the doorway to the kitchen, but she was not there. I saw Stella, though, at the top of the stairs. She was staring down at Vic, and I saw her face.

This all happened thirty years ago. I have forgotten much, and I will forget more, and in the end I will forget everything; yet, if I have any certainty of life beyond death, it is all wrapped up not in psalms or hymns, but in this one thing alone: I cannot believe that I will ever forget that moment, or forget the expression on Stella's face as she watched Vic hurrying away from her. Even in death I shall remember that.

Her clothes were in disarray, and there was makeup smudged across her face, and her eyes—

You wouldn't want to make a universe angry. I bet an angry universe would look at you with eyes like that.

We ran then, me and Vic, away from the party and the tourists and the twilight, ran as if a lightning storm was on our heels, a mad helter-skelter dash down the confusion of streets, threading through the maze, and we did not look back, and we did not stop until we could not breathe; and then we stopped and panted, unable to run any longer. We were in pain. I held on to a wall, and Vic threw up, hard and long, into the gutter.

He wiped his mouth.

"She wasn't a—" He stopped.

He shook his head.

Then he said, "You know . . . I think there's a thing. When you've gone as far as you dare. And if you go any further, you wouldn't be you anymore? You'd be the person who'd done that? The places you just can't go. . . . I think that happened to me tonight."

I thought I knew what he was saying. "Screw her, you mean?" I said.

He rammed a knuckle hard against my temple, and twisted it violently. I wondered if I was going to have to fight him—and lose—but after a moment he lowered his hand and moved away from me, making a low, gulping noise.

I looked at him curiously, and I realized that he was crying: his face was scarlet; snot and tears ran down his cheeks. Vic was sobbing in the street, as unselfconsciously and heartbreakingly as a little boy.

He walked away from me then, shoulders heaving, and he hurried down the road so he was in front of me and I could no longer see his face. I wondered what had occurred in that upstairs room to make him behave like that, to scare him so, and I could not even begin to guess.

The streetlights came on, one by one; Vic stumbled on ahead, while I trudged down the street behind him in the dusk, my feet treading out the measure of a poem that, try as I might, I could not properly remember and would never be able to repeat.

NINE-FINGER JACK
Anthony Boucher

A founding editor of The Magazine of Fantasy & Science Fiction *and one of the founders of* Mystery Writers of America, *Anthony Boucher's talent and passion for both genres, as a writer, editor and critic, is unquestionable. This combination also makes his rare stories that manage to combine his love for both special indeed.*

Originally published in Esquire, *"Nine-Finger Jack" even manages to pull in another of Boucher's great loves, his lifelong fascination with serial killers, with a wife-killing protagonist who finds his latest victim isn't so easy to kill—or entirely human. And things only get stranger from there, including multiple attempts at murder and a weaponized squirting lapel flower.*

🜚 🜚 🜚

John Smith is an unexciting name to possess, and there was of course no way for him to know until the end of his career that he would be forever famous among connoisseurs of murder as Nine-finger Jack. But he did not mind the drabness of Smith; he felt that what was good enough for the great George Joseph was good enough for him.

Not only did John Smith happily share his surname with George Joseph; he was proud to follow the celebrated G.J. in profession and even in method. For an attractive and plausible man of a certain age, there are few more satisfactory sources of income than frequent and systematic widowerhood; and of all the practitioners who have acted upon this practical principle, none have improved upon George Joseph Smith's sensible and unpatented Brides-in-the-Bath method.

John Smith's marriage to his ninth bride, Hester Pringle, took place on the morning of May the thirty-first. On the evening of May the thirty-first John Smith, having spent much of the afternoon pointing out to friends how much the wedding had excited Hester and how much he feared the effect on her notoriously weak heart, entered the bathroom and, with the careless ease of the practiced professional, employed five of his fingers to seize Hester's ankles and jerk her legs out of the tub while with the other five fingers he gently pressed her face just below water level.

So far all had proceeded in the conventional manner of any other wedding night; but the ensuing departure from ritual was such as to upset even John Smith's professional bathside manner. The moment Hester's face and neck were submerged below water, she opened her gills.

In his amazement, John released his grasp upon both ends of his bride.

Her legs descended into the water and her face rose above it. As she passed from the element of water to that of air, her gills closed, and her mouth opened.

"I suppose," she observed, "that in the intimacy of a long marriage you would eventually have discovered in any case that I am a Venusian. It is perhaps as well that the knowledge came early, so that we may lay a solid basis for understanding."

"Do you mean," John asked, for he was a precise man, "that you are a native of the planet Venus?"

"I do," she said. "You would be astonished to know how many of us there are already among you."

"I am sufficiently astonished," said John, "to learn of one. Would you mind convincing me that I did indeed see what I thought I saw?"

Obligingly, Hester lowered her head beneath the water. Her gills opened and her breath bubbled merrily. "The nature of our planet," she explained when she emerged, "has bred as its dominant race our species of amphibian mammals, in all other respects superficially identical with homo sapiens. You will find it all but impossible to recognize any of us, save perhaps by noticing those who, to avoid accidental opening of the gills, refuse to swim. Such concealment will of course be unnecessary soon when we take over complete control of your planet."

"And what do you propose to do with the race that already controls it?"

"Kill most of them, I suppose," said Hester; "and might I trouble you for that towel?"

"That," pronounced John, with any handcraftsman's abhorrence of mass production, "is monstrous. I see my duty to my race: I must reveal all."

"I am afraid," Hester observed as she dried herself, "that you will not. In the first place, no one will believe you. In the second place, I shall then be forced to present to the authorities the complete dossier which I have gathered on the cumulatively interesting deaths of your first eight wives, together with my direct evidence as to your attempt this evening."

John Smith, being a reasonable man, pressed the point no further. "In view of this attempt," he said, "I imagine you would like either a divorce or an annulment."

"Indeed, I should not," said Hester. "There is no better cover for my activities than marriage to a member of the native race. In fact, should you so much as mention divorce again, I shall be forced to return to the topic of that dossier. And now, if you will hand me that robe, I intend to do a little telephoning. Some of my better-placed colleagues will need to know my new name and address."

As John Smith heard her ask the long-distance operator for Washington, D.C., he realized with regretful resignation that he would be forced to depart from the methods of the immortal George Joseph.

Through the failure of the knife, John Smith learned that Venusian blood has extraordinary quick-clotting powers and Venusian organs possess an amazingly rapid system of self-regeneration. And the bullet taught him a further peculiarity of the blood: that it dissolves lead—in fact thrives upon lead.

His skill as a cook was quite sufficient to disguise any of the commoner poisons from human taste; but the Venusian palate not only detected but relished most of them. Hester was particularly taken with his tomato aspic à Varsénique and insisted on his preparing it in quantity for a dinner of her friends, along with his sole amandine to which the prussic acid lent so distinctively intensified a flavor and aroma.

While the faintest murmur of divorce, even after a year of marriage, evoked from Hester a frowning murmur of "Dossier..." the attempts at murder seemed merely to amuse her; so that finally John Smith was driven to seek out Professor Gillingsworth at the State University, recognized as the ultimate authority (on this planet) on life on other planets.

The professor found the query of much theoretical interest. "From what we are able to hypothesize of the nature of Venusian organisms," he announced, "I can almost assure you of their destruction by the forced ingestion of the best Beluga caviar, in doses of no less than one-half pound per diem."

Three weeks of the suggested treatment found John Smith's bank account seriously depleted and his wife in perfect health.

"That dear Gilly!" she laughed one evening. "It was so nice of him to tell you how to kill me; it's the first time I've had enough caviar since I came to earth. It's so dreadfully expensive."

"You mean," John demanded, "that Professor Gillingsworth is..."

She nodded.

"And all that money!" John protested. "You do not realize, Hester, how unjust you are. You have deprived me of my income, and I have no other source."

"Dossier," said Hester through a mouthful of caviar.

America's greatest physiologist took an interest in John Smith's problem. "I should advise," he said, "the use of crystallized carbon placed directly in contact with the sensitive gill area."

"In other words, a diamond necklace?" John Smith asked. He seized a water carafe, hurled its contents at the physiologist's neck, and watched his gills open.

The next day John purchased a lapel flower through which water may be squirted—an article which he thenceforth found invaluable for purposes of identification.

The use of this flower proved to be a somewhat awkward method of starting a conversation and often led the conversation into unintended paths; but it did establish a certain clarity in relations.

It was after John had observed the opening of the gills of a leading criminal psychiatrist that he realized where he might find the people who could really help him.

From then on, whenever he could find time to be unobserved while Hester was engaged in her activities preparatory to world conquest, he visited insane asylums, announced that he was a free-lance feature writer, and asked if they had any inmates who believed that there were Venusians at large upon earth and planning to take it over.

In this manner he met many interesting and attractive people, all of whom wished him godspeed in his venture, but pointed out that they would hardly be where they were if all of their own plans for killing Venusians had not miscarried as hopelessly as his.

From one of these friends, who had learned more than most because his Venusian wife had made the error of falling in love with him (an error which led to her eventual removal from human society), John Smith ascertained that Venusians may indeed be harmed and even killed by many substances on their own planet, but seemingly by nothing on ours—though (his) wife had once dropped a hint that one thing alone on earth could prove fatal to the Venusian system.

At last John Smith visited an asylum whose director announced that they had an inmate who thought he was a Venusian.

When the director had left them, a squirt of the lapel flower verified the claimant's identity.

"I am a member of the Coneiliationist Party," he explained, "the only member who has ever reached this earth. We believe that Earthmen and Venusians can live at peace as all men should, and I shall be glad to help you destroy all members of the opposition party.

"There is one substance on this earth which is deadly poison to any Venusian. Since in preparing and serving the dish best suited to its administration you must be careful to wear gloves, you should begin your campaign by wearing gloves at all meals..."

This mannerism Hester seemed willing to tolerate for the security afforded her by her marriage and even more particularly for the delights of John's skilled preparation of such dishes as spaghetti alVaglio ed ali'arsenico which is so rarely to be had in the average restaurant.

Two weeks later John finally prepared the indicated dish: ox tail according to the richly imaginative recipe of Simon Templar, with a dash of deadly nightshade added to the other herbs specified by *The*

Saint. Hester had praised the recipe, devoured two helpings, expressed some wonder as to the possibility of gills in its creator, whom she had never met, and was just nibbling at the smallest bones when, as the Conciliationist had foretold, she dropped dead.

Intent upon accomplishing his objective, John had forgotten the dossier, nor ever suspected that it was in the hands of a gilled lawyer who had instructions to pass it on in the event of Hester's death.

Even though that death was certified as natural, John rapidly found himself facing trial for murder, with seven other states vying for the privilege of the next opportunity should this trial fail to end in a conviction.

With no prospect in sight of a quiet resumption of his accustomed profession, John Smith bared his knowledge and acquired his immortal nickname. The result was a period of intense prosperity among manufacturers of squirting lapel flowers, bringing about the identification and exposure of the gilled masqueraders.

But inducing them, even by force, to ingest the substance poisonous to them was more difficult. The problem of supply and demand was an acute one, in view of the large number of the Venusians and the small proportion of members of the human race willing to perform the sacrifice made by Nine-finger Jack.

It was that great professional widower and amateur chef himself who solved the problem by proclaiming in his death cell his intention to bequeath his body to the eradication of Venusians, thereby pursuing after death the race which had ruined his career.

The noteworthy proportion of human beings who promptly followed his example in their wills has assured us of permanent protection against future invasions, since so small a quantity of the poison is necessary in each individual case; after all, one finger sufficed for Hester.

AN INCIDENT ON ROUTE 12

James H. Schmitz

James H. Schmitz was a lifelong favorite of the late great Eric Flint, to the point he spearheaded Baen Books' collecting and reprinting his entire bibliography, including his most famous novel, The Witches of Karres, *which had a trio of sequels written by Flint, Mercedes Lackey, and Dave Freer. It's easy to see why Flint loved him—the man was a master of classical space opera, with the right balance of whimsy and hard edge.*

This story from Schmitz couldn't be more different from his space operas, though nevertheless, his signature style shines through. This is the story of a bank robber on the lam, who quickly discovers there are things far more precious than the stolen loot in his passenger seat, and far more dangerous things on his tail than Johnny Law.

※ ※ ※

Phil Garfield was thirty miles south of the little town of Redmon on Route Twelve when he was startled by a series of sharp, clanking noises. They came from under the Packard's hood.

The car immediately began to lose speed. Garfield jammed down the accelerator, had a sense of sick helplessness at the complete lack of response from the motor. The Packard rolled on, getting rid of its momentum, and came to a stop.

Phil Garfield swore shakily. He checked his watch, switched off the headlights and climbed out into the dark road. A delay of even half an hour here might be disastrous. It was past midnight, and he had another hundred and ten miles to cover to reach the small private airfield where Madge waited for him and the thirty thousand dollars in the suitcase on the Packard's front seat.

If he didn't make it before daylight . . .

He thought of the bank guard. The man had made a clumsy play at being a hero, and that had set off the fool woman who'd run screaming into their line of fire. One dead. Perhaps two. Garfield hadn't stopped to look at an evening paper.

But he knew they were hunting for him.

He glanced up and down the road. No other headlights in sight at the moment, no light from a building showing on the forested hills. He reached back into the car and brought out the suitcase, his gun, a big flashlight and the box of shells which had been standing beside the suitcase. He broke the box open, shoved a handful of shells and the .38 into his coat pocket, then took suitcase and flashlight over to the shoulder of the road and set them down.

There was no point in groping about under the Packard's hood. When it came to mechanics, Phil Garfield was a moron and well aware of it. The car was useless to him now . . . except as bait.

But as bait it might be very useful.

Should he leave it standing where it was? No, Garfield decided. To anybody driving past it would merely suggest a necking party, or a drunk sleeping off his load before continuing home. He might have to wait an hour or more before someone decided to stop. He didn't have the time. He reached in through the window, hauled the top of the steering wheel towards him and put his weight against the rear window frame.

The Packard began to move slowly backwards at a slant across the road. In a minute or two he had it in position. Not blocking the road entirely, which would arouse immediate suspicion, but angled across it, lights out, empty, both front doors open and inviting a passerby's investigation.

Garfield carried the suitcase and flashlight across the right-hand shoulder of the road and moved up among the trees and undergrowth of the slope above the shoulder. Placing the suitcase between the bushes, he brought out the .38, clicked the safety off and stood waiting.

Some ten minutes later, a set of headlights appeared speeding up Route Twelve from the direction of Redmon. Phil Garfield went down on one knee before he came within range of the lights. Now he was completely concealed by the vegetation.

The car slowed as it approached, braking nearly to a stop sixty feet from the stalled Packard. There were several people inside it; Garfield heard voices, then a woman's loud laugh. The driver tapped his horn inquiringly twice, moved the car slowly forward. As the headlights went past him, Garfield got to his feet among the bushes, took a step down towards the road, raising the gun.

Then he caught the distant gleam of a second set of headlights approaching from Redmon. He swore under his breath and dropped back out of sight. The car below him reached the Packard, edged cautiously around it, rolled on with a sudden roar of acceleration.

The second car stopped when still a hundred yards away, the Packard caught in the motionless glare of its lights. Garfield heard the steady purring of a powerful motor.

For almost a minute, nothing else happened. Then the car came gliding smoothly on, stopped again no more than thirty feet to Garfield's left. He could see it now through the screening bushes—a big job, a long, low four-door sedan. The motor continued to purr. After a moment, a door on the far side of the car opened and slammed shut.

A man walked quickly out into the beam of the headlights and started towards the Packard.

Phil Garfield rose from his crouching position, the .38 in his right hand, flashlight in his left. If the driver was alone, the thing was now cinched! But if there was somebody else in the car, somebody capable of fast, decisive action, a slip in the next ten seconds might cost him the sedan, and quite probably his freedom and life. Garfield lined up the .38's sights steadily on the center of the approaching man's head. He let his breath out slowly as the fellow came level with him in the road and squeezed off one shot.

Instantly he went bounding down the slope to the road. The bullet had flung the man sideways to the pavement. Garfield darted past him to the left, crossed the beam of the headlights, and was in darkness again on the far side of the road, snapping on his flashlight as he sprinted up to the car.

The motor hummed quietly on. The flashlight showed the seats empty. Garfield dropped the light, jerked both doors open in turn, gun pointing into the car's interior. Then he stood still for a moment, weak and almost dizzy with relief.

There was no one inside. The sedan was his.

The man he had shot through the head lay face down on the road, his hat flung a dozen feet away from him. Route Twelve still stretched out in dark silence to east and west. There should be time enough to clean up the job before anyone else came along. Garfield brought the suitcase down and put it on the front seat of the sedan, then started back to get his victim off the road and out of sight. He scaled the man's hat into the bushes, bent down, grasped the ankles and started to haul him towards the left side of the road where the ground dropped off sharply beyond the shoulder.

The body made a high, squealing sound and began to writhe violently.

Shocked, Garfield dropped the legs and hurriedly took the gun from his pocket, moving back a step. The squealing noise rose in intensity as the wounded man quickly flopped over twice like a struggling fish, arms and legs sawing about with startling energy. Garfield clicked off the safety, pumped three shots into his victim's back.

The grisly squeals ended abruptly. The body continued to jerk for another second or two, then lay still.

Garfield shoved the gun back into his pocket. The unexpected interruption had unnerved him; his hands shook as he reached down again for the stranger's ankles. Then he jerked his hands back, and straightened up, staring.

From the side of the man's chest, a few inches below the right arm, something like a thick black stick, three feet long, protruded now through the material of the coat.

It shone, gleaming wetly, in the light from the car. Even in that first uncomprehending instant, something in its appearance brought a surge of sick disgust to Garfield's throat. Then the stick bent slowly halfway down its length, forming a sharp angle, and its tip opened into what could have been three blunt, black claws which scrabbled clumsily against the pavement. Very faintly, the squealing began again, and the body's back arched up as if another sticklike arm were pushing desperately against the ground beneath it.

Garfield acted in a blur of horror. He emptied the .38 into the thing at his feet almost without realizing he was doing it. Then, dropping the gun, he seized one of the ankles, ran backwards to the shoulder of the road, dragging the body behind him.

In the darkness at the edge of the shoulder, he let go of it, stepped around to the other side and with two frantically savage kicks sent the body plunging over the shoulder and down the steep slope beyond. He heard it crash through the bushes for some seconds, then stop. He turned, and ran back to the sedan, scooping up his gun as he went past. He scrambled into the driver's seat and slammed the door shut behind him.

His hands shook violently on the steering wheel as he pressed down the accelerator. The motor roared into life and the big car surged forward. He edged it past the Packard, cursing aloud in horrified shock, jammed down the accelerator and went flashing up Route Twelve, darkness racing beside and behind him.

What had it been? Something that wore what seemed to be a man's body like a suit of clothes, moving the body as a man moves, driving a man's car . . . roach-armed, roach-legged itself!

Garfield drew a long, shuddering breath. Then, as he slowed for a curve, there was a spark of reddish light in the rear-view mirror.

He stared at the spark for an instant, braked the car to a stop, rolled down the window and looked back.

Far behind him along Route Twelve, a fire burned. Approximately at the point where the Packard had stalled out, where something had gone rolling off the road into the bushes . . .

Something, Garfield added mentally, that found fiery automatic destruction when death came to it, so that its secrets would remain unrevealed.

But for him the fire meant the end of a nightmare. He rolled the window up, took out a cigarette, lit it, and pressed the accelerator . . .

In incredulous fright, he felt the nose of the car tilt upwards, headlights sweeping up from the road into the trees.

Then the headlights winked out. Beyond the windshield, dark tree branches floated down towards him, the night sky beyond. He reached frantically for the door handle.

A steel wrench clamped silently about each of his arms, drawing them in against his sides, immobilizing them there. Garfield gasped, looked up at the mirror and saw a pair of faintly gleaming red eyes watching him from the rear of the car. Two of the things . . . the second one stood behind him out of sight, holding him. They'd been in what had seemed to be the trunk compartment. And they had come out.

The eyes in the mirror vanished. A moist, black roach-arm reached over the back of the seat beside Garfield, picked up the cigarette he had dropped, extinguished it with rather horribly human motions, then took up Garfield's gun and drew back out of sight.

He expected a shot, but none came.

One doesn't fire a bullet through the suit one intends to wear . . .

It wasn't until that thought occurred to him that tough Phil Garfield began to scream. He was still screaming minutes later when, beyond the windshield, the spaceship floated into view among the stars.

THE GUY WITH THE EYES
Spider Robinson

*This was the first story Spider Robinson ever published, pulled out of
the* Analog *slush pile by editor Ben Bova way back in 1973. You can
immediately see why: it's the sort of debut story every author wishes
for, instantly memorable, vivid, inventive, and a perfect introduction to
everything readers have loved about both Robinson and his Callahan's
Place stories for the past fifty years.*

*Callahan's Place is a dive bar like any other—and unlike any other.
Your favorite drink is always on tap, the patrons always are ready to
lend a sympathetic ear, and the right solutions to whatever ails you—
no matter how cosmic in scope—are close at hand. Toss in Spider
Robinson's deliciously written prose and wry sense of humor, add ice,
shake twice, and savor every sip.*

Callahan's Place was pretty lively that night. Talk fought Budweiser
for mouth space all over the joint, and the beer nuts supply was
critical. But this guy managed to keep himself in a corner without
being noticed for nearly an hour. I only spotted him myself a few
minutes before all the action started, and I make a point of studying
everybody at Callahan's Place.

First thing, I saw those eyes. You get used to some haunted eyes
in Callahan's—the newcomers have 'em—but these reminded me of
a guy I knew once in Topeka, who got four people with an antique
revolver before they cut him down.

I hoped like hell he'd visit the fireplace before he left.

197

If you've never been to Callahan's Place, God's pity on you. Seek it in the wilds of Suffolk County, but look not for neon. A simple, hand-lettered sign illuminated by a single floodlight, and a heavy oaken door split in the center (by the head of one Big Beef McCaffrey in 1947) and poorly repaired.

Inside, several heresies.

First, the light is about as bright as you keep your living room. Callahan maintains that people who like to drink in caves are unstable.

Second, there's a flat rate. Every drink in the house is half a buck, with the option. The option operates as follows:

You place a one-dollar bill on the bar. If all you have on you is a fin, you trot across the street to the all-night deli, get change, come back and put a one-dollar bill on the bar. (Callahan maintains that nobody in his right mind would counterfeit one-dollar bills; most of us figure he just likes to rub fistfuls of them across his face after closing.)

You are served your poison-of-choice. You inhale this, and confront the option. You may, as you leave, pick up two quarters from the always full cigarbox at the end of the bar and exit into the night. Or you may, upon finishing your drink, stride up to the chalk line in the middle of the room, announce a toast (this is mandatory) and hurl your glass into the huge, old-fashioned fireplace which takes up most of the back wall. You then depart without visiting the cigarbox. Or, pony up another buck and exercise your option again.

Callahan seldom has to replenish the cigarbox. He orders glasses in such quantities that they cost him next to nothing, and he sweeps out the fireplace himself every morning.

Another heresy: no one watches you with accusing eyes to make sure you take no more quarters than you have coming to you. If Callahan ever happens to catch someone cheating him, he personally ejects them forever. Sometimes he doesn't open the door first. The last time he had to eject someone was in 1947, a gentleman named Big Beef McCaffrey.

Not too surprisingly, it's a damned interesting place to be. It's the kind of place you hear about only if you need to—and if you are very lucky. Because if a patron, having proposed his toast and smithereened his glass, feels like talking about the nature of his troubles, he receives the instant, undivided attention of everyone in the room. (That's why the toast is obligatory. Many a man with a hurt locked inside finds in the act of naming his hurt for the toast that he wants very much to talk about it. Callahan is one smart hombre.) On the other hand, even the most tantalizingly cryptic toast will bring no prying inquiries if the guy displays no desire to uncork. Anyone attempting to flout this custom is promptly blackjacked by Fast Eddie the piano player and dumped in the alley.

But somehow many do feel like spilling it in a place like Callahan's; and you can get a deeper insight into human nature in a week there than in ten years anywhere else I know. You can also quite likely find solace for most any kind of trouble, from Callahan himself if no one else. It's a rare hurt that can stand under the advice, help, and sympathy generated by upwards of thirty people that *care*. Callahan loses a lot of his regulars. After they've been coming around long enough, they find they don't need to drink any more.

It's that kind of a bar.

I don't want you to get a picture of Callahan's Place as an agonized, Alcoholics Anonymous type of group-encounter session, with Callahan as some sort of salty psychoanalyst-father-figure in the foreground. Hell, many's the toast provokes roars of laughter, or a shouted chorus of agreement, or a unanimous blitz of glasses from all over the room when the night is particularly spirited. Callahan is tolerant of rannygazoo; he maintains that a bar should be" merry," so long as no bones are broken unintentionally. I mind the time he helped Spud Flynn set fire to a seat cushion to settle a bet on which way the draft was coming. Callahan exudes, at all times, a kind of monolithic calm; and U.S.40 is shorter than his temper.

This night I'm telling you about, for instance, was nothing if not merry. When I pulled in around ten o'clock, there was an unholy shambles of a square dance going on in the middle of the floor. I laid a dollar on the bar, collected a glass of Tullamore Dew and a hello-grin from Callahan, and settled back in a tall chair—Callahan abhors barstools—to observe the goings-on. That's what I mean about Callahan's Place: most bars, men only dance if there're ladies around. Of one sex or another.

I picked some familiar faces out of the maelstrom of madmen

weaving and lurching over honest-to-God saw-dust, and waved a few greetings. There was Tom Flannery, who at that time had eight months to live, and knew it; he laughed a lot at Callahan's Place. There was Slippery Joe Maser, who had two wives, and Marty Matthias, who didn't gamble any more, and Noah Gonzalez, who worked on Suffolk County's bomb squad. Calling for the square dance while performing a creditable Irish jig was Doc Webster, fat and jovial as the day he pumped the pills out of my stomach and ordered me to Callahan's. See, I used to have a wife and daughter before I decided to install my own brakes. I saved thirty dollars, easy...

The Doc left the square-dancers to their fate—their creative individuality making a caller superfluous—and drifted over like a pink zeppelin to say hello. His stethoscope hung unnoticed from his ears, framing a smile like a sunlamp. The end of the 'scope was in his drink.

"Howdy, Doc. Always wondered how you kept that damned thing so cold," I greeted him.

He blinked like an owl with the staggers and looked down at the gently bubbling pickup beneath two fingers of scotch. Emitting a bellow of laughter at about force eight, he removed the gleaming thing and shook it experimentally.

"My secret's out, Jake. Keep it under your hat, will you?" he boomed.

"Maybe you better keep it under yours," I suggested. He appeared to consider this idea for a time, while I speculated on one of life's greatest paradoxes: Sam Webster, M.D. The Doc is good for a couple of quarts of Peter Dawson a night, three or four nights a week. But you won't find a better sawbones anywhere on Earth, and those sausage fingers of his can move like a tap-dancing centipede when they have to, with nary a tremor. Ask Shorty Steinitz to tell you about the time Doc Webster took out his appendix on top of Callahan's bar... while Callahan calmly kept the Scotch coming.

"At least then I could hear myself think," the Doc finally replied, and several people seated within earshot groaned theatrically.

"Have a heart, Doc," one called out.

"What a re-pulse-ive idea," the Doc returned the serve.

"Well, I know when I'm beat," said the challenger, and made as if to turn away.

"Why, you young whelp, aorta poke you one," roared the Doc, and the bar exploded with laughter and cheers. Callahan picked up a beer bottle in his huge hand and pegged it across the bar at the Doc's round skull. The beer bottle, being made of foam rubber, bounced gracefully into the air and landed in the piano, where Fast Eddie sat locked in mortal combat with the "C-Jam Blues."

Fast Eddie emitted a sound like an outraged transmission and kept right on playing, though his upper register was shot. "Little beer never hoit a piano," he sang out as he reached the bridge, and went over it like he figured to burn it behind him.

All in all it looked like a cheerful night, but then I saw the Janssen kid come in and I knew there was a trouble brewing.

This Janssen kid—look, I can't knock long hair, I wore mine long when it wasn't fashionable. And I can't knock pot for the same reason. But nobody I know ever had a good thing to say for heroin. Certainly not Joe Hennessy, who did two weeks in the hospital last year after he surprised the Janssen kid scooping junk-money out of his safe at four in the morning. Old Man Janssen paid Hennessy back every dime and disowned the kid, and he'd been in and out of sight ever since. Word was he was still using the stuff, but the cops never seemed to catch him holding. They sure did try, though. I wondered what the hell he was doing in Callahan's Place.

I should know better by now. He placed a tattered bill on the bar, took the shot of bourbon which Callahan handed him silently, and walked to the chalk line. He was quivering with repressed tension, and his boots squeaked on the sawdust. The place quieted down some, and his toast—"To smack !"—rang out clear and crisp. Then he downed the shot amid an expanding silence and flung his glass so hard you could hear his shoulder crack just before the glass shattered on unyielding brick.

Having created silence, he broke it. With a sob. Even as he let it out he glared around to see what our reactions were.

Callahan's was immediate, an "Amen!" that sounded like an echo of the smashing glass. The kid made a face like he was somehow satisfied in spite of himself, and looked at the rest of us. His gaze rested on Doc Webster, and the Doc drifted over and gently began rolling up the kid's sleeves. The boy made no effort to help or hinder him. When they were both rolled to the shoulder—phosphorescent purple I think they were—he silently held out his arms, palm-up.

They were absolutely unmarked. Skinny as hell and white as a piece of paper, but unmarked. The kid was clean.

Everyone waited in silence, giving the kid their respectful attention. It was a new feeling to him, and he didn't quite know how to handle it. Finally he said, "I heard about this place," just a little too truculently.

"Then you must of needed to," Callahan told him quietly, and the kid nodded slowly.

"I hear you get some answers in, from time to time," he half-asked.

"Now and again," Callahan admitted. "Some o' the damndest questions, too. What's it like, for instance?"

"You mean smack?"

"I don't mean bourbon." The kid's eyes got a funny, far-away look, and he almost smiled.

"It's . . ." He paused, considering. "It's like . . . being dead."

"Whooee!" came a voice from across the room. "That's a powerful good feeling indeed." I looked and saw it was Chuck Samms talking, and watched to see how the kid would take it.

He thought Chuck was being sarcastic and snapped back, "Well, what the hell do you know about it anyway?" Chuck smiled. A lot of people ask him that question, in a different tone of voice.

"Me?" he said, enjoying himself hugely. "Why, I've been dead is all."

"S'truth," Callahan confirmed as the kid's jaw dropped. "Chuck there was legally dead for five minutes before the Doc got his pacemaker going again. The crumb died owing me money, and I never had the heart to dun his widow."

"Sure was a nice feeling, too," Chuck said around a yawn." More peaceful than nap-time in a monastery. If it wasn't so pleasant I wouldn't be near so damned scared of it." There was an edge to his voice as he finished, but it disappeared as he added softly, "What the hell would you want to be dead for?"

The Janssen kid couldn't meet his eyes, and when he spoke his voice cracked. "Like you said, pop, peace. A little peace of mind, a little quiet. Nobody yammering at you all the time. I mean, if you're dead there's always the chance somebody'll mourn, right? Make friends with the worms, dig their side of it, maybe a little poltergeist action, who knows? I mean, what's the sense of talking about it, anyway? Didn't any of you guys ever just want to run away?"

"Sure thing," said Callahan. "Sometimes I do it too. But I generally run someplace I can find my way back from." It was said so gently that the kid couldn't take offense, though he tried.

"Run away from what, son?" asked Slippery Joe.

The kid had been bottled up tight too long; he exploded. "From what?" he yelled. "Jesus, where do I start? There was this war they wanted me to go and fight, see? And there's this place called college, I mean they want you to care, dig it, care about this education trip, and they don't care enough themselves to make it as attractive as the crap game across the street. There's this air I hear is unfit to breathe, and water that ain't fit to drink, and food that wouldn't nourish a vulture and a grand outlook for the future. You can't get to a job without the car you couldn't afford to run even if you were working, and if you *found* a job it'd pay five dollars less than the rent. The TV advertises karate classes for four-year-olds and up, the President's New Clothes didn't wear very well, the next Depression's around the corner and you ask me what in the name of God I'm running from?

"Man, I've been straight for seven months, what I mean, and in that seven god damned months I have been over this island like a fungus and there is *nothing* for me. No jobs, no friends, no place to live long enough to get the floor dirty, no money, and nobody that doesn't point and say 'Junkie' when I go by for seven *months* and you ask me what am I running from? Man, *everything* is all, just everything."

It was right then that I noticed that guy in the corner, the one with the eyes. Remember him? He was leaning forward in rapt attention, his mouth a black slash in a face pulled tight as a drumhead. Those ghastly eyes of his never left the Janssen kid, but somehow I was sure that his awareness included all of us, everyone in the room.

And no one had an answer for the Janssen boy. I could see, all around the room, men who had learned to *listen* at Callahan's Place, men who had learned to empathize, to want to understand and share the pain of another. And no one had a word to say. They were thinking past the blurted words of a haunted boy, wondering if this crazy world of confusion might not after all be one holy hell of a place to grow up. Most of them already had reason to know damn well that society never forgives the sinner, but they were realizing to their dismay how thin and uncomforting the straight and narrow has become these last few years.

Sure, they'd heard these things before, often enough to make them into cliches. But now I could see the boys reflecting that these were the cliches that made a young man say he liked to feel dead, and the same thought was mirrored on the face of each of them: *My God, when did we let these things become cliches!* The Problems of Today's Youth were no longer a Sunday supplement or a news broadcast or anything so remote and intangible, they had suddenly become a dirty, shivering boy who told us that in this world we had built for him with our sweat and our blood he was not only tired of living, but so scared of dying that he did it daily, sometimes, for recreation.

And silence held court in Callahan's Place. No one had a single thing to say, and that guy with the eyes seemed to know it, and to derive some crazy kind of bitter inner satisfaction from the knowledge. He started to settle back in his chair, when Callahan broke the silence.

"So run," he said.

Just like that, flat, no expression, just, "So run." It hung there for about ten seconds, while he and the kid locked eyes.

The kid's forehead started to bead with sweat. Slowly, with shaking fingers, he reached under his leather vest to his shirt pocket. Knuckles white, he hauled out a flat, shiny black case about four inches by two. His eyes never left Callahan's as he opened it and held it up so that we could all see the gleaming hypodermic. It didn't look like it had ever been used; he must have just stolen it.

He held it up to the light for a moment, looking up his bare, unmarked arm at it, and then he whirled and flung it case and all into the giant fireplace. Almost as it shattered he sent a cellophane bag of white powder after it, and the powder burned green while the sudden stillness hung in the air. The guy with the eyes looked oddly stricken in some interior way, and he sat absolutely rigid in his seat.

And Callahan was around the bar in an instant, handing the Janssen kid a beer that grew out of his fist and roaring, "Welcome home, Tommy!" and no one in the place was very startled to realize that only Callahan of all of us knew the kid's first name.

We all sort of swarmed around then and swatted the kid on the arm some and he even cried a little until we poured some beer over his head and pretty soon it began to look like the night was going to get merry again after all.

And that's when the guy with the eyes stood up, and everybody in the joint shut up and turned to look at him. That sounds melodramatic, but it's the effect he had on us. When he moved, he was the center of attention. He was tall, unreasonably tall, near seven foot, and I'll never know why we hadn't all noticed him right off. He was dressed in a black suit that fit worse than a Joliet Special, and his shoes didn't look right either. After a moment you realized that he had the left shoe on the right foot, and vice versa, but it didn't surprise you. He was thin and deeply tanned and his mouth was twisted up tight but mostly he was eyes, and I still dream of those eyes and wake up sweating now and again. They were like windows into hell, the very personal and private hell of a man faced with a dilemma he cannot resolve. They did not blink, not once.

He shambled to the bar, and something was wrong with his walk, too, like he was walking sideways on the wall with magnetic shoes and hadn't quite caught the knack yet. He took ten new singles out of his jacket pocket—which struck me as an odd place to keep cash—and laid them on the bar.

Callahan seemed to come back from a far place, and hustled around behind the bar again. He looked the stranger up and down and then placed ten shot glasses on the counter. He filled each with rye and stood back silently, running a big red hand through his thinning hair and regarding the stranger with clinical interest.

The dark giant tossed off the first shot, shuffled to the chalk line, and said in oddly-accented English, "To my profession," and hurled the glass into the fireplace.

Then he walked back to the bar and repeated the entire procedure. Ten times.

By the last glass, brick was chipping in the fireplace.

When the last, "To my profession," echoed in empty air, he turned and faced us. He waited, tensely, for question or challenge. There was none. He half turned away, paused, then swung back and took a couple of deep breaths. When he spoke his voice made you hurt to hear it.

"My profession, gentlemen," he said with that funny accent I couldn't place," is that of advance scout. For a race whose home is many light-years from here. Many, many light-years from here." He paused, looking for our reactions.

Well, I thought, *ten whiskeys and he's a Martian. Indeed. Pleased to meet you, I'm Popeye the Sailor.* I guess it was pretty obvious we were all thinking the same way, because he looked tired and said, "It would take far more ethanol than that to befuddle me, gentlemen." Nobody said a word to that, and he turned to Callahan. "You know I am not intoxicated," he stated.

Callahan considered him professionally and said finally, "Nope. You're not tight. I'll be a son of a bitch, but you're not tight."

The stranger nodded thanks, spoke thereafter directly to Callahan. "I am here now three days. In two hours I shall be finished. When I am finished I shall go home. After I have gone your planet will be vaporized. I have accumulated data which will ensure the annihilation of your species when they are assimilated by my Masters. To them, you will seem as cancerous cells, in danger of infecting all you touch. You will not be permitted to exist. You will be *cured*. And I repent me of my profession."

Maybe I wouldn't have believed it anywhere else. But at Callahan's Place *anything* can happen. Hell, we all believed him. Fast Eddie sang out, "Anyt'ing we can do about it?" and he was serious for sure. You can tell with Fast Eddie.

"I am helpless," the giant alien said dispassionately. "I contain... installations... which are beyond my influencing—or yours. They have recorded all the data I have perceived in these three days; in two hours a preset mechanism will be triggered and will transmit their contents to the Masters." I looked at my watch: it was eleven-fifteen. "The conclusions of the Masters are foregone. I cannot prevent the transmission; I cannot even attempt to. I am counter-programmed."

"Why are you in this line of work if it bugs you so much?" Callahan wanted to know. No hostility, no panic. He was trying to *understand*.

"I am accustomed to take pride in my work," the alien said. "I make safe the paths of the Masters. They must not be threatened by warlike species. I go before, to identify danger, and see to its neutralization. It is a good profession, I think. I thought."

"What changed your mind?" asked Doc Webster sympathetically.

"This place, this . . . 'bar' place we are in—this is not like the rest I have seen. Outside are hatred, competition, morals elevated to the status of ethics, prejudices elevated to the status of morals, whims elevated to the status of prejudices, all things with which I am wearily familiar, the classic symptoms of disease.

"But here is difference. Here in this place I sense qualities, attributes I did not know your species possessed, attributes which everywhere else in the known universe are mutually exclusive of the things I have perceived here tonight. They are good things . . . they cause me great anguish for your passing. They fill me with hurt.

"Oh, that I might lay down my geas," he cried. "I did not know that you had love!"

In the echoing stillness, Callahan said simply, "Sure we do, son. It's mebbe spread a little thin these days, but we've got it all right. Sure would be a shame if it all went up in smoke." He looked down at the rye bottle he still held in his big hand, and absently drank off a couple ounces. "Any chance that your masters might feel the same way?"

"None. Even I can still see that you must be destroyed if the Masters are to be safe. But for the first time in some thousands of years, I regret my profession. I fear I can do no more."

"No way you can gum up the works ?"

"None. So long as I am alive and conscious, the transmission will take place. I could not assemble the volition to stop it. I have said: I am counter-programmed."

I saw Noah Gonzalez' expression soften, heard him say, "Geez, buddy, that's hard lines." A mumbled agreement rose, and Callahan nodded slowly.

"That's tough, brother. I wouldn't want to be in your shoes."

He looked at us with absolute astonishment, the hurt in those terrible eyes of his mixed now with bewilderment. Shorty handed him another drink and it was like he didn't know what to do with it.

"You tell us how much it will take, mister," Shorty said respectfully, "and we'll get you drunk."

The tall man with star-burned skin groaned from deep within himself and backed away until the fireplace contained him. He and the flames ignored each other, and no one found it surprising.

"What is your matter?" he cried. "Why are you not destroying me? You fools, you need only destroy me and you are saved. I am your judge. I am your jury. I will be your executioner."

"You didn't ask for the job," Shorty said gently. "It ain't your doing."

"But you do not understand! If my data are not transmitted, the Masters will assume my destruction and avoid this system forever. Only the equal or superior of a Master could overcome my defenses, but I *can* control *them*. I will not use them. Do you comprehend me? I will not activate my defenses—you can destroy me and save yourselves and your species, and I will not hinder you.

"Kill me!" he shrieked.

There was a long, long pause, maybe a second or two, and then Callahan pointed to the drink Shorty still held out and growled, "You better drink that, friend. You need it. Talkin' of killin' in my joint. Wash your mouth out with bourbon and get outta that fireplace, I want to use it."

"Yeah, me too!" came the cry on all sides, and the big guy looked like he was gonna cry. Conversations started up again and Fast Eddie began playing "I Don't Want to Set the World On Fire," in very bad taste indeed.

Some of the boys wandered thoughtfully out, going home to tell their families, or settle their affairs. The rest of us, lacking either concern, drifted over to console the alien. I mean, where else would I want to be on Judgment Day?

He was sitting down, now, with booze of all kinds on the table before him. He looked up at us like a wounded giant. But none of us knew how to begin, and Callahan spoke first.

"You never did tell us your name, friend."

The alien looked startled, and he sat absolutely still, rigid as a fence post, for a long, long moment. His face twisted up awful, as though he was waging some titanic inner battle with himself, and cords of muscle stood up on his neck in what didn't seem to be the right places. Doc Webster began to talk to himself softly.

Then the alien went all blue and shivered like a steel cable under strain, and very suddenly relaxed all over with an audible gasp. He twitched his shoulders experimentally a few times, like he was making sure they were still there, and then he turned to Callahan and said, clear as a bell, "My name is Michael Finn."

It hung in the air for a very long time, while we all stood petrified, suspended.

Then Callahan's face split in a wide grin, and he bellowed, "Why of course! Why yes, yes of course, Mickey Finn. I didn't recognize you for a moment, Mr. Finn," as he trotted behind the bar. His big hands worked busily beneath the counter, and as he emerged with a tall glass of dark fluid the last of us got it. We made way eagerly as Callahan set the glass down before the alien, and stood back with the utmost deference and respect.

He regarded us for a moment, and to see his eyes now was to feel warm and proud. For all the despair and guilt and anguish and horror and most of all the hopelessness were gone from them now, and they were just eyes. Just like yours and mine.

Then he raised his glass and waited, and we all drank with him. Before the last glass was empty his head hit the table like an anvil, and we had to pick him up and carry him to the back room where Callahan keeps a cot, and you know, he was *heavy*.

And he snored in three stages.

CARTER'S DOG
Allen Steele

Be they the beamjacks of his novel Orbital Decay, *or the technicians and laborers of an undersea base in* Oceansphere, *Allen Steele has a knack for crafting tales of extraordinary futures of ordinary men, as well a gift for delightful retro scifi throwbacks like "The Death of Captain Future" and "The Emperor of Mars," which earned Allen two of his Hugo Awards.*

For our second original story in the anthology, Allen has given us a story about a man and his dog Houdini, who is an unusually expressive and intelligent dog at that. Of course, every dog owner thinks that about their dog… though as Houdini shall quickly prove, he's got more than enough tricks to live up to his name.

Carter didn't find the dog so much as it found him. Later, he discovered the difference was subtle yet nonetheless important. It wasn't that he'd gone searching for Houdini; it was more that Houdini had been waiting for him.

Some animal had been rooting through the garbage bins out by the carport. The last few mornings he'd found the tall plastic containers overturned, discarded food wrappers and used coffee filters and assorted other kitchen debris scattered about the side of his house near the kitchen door. The bins were supposed to be animal-proof, resistant to the raccoons and possums that occasionally emerged from the nearby woods at night to raid his trash, so whatever had done this was bigger and smarter than them, and larger animals like coyotes and bears only seldom visited his small-town Massachusetts neighborhood.

Oddly, the recycling bin—nearly identical except it was dark blue and had the recyclables trefoil stamped on its sides—went untouched. Noticing this the second time his garbage was raided, Carter figured there must not have been anything among the discarded newspapers and soft drink cans that smelled tempting. All the same, it seemed strange that particular bin had been left alone, not even explored.

After the second time his trash was raided, Carter went next door to see if his neighbors Warren and Angela had seen anything. Warren told him that he'd spotted a black dog loafing about the neighborhood; it wasn't one he recognized as belonging to anyone else on the street, nor did it appear to be wearing a collar. Probably a stray living in the woods who'd taken to rooting through garbage when he couldn't catch any squirrels or rabbits; no wonder, since autumn was almost over and most small undomesticated animals had gone into hibernation for the winter.

Carter decided to put a stop to it. He didn't want to do anything cruel, though, like leaving out poison, nor would he have shot it even if he'd owned a gun. Although he could've called the town animal control officer and had him come over to lay traps or something, on further reflection he realized, if he was caught, the dog would probably just end up in a pound, and if no one claimed it after a few days, the dog would be put to sleep. Carter didn't want to be responsible for having a death sentence given to some poor mutt just for rummaging through his garbage, so he decided to handle the matter himself, as humanely as possible.

Two nights later, the next time he took out the garbage, Carter removed the five-gallon plastic bag from the kitchen waste can, knotted the liner's drawstrings, then carried it out the side door to the place near the carport where the garbage and recycling bins awaited the weekly Wednesday morning pickup. But instead of immediately going back inside, Carter unfolded a camp chair under the carport's low roof, carefully positioning it so that he'd be hidden by the back of his Volvo, upwind of the cans and not within the light cast through the kitchen window. Then he sat out in the darkened carport, bundled up in a parka, cap, and gloves, reading a James Rollins thriller on his Kindle as he staked out his garbage cans with the quietly determined patience of a narcotics cop waiting for a neighborhood dope dealer. The night was cool but comfortable, and he figured he could stay out here for as long as needed.

Carter didn't have to wait very long. He'd just finished the first chapter and was a few pages into the second when his ears picked up something quietly moving in the darkened backyard not far from the carport. He didn't move a muscle. Still holding the ebook reader open in his lap, Carter fastened his gaze upon the garbage cans. They stood together just outside the carport, visible to him by the light cast from the kitchen window. A minute went by, and then another, and then the dog appeared.

The dog was not small but not very large either, taller than a border collie or a terrier but not quite as big as a Labrador retriever or a German shepherd. The dog was definitely a male; one glance at his hindquarters told Carter that he hadn't been neutered. His ears lay flat against the sides of a large head with a broad cranium and a long, slender snout, sort of like a cross between a bulldog and a hound. His fur was coal black, long without being shaggy or matted, completely dark with the exception of a white diamond on his chest. His paws were unusually wide, the toes invisible within thick thatches of black fur that padded every step he took, making him as stealthy as a fox. The furriest part of his body was his long tail, half-raised above his rear end like a shaggy black flag.

It was the dog's eyes, though, that really caught Carter's attention: deep, dark pupils surrounded by lovely silver-blue irises, both soulful and stunning. As the dog treaded softly toward the garbage bins, his eyes captured and reflected the light from the kitchen window, causing them to glow with an eerie luminescence. And when he stopped just short of the bins to turn his head and give the carport a quick look-around, Carter perceived within those eyes an intelligence that was beyond normal. This was a smart dog, streetwise and crafty, and nobody's pet.

When the dog didn't spot Carter sitting behind the car, he kept moving toward the bins. Carter waited silently until the dog reached the garbage. He was big enough to hop up on his hind legs and place his forepaws on the bin's closed lid. He had just begun to rock it back and forth when Carter jumped out from behind the car and yelled, "Hey! Hey, get outta here!"

The dog's head snapped around toward Carter and he immediately dropped back down on all fours. But yet, although he backed away from the bin, he didn't turn tail and dash off, as every other dog Carter had ever seen would've done. Instead, he stood his ground, placidly gazing back at the rightful owner of all that tempting garbage.

"Go on!" Carter shouted as he stepped around the Volvo, loudly clapping his hands. "Beat it! Scram." The dog still wouldn't move. "I mean it!" Carter yelled again as he kept walking toward him, clapping his hands again and again. "G'wan, get outta here! Move it or I'll get a stick!"

The dog still didn't run off. Instead, it sat down on its haunches, forepaws primly close together, tail gently waving back and forth as he calmly regarded Carter. Not arrogant, but not afraid either.

Carter was astounded. "Man, you got some balls," he murmured. As if he understood, the dog's mouth opened and a long red tongue lolled out, a canine grin if there had ever been one. "Look, that's mine, not yours," Carter went on, trying again to assert human authority. "I don't want you messing with it, okay?"

The dog stood up once more, but he didn't leave. Instead, he slowly but purposefully walked over to where Carter was standing, never taking his eyes off the man confronting him. Carter was surprised and, for a moment or two, afraid. But the dog's tail raised higher and continued to wag back and forth, and when he reached Carter, he indolently stretched out his forelegs, lowered the front of his body in a playful canine bow, then stood up straight and, still looking straight at him, let out a quick, friendly bark whose meaning was clear: *Hello, how are you? Want to make friends?*

"Oh man," Carter said, "you really do have some nerve, don't you?" The dog straightened up and took the last two steps he needed to take before reaching him. The dog's head was level with Carter's groin, yet there was no sign that he intended to bite a very sensitive part of him. Instead, he continued to gaze up at him with solemn friendliness, panting just a little, his tail swishing back and forth.

Carter slowly raised his right hand and hesitantly held it out, palm down, so that the dog could get his scent. The dog closed his mouth and stretched his muzzle forward to give his hand a perfunctory sniff. His nose brushed the back of Carter's fingers, cool and just a little moist, and yet this was more of a formality than anything else. It appeared that the dog had already accepted the man he'd just met as a friend.

Carefully, ready to yank back his hand at the first sign of trouble, Carter reached up to pat the top of the dog's head. His grin became a little larger and he panted a little harder; his ears raised, and his head tilted to one side, inviting Carter below his ears. No, the mutt wasn't hostile at all. He wanted the human he'd just met to accept him as a new pal, maybe even form a lasting friendship.

As Carter obliged him by gently scratching his neck, he noticed the dog wasn't wearing a collar, nor was there a faint furrow about his neck that would've indicated that he'd once worn one. The dog was a stray, yes, but not feral; he was well socialized, as if someone had once owned him and trained him to be accommodating to strangers. Yet he must be hungry; Carter could see his ribs through the fur along its sides, and he had little doubt that the dog was probably dehydrated as well.

"Tell you what," Carter said quietly, squatting down to look the dog straight in the eye, "if I give you something to eat, will you promise to stop going through my garbage? Do we have a deal?"

As if the dog had understood every word, he gave a short, enthusiastic bark: *Okay! It's a deal! Let's eat!* And when Carter stood up to walk to the kitchen door, intending to find the uneaten half of a tuna-and-cheese sub from Subway he'd brought home earlier that day, the dog unhesitatingly followed him through the door, into his house, and into his life.

That was how Carter met Houdini. Later, he'd wonder whether his kindness had been a mistake.

A few days after he took the dog in, Carter decided to give him the name Houdini, after Harry Houdini, the famous stage magician and escapist of the early twentieth century. By then, he had good reasons for making that choice.

The day after he found the dog, Carter took a few hours away from his desk—once the Covid-19 lockdown was over, his employer had allowed him to continue working out of his house—to try finding the dog's owners, assuming that he'd been lost by someone living in the same neighborhood. Searching the attic, he found an old leather dog collar and leash that his former wife had left behind when she walked out of his life, taking their dog with him; he missed one of them. The stray dog may have come to him collarless, but he didn't object when Carter put it around his neck and fastened its brass buckle, nor was he opposed to Carter attaching the four-foot nylon leash. In fact, the dog must have figured out what he meant to do, for when Carter left the dog downstairs hallway to go back up to his bedroom and get his wallet and keys, he came back to find the dog sitting patiently at the front door, giving him an expectant look: *Well, are you ready? I don't have all day, y'know.*

Again, it was as if the dog was communicating with him, a clear but silent voice in his mind, expressing replies to unspoken thoughts Carter just had. The dog wasn't just smart, he was also amazingly empathic, able to interpret human actions, facial expressions, and even body language, and respond in the correct way. This led Carter to conclude that the dog hadn't simply been lost; he'd deliberately run away from whoever owned him.

Yet as he escorted the dog door to door, block by block, and street by street all through the semirural neighborhood where he lived, he discovered that no one recognized the dog, let alone would claim him as their pet. Three people recognized him as the stray mutt whom they'd recently chased away from their own garbage. One little boy, infatuated with the dog, immediately wrapped his arms around his neck and childishly lied that the dog belonged to him. But his mother looked at Carter and quietly shook her head, and in the end, she had to pry her son loose from the doggie and pull him crying and screaming back inside. The dog was relieved; he actually sighed as Carter led him away.

Throughout the neighborhood, Carter found copies of a lost dog flyer stapled to telephone poles, but the snapshot of the missing dog, Charley, looked nothing like the dog Carter had found. When Carter called town hall and spoke to a police officer, the description he gave sounded nothing like any of the dogs that had been lately reported missing in town. There was nothing about a lost dog in the classified ads of his local newspaper, and when Carter posted a notice himself, no one called to ask about the dog he carefully described in the ad.

In the end, Carter had a choice: take the dog to the nearest animal shelter and give him up for adoption or adopt the dog himself. By then, the dog had grown on him. He ate whatever Carter put in front of him without fuss or complaint. He was already housebroken and signaled by pacing back and forth whenever he needed to go out. He slept on a throw rug at the foot of Carter's bed but figured out when Carter usually got up and took to hopping onto the bed and playfully licking his face just before the alarm clock went off. He didn't bark unnecessarily but instead stayed quiet most of the time, loyally staying by Carter's side and moving with him whenever he walked to another room.

Yet there were also some weird things about the dog. He watched TV with rapt attention, lying on his belly with his ears cocked straight up, studying everything on the screen whether it was the evening news, *Jeopardy*, an episode of a *Star Trek* show, or a classic detective movie on TCM. And when he wasn't engaged in anything else, he'd sit on the living room couch, which rested beneath the front window, and watch the sidewalk intently, ignoring cars but paying close attention to every person who walked or jogged by. Quite a few people used his street for exercise, and some of them walked their dogs. Carter's dog wasn't interested at all in people, and he never barked or growled at anyone, but he stared at other dogs with such silent intensity that many of them would notice. When they did, they either became infuriated and would lunge to the ends of their leashes, barking and snapping, until their owners managed to pull them away. Or they would immediately cower, their tails dropping between their legs as they shied away from the strange, staring dog in the wind, so fearful that sometimes they'd urinate then and there, the piss literally scared out of them.

Carter became concerned about this. He had no idea why his dog was behaving this way, but he was worried that it might cause trouble while he was alone in the house, so the next time he went out to do some errands he led the dog back upstairs and put him in his bedroom. Carter left a full bowl of water for him to drink, gave him a pat on the head, and told him he'd be home soon, then shut the door. There were no other doors into the bedroom save the one to the adjacent bathroom, and the only other way out was through a second-story window that was locked shut and weather-sealed for the winter.

Feeling a little foolish for being so cautious, Carter left the house.

He half-expected to hear the dog whimpering or scratching at the door, crying about being left alone and demanding to be let out, but he heard nothing. The dog had apparently resigned himself to being shut in for a little while. and that was that.

Carter was gone for a couple of hours. When he returned, he carried two bags of groceries from the car to the kitchen door, put them down, then used his house key to let himself in. And there was the dog, sitting on the kitchen floor calmly waiting for him. Seeing Carter's incredulous expression, the dog's mouth split into a wide, tongue-lolling grin. *I'm full of tricks, man,* he seemed to say. *A closed door means nothing to me.*

Incredulous, Carter went upstairs to the bedroom. Sure enough, the door was wide open. Yet there were no claw marks on the door or its frame, no drool on the doorknob, no clue as to how the dog had let himself out. The window was still sealed shut. Somehow, the dog had opened the door and walked out just as easily if he was human. He'd escaped a closed room, and for the life of him Carter couldn't figure out how he'd accomplished the feat.

That was why and when Carter gave his new dog the name Houdini.

Houdini wasn't the first dog Carter had. His first, of course, had been Prince, a German shepherd–black lab mix who'd been his companion through childhood and lived until Carter reached his teens; by then the dog was fifteen years old. Carter missed that old dog for the rest of his life, and always felt like he'd lost a brother the day he had to be put to sleep.

The next dog he had was Zack, the golden retriever mix whom he and his wife—his former wife, that is—adopted from an animal shelter shortly after they married and moved to the house he still owned. He'd loved Zack, too, but Zack always seemed to prefer his wife's company to his, so when she insisted on taking the dog with her when they divorced just three years later, Carter didn't fight it; he knew that Zack would be more upset by her departure than if he'd taken him when she went away, and it wasn't fair to make him stay if he didn't really want to remain with him. Still, he'd never forget the stunned look on the dog's face when his wife hauled him away by his collar to the moving van where the overaged jock whom she'd met at the gym waited to take both of them away. She could have the meathead and watch him get fat and lazy from all the beer he drank, but he realized too late that he should have fought to keep Zack.

So when Houdini came to him out of the October night, a hungry stray who clearly wanted to be brought in out of the cold, Carter was just as eager for companionship as the dog was. Obviously, it had always been in the back of his mind to eventually adopt another dog, for Zack's bed, food and water dishes, and even his toys were still in boxes down in the basement. Houdini took the bed and bowls as his own even though Zack's scent was undoubtedly still on them but ignored the toys as if such things were beneath him. Later, Carter would realize the significance of this.

When no one came forward to claim Houdini after a week, Carter began the process of officially adopting him. And since he'd need to have a rabies vaccination before Carter could obtain a tag from the town clerk—Carter had already learned from having Zack that his town had strict ordinances against unregistered dogs—the first step would be to take Houdini to a veterinarian for his shot. A routine medical exam wasn't a bad idea either.

Zack's vet was a middle-aged lady named Robin, a small-animal doctor who also took care of cats, rabbits, pot-bellied pigs, hedgehogs, baby box turtles, a boa constrictor, and even a South American iguana who'd been illegally smuggled into the U.S., don't ask how. She remembered Carter when he called to make an appointment and complimented him for being willing to take in a stray dog, but her eyes widened the moment Carter led Houdini into the examination room.

"Well, I'll be damned," she said, staring at the dog who passively regarded her with silver eyes. "Looks like you've found a Cumberland spook hound."

"A what?" Carter let go of Houdini's leash and let him walk over to Robin, who knelt down to offer him a dog cookie and let him give her a good sniff, which Houdini did in a disinterested manner, as if it was a formality he didn't care much about doing. Indeed, Houdini seemed to be more interested in her purple-and-silver dyed hair; he eyed her curiously, stepping closer to nuzzle her neck and the side of her head. "A Cumberland . . . what did you call him?"

"Cumberland spook hound." Now that Robin had introduced

herself, she scratched behind Houdini's ears as she began to look him over. "It's a new breed that's come out of nowhere over the last couple of years. They first showed up in Tennessee, on the Cumberland Plateau east of Nashville . . . rural farm country, not the sort of place you'd expect to find a new breed of anything except cattle." She cautiously brought her hands close to Houdini's mouth. "Here, boy . . . open up and let me look at your teeth."

Houdini didn't object at all when she gently pried open his jaws. "So why do they call them spook hounds?" Carter asked.

"'Cause they're spooky." Robin continued to closely look Houdini over. "Teeth look good. Ears are clean. They're always strays when someone finds them poking around in their garbage—"

"That's just how I found him."

"Typical. No one ever seems to own them. They're never wearing a collar and tags." Satisfied with what she'd found so far, Robin turned her attention to his back, belly, hips. "They appear to be a lab mix someone crossbred with other species. Someone at the University of Missouri vet school obtained a blood sample from a dog they picked up somewhere and ran a full DNA exam. They found black lab DNA along with several other species, everything from English foxhounds and Dobermans to ordinary beagles. It's like someone did controlled crossbreeding to create a new subspecies."

"Weird."

"You bet they're weird." She looked up at Carter. "Have you taken a close look at his paws since you've had him?"

"No. Why?"

"Come down here and take a look," she said, beckoning for him to come closer. Carter kneeled down beside her. "Look at this," she said as she grasped Houdini's left foreleg and gently turned it upward so that Carter could see the underside of the dog's large, thickly furred paw. "Good boy," Robin murmured to Houdini, then said to Carter, "Check it out. Notice anything?"

Carter peered at Houdini's paw. He'd noticed from the start that his paws seemed rather unproportionally large for a medium-size dog, like someone had grafted a St. Bernard's feet to a smaller dog's legs, but it wasn't until now that he'd given this part of Houdini's anatomy a closer look. At first, he didn't notice anything peculiar, but nonetheless something didn't look quite right. Then he saw it.

Houdini's paw had five toes. There were the usual two big toes in the middle of the paw, in front of the leaf-shaped pad at the center, with a small toe on either side of each big toe. Yet there was a third small toe on the inside of the paw, a fifth toe slightly larger than the fourth toe beside it.

"Five toes?" Carter said. Robin nodded. "Are there any other dogs like that?"

"A few breeds. Norwegian Lundehunds. Great Pyrenees. Rottweilers. Sometimes akitas. That extra toe is technically known as a polydactyl digit, commonly called a dewclaw. But when a dog has five toes, it's usually in the middle of the paw, between the two big toes . . . right here." Robin pointed to an imaginary location between the two middle toes. "They're in certain breeds to help balance their body mass, but until now no one has ever seen a dog with a polydactyl on the inside of the paw."

"Yeah . . . yeah, that is strange." Carter studied Houdini's leathery, oval-shaped toes for another moment. "Looks kind of like a thumb, doesn't it?"

"A little, but it couldn't serve the same purpose as an opposable thumb does for humans. The toes are much too short for their paws to function like hands." Robin dropped Houdini's paw, gave him another treat, then gently rubbed the back of his leg to make sure it didn't cramp. "If someone did this purposefully, then they're keeping quiet about it. No professional breeders have come forward to claim these dogs as their creations, and there's been no reports of an experimental breed accidentally escaping into the wild. Tennessee was just the first place they were found. They've been popping up all over, out of nowhere."

"Sounds spooky."

"That's why people in Tennessee called them spook hounds. But they're really nice dogs. Very friendly, even dispositions, good companions for children. No one's tried training them as service animals so far as I know, but I've heard they make excellent watchdogs. Nothing gets past them." Robin lightly ran her hands across Houdini's ribs. "A little underweight," she observed. "Feed him twice a day, morning and late afternoon, until his ribs aren't showing anymore, then cut him back to just one meal in the morning."

Leaning against a wall with his arms crossed, Carter watched as Robin lifted Houdini's tail to examine his anus. "I'll give him flea and heart worm shots, too" she added, "but I don't see any signs that he has them, and or any ticks either." She dropped Houdini's tail and gently massaged the top of Houdini's snout; the dog closed his eyes and grinned, enjoying the nose rub. "He hasn't been out in the wild for long. Wonder who's been taking care of him?"

"He's never done anything mean," Carter said. "But he's done things that are . . . well, kind of strange." He told her about what happened when he tried to leave him alone in a room while he went shopping. Robin listened attentively and nodded when he finished.

"I've read things that have been posted online in dog blogs by people who've adopted them," she said, "and they've said much the same thing. He's smart, isn't he?"

"Yeah . . . really smart." Carter hesitated, wondering how much he could say about Houdini that wouldn't sound crazy. "It's almost like . . . um, like he can understand everything I say."

"Uh-huh. I've heard that, too." Robin paused, then pointed to Houdini's hindquarters, down between his rear legs. "Are you going to have him neutered?" she said abruptly. "If you don't have him castrated, you'll have to pay a lot more when you register him."

When she said this, Houdini suddenly shied away from her. He growled softly, not baring his teeth but no longer trusting the vet as much as he had only a moment ago, as his tail went down between his legs, protectively curling around his balls.

Carter's eyes widened. Had there been a subtle change in her tone of voice, or had her scent suddenly become different in a way that only a dog's sensitive nose could pick up? Or had Houdini truly understood what she'd said?

Houdini turned his head then to look straight at him and for the first time since they'd met, there was strong disapproval, even suppressed anger, in his silver eyes. *Don't even think about it*, the dog seemed to say, wordlessly yet emphatically.

Robin noticed this. She spoke again, but silently this time, slowly moving her lips so that Carter could read them. *Smart dog*, she mouthed.

Carter nodded. Yeah. Smart dog, all right.

🐾 🐾 🐾

It wasn't long before Carter discovered just how smart the dog really was.

Houdini became part of his household, and his life, with an ease that Carter barely noticed. There was little that the dog did that he found objectionable or annoying, and if Carter expressed even the slightest disapproval, Houdini would immediately cease what he'd been doing and never do it again. He'd only sleep on furniture that Carter had covered with throw blankets to keep off the dog hair, and never made a fuss about having to take a bath, although he let it be known that he vastly preferred warm water when Carter bathed him in the upstairs bathroom. He was polite to everyone he met, and would even sit down and raise his left forepaw if someone asked, "Shake hands? Do you shake hands?"

Whenever he did this, Carter thought he detected a certain annoyed look in the dog's eerie eyes, as if Houdini was thinking—*Do you really have to be so condescending? I'm not a puppy, you know.*

There was just one major point of disagreement, and that was when it came to what Carter fed him for breakfast and dinner. Although Houdini obediently consumed the dry kibble that Carter picked up at a nearby convenience store that first night when the dog unexpectedly showed up, it was only a few days before Houdini went on his first food strike, turning around and haughtily walking away when Carter put down another bowl of the same. It took several more tries, with brands ranging from Pedigree to Alpo to Eukanuba to Blue, before Carter found something the damn mutt would eat more than once... and even then, Houdini would stick with it for only a few days before he'd stop eating again.

Like most dogs, Houdini showed a preference for human food. And yet, Carter discovered, this didn't necessarily mean his dog would eat just any scraps or leftovers put in front of him. After his wife left him, Carter struggled to learn how to cook for himself, and some of his attempts at mastering the recipes in *The Joy of Cooking* were rather unpalatable. But while Houdini would happily polish off the last few bites of something Carter had made successfully, he'd reject a botched effort at four-cheese lasagne or an undercooked pork loin. Some of his friends described their dogs as walking garbage disposals, but Carter began to wonder whether his dog had been a restaurant reviewer in a past life.

Indeed, over the weeks and months that followed Carter's adoption of a four-legged housemate, he found himself wondering just how intelligent this dog truly was. There were times when he'd be gazing into the dog's silver yet oddly soulful eyes, that he realized he, too, was being studied, by a mind that, while not exactly human, was definitely more than canine. Houdini wasn't just the "smart dog" Robin said, and he was way beyond being the "good boy" people use to praise a dog who's mastered a trick or two. There was more going on between Houdini's ears than thoughts of chasing squirrels or coaxing someone into giving him a belly rub.

Houdini was a dog, yes. But he was also something else.

Carter's occupation was electronic engineering, and his job was working as a systems manager for a large aerospace firm that was a major defense contractor. He worked at ongoing projects that his company did for the Navy and Air Force, and recently the Space Force had become another service branch that enlisted his special knowledge and talents.

Carter possessed Secret clearance (and occasionally he'd been uprated to Top Secret), and although it had been many years since he'd worn a uniform, quite a few people in the armed services still felt compelled to call him "sir" when they spoke on the phone or exchanged email. His neighbors and even close friends had only a vague idea of what he did for a living, but nonetheless Carter was respected as being a member of Uncle Sam's brain trust.

When the Covid-19 epidemic caused many American businesses to shut down their offices and send their employees home, Carter's company was among them. Instead of driving almost an hour each day to a campus-like industrial park surrounded by a chain-link fence, where a uniformed guard in a gatehouse checked his windshield sticker and lanyard I.D. before letting him in, Carter found himself working at home, in an old dining room next to the kitchen that he'd turned into an office. But when the lockdown ended and people began returning to their workplaces, Carter was one of those whom his employers decided could continue working from home if they wished. Carter loved the small town and the old Victorian farmhouse where he lived but never enjoyed making the long commute, and since his divorce had been finalized before the pandemic, he needn't worry any longer about someone else in his house stumbling upon sensitive material. So, he opted for the work-at-home option.

To ensure electronic privacy for the Space Force project he was currently working on, Carter's employers mandated new security measures. They gave him two new computers for his office, both of which were manufactured to military specifications and were to be used only for his work. The desktop system was very powerful, with a twelve-gigabyte memory, but it wasn't networked in any way; no ground lines were attached to it, nor was it hooked up to any sort of cell modem or satellite dish.

The second computer was a laptop used primarily for communications. It was encrypted and shielded, with so much advanced software protection that it had to be upgraded nearly every day. Both computers were equipped with old-fashioned CDR drives; information from the desktop system was downloaded onto a disc, which then was inserted into the laptop's CDR drive to be uploaded via satphone hookup. Once the files were sent, Carter would totally delete them from the laptop's hard drive and destroy the disk. Even if anyone managed to hack into the laptop or even steal it, they wouldn't get any valuable information because the files were in an isolated computer beyond their reach.

This method was cumbersome, yet it was a simple and efficient way of ensuring that he was invulnerable to cyber espionage. And if Carter didn't think even this was secure enough, he could always resort to an even simpler method of transferring classified material; he'd call the company and request a courier.

When Carter adopted Houdini, he soon discovered that the dog was a creature of habit. That wasn't unusual; as Robin told him, "A dog's idea of a perfect day is when they can eat the same meals, take naps at the same time, and go for a walk just the same way they did yesterday and the day before that. They don't want variety. They want dependability."

Except for having gourmet (and rather expensive) tastes in food, Carter soon discovered that Houdini had the same behavioral pattern in the way he spent the day with him. Every morning Carter would get out of bed, have breakfast, shower, shave, and get dressed, and Houdini would quietly follow him around the house like a four-legged aide-de-camp, until they finally arrived in the office. Carter would sit down at his desk, power up the desktop computer with its two flatscreen monitors and the auxiliary laptop parked on a side table, then pick up where he'd left off the day before. And while he went about today's tasks, Houdini would climb onto an old couch Carter had picked up at a flea market for him, and there he would stretch out and nap until Carter broke for lunch, and return to once lunch was over and stay until late in the day when Carter would take him for a walk before dinnertime.

On several occasions, though, Carter would happen to glance over his shoulder to see what the dog was doing. Most of the time, Houdini was asleep, but every so often his eyes were open, and although he still was stretched out across the couch, the dog would be watching him. As soon as he was noticed, Houdini would lazily thump his tail a few times, then his mouth would open in a languorous, tongue-lolling yawn and he'd close his eyes and go back to sleep again.

But there were times when Carter would have the distinct feeling that he was being closely observed, that everything he did at his desk was the subject of careful scrutiny. And if he quickly looked around, or managed to catch a reflection behind himself on one of the screens, he'd discover Houdini sitting up on his haunches, head canted forward with his ears raised, silver eyes staring straight ahead . . . not at Carter, though, but at whatever data was presently displayed on the computer's dual screens, which at those moments almost always displayed something very important and very classified.

Was Carter imagining things, or was the dog spying on him?

The idea was so absurd, Carter had trouble believing that it had even occurred to him. He had to be getting paranoid if he imagined for even a moment that his dog was peering over his shoulder to see what he was doing. Houdini was smart, yes, and in fact more intelligent than any dog he'd ever heard about, but . . .

No. That was the craziest thought he'd ever had. Carter figured he must be working too hard if his mind was concocting suspicions like that. He was overdue for a vacation. Once this project was wrapped up and the final work was submitted to the Space Force, he'd make a trip to the Bahamas. Houdini could take a vacation of his own in a kennel. Might do him some good if he associated with other dogs, even meet a nice bitch.

Then came the Saturday night when he discovered who Houdini really was and why he was there.

Carter wasn't entirely a loner. He had a few friends, although most were people he knew from work, and once the pandemic was over and folks were able to socialize again without having to wear masks or maintain social distance, he began to pay attention once more to a young lady at the company, an assistant project manager who had also recently divorced her spouse. They'd just started dating when Covid-19 put on hold a lot of budding romances, but when Carter travelled to the company HQ for an in-person meeting with his team, he ran into Anne, and she let him know that she'd like to start seeing him again.

Carter knew that he really needed to get out more often, anyway, so he called Anne and suggested getting together for dinner and a movie. She liked the idea, so that next Saturday evening Carter washed behind his ears, put on his best clothes, and headed out for a night on the town. Houdini didn't seem to mind; he didn't insist on coming along, as some dogs often do, but instead calmly walked him to the door. As Carter was backing his car out of the driveway, he looked back to see the dog standing at the living room window where he'd left a light on, head pushed through the curtains as he watched his human companion go out for the night.

Unfortunately, the date didn't work out as planned. January weather is always unpredictable in New England, and the mild snowfall that the local TV weatherman had earlier forecast as being moderate developed into something much worse. The sky was already filled with fat, wet snowflakes when Carter picked up Anne at her apartment house, and by the time the two of them finished dinner and left the restaurant, there were already four inches of fresh snow on the sidewalk and the streets were becoming slick with ice and slush. Plows hadn't yet gone through that part of town, and to make matters worse Carter hadn't replaced the old, balding tires on his car. So when the driver of an enormous pickup truck carelessly crossed over the center line and caused Carter to swerve hard to the right, his car hit a icy patch, spun out, and slid head-on into a snow bank. It would've been a minor, slow-speed collision except for the fact that there was a fire hydrant half-buried in the snowbank, and that's what Carter smashed into.

Neither he nor his lady friend were harmed in any way—the impact didn't even trigger the air bags, much to Carter's annoyance—but with the left headlight shattered, the hood caved in, and the bumper dragging on the pavement, the car was clearly unroadworthy until its front end could be repaired. So after the cop who'd arrived on the scene called a tow truck to haul the car to a nearby garage, Carter reluctantly called an end to the date. Anne was shaken up and no longer wanted to do anything but go home, so he gallantly phoned Uber to get someone to pick them up. Anne let Carter give her an apologetic kiss before she got out at her apartment house; Carter then instructed the college kid who was his Uber driver how to get to his place.

The snowstorm had ended by the time they reached the street where Carter lived. The town's plows hadn't yet reached his neighborhood, and so the street was covered with six or more inches of snow that lay deeper in places near the curb where the wind had created dense drifts. The driver was hesitant to go down the street; he was familiar with the neighborhood, and knew this street was narrow and ended in a cul-de-sac where turning about would be difficult. The odds of getting stuck were high, and since the last thing Carter wanted was to have to muscle a car out of a snowbank, he let the kid drop him off at the top of the street. His house was only a couple of hundred yards away; he'd walk the rest of the way home.

A hole had opened in the clouds just as he reached his mailbox, revealing a full moon that cast its brilliance upon his lawn and created skeletal shadows from the willow tree by the driveway. The snow lay as white and unbroken as a glacial plain, and since he knew that drifts could get knee-deep near his front door, Carter decided instead to enter through the kitchen door on the side of the house where the carport awning would protect it from the wind.

The snow muffled his steps as he marched down the driveway, and he'd almost reached the kitchen door when he noticed something unusual.

The lights in his office were on. That shouldn't be; Carter was very conscientious about energy conservation, and always turned lights off when he left the house save for a table lamp in the front room that he kept on to deter break-ins. So he was *positive* that his office had been dark when he'd gone out a few hours ago. But now the lights were on, and that couldn't be good.

His office had a window next to the kitchen door; its sill was only waist high, making it easy for him to peer into the room. As Carter crept up on the window, keeping close to the wall and carefully making sure each step was as quiet as possible, in the cold stillness of the night his ears picked up a familiar sound: the soft click of fingers typing at his computer keyboard.

Yes, someone had managed to break into his house, and if they were seated at his desk and working at his computer, it was a good bet they weren't here to steal the TV and stereo. Well, Carter wasn't carrying a gun—he didn't even own one, nor had he fired anything since basic training in Navy—but he did have his cell phone. One quick look to see who was there, and then he'd back away, call 911, and get the cops sent over here.

Two more steps, then one, and then he was looking through the window, peeking around the side so that he couldn't be clearly seen from whoever was at his desk. And sure enough, someone was seated at his desk.

Houdini.

For a couple of seconds, Carter's mind refused to accept what his eyes were seeing. He *must* be mistaken; this *had* to be a hallucination. What he saw couldn't possibly be real. But the longer he stared, the more certain he became that what he was seeing was reality, not fantasy.

His dog was sitting in his chair, squatting upon his haunches with his back hunched forward, his head turned directly toward the screens. His forepaws were at the keyboard; they weren't resting upon the keys, though, but instead were in constant, deliberate motion, quickly typing commands that rapidly opened files and changed pages on the screen.

Straining his eyes, Carter peered more closely at Houdini's paws. They no longer resembled a normal dog's paws; each of the five toes on each paw had become longer, becoming actual fingers with two knuckles on each digit, the unusual fifth toe of each paw now forming an opposing thumb. At the same time, the claws of each toe had retracted, pulled back into sheaths so that they'd be out of the way. The paws were now nimble hands, hairy but dexterous.

The dog's eyes were in motion, too. As his head shifted from one side to the other, reading first one screen, then the next, Houdini's silver eyes tracked the lines scrolling down each screen, pausing now and then to read—yes, *read*—the material he'd found. There was an expression on his canine face that reflected not just comprehension, but intense interest.

This wasn't a trick. Houdini's behavior definitely was not that of an ordinary dog, if he was even a dog at all. Seeing Houdini this way, doing something no one else had probably ever seen a dog do before, struck Carter as being like a scene from some cheesy animal comedy Disney might have done back in the '60s, like *Secret Agent Double-0 Canine*. Or *The Spy Who Sniffed Me,* or maybe even *Thunderbone.*

This thought forced involuntary laughter from him, an amused chuckle that came out before he could stop himself. Carter clamped a hand over his mouth, but it was too late. Whatever Houdini really was, he had a dog's sharp hearing. His head jerked toward the window, and for just a moment his eyes met Carter's.

Man and dog stared at one another, each just as shocked by whom they saw through the window. Then Houdini leaped from the chair, his strong hind legs causing it to fall over and crash to the floor. Before Houdini's paws even touched the carpet, though, Carter was rushing from the window toward the kitchen door. He fumbled in his parka's right front pocket for his house keys as he struggled through cold, deep snow that pulled at his boots like glue. He found the key for the kitchen door and had just managed to fit it into the lock when the door was yanked open from inside and out charged Houdini.

The dog barreled through the door as if he was back to being just another mutt deliriously happy to see his master home at last. Houdini had done just that many times over the past few months when Carter had returned from shopping or another errand, but this time was different. Carter had just a second to wonder whether the dog had been faking his earlier displays of enthusiasm before Houdini bowled him over.

Carter yelled as he fell backward, hitting the snow-covered carport pavement hard enough to knock the wind out of him. He tried to grab Houdini, but his hands came away with nothing but loose black fur as the dog raced away.

"Houdini, stop!" he shouted. "Stop, Houdini!" But the dog was already gone, disappearing into the night once again made dark by returning clouds. In the wane houselight cast through the open door, Carter saw the tracks Houdini left in the snow. They were ordinary paw prints again, just like those any five-toed dog would leave behind.

But they'd once been hands. Of that, he was absolutely certain.

Carter spent the next several hours in his office, first checking to see which files Houdini had been reading, then pacing back and forth, wondering what to do about the unbelievable thing he'd seen... because, indeed, the whole affair truly was incredible, in the strictest sense of the term: a story not to be considered credible by anyone who heard it.

First, the files. It took only a few minutes for Carter to discover which password-protected programs Houdini had managed to hack into, then search their activity logs to find out which docs he'd opened and read over the past few hours. There were six in all, and Carter's blood went cold when he found that every once of them were classified either Secret or Top Secret. In some way, Houdini had managed to discover and enter passwords that the company randomly generated and changed every week, and once in the system he'd decrypted those documents he'd painstakingly encrypted for further protection. And once he'd found what he wanted, it appeared that Houdini had done just what Carter did: copy the material onto a disc, then use the networked laptop computer to send the info... well, somewhere, because the dog had also been smart enough to erase that address from the email buffer.

How had Houdini learned all his passwords? Carter figured that out almost at once. The dog had simply lay or sat on the couch behind him and watched over his shoulder as Carter got in, memorizing each eight-digit string that had been sent to him through the laptop computer and then typed into the desktop system. Carter recalled occasions when Houdini had casually got off the couch, stretched, then sauntered over to Carter's chair and rested his head in his lap; thinking the dog was just bored, Carter had stopped to pet Houdini, scratch behind his ears... and all the while the damn mutt had been staring straight at the computer screen, getting a closer look at the something he wanted to see. A CIA agent couldn't have done better.

Which led him to even more mysterious questions. What sort of advanced technology was responsible for espionage as sophisticated as this? Had Houdini been genetically engineered somehow to give him hands disguised as paws, a brain capable of understanding not just human language but also human science? Could a dog be physically altered and trained to do all that by the Russians or the Chinese or even certain Middle East countries?

Was Houdini even a dog at all? Perhaps, just maybe, he was actually a robot, or perhaps an android (although androids by definition are artificial humans, not dogs). If so, then Houdini must represent a level of cybernetic technology far beyond anything previously imagined, because the dog certainly looked and behaved like a living creature.

Carter shook his head. No, that was out of the question. Whatever else he might be, Houdini was definitely a dog. At least, so he thought . . .

Finally, there was the most important question of all: what was Carter going to do about it? The security agreements he'd signed with both the company and the government obligated him to report any incidents of espionage where it appeared that project secrecy had been compromised. Coming home to find a spy in your office obviously qualified as a security breach, but how could he tell anyone that the dog he'd recently adopted was actually a secret agent?

There was no way, no way in hell, he could possibly explain that to anyone without sounding like he'd gone completely off the deep end. Instead of examining Houdini's paws, they'd want to examine his head. And when they were done, they'd doubtless pull him off the project, revoke his security clearance, and send him somewhere for a nice long rest, playing checkers all day long.

And meanwhile, the dog had vanished. The instant he'd seen Carter at the office window, Houdini knew the jig was up. Carter couldn't get over the fact that, while he was fumbling with his house keys, the kitchen door had swung open from the *inside*. The only way anyone could do that was by first turning the knob, then pulling open the door. Simple for a human, but difficult if not impossible for a dog, especially if that dog was in a hurry to escape. But if that dog had hands . . .

Too much to absorb, too much to consider, too many mysteries unresolved. His head throbbing, his eyes beginning to itch, Carter decided that he needed sleep. Besides, he still had a wrecked car that he needed to get fixed; he'd forgotten all about that, but it couldn't be ignored. He'd take care of things in the morning; for now, the only place for him to go was bed.

Knowing that the events of the evening would keep him awake if he let them, Carter did the things he always did to make sure he slept soundly. He drank a glass of milk, put on socks as well as pajamas to keep his feet warm, threw an extra blanket on the bed.

But he didn't close the curtains of the bedroom window. And he forgot to lock the kitchen door.

Carter had been asleep for just a while when he felt a weight softly settle upon the other side of the bed. He'd always let Houdini sleep on the bed with him, so at first, he didn't think anything unusual about feeling the dog climbing up. Then conscious thought penetrated the fog of sleep, and he suddenly recalled what had happened just a few hours earlier.

With a start, he rolled over to see, just above the foot of the bed, a pair of silver eyes reflecting the cold winter moonlight as they stared down at him. Houdini had come home.

—*Hello, Carter. Wake up. We need to talk.*

The voice he heard wasn't in his ears but in his mind. It sounded so much like his own that Carter thought at first he was listening to his own thoughts, the internal dialogue that everyone has with himself. But that wasn't anything he'd just thought, and the voice was different enough that he knew that it was his.

"Houdini?" he asked, a dry-throated whisper in the dark. "Is that you? Are you . . . talking to me?"

—*This is me, yes, but verbal conversation is something I cannot do.* Houdini panted a little, the manner by which a dog laughs.—*So I'm telepathically speaking to you, which is how my kind can converse with humans if we allow ourselves to do so. Which is rare, and only if necessary.*

Carter tried to reply to Houdini the same way, by concentrating on sending thoughts toward the dog, or whatever he was. After a few moments, Houdini spoke to him again.—*The silence we've just shared tells me you've attempted telepathic communication yourself. If that's* true, I hate to inform you that I didn't receive any thoughts you tried to send me. Very few humans have that ability. Telepathy is a rare trait among your kind. So please speak out loud, because that's your way, and let me answer you with directed thoughts, which is my way. All right?*

"Okay, Houdini," Carter replied, and the dog nodded his head. "So . . . what do you want to talk about?"

Houdini panted again.—*As if you have to ask. You caught me doing something earlier tonight that you shouldn't have seen. I can't read your mind even though I can address myself directly to it, so I have to assume this was by accident and that you weren't deliberately spying on me. Is that right?*

"Yeah, that's right." Carter sat up a little more, propping his head and shoulders against the backboard behind him. "I had a car accident and my date decided she wanted to go home, so I got an Uber . . . do you know what Uber is?" Houdini nodded again "Okay, I called an Uber driver to pick us up and carry us both home. That's why I didn't drive back tonight. I walked part of the way so—"

—*I understand. You may skip the rest.* Houdini looked away to gaze out the bedroom window for a few moments, as if pondering some private thought he didn't want to share with Carter.—*This is very fortunate. I'm glad it was an accident. If you'd become suspicious of me, suspicious enough to try sneaking up on me to catch me as you did, then this conversation would be different . . . much different.*

"How so?"

—*At this moment, my teeth would be at your throat and I would be ending your life.* Another pause—*And as I did so, I would also be telling you how sorry I was to have to do that, even though I doubt very much you'd hear me or even care.*

A cold wind gust rattled the windowpane and seemed to penetrate the weather stripping Carter had put up all around the house last fall. Yet the chill he felt didn't come from the wind. "Would you have done that? Really? I thought we were friends."

—*And we still are. I became your friend the night you showed me kindness and mercy by taking me in after you caught me rummaging through your garbage cans.* Houdini lay down on his belly, folding his forepaws together before him in a humanistic pose that Carter had assumed wasn't deliberate until now.—*That encounter wasn't by accident. This you should now know . . . my people had always planned for you and I to meet under circumstances that we hoped would lead to you adopting me and bringing me into your home. I'm sorry, Carter, but that's the truth. I'm just happy to have learned that you're a better person than they'd estimated. So, yes, you're my friend . . . that is, unless you give me a reason to change my mind.*

Hearing this, Carter felt his mind spinning, his mental equilibrium destabilized and disturbed by what he'd just heard. As the dog spoke, he reached over to the bedside table to switch on the light. When the light came on and Houdini didn't vanish, he knew for certain none of this was a dream.

I'm talking to my dog, he thought, *and my dog is talking back. I must be losing my mind.* But if he hadn't gone crazy, then as unbelievable as everything seemed, what Houdini was telling him must be true.

"Then . . . why did you come find me?" He sat up higher in bed. "Was it to spy on me, find out what I've been working on?"

—*Yes. That's right. It's taken me awhile to learn all your passwords and decryption protocols I needed to know to open your files and thoroughly study your work. In fact, tonight was the first opportunity I've had to do that, since I believed you'd be gone longer . . . perhaps even overnight if your date had invited you to spend the night with her.*

"Most women won't do that on their first date."

—*So I've learned. Obviously your mating customs aren't quite the same way as they're frequently shown to be on TV. That's how my people have learned much of what we know about your race . . .*

"My race?" Something seemed to jab him in the guts. "Are you saying you're . . . you're not from here?"

Carter had a hard time giving voice to the obvious conclusion; Houdini solved the problem for him.—*Yes. My kind isn't from Earth, or indeed from any nearby solar system. However, I'm not totally what you'd call an "alien" either. The situation is a bit more complicated than that.*

"So then you're a shape-changer." Carter recalled a half dozen science fiction movies and TV shows he'd seen.

—*No, no, I really am a dog. As your veterinarian friend told you, my genome is completely canine, native to this world. My body is the result of gene-splicing several different canine breeds, selecting particular traits from different kinds of dogs. Once a hybrid was successfully produced, its fetus was altered in situ to give me certain hidden advantages, such as a higher cerebral capacity and the ability to reshape my paws into functional hands, along with ... well, other abilities. But my consciousness, my intelligence, came from elsewhere. Once the body was complete ... a process much like cloning, but more advanced than that ... then my mind was transferred from my original body to the one I inhabit now.*

Houdini paused, then his tail began to wag, his ears lifted, and his mouth widened into a toothy grin.—*By the way, thanks for giving me such a good name. I've learned who the original Harry Houdini was, and I'm flattered by the comparison.* His ears and tail went down.—*Some of my brethren haven't been so fortunate. Some of them have been given names that are quite awful ... Butthead or Mr. Goofy, for instance.*

"Then there are others like you?" Carter asked, and Houdini affirmatively thumped his tail against the bed a couple of times. "So, what Robin said about Cumberland spook hounds suddenly showing up everywhere ..."

—*Those are also my people. And we've established a presence not only in this country, but in others as well, although some of us came to this continent first as a test to make sure we'd be accepted. For the most part, we have. A few of my kind have been killed, sometimes deliberately.* Houdini's lipless mouth pulled back in a silent and uncharacteristic snarl and a low growl came from deep inside—*Unfortunately, we've also learned that your people can sometimes be quite cruel, to even a psychotic degree, toward creatures as selflessly loyal and trusting as dogs. But most occasions, we've been accepted as what we appear to be.*

"Is this an invasion?" He spoke the question more bluntly than he'd planned, but he had to know. "Are you ... a scout of some kind, someone sent ahead to—?"

—*No!* Houdini said this forcefully and immediately, interrupting Carter as if his question needed to be answered at once.—*Whatever else we may be, we're not conquerors, and our intent isn't to take over the world. You needn't fear us any more than if we actually were dogs ... which we are, really, just ones from a distant planet not unlike your own.*

"Colonists?"

—*Yes, but secretly. Hundreds of my kind reside here already. Soon there will be thousands.*

"Why?"

—*Our home world was on the brink of planetary catastrophe when our first refugees departed, two hundred years ago by your reckoning. For all I know, it may already be uninhabitable, the only survivors those who managed to escape in tine. So we must learn to live here, because planets like yours and mine are not commonplace in the galaxy.*

"And the reason why you've come here? To my house, my home?"

—*I was given a mission, Carter. The reason why I was sent to meet you and to be accepted into your home was so that I could examine the files you're able to access regarding advanced defense research. We need to learn the extent of your military technology, so that if our presence is discovered and our vessels are detected in lunar orbit, we'll be able to defend ourselves if attacked.*

"Or give you an edge when you attack us." Carter tried to hide his anger, but couldn't.

Again, Houdini's tail wagged.—*Trust me, my friend. Flying saucers piloted by alien dogs will never attack your cities. This is not like one of your movies. We want to be your friends much more than we want to be your enemies.*

Carter didn't know whether he fully trusted this creature, but at least now he knew for certain that he hadn't lost his mind, that what was happening was not a paranoid hallucination. As he let that sink in, Houdini quietly gazed back at him, his canine expression as warm and accepting as it had been just yesterday afternoon, before Carter went out for the evening and came home to find that his dog wasn't the dog he'd thought him to be.

"Just one more question," Carter said at last. "Why make yourselves look like dogs? Why not look like humans instead?"

—*For the simple reason that my race is also a four-legged, warm-blooded mammal species not unlike Earth's dogs. We're much more similar to dogs than we are to humans. This makes it easier for us to adapt ourselves to their forms.*

Houdini paused, then added—*This is important, for the consciousness transferral is not reversible. Once we've become dogs, what you called Cumberland spook hounds, there is no going back. My original body has already been rendered lifeless. I cannot resume its form again.*

"So you're here for good?"

—Yes we are . . . and if you'll have me, I'll always be here with you, as your friend. Houdini sat up again.*—I know you'll never betray me, because who would ever believe you? A few other humans have also discovered the truth about my so-called breed, but they've also remained silent. As I know you will.*

"Guess I don't have much choice, do I?"

—Yes, you do have a choice. Tell me to leave, and I'll go. My mission has been accomplished, so I don't have to stay here. But I'd rather stay. I like this house, and I like you.

Houdini lifted his right foreleg, the familiar hand-shake pose dogs have often been trained to make but which Carter didn't bother to do with his previous dogs. As he watched, Houdini's toes elongated again, their claws restricting as slender, knuckled digits slipped forward from their sheaths, becoming fingers. It was eerie to see a dog's paw become something resembling a human hand, but it wasn't as startling as the first time he'd seen it . . . nor as threatening.

—Friends? Houdini expectantly cocked his head to one side.

Carter hesitated, then gently clasped Houdini's hand with his own. "Friends. Yeah, you can stay."

—Good. I'm very glad to hear it. Now if you'll excuse me, I must answer the call of the wild.

Houdini jumped off the bed, sauntered toward the door. Carter started to get out of bed, but then the dog paused to look back at him, a happy smile on his face.

—Don't worry about letting me out and bringing me back in. I can do that on my own now. Then his smile faded.*—Just one more thing, and this is important.*

"Sure. What's that?"

*—Don't even think about having me neutered. I have plans for those things, and if you let that vet get anywhere near me with a knife—*the dog turned about and continued to walk out the door—*I really will rip your throat out.*

Carter watched Houdini leave. A couple of moments later, he

heard the kitchen door open, and then shut. Confident that the dog could come in out of the cold without help, he lay back down in bed, closed his eyes, and tried to go back to sleep.

But he left the light on, and it was a long while before he was able to sleep again.

POTTAGE
Zenna Henderson

On the surface, the various elements of "Pottage" are so classic it almost seems cliché—a small, isolated town with an even smaller schoolhouse, filled with strange children who never smile. An idealistic young teacher desperate to light a spark in her students, even if it means butting heads with local attitudes. A group of aliens seeking refuge on Earth, going to desperate lengths to avoid discovery. Of course, of the many words one could use to describe Zenna Henderson's stories about The People, surface-level isn't one of them.

No, this is a wonderfully complex tale that, much like the children at the center of the story, blends those elements into something exciting and new. "Pottage" is a tale of a diaspora desperately trying to walk the line between assimilation and retaining their heritage, and a group of children learning to open up and become comfortable with who they are, and perhaps providing a roadmap for people from two different worlds to follow in their footsteps.

You get tired of teaching after a while. Well, maybe not of teaching itself, because it's insidious and remains a tug in the blood for all of your life, but there comes a day when you look down at the paper you're grading or listen to an answer you're giving a child and you get a *boinnng!* feeling. And each reverberation of the *boing* is a year in your life, another set of children through your hands, another beat in monotony, and it's frightening. The value of the work you're doing doesn't enter into it at that moment and the monotony is bitter on your tongue.

241

Sometimes you can assuage that feeling by consciously savoring those precious days of pseudofreedom between the time you receive your contract for the next year and the moment you sign it. Because you *can* escape at that moment, but somehow—you don't.

But I did, one spring. I quit teaching. I didn't sign up again. I went chasing after—after what? Maybe excitement—maybe a dream of wonder—maybe a new bright wonderful world that just *must* be somewhere else because it isn't here-and-now. Maybe a place to begin again so I'd never end up at the same frightening emotional dead end. So I quit.

But by late August the emptiness inside me was bigger than boredom, bigger than monotony, bigger than lusting after freedom. It was almost terror to be next door to September and not care that in a few weeks school starts—tomorrow school starts—first day of school. So, almost at the last minute, I went to the placement bureau. Of course it was too late to try to return to my other school, and besides, the mold of the years there still chafed in too many places.

"Well," the placement director said as he shuffled his end-of-the-season cards, past Algebra and Home Ec and PE and High School English, "there's always Bendo." He thumbed out a battered-looking three-by-five. "There's *always* Bendo."

And I took his emphasis and look for what they were intended as and sighed.

"Bendo?"

"Small school. One room. Mining town, or used to be. Ghost town now." He sighed wearily and let down his professional hair. "Ghost people, too. Can't keep a teacher there more than a year. Low pay—fair housing—at someone's home. No community activities— no social life. No city within fifty or so miles. No movies. No nothing but children to be taught. Ten of them this year. All grades."

"Sounds like the town I grew up in," I said. "Except we had two rooms and lots of community activities."

"I've been to Bendo." The director leaned back in his chair, hands behind his head. "Sick community. Unhappy people. No interest in anything. Only reason they have a school is because it's the law. Law-abiding anyway. Not enough interest in anything to break a law, I guess."

"I'll take it," I said quickly before I could think beyond the feeling that this sounded about as far back as I could go to get a good running start at things again.

He glanced at me quizzically. "If you're thinking of lighting a torch of high reform to set Bendo afire with enthusiasm, forget it. I've seen plenty of king-sized torches fizzle out there."

"I have no torch," I said. "Frankly I'm fed to the teeth with bouncing bright enthusiasm and huge PTA's and activities until they come out your ears. They usually turn out to be the most monotonous kind of monotony. Bendo will be a rest."

"It will that," the director said, leaning over his cards again. "Saul Diemus is the president of the board. If you don't have a car, the only way to get to Bendo is by bus—it runs once a week."

I stepped out into the August sunshine after the interview and sagged a little under its savage pressure, almost hearing a hiss as the refrigerated coolness of the placement bureau evaporated from my skin.

I walked over to the quad and sat down on one of the stone benches I'd never had time to use, those years ago when I had been a student here. I looked up at my old dorm window and, for a moment, felt a wild homesickness—not only for years that were gone and hopes that had died and dreams that had had grim awakenings, but for a special magic I had found in that room. It was a magic—a true magic—that opened such vistas to me that for a while anything seemed possible, anything feasible—if not for me right now, then for others, someday. Even now, after the dilution of time, I couldn't quite believe that magic, and even now, as then, I wanted fiercely to believe it. If only it could be so! If only it could be so!

I sighed and stood up. I suppose everyone has a magic moment somewhere in his life and, like me, can't believe that anyone else could have the same—but mine was different! No one else could have had the same experience! I laughed at myself. Enough of the past and of dreaming. Bendo waited. I had things to do.

I watched the rolling clouds of red-yellow dust billow away from the jolting bus, and cupped my hands over my face to get a breath of clean air. The grit between my teeth and the smothering sift of dust across my clothes was familiar enough to me, but I hoped by the time we reached Bendo we would have left this dust plain behind and come into a little more vegetation. I shifted wearily on the angular seat, wondering if it had ever been designed for anyone's comfort, and caught myself as a sudden braking of the bus flung me forward.

We sat and waited for the dust of our going to catch up with us, while the last-but-me passenger, a withered old Indian, slowly gathered up his gunny-sack bundles and his battered saddle and edged his Levied velveteen-bloused self up the aisle and out to the bleak roadside.

We roared away, leaving him a desolate figure in a wide desolation. I wondered where he was headed. How many weary miles to his hogan in what hidden wash or miniature greenness in all this wilderness.

Then we headed straight as a die for the towering redness of the bare mountains that lined the horizon. Peering ahead I could see the road, ruler straight, disappearing into the distance. I sighed and shifted again and let the roar of the motor and the weariness of my bones lull me into a stupor on the border between sleep and waking.

A change in the motor roar brought me back to the jouncing bus. We jerked to a stop again. I looked out the window through the settling clouds of dust and wondered who we could be picking up out here in the middle of nowhere. Then a clot of dust dissolved and I saw

BENDO POST OFFICE
GENERAL STORE
Garage & Service Station
Dry Goods & Hardware
Magazines

in descending size on the front of the leaning, weather-beaten building propped between two crumbling smoke-blackened stone ruins. After so much flatness it was almost a shock to see the bare tumbled boulders crowding down to the roadside and humping their lichen-stained shoulders against the sky.

"Bendo," the bus driver said, unfolding his lanky legs and hunching out of the bus. "End of the line—end of civilization—end of everything!" He grinned and the dusty mask of his face broke into engaging smile patterns.

"Small, isn't it?" I grinned back.

"Usta be bigger. Not that it helps now. Roaring mining town years ago." As he spoke I could pick out disintegrating buildings dotting the rocky hillsides and tumbling into the steep washes. "My dad can remember it when he was a kid. That was long enough ago that there was still a river for the town to be in the bend o."

"Is that where it got its name?"

"Some say yes, some say no. Might have been a feller named Bendo." The driver grunted as he unlashed my luggage from the bus roof and swung it to the ground.

"Oh, hi!" said the driver.

I swung around to see who was there. The man was tall, well built, good-looking—and old. Older than his face—older than years could have made him because he was really young, not much older than I. His face was a stern unhappy stillness, his hands stiff on the brim of his Stetson as he held it waist high.

In that brief pause before his "Miss Amerson?" I felt the same feeling coming from him that you can feel around some highly religious person who knows God only as a stern implacable vengeful deity, impatient of worthless man, waiting only for an unguarded moment to strike him down in his sin. I wondered who or what his God was that prisoned him so cruelly. Then I was answering, "Yes, how do you do?" And he touched my hand briefly with a "Saul Diemus" and turned to the problem of my two large suitcases and my record player.

I followed Mr. Diemus' shuffling feet silently, since he seemed to have slight inclination for talk. I hadn't expected a reception committee, but kids must have changed a lot since I was one, otherwise curiosity about teacher would have lured out at least a couple of them for a preview look. But the silent two of us walked on for a half block or so from the highway and the post office and rounded the rocky corner of a hill. I looked across the dry creek bed and up the one winding street that was residential Bendo. I paused on the splintery old bridge and took a good look. I'd never see Bendo like this again. Familiarity would blur some outlines and sharpen others, and I'd never again see it, free from the knowledge of who lived behind which blank front door.

The houses were scattered haphazardly over the hillsides, and erratic flights of rough stone steps led down from each to the road that paralleled the bone-dry creek bed. The houses were not shacks but they were unpainted and weathered until they blended into the background almost perfectly. Each front yard had things growing in it, but such subdued blossoming and unobtrusive planting that they could easily have been only accidental massings of natural vegetation.

Such a passion for anonymity . . .

"The school—" I had missed the swift thrust of his hand.

"Where?" Nothing I could see spoke school to me.

"Around the bend." This time I followed his indication and suddenly, out of the featurelessness of the place, I saw a bell tower barely topping the hill beyond the town, with the fine pencil stroke of a flagpole to one side. Mr. Diemus pulled himself together to make the effort.

"The school's in the prettiest place around here. There's a spring and trees, and—" He ran out of words and looked at me as though trying to conjure up something else I'd like to hear. "I'm board president," he said abruptly. "You'll have ten children from first grade to second-year high school. You're the boss in your school. Whatever you do is your business. Any discipline you find desirable—use. We don't pamper our children. Teach them what you have to. Don't bother the parents with reasons and explanations. The school is yours."

"And you'd just as soon do away with it and me, too." I smiled at him.

He looked startled. "The law says school them." He started across the bridge. "So school them."

I followed meekly, wondering wryly what would happen if I asked Mr. Diemus why he hated himself and the world he was in and even—oh, breathe it softly—the children I was to "school."

"You'll stay at my place," he said. "We have an extra room."

I was uneasily conscious of the wide gap of silence that followed his pronouncement, but couldn't think of a thing to fill it. I shifted my small case from one hand to the other and kept my eyes on the rocky path that protested with shifting stones and vocal gravel every step we took. It seemed to me that Mr. Diemus was trying to make all the noise he could with his shuffling feet. But, in spite of the amplified echo from the hills around us, no door opened, no face pressed to a window. It was a distinct relief to hear suddenly the happy unthinking rusty singing of hens as they scratched in the coarse dust.

I hunched up in the darkness of my narrow bed trying to comfort my uneasy stomach. It wasn't that the food had been bad—it had been quite adequate—but such a dingy meal! Gloom seemed to festoon itself from the ceiling and unhappiness sat almost visibly at the table.

I tried to tell myself that it was my own travel weariness that slanted my thoughts, but I looked around the table and saw the hopeless endurance furrowed into the adult faces and beginning faintly but unmistakably on those of the children. There were two children there. A girl, Sarah (fourth grade, at a guess), and an adolescent boy, Matt (seventh?)—too silent, too well mannered, too controlled, avoiding much too pointedly looking at the empty chair between them.

My food went down in lumps and quarreled fiercely with the coffee that arrived in square-feeling gulps. Even yet—long difficult hours after the meal—the food still wouldn't lie down to be digested.

Tomorrow I could slip into the pattern of school, familiar no matter where school was, since teaching kids is teaching kids no matter where. Maybe then I could convince my stomach that all was well, and then maybe even start to thaw those frozen unnatural children. Of course they well might be little demons away from home—which is very often the case. Anyway I felt, thankfully, the familiar September thrill of new beginnings.

I shifted in bed again, then, stiffening my neck, lifted my ears clear of my pillow.

It was a whisper, the intermittent hissing I had been hearing. Someone was whispering in the next room to mine. I sat up and listened unashamedly. I knew Sarah's room was next to mine, but who was talking with her? At first I could get only half words and then either my ears sharpened or the voices became louder.

"... and did you hear her laugh? Right out loud at the table!" The quick whisper became a low voice. "Her eyes crinkled in the corners and she laughed."

"Our other teachers laughed, too." The uncertainly deep voice must be Matt.

"Yes," Sarah whispered. "But not for long. Oh, Matt! What's wrong with us? People in our books have fun. They laugh and run and jump and do all kinds of fun stuff and nobody—" Sarah faltered, "no one calls it evil."

"Those are only stories," Matt said. "Not real life."

"I don't believe it!" Sarah cried. "When I get big I'm going away from Bendo. I'm going to see—"

"Away from Bendo!" Matt's voice broke in roughly.

"Away from the Group?" I lost Sarah's reply. I felt as though I had missed an expected step. As I wrestled with my breath, the sights and sounds and smells of my old dorm room crowded back upon me. Then I caught myself. It was probably only a turn of phrase. This futile desolate unhappiness couldn't possibly be related in any way to *that* magic . . .

"Where is Dorcas?" Sarah asked, as though she knew the answer already.

"Punished." Matt's voice was hard and unchildlike. "She jumped."

"Jumped!" Sarah was shocked.

"Over the edge of the porch. Clear down to the path. Father saw her. I think she let him see her on purpose." His voice was defiant. "Someday when I get older I'm going to jump, too—all I want to— even over the house. Right in front of Father."

"Oh, Matt!" The cry was horrified and admiring. "You wouldn't! You couldn't. Not so far, not right in front of Father!"

"I would so," Matt retorted. "I could so, because I—" His words cut off sharply. "Sarah," he went on, "can you figure any way, any way, that jumping could be evil? It doesn't hurt anyone. It isn't ugly. There isn't any law—"

"Where is Dorcas?" Sarah's voice was almost inaudible. "In the hidey hole again?" She was almost answering Matt's question instead of asking one of her own.

"Yes," Matt said. "In the dark with only bread to eat. So she can learn what a hunted animal feels like. An animal that is different, that other animals hate and hunt." His bitter voice put quotes around the words.

"You see," Sarah whispered. "You see?"

In the silence following I heard the quiet closing of a door and the slight vibration of the floor as Matt passed my room. I eased back onto my pillow. I lay back, staring toward the ceiling. What dark thing was here in this house? In this community? Frightened children whispering in the dark. Rebellious children in hidey holes learning how hunted animals feel. And a Group...? No, it couldn't be. It was just the recent reminder of being on campus again that made me even consider that this darkness might in some way be the reverse of the golden coin Karen had shown me.

My heart almost failed me when I saw the school. It was one of those monstrosities that went up around the turn of the century. This one had been built for a boom town, but now all the upper windows were boarded up and obviously long out of use. The lower floor was blank, too, except for two rooms—though with the handful of children quietly standing around the door it was apparent that only one room was needed. And not only was the building deserted, the yard was swept clean from side to side, innocent of grass or trees— or playground equipment. There was a deep grove just beyond the school, though, and the glint of water down canyon.

"No swings?" I asked the three children who were escorting me. "No slides? No seesaws?"

"No!" Sarah's voice was unhappily surprised. Matt scowled at her warningly.

"No," he said, "we don't swing or slide—nor see a saw!" He grinned up at me faintly.

"What a shame!" I said. "Did they all wear out? Can't the school afford new ones?"

"We don't swing or slide or seesaw." The grin was dead. "We don't believe in it."

There's nothing quite so flat and incontestable as that last statement. I've heard it as an excuse for practically every type of omission, but, so help me, never applied to playground equipment. I couldn't think of a reply any more intelligent than "Oh," so I didn't say anything.

All week long I felt as if I were wading through knee-deep Jell-O or trying to lift a king-sized feather bed up over my head. I used up every device I ever thought of to rouse the class to enthusiasm— about anything, *anything*! They were polite and submissive and did what was asked of them, but joylessly, apathetically, enduringly.

Finally, just before dismissal time on Friday, I leaned in desperation across my desk.

"Don't you like *anything*?" I pleaded. "Isn't *anything* fun?"

Dorcas Diemus' mouth opened into the tense silence. I saw Matt kick quickly, warningly, against the leg of the desk. Her mouth closed.

"I think school is fun," I said. "I think we can enjoy all kinds of things. I want to enjoy teaching but I can't unless you enjoy learning."

"We learn," Dorcas said quickly. "We aren't stupid."

"You learn," I acknowledged. "You aren't stupid. But don't any of you like school?"

"I like school," Martha piped up, my first grade. "I think it's fun!"

"Thank you, Martha," I said. "And the rest of you—" I glared at them in mock anger, "you're going to have fun if I have to beat it into you!"

To my dismay they shrank down apprehensively in their seats and exchanged troubled glances. But before I could hastily explain myself, Matt laughed and Dorcas joined him. And I beamed fatuously to hear the hesitant rusty laughter spread across the room, but I saw ten-year-old Esther's hands shake as she wiped tears from her eyes. Tears—of laughter?

That night I twisted in the darkness of my room, almost too tired to sleep, worrying and wondering. What had blighted these people? They had health, they had beauty—the curve of Martha's cheek against the window was a song, the lift of Dorcas' eyebrows was breathless grace. They were fed—adequately, clothed—adequately, housed—adequately, but nothing like they could have been. I'd seen more joy and delight and enthusiasm from little campground kids who slept in cardboard shacks and washed—if they ever did—in canals and ate whatever edible came their way, but grinned, even when impetigo or cold sores bled across their grins.

But these lifeless kids! My prayers were troubled and I slept restlessly.

A month or so later things had improved a little bit, but not much. At least there was more relaxation in the classroom. And I found that they had no deep-rooted convictions against plants, so we had things growing on the deep window sills—stuff we transplanted from the spring and from among the trees. And we had jars of minnows from the creek and one drowsy horned toad that roused in his box of dirt only to flick up the ants brought for his dinner. And we sang, loudly and enthusiastically, but, miracle of miracles, without even one monotone in the whole room. But we didn't sing "Up, Up in the Sky" or "How Do You Like to Go Up in a Swing?" My solos of such songs were received with embarrassed blushes and lowered eyes!

There had been one dust-up between us, though—this matter of shuffling everywhere they walked.

"Pick up your feet, for goodness' sake," I said irritably one morning when the *shoosh, shoosh, shoosh* of their coming and going finally got my skin off. "Surely they're not so heavy you can't lift them."

Timmy, who happened to be the trigger this time, nibbled unhappily at one finger. "I can't," he whispered.

"Not supposed to."

"Not supposed to?" I forgot momentarily how warily I'd been going with these frightened mice of children. "Why not? Surely there's no reason in the world why you can't walk quietly."

Matt looked unhappily over at Miriam, the sophomore who was our entire high school. She looked aside, biting her lower lip, troubled. Then she turned back and said, "It is customary in Bendo."

"To shuffle along?" I was forgetting any manners I had. "Whatever for?"

"That's the way we do in Bendo." There was no anger in her defense, only resignation.

"Perhaps that's the way you do at home. But here at school let's pick our feet up. It makes too much disturbance otherwise."

"But it's bad—" Esther began.

Matt's hand shushed her in a hurry.

"Mr. Diemus said what we did at school was my business," I told them. "He said not to bother your parents with our problems. One of our problems is too much noise when others are trying to work. At least in our schoolroom let's lift our feet and walk quietly."

The children considered the suggestion solemnly and turned to Matt and Miriam for guidance. They both nodded and we went back to work. For the next few minutes, from the corner of my eyes, I saw with amazement all the unnecessary trips back and forth across the room, with high-lifted feet, with grins and side glances that marked such trips as high adventure—as a delightfully daring thing to do! The whole deal had me bewildered. Thinking back, I realized that not only the children of Bendo scuffled but all the adults did, too—as though they were afraid to lose contact with the earth, as though . . . I shook my head and went on with the lesson.

Before noon, though, the endless *shoosh, shoosh, shoosh* of feet began again. Habit was too much for the children. So I silently filed the sound under "Uncurable, Endurable," and let the matter drop.

I sighed as I watched the children leave at lunchtime. It seemed to me that with the unprecedented luxury of a whole hour for lunch they'd all go home. The bell tower was visible from nearly every house in town. But instead they all brought tight little paper sacks with dull crumbly sandwiches and unimaginative apples in them. And silently with their dull scuffly steps they disappeared into the thicket of trees around the spring.

"Everything is dulled around here," I thought. "Even the sunlight is blunted as it floods the hills and canyons. There is no mirth, no laughter. No high jinks or cutting up. No preadolescent silliness. No adolescent foolishness. Just quiet children, enduring."

I don't usually snoop but I began wondering if perhaps the kids were different when they were away from me—and from their parents. So when I got back at twelve thirty from an adequate but uninspired lunch at the Diemuses' house I kept on walking past the schoolhouse and quietly down into the grove, moving cautiously through the scanty undergrowth until I could lean over a lichened boulder and look down on the children.

Some were lying around on the short still grass, hands under their heads, blinking up at the brightness of the sky between the leaves. Esther and little Martha were hunting out fillaree seed pods and counting the tines of the pitchforks and rakes and harrows they resembled. I smiled, remembering how I used to do the same thing.

"I dreamed last night." Dorcas thrust the statement defiantly into the drowsy silence. "I dreamed about the Home."

My sudden astonished movement was covered by Martha's horrified "Oh, Dorcas!"

"What's wrong with the Home?" Dorcas cried, her cheeks scarlet. "There was a Home! There was! There was! Why shouldn't we talk about it."

I listened avidly. This couldn't be just coincidence—a Group and now the Home. There must be some connection... I pressed closer against the rough rock.

"But it's bad!" Esther cried. "You'll be punished! We can't talk about the Home!"

"Why not?" Joel asked as though it had just occurred to him, as things do just occur to you when you're thirteen. He sat up slowly. "Why can't we?"

There was a short tense silence.

"I've dreamed, too," Matt said. "I've dreamed of the Home—and it's good, it's good!"

"Who hasn't dreamed?" Miriam asked. "We all have, haven't we? Even our parents. I can tell by Mother's eyes when she has."

"Did you ever ask how come we aren't supposed to talk about it?" Joel asked. "I mean and ever get any answer except that it's bad."

"I think it has something to do with a long time ago," Matt said. "Something about when the Group first came—"

"I don't think it's just dreams," Miriam declared, "because I don't have to be asleep. I think it's remembering."

"Remembering?" asked Dorcas. "How can we remember something we never knew?"

"I don't know," Miriam admitted, "but I'll bet it is."

"I remember," volunteered Talitha, who never volunteered anything.

"Hush!" whispered Abie, the second-grade next-to-youngest who always whispered.

"I remember," Talitha went on stubbornly. "I remember a dress that was too little so the mother just stretched the skirt till it was long enough and it stayed stretched. 'Nen she pulled the waist out big enough and the little girl put it on and flew away."

"Hoh!" Timmy scoffed. "I remember better than that." His face stilled and his eyes widened. "The ship was so tall it was like a mountain and the people went in the high high door and they didn't have a ladder. 'Nen there were stars, big burning ones—not squinchy little ones like ours."

"It went too fast!" That was Abie! Talking eagerly! "When the air came it made the ship hot and the little baby died before all the little boats left the ship." He scrunched down suddenly, leaning against Talitha and whimpering.

"You see!" Miriam lifted her chin triumphantly. "We've all dreamed—I mean remembered!"

"I guess so," said Matt. "I remember. It's *lifting*, Talitha, not flying. You go and go as high as you like, as far as you want to and don't *ever* have to touch the ground—at all! At all!" He pounded his fist into the gravelly red soil beside him.

"And you can dance in the air, too," Miriam sighed. "Freer than a bird, lighter than—"

Esther scrambled to her feet, white-faced and panic-stricken. "Stop! Stop! It's evil! It's bad! I'll tell Father! We can't dream—or lift— or dance! It's bad, it's bad! You'll die for it! You'll die for it!"

Joel jumped to his feet and grabbed Esther's arm.

"Can we die any deader?" he cried, shaking her brutally. "You call *this* being alive?" He hunched down apprehensively and shambled a few scuffling steps across the clearing.

I fled blindly back to school, trying to wink away my tears without admitting I was crying, crying for these poor kids who were groping so hopelessly for something they knew they should have. Why was it so rigorously denied them? Surely, if they were what I thought them . . . And they could be! They could be!

I grabbed the bell rope and pulled hard. Reluctantly the bell moved and rolled.

One o'clock, it clanged. *One o'clock!*

I watched the children returning with slow uneager shuffling steps.

That night I started a letter:

"Dear Karen,

"Yep, 'sme after all these years. And, oh, Karen! I've found some more! Some more of the People! Remember how much you wished you knew if any other Groups besides yours had survived the Crossing? How you worried about them and wanted to find them if they had? Well, *I've* found a whole Group! But it's a sick unhappy group. Your heart would break to see them. If you could come and start them on the right path again..."

I put my pen down. I looked at the lines I had written and then crumpled the paper slowly. This was *my* Group. I had found them. Sure, I'd tell Karen—but later. Later, after—well, after I had tried to start them on the right path—at least the children.

After all, I knew a little of their potentialities. Hadn't Karen briefed me in those unguarded magical hours in the old dorm, drawn to me as I was to her by some mutual sympathy that seemed stronger than the usual roommate attachment, telling me things no Outsider had a right to hear? And if, when I finally told her and turned the Group over to her, if it could be a joyous gift, then I could feel that I had repaid her a little for the wonder world she had opened for me.

"Yes," I thought ruefully, "and there's nothing like a large portion of ignorance to give one a large portion of confidence." But I did want to try—desperately. Maybe if I could break prison for someone else, then perhaps my own bars... I dropped the paper in the wastebasket.

But it was several weeks before I could bring myself to do anything to let the children know I knew about them. It was such an impossible situation, even if it was true—and if it wasn't, what kind of lunacy would they suspect me of?

When I finally set my teeth and swore a swear to myself that I'd do something definite, my hands shook and my breath was a flutter in my dry throat.

"Today—" I said with an effort, "today is Friday." Which gem of wisdom the children received with charitable silence. "We've been working hard all week, so let's have fun today." This stirred the children—half with pleasure, half with apprehension. They, poor kids, found my "fun" much harder than any kind of work I could give them. But some of them were acquiring a taste for it. Martha had even learned to skip!

"First, monitors pass the composition paper." Esther and Abie scuffled hurriedly around with the paper, and the pencil sharpener got a thorough workout. At least these kids didn't differ from others in their pleasure in grinding their pencils away at the slightest excuse.

"Now," I gulped, "we're going to write." Which obvious asininity was passed over with forbearance, though Miriam looked at me wonderingly before she bent her head and let her hair shadow her face. "Today I want you all to write about the same thing. Here is our subject."

Gratefully I turned my back on the children's waiting eyes and printed slowly:

I Remember the Home

I heard the sudden intake of breath that worked itself downward from Miriam to Talitha and then the rapid whisper that informed Abie and Martha. I heard Esther's muffled cry and I turned slowly around and leaned against the desk.

"There are so many beautiful things to remember about the Home," I said into the strained silence. "So many wonderful things. And even the sad memories are better than forgetting, because the Home was good. Tell me what you remember about the Home."

"We can't!" Joel and Matt were on their feet simultaneously.

"Why can't we?" Dorcas cried. "Why can't we?"

"It's bad!" Esther cried. "It's evil!"

"It ain't either!" Abie shrilled, astonishingly. "It ain't either!"

"We shouldn't." Miriam's trembling hands brushed her heavy hair upward. "It's forbidden."

"Sit down," I said gently. "The day I arrived at Bendo, Mr. Diemus told me to teach you what I had to teach you. I have to teach you that remembering the Home is good."

"Then why don't the grownups think so?" Matt asked slowly. "They tell us not to talk about it. We shouldn't disobey our parents."

"I know," I admitted. "And I would never ask you children to go against your parents' wishes, unless I felt that it is very important. If you'd rather they didn't know about it at first, keep it as our secret. Mr. Diemus told me not to bother them with explanations or reasons. I'll make it right with your parents when the time comes." I paused to swallow and blink away a vision of me leaving town in a cloud of dust, barely ahead of a posse of irate parents. "Now, everyone, busy," I said briskly. "'I Remember the Home.'"

There was a moment heavy with decision and I held my breath, wondering which way the balance would dip. And then—surely it must have been because they wanted so to speak and affirm the wonder of what had been that they capitulated so easily. Heads bent and pencils scurried. And Martha sat, her head bowed on her desk with sorrow.

"I don't know enough words," she mourned. "How do you write '*toolas*'?"

And Abie laboriously erased a hole through his paper and licked his pencil again.

"Why don't you and Abie make some pictures?" I suggested. "Make a little story with pictures and we can staple them together like a real book."

I looked over the silent busy group and let myself relax, feeling weakness flood into my knees. I scrubbed the dampness from my palms with Kleenex and sat back in my chair. Slowly I became conscious of a new atmosphere in my classroom. An intolerable strain was gone, an unconscious holding back of the children, a wariness, a watchfulness, a guilty feeling of desiring what was forbidden.

A prayer of thanksgiving began to well up inside me. It changed hastily to a plea for mercy as I began to visualize what might happen to me when the parents found out what I was doing. How long must this containment and denial have gone on? This concealment and this carefully nourished fear? From what Karen had told me it must be well over fifty years—long enough to mark indelibly three generations.

And here I was with my fine little hatchet trying to set a little world afire! On which very mixed metaphor I stiffened my weak knees and got up from my chair. I walked unnoticed up and down the aisles, stepping aside as Joel went blindly to the shelf for more paper, leaning over Miriam to marvel that she had taken out her Crayolas and part of her writing was with colors, part with pencil— and the colors spoke to something in me that the pencil couldn't reach, though I'd never seen the forms the colors took.

The children had gone home, happy and excited, chattering and laughing, until they reached the edge of the school grounds. There, smiles died and laughter stopped and faces and feet grew heavy again. All but Esther's. Hers had never been light. I sighed and turned to the papers. Here was Abie's little book. I thumbed through it and drew a deep breath and went back through it slowly again.

A second grader drawing this? Six pages—six finished adult-looking pages. Crayolas achieving effects I'd never seen before—pictures that told a story loudly and clearly.

Stars blazing in a black sky, with the slender needle of a ship, like a mote in the darkness.

The vasty green cloud-shrouded arc of Earth against the blackness. A pink tinge of beginning friction along the ship's belly. I put my finger to the glow. I could almost feel the heat.

Inside the ship, suffering and pain, heroic striving, crumpled bodies and seared faces. A baby dead in its mother's arms. Then a swarm of tinier needles erupting from the womb of the ship. And the last shriek of incandescence as the ship volatilized against the thickening drag of the air.

I leaned my head on my hands and closed my eyes. All this, all *this* in the memory of an eight-year-old? All *this* in the feelings of an eight-year-old? Because Abie knew—he *knew* how this felt. He knew the heat and strivings and the dying and fleeing. No wonder Abie whispered and leaned. Racial memory was truly a two-sided coin.

I felt a pang of misgivings. Maybe I was wrong to let him remember so vividly. Maybe I shouldn't have let him . . .

I turned to Martha's papers. They were delicate, almost spidery drawings of some fuzzy little animal (*toolas*?) that apparently built a hanging hammocky nest and gathered fruit in a huge leaf basket and had a bird for a friend. A truly out-of-this-world bird. Much of her story escaped me because first graders—if anyone at all—produce symbolic art and, since her frame of reference and mine were so different, there was much that I couldn't interpret. But her whole booklet was joyous and light.

And now, the stories . . .

I lifted my head and blinked into the twilight. I had finished all the papers except Esther's. It was her cramped writing, swimming in darkness, that made me realize that the day was gone and that I was shivering in a shadowy room with the fire in the old-fashioned heater gone out.

Slowly I shuffled the papers into my desk drawer, hesitated and took out Esther's. I would finish at home. I shrugged into my coat and wandered home, my thoughts intent on the papers I had read. And suddenly I wanted to cry—to cry for the wonders that had been and were no more. For the heritage of attainment and achievement these children had but couldn't use. For the dream-come-true of what they were capable of doing but weren't permitted to do. For the homesick yearning that filled every line they had written—these unhappy exiles, three generations removed from any physical knowledge of the Home.

I stopped on the bridge and leaned against the railing in the half dark. Suddenly *I* felt a welling homesickness. *That* was what the world should be like—what it *could* be like if only—if only . . .

But my tears for the Home were as hidden as the emotions of Mrs. Diemus when she looked up uncuriously as I came through the kitchen door.

"Good evening," she said. "I've kept your supper warm."

"Thank you." I shivered convulsively. "It *is* getting cold."

I sat on the edge of my bed that night, letting the memory of the kids' papers wash over me, trying to fill in around the bits and snippets that they had told of the Home. And then I began to wonder. All of them who wrote about the actual Home had been so happy with their memories. From Timmy and his *Shinny ship as high as a montin and faster than two jets*, and Dorcas' wandering tenses as though yesterday and today were one: *The flowers were like lights. At night it isn't dark becas they shine so bright and when the moon came up the breeos sing and the music was so you can see it like rain falling around only happyer*; up to Miriam's wistful *On Gathering Day there was a big party. Everybody came dressed in beautiful clothes with* flahmen *in the girls' hair.* Flahmen *are flowers but they're good to eat. And if a girl felt her heart sing for a boy they ate a* flahmen *together and started two-ing.*

Then, if all these memories were so happy, why the rigid suppression of them by grownups? Why the pall of unhappiness over everyone? You can't mourn forever for a wrecked ship. Why a hidey hole for disobedient children? Why the misery and frustration when, if they could do half of what I didn't fully understand from Joel and Matt's highly technical papers, they could make Bendo an Eden?

I reached for Esther's paper. I had put it on the bottom on purpose. I dreaded reading it. She had sat with her head buried on her arms on her desk most of the time the others were writing busily. At widely separated intervals she had scribbled a line or two as though she were doing something shameful. She, of all the children, had seemed to find no relief in her remembering.

I smoothed the paper on my lap.

I remember, she had written. *We were thursty. There was water in the creek we were hiding in the grass. We could not drink. They would shoot us. Three days the sun was hot. She screamed for water and ran to the creek. They shot. The water got red.*

Blistered spots marked the tears on the paper.

They found a baby under a bush. The man hit it with the wood part of his gun. He hit it and hit it and hit it. I hit scorpins like that.

They caught us and put us in a pen. They built a fire all around us. Fly "they said," fly and save yourselfs. We flew because it hurt. They shot us.

Monster "they yelled" evil monsters. People can't fly. People can't move things. People are the same. You aren't people, Die die die.

Then blackly, traced and retraced until the paper split:

If anyone finds out we are not of earth we will die.

Keep your feet on the ground.

Bleakly I laid the paper aside. So there was the answer, putting Karen's bits and snippets together with these. The shipwrecked ones finding savages on the desert island. A remnant surviving by learning caution, suppression, and denial. Another generation that pinned the *evil* label on the Home to insure continued immunity for their children, and now, a generation that questioned and wondered—and rebelled.

I turned off the light and slowly got into bed. I lay there staring into the darkness, holding the picture Esther had evoked. Finally I relaxed. "God help her," I sighed. "God help us all."

Another week was nearly over. We cleaned the room up quickly, for once anticipating the fun time instead of dreading it. I smiled to hear the happy racket all around me, and felt my own spirits surge upward in response to the lightheartedness of the children. The difference that one afternoon had made in them! Now they were beginning to feel like children to me. They were beginning to accept me. I swallowed with an effort. How soon would they ask, "How come? How come you knew?" There they sat, all nine of them—nine, because Esther was my first absence in the year—bright-eyed and expectant.

"Can we write again?" Sarah asked. "I can remember lots more."

"No," I said. "Not today." Smiles died and there was a protesting wiggle through the room. "Today we are going to *do*. Joel." I looked at him and tightened my jaws. "Joel, give me the dictionary." He began to get up. "*Without leaving your seat!*"

"But I—!" Joel broke the shocked silence. "I can't!"

"Yes, you can," I prayed. "Yes, you can. Give me the dictionary. Here, on my desk."

Joel turned and stared at the big old dictionary that spilled pages 1965 to 1998 out of its cracked old binding. Then he said, "Miriam?" in a high tight voice. But she shook her head and shrank back in her seat, her eyes big and dark in her white face.

"You can." Miriam's voice was hardly more than a breath. "It's just bigger—"

Joel clutched the edge of his desk and sweat started out on his forehead. There was a stir of movement on the bookshelf. Then, as though shot from a gun, pages 1965 to 1998 whisked to my desk and fell fluttering. Our laughter cut through the blank amazement and we laughed till tears came.

"That's a-doing it, Joel!" Matt shouted. "That's showing them your muscles!"

"Well, it's a beginning." Joel grinned weakly. "You do it, brother, if you think it's so easy."

So Matt sweated and strained and Joel joined with him, but they only managed to scrape the book to the edge of the shelf, where it teetered dangerously. Then Abie waved his hand timidly. "I can, teacher."

I beamed that my silent one had spoken and at the same time frowned at the loving laughter of the big kids.

"Okay, Abie," I encouraged. "You show them how to do it."

And the dictionary swung off the shelf, and glided unhastily to my desk, where it came silently to rest.

Everyone stared at Abie and he squirmed. "The little ships," he defended. "That's the way they moved them out of the big ship. Just like that."

Joel and Matt turned their eyes to some inner concentration and then exchanged exasperated looks.

"Why, sure," Matt said. "Why, sure." And the dictionary swung back to the shelf.

"Hey!" Timmy protested. "It's my turn!"

"That poor dictionary," I said. "It's too old for all this bouncing around. Just put the loose pages back on the shelf."

And he did.

Everyone sighed and looked at me expectantly.

"Miriam?" She clasped her hands convulsively. "*You* come to me," I said, feeling a chill creep across my stiff shoulders. "*Lift* to me, Miriam."

Without taking her eyes from me she slipped out of her seat and stood in the aisle. Her skirts swayed a little as her feet lifted from the floor. Slowly at first and then more quickly she came to me, soundlessly, through the air, until in a little flurried rush her arms went around me and she gasped into my shoulder. I put her aside, trembling. I groped for my handkerchief. I said shakily, "Miriam, help the rest. I'll be back in a minute."

And I stumbled into the room next door. Huddled down in the dust and debris of the catchall storeroom it had become, I screamed soundlessly into my muffling hands. And screamed and screamed! Because after all—*after all*!

And then suddenly, with a surge of pure panic, I heard a sound—the sound of footsteps, many footsteps, approaching the schoolhouse. I jumped for the door and wrenched it open just in time to see the outside door open. There was Mr. Diemus and Esther and Esther's father, Mr. Jonso.

In one of those flashes of clarity that engrave your mind in a split second, I saw my whole classroom.

Joel and Matt were chinning themselves on nonexistent bars, their heads brushing the high ceiling as they grunted upward. Abie was swinging in a swing that wasn't there, arcing across the corner of the room, just missing the stovepipe from the old stove, as he chanted, "Up in a swing, up in a swing!" This wasn't the first time they had tried their wings! Miriam was kneeling in a circle with the other girls and they were all coaxing their books up to hover unsupported above the door, while Jimmy vroom-vroomed two paper jet planes through intricate maneuvers in and out the rows of desks.

My soul curdled in me as I met Mr. Diemus' eyes. Esther gave a choked cry as she saw what the children were doing, and the girls' stricken faces turned to the intruders. Matt and Joel crumpled to the floor and scrambled to their feet. But Abie, absorbed in his wonderful new accomplishment, swung on, all unconscious of what was happening until Talitha frantically screamed, "Abie!"

Startled, he jerked around and saw the forbidding group at the door. With a disappointed cry, as though a loved toy had been snatched from him, he stopped there in midair, his fists clenched. And then, realizing, he screamed, a terrified panic-stricken cry, and slanted sharply upward, trying to escape, and ran full tilt into the corner of the high old map case, sideswiping it with his head, and, reeling backward, fell!

I tried to catch him. I did! I did! But I caught only one small hand as he plunged down onto the old wood-burning heater beneath him. And the crack of his skull against the ornate edge of the cast-iron lid was loud in the silence.

I straightened the crumpled little body carefully, not daring to touch the quiet little head. Mr. Diemus and I looked at each other as we knelt on opposite sides of the child. His lips opened, but I plunged before he could get started.

"If he dies," I bit my words off viciously, "you killed him!"

His mouth opened again, mainly from astonishment. "I—" he began.

"Barging in on my classroom!" I raged. "Interrupting classwork! Frightening my children! It's all your fault, your fault!" I couldn't bear the burden of guilt alone. I just had to have someone share it with me. But the fire died and I smoothed Abie's hand, trembling.

"Please call a doctor. He might be dying."

"Nearest one is in Tortura Pass," Mr. Diemus said. "Sixty miles by road."

"Cross country?" I asked.

"Two mountain ranges and an alkali plateau."

"Then—then—" Abie's hand was so still in mine.

"There's a doctor at the Tumble A Ranch," Joel said faintly. "He's taking a vacation."

"Go get him." I held Joel with my eyes. "*Go as fast as you know how!*"

Joel gulped miserably. "Okay."

"They'll probably have horses to come back on," I said. "Don't be too obvious."

"Okay," and he ran out the door. We heard the thud of his running feet until he was halfway across the schoolyard, then silence. Faintly, seconds later, creek gravel crunched below the hill. I could only guess at what he was doing—that he couldn't lift all the way and was going in jumps whose length was beyond all reasonable measuring.

The children had gone home, quietly, anxiously. And after the doctor arrived we had improvised a stretcher and carried Abie to the Peterses' home. I walked along close beside him watching his pinched little face, my hand touching his chest occasionally just to be sure he was still breathing.

And now—the waiting...

I looked at my watch again. A minute past the last time I looked. Sixty seconds by the hands, but hours and hours by anxiety.

"He'll be all right," I whispered, mostly to comfort myself. "The doctor will know what to do."

Mr. Diemus turned his dark empty eyes to me. "Why did you do it?" he asked. "We almost had it stamped out. We were almost free."

"Free of what?" I took a deep breath. "Why did *you* do it? Why did you deny your children their inheritance?"

"It isn't your concern—"

"Anything that hampers my children is my concern. Anything that turns children into creeping frightened mice is wrong. Maybe I went at the whole deal the wrong way, but you told me to teach them what I had to—and I did."

"Disobedience, rebellion, flouting authority—"

"They obeyed *me*," I retorted. "They accepted *my* authority!" Then I softened. "I can't blame them," I confessed. "They were troubled. They told me it was wrong—that they had been *taught* it was wrong. I argued them into it. But oh, Mr. Diemus! It took so little argument, such a tiny breach in the dam to loose the flood. They never even questioned my knowledge—any more than you have, Mr. Diemus! All this—this *wonder* was beating against their minds, fighting to be set free. The rebellion was there long before I came. I didn't incite them to something new. I'll bet there's not one, except maybe Esther, who hasn't practiced and practiced, furtively and ashamed, the things I permitted—demanded that they do for me.

"It wasn't fair—not fair at all—to hold them back."

"You don't understand." Mr. Diemus' face was stony. "You haven't all the facts—"

"I have enough," I replied. "So you have a frightened memory of an unfortunate period in your history. But what people *doesn't* have such a memory in larger or lesser degree? That you and your children have it more vividly should have helped, not hindered. You should have been able to figure out ways of adjusting. But leave that for the moment. Take the other side of the picture. What possible thing could all this suppression and denial yield you more precious than what you gave up?"

"It's the only way," Mr. Diemus said. "We are unacceptable to Earth but we have to stay. We have to conform—"

"Of course you had to conform," I cried. "Anyone has to when they change societies. At least enough to get them by until others can adjust to them. But to crawl in a hole and pull it in after you! Why, the other Group—"

"Other Group!" Mr. Diemus whitened, his eyes widening. "Other Group? There are others? There are others?" He leaned tensely forward in his chair. "Where? Where?" And his voice broke shrilly on the last word. He closed his eyes and his mouth trembled as he fought for control. The bedroom door opened. Dr. Curtis came out, his shoulders weary.

He looked from Mr. Diemus to me and back. "He should be in a hospital. There's a depressed fracture and I don't know what all else. Probably extensive brain involvement. We need X rays and—and—" He rubbed his hand slowly over his weary young face. "Frankly, I'm not experienced to handle cases like this. We need specialists. If you can scare up some kind of transportation that won't jostle—" He shook his head, seeing the kind of country that lay between us and anyplace, and went back into the bedroom.

"He's dying," Mr. Diemus said. "Whether you're right or we're right, he's dying."

"Wait! Wait!" I said, catching at the tag end of a sudden idea. "Let me think." Urgently I willed myself back through the years to the old dorm room. Intently I listened and listened and remembered.

"Have you a—a—*Sorter* in this Group?" I asked, fumbling for unfamiliar terms.

"No," said Mr. Diemus. "One who could have been, but isn't."

"Or *any* Communicator? Anyone who can send or receive?"

"No," Mr. Diemus said, sweat starting on his forehead. "One who could have been, but—"

"See?" I accused. "See what you've traded for—for what? Who are the could-but-can'ts? Who are they?"

"I am," Mr. Diemus said, the words a bitterness in his mouth. "And my wife."

I stared at him, wondering confusedly. How far did training decide? What could we do with what we had?

"Look," I said quickly. "There is another Group. And they—they have all the Persuasions and Designs. Karen's been trying to find you—to find any of the People. She told me—oh, Lord, it's been years ago, I hope it's still so—every evening they send out calls for the People. If we can catch it—if *you* can catch the call and answer it, they can help. I know they can. Faster than cars, faster than planes, more surely than specialists—"

"But if the doctor finds out—" Mr. Diemus wavered fearfully.

I stood up abruptly. "Good night, Mr. Diemus," I said, turning to the door. "Let me know when Abie dies."

His cold hand shook on my arm.

"Can't you see!" he cried. "I've been taught, too—longer and stronger than the children! We never even dared think of rebellion! Help me, help me!"

"Get your wife," I said. "Get her and Abie's mother and father. Bring them down to the grove. We can't do anything here in the house. It's too heavy with denial."

I hurried on ahead and sank on my knees in the evening shadows among the trees.

"I don't know what I'm doing," I cried into the bend of my arm. "I have an idea but I don't know! Help us! Guide us!"

I opened my eyes to the arrival of the four.

"We told him we were going out to pray," said Mr. Diemus.

And we all did.

Then Mr. Diemus began the call I worded for him, silently, but with such intensity that sweat started again on his face. *Karen, Karen. Come to the People, Come to the People.* And the other three sat around him, bolstering his effort, supporting his cry. I watched their tense faces, my own twisting in sympathy, and time was lost as we labored.

Then slowly his breathing calmed and his face relaxed and I felt a stirring as though something brushed past my mind. Mrs. Diemus whispered, "He remembers now. He's found the way."

And as the last spark of sun caught mica highlights on the hilltop above us, Mr. Diemus stretched his hands out slowly and said with infinite relief, "There they are."

I looked around startled, half expecting to see Karen coming through the trees. But Mr. Diemus spoke again.

"Karen, we need help. One of our Group is dying. We have a doctor, an Outsider, but he hasn't the equipment or the know-how to help. What shall we do?"

In the pause that followed I became slowly conscious of a new feeling. I couldn't tell you exactly what it was—a kind of unfolding—an opening—a relaxation. The ugly tight defensiveness that was so characteristic of the grownups of Bendo was slipping away.

"Yes, Valancy," said Mr. Diemus. "He's in a bad way. We can't help because—" His voice faltered and his words died. I felt a resurgence of fear and unhappiness as his communication went beyond words and then ebbed back to speech again.

"We'll expect you then. You know the way."

I could see the pale blur of his face in the dusk under the trees as he turned back to us.

"They're coming," he said, wonderingly. "Karen and Valancy. They're so pleased to find us—" His voice broke. "We're *not* alone—"

And I turned away as the two couples merged in the darkness. I had pushed them somewhere way beyond me.

It was a lonely lonely walk back to the house for me—alone.

They dropped down through the half darkness—four of them. For a fleeting second I wondered at myself that I could stand there matter-of-factly watching four adults slant calmly down out of the sky. Not a hair ruffled, not a stain of travel on them, knowing that only a short time before they had been hundreds of miles away—not even aware that Bendo existed.

But all strangeness was swept away as Karen hugged me delightedly.

"Oh, Melodye," she cried, "it is you! He said it was, but I wasn't sure! Oh, it's so good to see you again! Who owes who a letter?"

She laughed and turned to the smiling three. "Valancy, the Old One of our Group." Valancy's radiant face proved the Old One didn't mean age. "Bethie, our Sensitive." The slender fair-haired young girl ducked her head shyly. "And my brother Jemmy. Valancy's his wife."

"This is Mr. and Mrs. Diemus," I said. "And Mr. and Mrs. Peters, Abie's parents. It's Abie, you know. My second grade." I was suddenly overwhelmed by how long ago and far away school felt. How far I'd gone from my accustomed pattern!

"What shall we do about the doctor?" I asked. "Will he have to know?"

"Yes," said Valancy. "We can help him but we can't do the actual work. Can we trust him?"

I hesitated, remembering the few scanty glimpses I'd had of him. "I—" I began.

"Pardon me," Karen said. "I wanted to save time. I went in to you. We know now what you know of him. We'll trust Dr. Curtis."

I felt an eerie creeping up my spine. To have my thoughts taken so casually! Even to the doctor's name!

Bethie stirred restlessly and looked at Valancy. "He'll be in convulsions soon. We'd better hurry."

"You're sure you have the knowledge?" Valancy asked.

"Yes," Bethie murmured. "If I can make the doctor see—if he's willing to follow."

"Follow what?"

The heavy tones of the doctor's voice startled us all as he stepped out on the porch.

I stood aghast at the impossibility of the task ahead of us and looked at Karen and Valancy to see how they would make the doctor understand. They said nothing. They just looked at him. There was a breathless pause. The doctor's startled face caught the glint of light from the open door as he turned to Valancy. He rubbed his hand across his face in bewilderment and, after a moment, turned to me.

"Do *you* hear her?"

"No," I admitted. "She isn't talking to me."

"Do you *know* these people?"

"Oh, yes!" I cried, wishing passionately it were true. "Oh, yes!"

"And believe them?"

"Implicitly."

"But she says that Bethie—who's Bethie?" He glanced around.

"She is," Karen said, nodding at Bethie.

"*She* is?" Dr. Curtis looked intently at the shy lovely face. He shook his head wonderingly and turned back to me.

"Anyway this one, Valancy, says Bethie can sense every condition in the child's body and that she will be able to tell all the injuries, their location and extent without X rays! Without equipment!"

"Yes," I said. "If they say so."

"You would be willing to risk a child's life—?"

"Yes. They know. They really do." And I swallowed hard to keep down the fist of doubt that clenched in my chest.

"You believe they can see through flesh and bone?"

"Maybe not see," I said, wondering at my own words. "But know with a knowledge that is sure and complete." I glanced, startled, at Karen. Her nod was very small but it told me where my words came from.

"Are *you* willing to trust these people?" The doctor turned to Abie's parents.

"They're *our* People," Mr. Peters said with quiet pride. "I'd operate on him myself with a pickax if they said so."

"Of all the screwball deals—!" The doctor's hand rubbed across his face again. "I know I needed this vacation, but this is ridiculous!"

We all listened to the silence of the night and—at least I—to the drumming of anxious pulses until Dr. Curtis sighed heavily.

"Okay, Valancy. I don't believe a word of it. At least I wouldn't if I were in my right mind, but you've got the terminology down pat as if you knew something—Well, I'll do it. It's either that or let him die. And God have mercy on our souls!"

I couldn't bear the thought of shutting myself in with my own dark fears, so I walked back toward the school, hugging myself in my inadequate coat against the sudden sharp chill of the night. I wandered down to the grove, praying wordlessly, and on up to the school. But I couldn't go in. I shuddered away from the blank glint of the windows and turned back to the grove. There wasn't any more time or direction or light or anything familiar, only a confused cloud of anxiety and a final icy weariness that drove me back to Abie's house.

I stumbled into the kitchen, my stiff hands fumbling at the doorknob. I huddled in a chair, gratefully leaning over the hot wood stove that flicked the semidarkness of the big homey room with warm red light, trying to coax some feeling back into my fingers.

I drowsed as the warmth began to penetrate, and then the door was flung open and slammed shut. The doctor leaned back against it, his hand still clutching the knob.

"Do you know what they did?" he cried, not so much to me as to himself. "What they made *me* do? Oh, Lord!" He staggered over to the stove, stumbling over my feet. He collapsed by my chair, rocking his head between his hands. "They made me operate on his brain! *Repair* it. Trace circuits and rebuild them. *You can't do that*! It can't be done! Brain cells damaged can't be repaired. No one can restore circuits that are destroyed! It can't be done. But I did it! *I did it*!"

I knelt beside him and tried to comfort him in the circle of my arms.

"There, there, there," I soothed.

He clung like a terrified child. "No anesthetics!" he cried. "*She* kept him asleep. And no bleeding when I went through the scalp! *They* stopped it. And the impossible things I did with the few instruments I have with me! And the brain starting to mend right before my eyes! Nothing was right!"

"But nothing was wrong," I murmured. "Abie will be all right, won't he?"

"How do I know?" he shouted suddenly, pushing away from me. "I don't know anything about a thing like this. I put his brain back together and he's still breathing, but how do I know!"

"There, there," I soothed. "It's over now."

"It'll never be over!" With an effort he calmed himself, and we helped each other up from the floor. "You can't forget a thing like this in a lifetime."

"We can give you forgetting," Valancy said softly from the door.

"If you *want* to forget. We can send you back to the Tumble A with no memory of tonight except a pleasant visit to Bendo."

"You can?" He turned speculative eyes toward her. "You can," he amended his words to a statement.

"Do you want to forget?" Valancy asked.

"Of course not," he snapped. Then, "I'm sorry. It's just that I don't often work miracles in the wilderness. But if I did it once, maybe—"

"Then you understand what you did?" Valancy asked, smiling.

"Well, no, but if I could—if you would—There must be some way—"

"Yes," Valancy said, "but you'd have to have a Sensitive working with you, and Bethie is it as far as Sensitives go right now."

"You mean it's true what I saw—what you told me about the—the Home? You're extraterrestrials?"

"Yes," Valancy sighed. "At least our grandparents were." Then she smiled. "But we're learning where we can fit into this world. Someday—someday we'll be able—" She changed the subject abruptly.

"You realize, of course, Dr. Curtis, that we'd rather you wouldn't discuss Bendo or us with anyone else. We would rather be just people to Outsiders."

He laughed shortly, "Would I be believed if I did?"

"Maybe no, maybe so," Valancy said. "Maybe only enough to start people nosing around. And that would be too much. We have a bad situation here and it will take a long time to erase—" Her voice slipped into silence, and I knew she had dropped into thoughts to brief him on the local problem. How long is a thought? How fast can you think of hell—and heaven? It was that long before the doctor blinked and drew a shaky breath.

"Yes," he said. "A long time."

"If you like," Valancy said, "I can block your ability to talk of us."

"Nothing doing!" the doctor snapped. "I can manage my own censorship, thanks."

Valancy flushed. "I'm sorry. I didn't mean to be condescending."

"You weren't," the doctor said. "I'm just on the prod tonight. It has been *a day*, and that's for sure!"

"Hasn't it, though?" I smiled and then, astonished, rubbed my cheeks because tears had begun to spill down my face. I laughed, embarrassed, and couldn't stop. My laughter turned suddenly to sobs and I was bitterly ashamed to hear myself wailing like a child. I clung to Valancy's strong hands until I suddenly slid into a warm welcome darkness that had no thinking or fearing or need for believing in anything outrageous, but only in sleep.

It was a magic year and it fled on impossibly fast wings, the holidays flicking past like telephone poles by a railroad. Christmas was especially magical because my angels actually flew and the glory actually shone round about because their robes had hems woven of sunlight—I watched the girls weave them. And Rudolph the red-nosed reindeer, complete with cardboard antlers that wouldn't stay straight, really took off and circled the room. And as our Mary and Joseph leaned raptly over the manger, their faces solemn and intent on the miracle, I felt suddenly that they were really seeing, really kneeling beside the manger in Bethlehem.

Anyway the months fled, and the blossoming of Bendo was beautiful to see. There was laughter and frolicking and even the houses grew subtly into color. Green things crept out where only rocks had been before, and a tiny tentative stream of water had begun to flow down the creek again. They explained to me that they had to take it slow because people might wonder if the creek filled overnight! Even the rough steps up to the houses were being overgrown because they were so seldom used, and I was becoming accustomed to seeing my pupils coming to school like a bevy of bright birds, playing tag in the treetops. I was surprised at myself for adjusting so easily to all the incredible things done around me by the People, and I was pleased that they accepted me so completely. But I always felt a pang when the children escorted me home—with me, they had to walk.

But all things have to end, and one May afternoon I sat staring into my top desk drawer, the last to be cleaned out, wondering what to do with the accumulation of useless things in it. But I wasn't really seeing the contents of the drawer, I was concentrating on the great weary emptiness that pressed my shoulders down and weighted my mind. "It's not fair," I muttered aloud and illogically, "to show me heaven and then snatch it away."

"That's about what happened to Moses, too, you know."

My surprised start spilled an assortment of paper clips and thumbtacks from the battered box I had just picked up.

"Well, forevermore!" I said, righting the box. "Dr. Curtis! What are you doing here?"

"Returning to the scene of my crime," he smiled, coming through the open door. "Can't keep my mind off Abie. Can't believe he recovered from all that—shall we call it repair work? I have to check him every time I'm anywhere near this part of the country—and I still can't believe it."

"But he has."

"He has for sure! I had to fish him down from a treetop to look him over—" The doctor shuddered dramatically and laughed. "To see him hurtling down from the top of that tree curdled my blood! But there's hardly even a visible scar left."

"I know," I said, jabbing my finger as I started to gather up the tacks. "I looked last night. I'm leaving tomorrow, you know." I kept my eyes resolutely down to the job at hand. "I have this last straightening up to do."

"It's hard, isn't it?" he said, and we both knew he wasn't talking about straightening up.

"Yes," I said soberly. "Awfully hard. Earth gets heavier every day."

"I find it so lately, too. But at least you have the satisfaction of knowing that you—"

I moved uncomfortably and laughed.

"Well, they do say: those as can, do; those as can't, teach."

"Umm," the doctor said noncommittally, but I could feel his eyes on my averted face and I swiveled away from him, groping for a better box to put the clips in.

"Going to summer school?" His voice came from near the windows.

"No," I sniffed cautiously. "No, I swore when I got my Master's that I was through with education—at least the kind that's come-every-day-and-learn-something."

"Hmm!" There was amusement in the doctor's voice. "Too bad. I'm going to school this summer. Thought you might like to go there, too."

"Where?" I asked bewildered, finally looking at him.

"Cougar Canyon summer school," he smiled. "Most exclusive."

"Cougar Canyon! Why, that's where Karen—"

"Exactly," he said. "That's where the other Group is established. I just came from there. Karen and Valancy want us both to come. Do you object to being an experiment?"

"Why, no—" I cried, and then, cautiously, "What kind of an experiment?" Visions of brains being carved up swam through my mind.

The doctor laughed. "Nothing as gruesome as you're imagining, probably." Then he sobered and sat on the edge of my desk. "I've been to Cougar Canyon a couple of times, trying to figure out some way to get Bethie to help me when I come up against a case that's a puzzler. Valancy and Karen want to try a period of training with Outsiders—" he grimaced wryly, "—that's us—to see how much of what *they* are can be transmitted by training. You know Bethie is half Outsider. Only her mother was of the People."

He was watching me intently.

"Yes," I said absently, my mind whirling. "Karen told me."

"Well, do you want to try it? Do you want to go?"

"Do I want to go!" I cried, scrambling the clips into a rubber-band box. "How soon do we leave? Half an hour? Ten minutes? Did you leave the motor running?"

"Woops, woops!" The doctor took me by both arms and looked soberly into my eyes.

"We can't set our hopes too high," he said quietly. "It may be that for such knowledge we aren't teachable—"

I looked soberly back at him, my heart crying in fear that it might be so.

"Look," I said slowly. "If you had a hunger, a great big gnawing-inside hunger and no money and you saw a bakery shop window, which would you do? Turn your back on it? Or would you press your nose as close as you could against the glass and let at least your eyes feast? I know what I'd do." I reached for my sweater.

"And, you know, you never can tell. The shop door might open a crack, maybe—someday—"

AUTHOR BIOGRAPHIES

Poul Anderson (1926–2001) was one of the most prolific and popular writers in science fiction. He won the Hugo Award seven times and the Nebula Award three times, as well as many other awards, notably including the Grand Master Award of the Science Fiction Writers of America for a lifetime of distinguished achievement.

With a degree in physics and a wide knowledge of other fields of science, as well as a passion for history and mythology, he was noted for building stories on a solid foundation of real science, as well as for being one of the most skilled creators of fast-paced adventure stories. He was the author of more than one hundred science fiction and fantasy novels and story collections, and several hundred short stories, as well as historical novels, mysteries, and nonfiction books.

He wrote several series, notably the Technic Civilization novels and stories, the Psychotechnic League series, the Harvest of Stars novels, and his Time Patrol series, along with novels such as *The High Crusade*, *Three Hearts and Three Lions*, and *The Broken Sword*.

Anthony Boucher (1911–1968) began publishing stories in 1941. His first published story was "Snulbug," which was published in *Unknown Worlds*, and he was a regular contributor to that magazine and to *Astounding Science Fiction* for the next two decades.

As a writer and reviewer Anthony Boucher had a considerable effect on science fiction, but it was as cofounder (with J. Francis McComas) and longtime editor of *The Magazine of Fantasy & Science Fiction*, which he edited until his retirement in 1958, that he really became a seminal influence on the field. Founded in 1949, *F&SF* soon became a showcase for the most literate and sophisticated work being done in the field, and Boucher earned himself a secure place in the pantheon of science fiction's greatest editors.

As a writer, he is best remembered for wry and ironic stories such as "The Quest for St. Aquin," "Barrier," "Snulbug," and "The Compleat Werewolf."

He also had a separate and very successful career as a writer and critic in the mystery genre, and was a recipient of the prestigious Edgar Allan Poe Award of the Mystery Writers of America, and became the namesake for the Boucher Award.

Steve Diamond is a horror, fantasy, and science fiction author for Baen Books, Wordfire Press, Gallant Knight Games, and numerous small publications. He is the author of *Residue*, a YA supernatural thriller, a collection of short fiction, *What Hellhounds Dream*, and his most recent work is a dark fantasy/horror novel cowritten with Larry Correia, *Servants of War*. He is also the cohost of the writing advice podcast, *The WriterDojo*. Steve lives in Utah with his wife and two kids.

Neil Gaiman is the #1 *New York Times* bestselling author of books, short stories, films and graphic novels for adults and children.

Some of his most notable titles include the novels *The Graveyard Book* (the first book to ever win both the Newbery and Carnegie medals), the Vertigo comic book series *Sandman*, *American Gods*, and the UK's National Book Award 2013 Book of the Year, *The Ocean at the End of the Lane*. His latest collection of short stories, *Trigger Warning*, was an immediate *New York Times* bestseller and was named a NYT Editors' Choice.

Among his numerous literary awards are the Newbery and Carnegie medals, and the Hugo, Nebula, World Fantasy, and Will Eisner awards.

Zenna Henderson (1917–1983) published her first science fiction story, "Come On, Wagon!," in the *Magazine of Fantasy & Science Fiction* in December 1951 and was quickly singled out for praise by Sam Merwyn in an essay celebrating what was then seen as a new boom of women science fiction writers. In 1959, her long story "Captivity" received a Hugo nomination.

She is most widely remembered for The People, a series of stories first published between 1952 and 1980 about a group of humanoid aliens stranded on Earth who represent our better selves. Along with *Pilgrimage: The Book of the People* (1961) and *The People: No Different Flesh* (1966), Henderson's short fiction is collected in *The*

Anything Box (1965) and *Holding Wonder* (1971). *The People*, a made-for-TV movie based on her series of the same name and starring Kim Darby and William Shatner, was released in 1972. *Ingathering: The Complete People Stories* (1995), including previously uncollected material, was published after Henderson's death in Tucson at the age of sixty-five.

Nina Kiriki Hoffman has sold novels, juvenile and media tie-in books, short story collections, and more than two hundred short stories over the past forty years.

Her first solo novel, *The Thread That Binds the Bones*, won the Bram Stoker Award for first novel; her second novel, *The Silent Strength of Stones*, was a finalist for the Nebula and World Fantasy Awards. *A Red Heart of Memories* (part of her Matt Black series), nominated for a World Fantasy Award, was followed by the sequel *Past the Size of Dreaming*.

Much of her work to date is short fiction, including the "Matt Black" novella "Unmasking," nominated for a World Fantasy Award, and the "Matt Black" novelette "Home for Christmas," which was nominated for the Nebula, World Fantasy, and Sturgeon awards.

In addition to writing, Hoffman has taught, worked part-time at a B. Dalton bookstore, and done production work on *The Magazine of Fantasy & Science Fiction*. An accomplished fiddle player, she has played regularly at various granges near her home in Eugene, Oregon.

Sean CW Korsgaard is a U.S. Army veteran, historian, award-winning journalist, and an editor and author at Baen Books.

As a reporter, he's had over fifteen hundred articles published across dozens of newspapers in Virginia over the past seven years, including the *Richmond Times-Dispatch* and the *Daily Press*, and nationally, in outlets ranging from *The New York Times* to io9 to *VFW Magazine*, and most recently, as a columnist for *Analog Science Fiction & Fact*.

His work has seen him interview two U.S. Presidents, walk the grounds of Auschwitz beside Holocaust survivors, party with Swedish metal bands, get caught in the thick of riots, and even be attacked by a shark. He was a finalist for the Baen Fantasy Adventure Award and Writers of the Future, and recently saw the publication of his first anthology, *Worlds Long Lost*, and his first published short story, "Black Box."

Sean lives in Richmond, Virginia, with his wife and son, and is always looking for his next great adventure and his next big byline, and you can follow him and his work at www.korsgaards commentary.com or on Twitter @SCWKorsgaard.

Richard Matheson (1926–2013) served with the U.S. Army in Europe during World War II, graduated from the Missouri School of Journalism at the University of Missouri, and was the author of many classic novels and short stories. He wrote in a variety of genres including terror, fantasy, horror, paranormal, suspense, science fiction and western.

His short stories appeared in magazines as diverse as *Playboy*, *The Magazine of Fantasy & Science Fiction*, *Galaxy*, *Detective Story*, *Weird Tales*, *Western Stories*, *Stag* and *For Men Only*. His novels, meanwhile, often blended science fiction and fantasy, be it the postapocalyptic vampires of *I Am Legend* or the exploration of the afterlife in *What Dreams May Come*.

In addition to books, he wrote prolifically for television (including *The Twilight Zone*, *Night Gallery*, *Star Trek*) and numerous feature films. Many of Matheson's novels and stories have been made into movies including *I Am Legend*, *Somewhere in Time*, and *The Shrinking Man*, and he worked with filmmakers ranging from Roger Corman to Steven Spielberg.

His many awards include the World Fantasy and Bram Stoker Awards for Lifetime Achievement, the Hugo Award, Edgar Award, Spur Award for Best Western Novel, and Writer's Guild awards. Matheson received the World Fantasy Award for Life Achievement in 1984, the Bram Stoker Award for Lifetime Achievement from the Horror Writers Association in 1991, and the Science Fiction Hall of Fame inducted him in 2010.

Larry Niven is known as an author for his hard science fiction, using big but authentic scientific concepts and theoretical physics. His Known Space series is one of the most popular "future history" sagas in SF and includes the epic novel *Ringworld*, one of the few novels to have won both the Hugo and Nebula awards, as well as the Locus and Ditmar awards, and which is recognized as a milestone in modern science fiction.

Niven also often includes elements of detective fiction and adventure stories. His fantasy includes his The Magic Goes Away series, which utilizes an exhaustible resource, called mana, to make magic a nonrenewable resource. Niven created an alien species, the Kzin, which were featured in a series of collections, the Man-Kzin Wars. He co-authored a number of novels with Jerry Pournelle. In fact, much of his writing since the 1970s has been in collaboration, particularly with Pournelle, Steven Barnes, Brenda Cooper, or Edward M. Lerner. His *Beowulf's Children*, co-authored with Jerry Pournelle and Steven Barnes, was a *New York Times* bestseller.

He has also written for the DC Comics character Green Lantern, including in his stories hard science fiction concepts such as universal entropy and the redshift effect, which are unusual in comic books, as is his "Man of Steel, Woman of Kleenex," a memorable if not-quite-serious essay on Superman and the problems of his having a sex life.

He has received the Nebula Award, five Hugos, four Locus Awards, two Ditmars, the Prometheus, and the Robert A. Heinlein Award, among other honors. Most recently, the Science Fiction and Fantasy Writers of America have presented him with the Damon Knight Memorial Grand Master Award, given for Lifetime Achievement in the field. He lives in Chatsworth, California.

Lester del Rey (1915–1993) was a man of multiple talents, a writer not just of SF and fantasy but of many other forms of more mundane fiction, as well as many nonfiction books. He was editor of many SF magazines, from the early 1950s to the late 1960s, an authors' agent, a book reviewer, and probably most influentially, an editor, with his wife, Judy-Lynn del Rey, at Del Rey books for over two decades. (Incidentally, Del Rey Books, one of the strongest SF lines in the late twentieth century, was named for the lady, not Lester.)

In person, he was a superb, if controversial, speaker, an energetic debater, and if he didn't have the entire history of SF and fantasy stored in his head, anything left out was probably unimportant.

Lester del Rey was diminutive in physical stature, but a titan in his influence on SF and fantasy or, to put it another way, a master of the genre—and the Science Fiction Writers of America made it official, awarding him the Grand Master Award for a lifetime of distinguished service to the field, an obvious and inevitable honor.

Spider Robinson began writing professionally in 1972, and since then, he has won the John W. Campbell Award for Best New Writer, three Hugo Awards, a Nebula Award, and countless other international and regional awards. Most of his thirty-six books are still in print, in ten languages. His short work has appeared in magazines around the planet, from *Omni* and *Analog* to *Xhurnal Izobretatel i Rationalizator* (Moscow), and in numerous anthologies. The Usenet newsgroup alt.callahans and its many internet offshoots, inspired by his Callahan's Place series, for many years constituted one of the largest non-porn networks in cyberspace.

In 2006 he became the only writer ever to collaborate on a novel with First Grandmaster of Science Fiction Robert A. Heinlein, posthumously completing *Variable Star*. That same year the Library of Congress invited him to Washington, D.C., to be a guest of the First Lady at the White House for the National Book Festival. In 2008 he won the Robert A. Heinlein Award for Lifetime Excellence in Literature.

Spider was a regular book reviewer for *Galaxy, Analog,* and *New Destinies* magazines for nearly a decade, and contributes occasional book reviews to *The Globe and Mail*, Canada's national newspaper, for which he wrote a regular Op-Ed column from 1996–2004.

James H. Schmitz (1911–1981) was born in Hamburg, Germany, to American parents. Aside from several trips to the USA, he lived in Germany until 1938, when the outbreak of WWII prompted his family to move to America. He sold his first story, "Greenface," to the now-legendary magazine *Unknown Worlds* shortly before Pearl Harbor. By the time it was published, he was flying with the Army Air Corps in the South Pacific.

In 1949, he began publishing his Agents of Vega series in *Astounding* (later *Analog*), and was one of that magazine's most popular contributors over the next three decades, introducing Telzey Amberdon and Trigger Argee, the heroines of his Federation of the Hub series. He was a master of space opera adventure, notably represented in his classic novel, *The Witches of Karres*, but also demonstrated in many other novels and shorter works.

Michael Shaara (1928–1988) was an American writer of science fiction, sports fiction, and historical fiction. He was born to Italian immigrant parents (the family name was originally spelled Sciarra, which in Italian is pronounced the same way) in Jersey City, New Jersey, graduated from Rutgers University in 1951, and served as a sergeant in the 82nd Airborne division prior to the Korean War.

Before Shaara began selling science fiction stories to fiction magazines in the 1950s, he was an amateur boxer and police officer. Shaara was an early pioneer of military science fiction, with his most iconic short story, "Soldier Boy," serving as an early work of the subgenre, and lending its name to a later collection of his short genre fiction.

He later taught literature at Florida State University while continuing to write fiction. The stress of this and his smoking caused him to have a heart attack at the early age of thirty-six, from which he fully recovered. His novel about the Battle of Gettysburg, *The Killer Angels*, won the Pulitzer Prize for Fiction in 1975.

Alex Shvartsman is the author of *Kakistocracy* (2023), *The Middling Affliction* (2022), and *Eridani's Crown* (2019) fantasy novels. Over 120 of his short stories have appeared in *Analog*, *Nature*, *Strange Horizons*, *Fireside*, *Weird Tales*, *Galaxy's Edge*, and many other venues. He won the WSFA Small Press Award for Short Fiction in 2014 and was a three-time finalist for the Canopus Award for Excellence in Interstellar Fiction.

Alex's translations from Russian have appeared in *The Magazine of Fantasy & Science Fiction*, *Clarkesworld*, Tor.com, *Asimov's*, *Apex*, *Strange Horizons*, and elsewhere.

He's the editor of the Unidentified Funny Objects series of humorous SF/F, as well as a variety of other anthologies, including *The Cackle of Cthulhu* (Baen), *Humanity 2.0* (Arc Manor), and *Funny Science Fiction* (UFO). For five years he edited *Future Science Fiction Digest*, a magazine that focused on international fiction.

His website is www.alexshvartsman.com and his Twitter handle is @AShvartsman.

Robert Silverberg sold his first SF story, "Gorgon Planet," before he was out of his teens, to the British magazine *Nebula*. Two years later, his first SF novel, a juvenile, *Revolt on Alpha C*, followed. Decades later, his total SF titles, according to his semiofficial website, stands at 82 SF novels and 457 short stories. Early on, he won a Hugo Award for most promising new writer—rarely have the Hugo voters been so perceptive.

Toward the end of the 1960s and continuing into the 1970s, he wrote a string of novels much darker in tone and deeper in characterization than his work of the 1950s, such as the novels *Nightwings*, *Dying Inside*, *The Book of Skulls*, and many others. He took occasional sabbaticals from writing to later return with new works, such as the Majipoor series. His most recent novels include *The Alien Years*, *The Longest Way Home*, and a new trilogy of Majipoor novels, and he has edited three big collections: *Legends* and *Legends II* (fantasy) and *Far Horizons* (SF).

The Science Fiction and Fantasy Hall of Fame inducted him in 1999. In 2004, the Science Fiction Writers of America presented him with the Damon Knight Memorial Grand Master Award. For more information see his "quasi-official" website at www.majipoor.com, heroically maintained by Jon Davis (no relation).

Allen Steele is a science fiction writer with twenty-three novels and eight collections of short fiction to his credit. His works have been translated worldwide and have received the Hugo, Locus, and Seiun awards, and have been nominated for the Nebula, Sturgeon, and Sidewise Awards. He is also a recipient of the Robert A. Heinlein Award.

His first published story, "Live from the Mars Hotel," was published in 1988, and his first novel, *Orbital Decay*, was published in 1989. His best-known work is the Coyote series—*Coyote*, *Coyote Rising*, *Coyote Frontier*, *Coyote Horizon*, and *Coyote Destiny*—and the associative novels set in the same universe: *Spindrift*, *Galaxy Blues*, and *Hex*. His novella "The Death Of Captain Future" received the Hugo Award, as did his novella "'. . . Where Angels Fear to Tread,'" and his novelette, "The Emperor of Mars."

A graduate of New England College and the University of Missouri, he is a former journalist, and once spent a brief tenure as a Washington correspondent. He was born and raised in Nashville, Tennessee, and lives in western Massachusetts with his wife Linda and their dogs.

Theodore Sturgeon (1918–1985) was considered one of the most influential writers of the so-called Golden Age of science fiction, though he wrote well into the 1970s. He was particularly appreciated for his prose style, his attention to character, and his treatment of important social issues such as sex, war, and difference. Sturgeon's stories such as "It," "Microcosmic God," "Killdozer," "Bianca's Hands," "Maturity," "The Other Man," and the brilliant "Baby Is Three"— which was eventually expanded into Sturgeon's most famous novel, *More Than Human*—helped to expand the boundaries of the SF story, and push it in the direction of artistic maturity.

Best known as a science fiction writer, he also wrote horror, fantasy, comedy, westerns, and historical fiction, as well as two popular *Star Trek* scripts, "Amok Time" and "Shore Leave." His influence extended beyond even genre fiction, seen everywhere from the Grateful Dead to Stan Lee, and his work presaged the invention of Velcro and the discovery of the double helix in DNA. He is frequently quoted in what became popularly known as Sturgeon's Law ("ninety percent of everything is crap"), though he himself referred to it as Sturgeon's Revelation. He was an extensive reviewer and teacher of science fiction. For his lifetime of work, he was awarded a World Fantasy Achievement Award, and was inducted into the Science Fiction Hall of Fame in 2000.